Longbourn's Unexpected Matchmaker

A fan fiction novel based on Jane Austen's Pride and Prejudice.

Emma Hox

To order additional copies of this title, contact your favorite local bookstore or online distributor and use the following ISBN:

ISBN-13: 978-0-6153-2885-0
ISBN-10: 0-6153-2885-7

Manufactured in the United States of America.

Cover design by Rhemalda Corporation.

For additional information about the author Emma Hox and her other writings, visit www.EmmaHox.com

To my husband with Love!
-Love Eternal-

Would Pride and Prejudice have been different if Colonel Fitzwilliam had accompanied Mr. Bingley and Mr. Darcy to Netherfield?

What would happen if Mr. Darcy made friends with a mysterious member of the Meryton neighborhood who refuses an introduction but who has a close relationship with the Bennet household?

Mr. Bingley had not been of age two years, when he was tempted by an accidental recommendation to look at Netherfield House. He did look at it, and into it for half an hour, was pleased with the situation and the principal rooms, satisfied with what the owner said in its praise, and took it immediately...

It is a truth universally acknowledged that a true lady must possess the attributes of sincerity, generosity, sympathy, modesty, and serenity. Once a single lady is in sufficient possession of these attributes it then becomes her desire to find a single man who possesses a good fortune and is in want of a wife.

Miss Jane Bennet and Miss Elizabeth Bennet were just such ladies.

Chapter 1
Netherfield Park is Let at Last

"My dear Jane," Elizabeth exclaimed as she ungracefully lunged into the middle of Jane's bed to have their nightly chat, "Have you heard that Netherfield Park is let at last?"

Jane replied that she had not.

"But it is," returned she; "for I have just overheard Mama telling Papa."

Jane nodded, but made no answer.

"Do you not want to know who has taken it?" continued Lizzy in her best imitation of their mother's voice.

"YOU want to tell me, and I have no objection to hearing it." giggled Jane as she attempted to imitate their father.

This was invitation enough. "Well then, dearest Jane, you must know that Mama told Papa that Mrs. Long said that Netherfield is taken by a young man of large fortune from the North of England; that he came down on Monday with his two closest friends to see the place, and was so much delighted with it, that he agreed with Mr. Morris immediately; that he is to take possession before Michaelmas, and some of his servants are to be in the house by the end of next week."

"What are their names?"

"Bingley, Fitzwilliam, and Darcy."

"Are others to be joining them for their stay?" asked Jane.

Elizabeth laughed, "Why Jane, that is not the correct question to ask, don't you mean to ask the same one that Papa asked?"

"What did Papa ask, dearest Lizzy?"

"Why, are they married or single, of course."

Jane laughed at Lizzy's frightfully accurate representation of their mother's voice as she continued entirely on her own imitating both her mothers and fathers voices.

"Oh! Single, my dear, to be sure! Three single men of independent fortunes; Bingley is said to have four or five thousand a year, Fitzwilliam is a second son to an Earl and a Colonel in the militia and Darcy, why this is the best of all, he is said to have a clear ten thousand a year. What a fine thing for our girls!"

"How so? How can it affect them?"

"My dear, how can you be so tiresome? You must know that I am thinking of them marrying two or three of them."

"Is that their design in settling here?"

"Design! Nonsense, how can you talk so! But it is very likely that they MAY fall in love with them, they are the most beautiful girls in the entire county I have been told more than once, and therefore you must visit them as soon as they come."

It was here that Jane interrupted Lizzy since she could bear no more. Her face and sides hurt from smiling and laughing so much at Lizzy's crazy antics. "Is Father actually taking the time to go and visit the Netherfield gentlemen? He rarely takes the time to visit any newcomers."

"No Jane, you are correct in your implied meaning behind your question, Father will not be visiting them, much to our mother's vexation, which I am sure we will be hearing about until the night of the Meryton Assembly Ball."

Mr. Bennet had been among the earliest of those who waited on Mr. Bingley of Netherfield. He had always intended to visit him, though assuring his wife and daughters until the night of the Meryton Assembly that he should not go.

All intelligence that the ladies had learned of the Netherfield gentlemen was gathered from Elizabeth's close friend Miss Charlotte Lucas' father. Sir William Lucas informed them that it was Mr. Bingley that had leased Netherfield and he stated that he was delighted with him. He was quite young, he appeared to be wonderfully handsome, extremely agreeable and to crown the whole, he means to be at the next assembly with his entire party. Nothing could be more delightful! To be fond of dancing was a certain step towards falling in love; and very lively hopes of Mr. Bingley's heart were entertained.

The Longbourn ladies were discussing their appearances and whether Mr. Bingley and his friends Colonel Fitzwilliam and Mr. Darcy would approve of them as they rounded the bend into the town of Meryton the night of the assembly ball. It was now that Mr. Bennet revealed to the ladies that he had visited Mr. Bingley. He did so in the following manner.

"I know each of you has thoughts of entertaining the Netherfield gentlemen this night with your elegant dancing, but dearest daughters I do not think any of you has a chance since not one of you are wearing blue and I am positive I heard Mr. Bingley say that his favorite color was blue".

Mrs. Bennet was all in confusion exclaiming, "Of what are you talking of Mr. Bennet, I am sure not one of us understand you".

"Of Mr. Bingley of course, why just last week as I visited him I am sure he said he loved to dance, especially if the lady was wearing blue".

The astonishment of the ladies was just what he wished; and the ladies instantly accosted him with barefaced questions, ingenious suppositions, and distant surmises, but he eluded the skill of them all. The only information the Longbourn ladies could determine was that Mr. Bennet only met Mr. Bingley and not the Colonel or Mr. Darcy.

The carriage finally pulled up in front of the Meryton Assembly Hall and the footman opened the door. Mr. Bennet was the first to depart from the carriage. He first stretched his back and legs, chuckled to himself that each of the ladies was wishing they wore blue, and cringed as Mrs. Bennet exclaimed to Jane "Why did you not listen to me, I told you to wear your blue dress." Jane ignored her mother as her father began to hand down his wife and five daughters. They all proceeded inside to enjoy the festivities of the night.

When the Netherfield party arrived, fashionably late, all activity stopped and every person in the assembly hall turned to observe the four gentlemen and two ladies that entered the room.

Mr. Bingley was good-looking and gentleman-like; he had a pleasant countenance, and easy, unaffected manners. Colonel Fitzwilliam was also noted to have an easy disposition and pleasant manners. The two had soon made themselves acquainted with all the principal people in the room; they were both lively and unreserved, danced every dance, were angry that the ball planned to close so early, and Mr. Bingley talked of giving one himself at Netherfield. Such amiable qualities must speak for themselves. What a contrast between them and their friend. Mr. Darcy, although tall, extremely handsome, rich, and having the appearance of having everything, rarely danced, avoided being introduced to any other lady, and spent much of the evening in walking about the room, speaking occasionally to one of his own party. These manners did not present him in a favorable light and so his fine, tall person, handsome features, noble mien, large estate, and ten thousand a year could not dispel him of being labeled a disagreeable man and unworthy of being compared with his friends. His character was decided. He was the proudest, most disagreeable man in the world, and everybody hoped that he would never come there again.

Elizabeth Bennet took advantage of a pause in the music to compose herself by walking to the refreshment table and partaking of some lemonade. She was thirsty from all of the dancing and needed to quench her thirst before her next dance partner sought her out. This assembly ball had been particularly wonderful for Lizzy since she had not yet sat out a single set and her dance card was already full for the remainder of the evening, thus fulfilling any young lady's wish of a partner for every dance at the ball. With her refreshment in hand Elizabeth took a seat to enjoy the entertainment. Maria Lucas was currently performing a simple but very pretty lullaby. She received a genuine applause from those assembled and was followed by none other than Elizabeth's sister Miss Mary Bennet. Although Mary played all of the notes of her piece perfectly it lacked emotion and feeling. When the singing portion of the song arrived her voice was weak and not suited for the song. Although those assembled applauded at the conclusion of her display it was more for wanting her to desist rather than to commend her performance. Looking about the room Elizabeth could read the derision upon the faces and in the eyes of many looking upon her display. As always though Mary was succeeded by another and her performance was soon forgotten by all in attendance. Elizabeth continued to sip her lemonade and began to study and turn her focus to everyone around her as she liked to do when alone.

Mr. Bingley and Colonel Fitzwilliam were standing near Lizzy and as she focused on everyone around her she accidentally overheard them talking about the current poor disposition of Mr. Darcy and their resolution to discuss it with him. This interested Lizzy because their discussion made it sound like Mr. Darcy was acting outside of his normal character; this is always interesting to a studier of human folly such as she was.

Mr. Darcy had just arrived at the refreshment table when Mr. Bingley and Colonel Fitzwilliam reached their resolution to talk to him. Colonel Fitzwilliam began by saying: "Come, Darcy, I must have you dance. I hate to see you standing about by yourself in this stupid manner. You had much better dance."

"I certainly shall not cousin. You of all people know how I detest it, unless I am particularly acquainted with my partner, plus you both are aware that I am presently in no mood to meet new ladies. Bingley's sisters are engaged, and there is not another woman in the room whom I know well enough to stand up with without them thinking it was a punishment."

"I would not be as fastidious as you are," cried Mr. Bingley, "for a kingdom! Upon my honor, I never met with so many pleasant girls in my life as I have this evening; and there are several of them you see uncommonly pretty. They seem to be easy enough to get to know."

"You two may consider the women of the Hertfordshire society pretty and pleasant, but you are too easily impressed, there are none here that have yet caught my eye" said Mr. Darcy, looking around the room. It was at this point that he paused as he first caught a glimpse of Miss Elizabeth Bennet. To him it appeared as if she was listening to their conversation. However at the point he looked over she began to walk away and he decided that he must be paranoid and she must have not in fact been listening.

It was not lost upon Colonel Fitzwilliam that Darcy had paused upon the sight of Miss Elizabeth Bennet. He would have to remember this and see if it could be used to his advantage at some future date.

It was now that the orchestra began to be seated to resume their playing and Mr. Darcy told his companions "I assume each of you has already engaged pretty ladies to do you the honor of the next dance, therefore you had better go back to your partners and enjoy their smiles. You are both wasting your time with me."

Mr. Bingley and Colonel Fitzwilliam shrugged shoulders at each other and followed his advice to find their dance partners as Mr. Darcy walked off to brood in the corner.

Prior to Elizabeth's partner claiming her for the dance she had a chance to sit and think about what the three gentlemen had said. To Elizabeth it seemed as if Mr. Darcy was not acting in a manner that his friends were used to. She had just started to consider what could be the cause of such a change in one's character when Colonel Fitzwilliam claimed her for the next set.

Mr. Darcy paced the length of the room during the first dance of the set until he realized that Colonel Fitzwilliam was dancing with the young lady he had seen from the refreshment table. Darcy noted that her eyes seemed to turn and dance as she did and her smile... oh "that smile"... he was resolved that maybe; just maybe, he would dance a set with a lady other than one of his party.

Mr. Darcy waited for the set to end and moved in the same direction that Colonel Fitzwilliam was heading to deposit the lady. Upon reaching them the

Colonel had not yet departed and Darcy nodded to him to introduce his latest partner.

"Miss Elizabeth Bennet I would be pleased to introduce you to my cousin and good friend Mr. Darcy."

Elizabeth curtsied to Mr. Darcy.

"It is my pleasure to make your acquaintance Miss Bennet; would you do me the honor of dancing the next set?" Mr. Darcy asked with slight hesitation. He was never at ease conversing in society, especially with ladies.

"It would be my honor Mr. Darcy..." Mr. Darcy began to release the breath he had been holding in nervousness when he heard her further reply "...but I am already engaged for the next set. I do apologize, perhaps another time."

Mr. Darcy, taking another breath and holding it said, "No apology is needed, I would be pleased to stand up with you for whichever set you have available this evening."

Miss Elizabeth colored, as she had to reply, "I must apologize again Mr. Darcy however all of my dance sets have already been claimed for this evening."

Once Elizabeth finished, an extremely embarrassed Mr. Darcy bowed said "Miss Bennet... Colonel Fitzwilliam," and began to stalk away, angry at himself for letting his impulses guide his actions and allowing himself to be so embarrassed.

Colonel Fitzwilliam quickly stopped him by placing a hand on his shoulder. He held on to Darcy as he began to address Elizabeth. "Miss Bennet, I have just had the honor and privilege of your dancing pleasure this evening and I believe I am one of the lucky gentlemen to have engaged with you for another set of the night, in fact I believe I have the final set of the night. I by no means want to be released from our dance; however I would also let you know that there can be no finer dance partner than Mr. Darcy and if you would like him as your partner for the final set of the evening I give you leave to accept him. I will not be offended to allow my cousin your dancing pleasure."

Mistaking Elizabeth's look for uneasiness at having to choose between the two Mr. Darcy quickly stopped him "Colonel Fitzwilliam, you by no means should punish yourself by quitting the dance to allow me one in which I had not the foresight to plan in advance for a partner."

Elizabeth was enjoying the scene before her but also saw her next dance partner coming to claim her and so thought it prudent to bring the discussion to an end. "Gentlemen, I would indeed be honored to dance with either of you. The Colonel is correct; we have already enjoyed a set this evening and he and I are engaged for the final. As much as I enjoy dancing with him I would also be very pleased to dance with and become acquainted with you Mr. Darcy." This was said as she looked towards and nodded at Mr. Darcy. Elizabeth's eyebrows quickly rose in a becoming arch and she stated "I have an idea. I leave it to you gentlemen to surprise me at the last dance. Whoever reaches me first to claim my hand shall be the one I have the honor of dancing with." Elizabeth flashed a stunning smile and curtsied as her next partner claimed her for their dance.

The remainder of the evening passed slowly for Darcy and at last it was nearing time for the final set of the evening. Darcy had watched Elizabeth since she had left the Colonel and himself earlier in the evening. As he watched her he became resolute and determined that the final set with Miss Elizabeth would be his.

Colonel Fitzwilliam had watched Darcy as he watched Miss Elizabeth and was resolute that the final set should be his.

As Darcy watched Miss Elizabeth he delighted in his discovery that at the conclusion of the sets she had her partner lead her either to her sister or her friend Miss Charlotte Lucas, but in actuality it was wherever her mother was not. Based on these observations he concluded that upon completion of this set she would place herself next to her friend Charlotte and therefore it was near there that he was determined to wait.

Elizabeth had noticed Mr. Darcy watching her since their introduction and his offering of a dance and was beginning to hope that it was him who was able to claim her for the final set. As her dance was ending she had two options of where to have her partner escort her. She could be dropped off by her dearest sister Jane who was presently at the refreshment table talking with Miss Bingley and her mother or by her good friend Charlotte. Elizabeth had decided she would go to whoever was closest to Mr. Darcy. Upon seeing Mr. Darcy by Charlotte that is where she had her partner deposit her.

Darcy was not disappointed, at the conclusion of the dance arrived Miss Elizabeth and he was easily able to claim her for the final set of the evening before the Colonel had even been seen. "Miss Bennet, I come to claim you for the final set of the evening. While the musicians are pausing for a rest would you allow me to escort you for some refreshment?"

"It would be my pleasure Mr. Darcy" she smiled lightly at her friend Charlotte as she departed on Mr. Darcy's arm.

At the refreshment table Darcy and Elizabeth met the Colonel. "Well Darcy I see you wasted no time in beating me to the prize by claiming Miss Elizabeth for the final set."

Darcy was not quite sure how to respond but slightly bowed and said "Yes, Fitzwilliam, as you see I have claimed Miss Bennet already and encourage you to find another lovely lady to partner with. I thank you for your thoughtfulness in allowing me the pleasure of dancing with Miss Bennet this evening."

Colonel Fitzwilliam grinned, bowed, and departed.

Darcy obtained a glass of lemonade for Miss Elizabeth and presented her with it. She thanked him and sipped it silently until the dance began. Darcy had not said a word to her but was content with occasionally looking at her to admire her features. Elizabeth was beginning to be uncomfortable under his scrutiny and was ready for the dance to begin to rid her thoughts of the many questions she was having. *Why is he looking at me in that stern way for? Is he looking at me only to see fault? Is he regretting asking me to dance? If he is, why did he not just let the Colonel reach me first to claim the dance? Was it because I ceremoniously placed myself so near him at the end of the last set?* She longed to ask him and make him as uncomfortable as she was but she held her tongue and waited for the dance to begin.

As the dance set was beginning Darcy put away Elizabeth's lemonade and then offered her his arm. As he led her Elizabeth was conscious of all the murmuring that the sight of her dancing with Mr. Darcy was causing and hoped that he did not hear it or at a minimum hoped he would not be affected or offended by it.

The dance was pleasant enough for both of them despite the fact that the first of the set was danced in almost complete silence. The second dance of the set had a bit of conversation, although very little. Darcy was able to determine that Elizabeth was the second of five sisters and Elizabeth found out that Darcy had one. Elizabeth soon realized that Darcy felt comfortable talking of his sister and further encouraged him to speak of her. The remainder of the dance was spent with Elizabeth persuading Darcy to expound on the beauty, sereneness, and talents of his almost angelic sister. Elizabeth smiled as she recognized the protectiveness that Darcy had for his almost perfect sister, much the same as she towards her dearest Jane.

At the conclusion of the dance Mr. Darcy led Elizabeth to her sister Jane. "Thank you Mr. Darcy, I truly had an enjoyable dance with you and am glad it was you who reached me first. I hope it was pleasant for you as well."

"Yes Miss Bennet it was." With that said Mr. Darcy bowed and departed with one last long look at Elizabeth. His hope was granted when she graced him with "that smile" he had seen her give others earlier.

Chapter 2
The Party at Lucas Lodge

The evening altogether passed off pleasantly for the whole family. Mrs. Bennet had seen her eldest two daughters much admired by the Netherfield gentlemen. Mr. Bingley had danced with Jane twice, and his sisters had distinguished her. Jane was as much gratified by this as her mother could be, though in a quieter way. Elizabeth likewise had danced once with Mr. Bingley, once with Colonel Fitzwilliam and once with Mr. Darcy. That was enough for Mrs. Bennet to be proud of. Mary had heard herself mentioned to Miss Bingley as the most accomplished girl in the neighborhood; and Catherine and Lydia had also been fortunate enough never to be without partners, which was all that they had yet learnt to care for at a ball. They returned, therefore, in good spirits to Longbourn.

Mrs. Bennet rambled on about the evening as long as anyone would listen to her and finally gave up trying to discuss the dance and continued on in a different vein.

"What a successful evening, was it not, girls?"

"Yes, Mama, it was." Jane sweetly answered.

"Why, I noticed that even Lizzy was not obliged to sit out any sets as she generally does."

With that Mr. Bennet got up and departed the room with a sad look at his dear Lizzy. She had been his favorite daughter since it was determined in her young age that she had as much or more wit than he did. He despised it when his wife demeaned her, however he had learned over the years to walk out and ignore it and luckily his Lizzy never took it to heart.

That evening, despite the late hour, when Jane and Elizabeth were alone for their nightly chat, the former, who had been cautious in her praise of Mr. Bingley before, expressed to her sister just how very much she admired him. "He is just what a young man ought to be," said she, "sensible, good-humored, lively, and I never saw such happy manners! So much ease, with such perfect good breeding!"

"He is also handsome," replied Elizabeth, "which a young man ought likewise to be, if he possibly can. His character is thereby complete."

"I was very much flattered by his asking me to dance a second time. I did not expect such a compliment."

"Did not you? I did for you. But that is one great difference between us. Compliments always take you by surprise and me never. What could be more natural than his asking you again? He could not help seeing that you were about five times as pretty as every other woman in the room. No thanks to his gallantry for that. Well, he certainly is very agreeable, and I give you leave to like him. You have liked many a stupider person."

"Dear Lizzy!"

"Do not 'Dear Lizzy' me, Jane; you know I speak the truth."

Bingley and the Colonel had not been friends nearly as long as he and Darcy but Bingley had been introduced to the Colonel at one of the clubs that he and Darcy frequented while residing in London. Bingley and the Colonel had become fast friends on account that they had nearly the same easy disposition and had many of the same interests and hobbies, not to mention their joint friendship with Mr. Darcy. The main difference between the Colonel and Mr. Bingley being that the Colonel as a member of the military did not trust all he met as easily as Bingley did upon first meeting them.

Between Bingley and Darcy there was a very steady friendship, in spite of great opposition of character. Bingley was endeared to Darcy by the easiness, openness, and ductility of his temper, though no disposition could offer a greater contrast to his own, and though with his own he never appeared dissatisfied.

On the strength of Darcy's regard, Bingley had the firmest reliance, and of his judgment the highest opinion. In understanding, Darcy was the superior. Bingley was by no means deficient, but Darcy was clever. He was at the same time haughty, reserved, and fastidious, and his manners, though well bred, were not inviting. In that respect his friend had greatly the advantage. Bingley was sure of being liked wherever he appeared. Darcy was continually giving offense.

Mr. Darcy and Colonel Fitzwilliam had the closest connection of all. They had not only known each other since infancy, but they were also cousins. Although they were cousins by blood they were brothers by heart. The two could not have a closer bond with anyone. They knew each other's thoughts and actions almost before they themselves knew them and were close enough that they had no reserve in talking to each other about everything.

The manner in which they spoke of the Meryton assembly was sufficiently characteristic of each of their personalities. Bingley and Fitzwilliam had never met with more pleasant people or prettier girls in their life; everybody had been most kind and attentive to them; there had been no formality, no stiffness; they both had soon felt acquainted with all the room; Bingley stated that as to Miss Jane Bennet, he could not conceive an angel more beautiful, Colonel Fitzwilliam agreed with him and said there were a few others that were uncommonly pretty and he should like to know them better. Darcy had maintained his quiet observation and was ruminating about them to himself when the Colonel interrupted his thoughts. "Darcy, what thought you about the dance? I seem to recall a look upon your face that indicated you were pleased with your partner of the fairer sex."

"Indeed I did, although the assembly in general only had a very minimal amount of fashion and a few were rather boorish, I see no harm in staying and getting to know a few of them a bit more."

The Colonel and Mr. Bingley just smiled at the typical Darcy response.

The morning after the assembly brought Miss Charlotte and Miss Maria Lucas to Longbourn to hear and to communicate with the ladies about the ball. Charlotte, Jane, and Elizabeth went to the garden bench to sit and discuss while Maria kept Kitty and Lydia occupied.

As soon as they settled, Elizabeth asked "Charlotte, what thought you of last evening?"

Charlotte was pleased to be able to answer "Oh, Jane and Lizzy, I had a most enjoyable evening. I was so pleased to be asked to dance four sets. I danced with Mr. Sharp, Mr. Bates, Mr. Bingley, and Colonel Fitzwilliam. Oh you know how I dread my frequent dances with Mr. Bates, however Mr. Sharp loves to dance and I enjoy getting away from the wall."

Jane and Lizzy both smiled at this. Charlotte was indeed getting beyond the age of being marriageable and frequently only danced one or two dances all evening as a result. Every ball one of those two dances was Mr. Sharp. Mr. Sharp was a widower of the past five years with three grown children. He dearly loved his departed wife and vowed to never remarry; however he loved to dance. Upon moving into Meryton two years past he noted that the eldest Lucas girl was frequently without dance partners. He made it a point to ask her to dance at every ball, therefore fulfilling a joy for both of them.

Mr. Bates was another matter altogether. Charlotte only endured his dances because if she refused them she would no longer be able to accept the offer of others. He early on in their acquaintance, while trampling on her feet, let her know in no uncertain terms that he would never pay her more notice than a dance at each assembly due to her lack of dowry.

Elizabeth then asked Charlotte with a half-cocked smile and an odd twinkle in her eye "Did you enjoy dancing with Mr. Bingley?"

Jane began to blush as Charlotte answered, "I did!" Jane knew where Lizzy was heading and knew that her cheeks would become redder as her sister's questioning continued. Jane desperately tried to think of something to interject, but too late Lizzy had continued.

"As well as Jane did?"

At this all Charlotte could do was laugh and they continued on in their pleasant conversation until Charlotte announced that she must be heading home. They wandered back to the house to gather Miss Maria Lucas, Charlotte's younger sister and as they were leaving Maria reminded Charlotte of the invitation.

"Oh dear, how could I have forgotten? My father is to give a party at Lucas Lodge and you are all invited." With the invitation made the Lucas ladies departed for home.

A few days after the Meryton Assembly the ladies of Longbourn waited on those of Netherfield. The visit was soon returned in due form. Miss Bennet's pleasing manners grew on the goodwill of Mrs. Hurst and Miss Bingley; and though the mother was found to be intolerable, and the younger sisters not worth speaking to, a wish of being better acquainted with the two eldest was expressed. By Jane, this attention was received with the greatest pleasure, but Elizabeth still saw superciliousness in their treatment of everybody, hardly excepting even her sister, and could not like them; though their kindness to Jane, such as it was, had a value as arising in all probability from the influence of their brother's admiration.

It was generally evident whenever they met, that Mr. Bingley did admire Jane and to Elizabeth it was equally evident that Jane was yielding to him and was on her way to be very much in love; but she considered that it was not likely to be discovered by the world in general, since Jane, united with great strength of feeling, a composure of temper and a uniform cheerfulness of manner which would guard her from the suspicions of the impertinent. She mentioned this to her friend Miss Lucas at the party at Lucas Lodge.

"It may perhaps be pleasant," replied Charlotte, "to be able to impose on the public in such a case; but it is sometimes a disadvantage to be so very guarded. If a woman conceals her affection with the same skill from the object of it, she may lose the opportunity of fixing him; we can all begin freely – a slight preference is natural enough; but there are very few of us who have heart enough to be really in love without encouragement. In nine cases out of ten a women had better show more affection than she feels. Bingley likes your sister undoubtedly; but he may never do more than like her, if she does not help him on."

"But she does help him on, as much as her nature will allow. If I can perceive her regard for him, he must be a simpleton, indeed, not to discover it too."

"Remember, Lizzy, that he does not know Jane's disposition as you do."

"But if a woman is partial to a man, and does not endeavor to conceal it, he must find it out."

"Perhaps he must, I suppose, but Jane should make the most of every half hour in which she can command his attention. When she has secured him, there will be more leisure for falling in love as much as she chooses."

"Secure him," laughed Elizabeth, "where nothing is in question but the desire of being well married, and if I were determined to get a rich husband, or any husband, I dare say I should adopt it. But these are not Jane's feelings; she is not acting by design. As yet, she cannot even be certain of the degree of her own regard nor of its reasonableness. She has known him only a fortnight. She danced two sets with him at Meryton; she saw him one morning at his own house, and has since dined with him in company four times. This is not quite enough to make her understand his character."

"Not as you represent it. Had she merely dined with him, she might only have discovered whether he had a good appetite; but you must remember that four evenings have also been spent together—and four evenings may do a great deal."

"Yes; these four evenings have enabled them to ascertain that they both like Vingtet-un better than Commerce; but with respect to any other leading characteristic, I do not imagine that much has been unfolded."

"Well," said Charlotte, "I wish Jane success with all my heart; and if she were married to him tomorrow, I should think she had as good a chance of happiness as if she were to be studying his character for a twelvemonth. Happiness in marriage is entirely a matter of chance. If the dispositions of the parties are ever so well known to each other or ever so similar beforehand, it does not advance their felicity in the least. They always continue to grow sufficiently unlike afterwards to have their share of vexation; and it is better to know as little as possible of the defects of the person with whom you are to pass your life."

"You make me laugh, Charlotte; but it is not sound. You know it is not sound, and that you would never act in this way yourself and I am positive I never would and neither would Jane. You know Jane and I will only marry for the deepest love."

"Yes Lizzy, I am aware of that, but as you are aware, I do not have the same belief. I just wish to marry regardless of other considerations."

"Well Charlotte, I will not relent, so as you may well imagine Jane will marry for love and have many children and I shall be content to love them as my own and teach them all that I know."

Colonel Fitzwilliam had been standing with his back to Miss Bennet and Miss Lucas trying to attend to Colonel Forster and some officers that were inquiring about the news from Spain during the ladies' conversation. Although he was finding it hard to comment to Colonel Forster he was quite pleased with the feelings that Miss Bennet related to her friend. Especially after meeting her family at the past few assemblies, he was pleased that she was different than her mother and younger sisters and it appeared as her sister felt the same way. Although a bit jealous of his friend's good fortune with regards the lady, he was also delighted that it appeared as Miss Jane Bennet liked Bingley as much as he liked her. He would be sure to let Bingley know.

Occupied in observing Mr. Bingley's attentions to her sister Jane and trying to intercede prior to her remaining sisters bringing undue attention to themselves by either playing the piano or chasing after the officers, Elizabeth was far from suspecting that she was herself becoming an object of some interest in the eyes of his friend. Mr. Darcy, who had at first scarcely allowed any woman to catch his eye, was beginning to find that Elizabeth's face was rendered uncommonly intelligent by the beautiful expression of her dark eyes, "that smile" and her frame that was light and pleasing. To this discovery succeeded some others equally pleasing as he realized that her manners were all ease and playfulness, yet had something of quickness and intelligence that he had yet to encounter in any lady of his acquaintance.

Of this observation Miss Elizabeth was perfectly unaware.

Mr. Darcy began to wish to know more of her, yet he also knew that his disposition did not render him easy in others company. Darcy determined to speak to his cousin and get some assistance to aide his endeavors, but until he could speak to him he would not delay an attempt on his own.

Darcy had danced with her at the Meryton Assembly and received such pleasure that he was now determined to repeat it.

His thoughts were so much engrossed on determining how he would accomplish this that he did not perceive that Sir William Lucas was his neighbor, until Sir William thus began: "What a charming amusement for young people this is, Mr. Darcy! There is nothing like dancing after all. I consider it as one of the first refinements of polished society."

"Certainly, sir; and it has the advantage also of being in vogue amongst the less polished societies of the world. Every savage can dance."

Sir William only smiled. "Your friends perform delightfully," he continued after a pause, on seeing Bingley and Fitzwilliam join the group; "and I doubt not that you are an adept in the science yourself, Mr. Darcy."

"You saw me dance at Meryton, I believe, sir."

"Yes, indeed, and received no inconsiderable pleasure from the sight of you with our own Miss Elizabeth. Do you often dance at St. James's?"

"Never, sir."

"Do you not think it would be a proper compliment to the place?"

"It is a compliment which I prefer not to pay to any place unless I am acquainted with my partner."

"Oh I see." Stated Sir William "Well we shall have to find someone in which you are acquainted with then."

Darcy began to answer that he knew Miss Elizabeth Bennet and would be pleased to dance with her when Sir William without hearing him interrupted saying, "Well your friend's sisters are presently engaged in delightful conversation with my wife and I am sure they do not wish to be interrupted, but ah ha…" and speaking to Darcy as if it was a secret he leaned in and said quietly as he nodded to Elizabeth, "I am certain that with the familiarity that your friend shows to the family and your own previous dance with her you must be sufficiently acquainted with her."

Darcy was shocked by his statement regarding Mr. Bingley and before he could think or react Sir William had began. "My dear Miss Eliza, why are you not dancing? Mr. Darcy here was just saying how he did not wish to dance unless he was acquainted with his partner. I know that he and his friends know you and Miss Jane and as you are most proficient and excel in dancing you must allow me to present you as a very desirable partner. Mr. Darcy, you cannot refuse to dance, I am sure when so much beauty is before you." And, taking her hand, he gave it to Mr. Darcy, turned on his heel and rushed away.

Mr. Darcy, though still extremely surprised from Sir William Lucas' last statement, was not unwilling to receive Miss Bennet. He started to stammer "Miss... B.... Bennet."

Elizabeth who was equally surprised but more in control of her speech as her wit ran strong rushed in stating "Mr. Darcy, you are all politeness as Sir William forces you to dance with the first lady who walks by that he can decipher a connection in any possible way between you and her or her family. I do not think that you truly wish to dance. I think Sir William was making that decision for you."

The pause which ensued was enough for Elizabeth to surmise that she had been correct. Not wanting to embarrass herself or Mr. Darcy she stated "Mr. Darcy" with a slight smile and curtsey and walked away.

All sorts of thoughts were streaming through Darcy's head and not a one of them was coherent and reasonable. All he could think was that he did want to dance, at least if it was with her, but he could not get his mind and mouth to cooperate with him. That was it, she had walked away. He was about ready to seek his cousin's advice over the event when he saw it, "that smile." Unfortunately, "that smile" was not on Elizabeth's face, it was on none other than Colonel Fitzwilliam's.

The current dance was ending and preparation for the next was occurring. The Colonel was depositing one partner and set off towards none other than Miss Elizabeth Bennet with ... "that smile". Darcy knew "that smile" well... it was the smile that Colonel Fitzwilliam had every time he meant to disconcert someone based on an observation he had made. Darcy suspected as he looked at the Colonel that he had overseen the interaction between himself and Miss Elizabeth but seeing "that smile" confirmed it. The Colonel usually used his charms to disentangle a lady from his much sought after cousin and "that smile" was always present when he did it. "That smile" had been frequent over the past years and in all instances they came to nothing good in the end, at least for the lady, the good was that Mr. Darcy was left alone. Darcy felt a pang in his chest... something he had never felt before on seeing "that smile". What did that feeling mean? The sensation had never accompanied him as his cousin bestowed "that smile" upon his face, until now.

Mr. Darcy's mind raced. *As the Colonel watched me did he detect that I no longer wish Miss Elizabeth's company? What is this that I feel... regret? Why do I feel regret? What do I regret? Certainly not this woman, I would never regret a woman... would I? What does she think of me? Does she want to dance with me or with my cousin?* He had not time to ponder it though, he wanted the next dance with Miss Elizabeth and he must beat the Colonel to her side or else irreparable damage may occur.

If Darcy had known the Colonel's thoughts this time though he may have let the Colonel have this dance and wait for another after he had talked with the Colonel. What Darcy did not know is the Colonel also used "that smile" when he was about to aid a friend in catching a certain lady. Darcy had never had that privilege though and so he did not know this.

Luckily for Darcy, Colonel Fitzwilliam had decided to partake of some refreshment along his path to Elizabeth and so Darcy was able to make it to her side as the music was beginning and right before Colonel Fitzwilliam.

"Miss Bennet, may I have the pleasure of this dance?"

20

Elizabeth looked up shocked; it was not five minutes since she had left Mr. Darcy, slightly regretting that he would never want to dance with her and now here he was asking her to dance. All she could do was stare... then ... ouch ... what was that?

Charlotte saw that Elizabeth had not answered Mr. Darcy and the stress was beginning to form on his face. She had already decided after the Meryton Assembly in her own mind that the two were perfect for each other and did not want Lizzy to screw it up, but if Lizzy did not answer he would leave. She needed to bring Lizzy back to reality so she pinched her.

Lizzy realized what had occurred and quickly though not elegantly stated a blunt "Yes".

Mr. Darcy gave her his arm and as he turned to walk her to the floor came face to face with the Colonel. Fitzwilliam gave Darcy a smile and continued to ask Miss Lucas to dance.

Miss Lucas was pleased to be asked to dance, but also slightly disappointed that of all the dances she always had free she had been asked to dance on the one that she would have actually enjoyed observing.

A few steps into the dance Elizabeth realized this dance was beginning as silently as the one at the Meryton Assembly and began to wonder if she and Mr. Darcy would have any conversation at all. Elizabeth decided to try her luck with conversing about the neighborhood. "So Mr. Darcy, do you like our Meryton?"

"It is a pleasant country with nice trails for riding and game for hunting." Stated Mr. Darcy flatly as his thoughts flew with the answer *Oh yes indeed, a few of the ladies are absolutely gorgeous and they fill my dreams most pleasantly, particularly you my gorgeous goddess.*

Elizabeth thought that though the answer was rather short and dully stated, it was reasonable enough and she could reply. "So you enjoy hunting and riding do you Mr. Darcy?"

"Indeed I do Miss Bennet." To himself he added *particularly if the game has gorgeous dancing eyes, ravishing chestnut hair and occasionally flashes "that smile"*...

Elizabeth was discouraged that the reply left nothing for a response and decided to wait and let him continue the conversation.

Mr. Darcy sensing that it was his turn for comment replied with "Do you ride, Miss Bennet?"

Miss Elizabeth laughingly stated "Certainly not sir."

Darcy was mesmerized by her heavenly laugh and "that smile", which had reached her dancing eyes and could not reply for fear of letting his feelings slip where and be known to the world at large.

Elizabeth feared she had offended him when he did not answer and so she continued in a stumbling manner "I do not mean to imply that it is not a respectable pastime for any lady, it is just not a perfectly respectable pastime for me."

Darcy realized that she thought she had offended him and was now dedicated to making her feel more at ease, even if it meant he had to trouble himself with conversation. She had not offended him; in fact it was quite the opposite. The last thing he wanted was her to be uncomfortable around him. "Why do you say that,

Miss Bennet? Do you not enjoy riding?" Darcy was indeed curious about anything she would reveal about herself.

"Well, if you must know, Mr. Darcy, my father is a favorite of mine and as I grew I often went with him onto the estate to check on tenants and the sort. I always rode with him so that I would be safe; to own, I am rather afraid of moving heights, specifically horses. Well as I turned ten years of age my father decided I must seat myself upon my own horse if I was to go with him. For weeks I instead stayed home thinking my father would relent and let me ride with him rather than lose my company. However, it was not to be, he was firm on me learning to ride on my own. One day my mother was being particularly vocal and I longed to be with my father to escape. I ran to the stables and demanded to have my father's fastest horse so I could catch up with him. Mr. Hill tried to give me the old mare, but you see I am familiar with the entire estate, almost as a son would be, and I knew what he was up to. I demanded to ride Lightning and so it was, Mr. Hill saddled Lightning and off I went in search of my beloved father. Well Mr. Darcy, I never found my father but he found me crying under the apple tree at the farthest point of the estate from the house and without my mount."

Elizabeth concluded her story with a delightful laugh, "that smile" and an "I have never rode since, I prefer my two sturdy legs to any animal's four."

Mr. Darcy could not help but laugh at this and Elizabeth could not help noticing his smile. *"That smile" should grace his features more often; it is so pleasant* she thought to herself.

"So you are close with your father?"

"Oh yes indeed sir, as I told you at the Meryton Assembly, I have no brothers. I am the second of five sisters. As my father has no sons I am he. What you may not know is that our estate is entailed to heirs male."

Mr. Darcy had thus far learned her playful spirit and knew that this was a prime opportunity for him to attempt teasing. "Do not tell me that as your father's son you dress as a male, aid in the management of the estate, court young ladies and will eventually inherit?"

Elizabeth saw his slight smile and the gleam in his eye and heartily laughed "Oh no, Mr. Darcy, do you tease? As much as I wish I could inherit to save my family I cannot. I am only expected to marry and leave so that there is one less mouth to feed and one less body to worry about."

Mr. Darcy was not sure if he was pleased at her openness or afraid that she was going to turn into one of those ladies of the ton that flaunted themselves about his person exclaiming why they would be the best mistress for his "Dear Pemberley." He had thought her different than her mother, but he could not deny who her mother was and knew not that lady's influence over her. He knew she had been teasing and that he had encouraged it, but had he gone too far? With that in mind he was determined to expedite her response to his thought and without realizing how he said it, did so in a rather cold and rude manner instead of the teasing one that he had intended. "So Miss Bennet, you are expected to marry WELL and leave, are you?"

The statement was said in such a way that Elizabeth could not miss the rude tone and his meaning and was furious about it. Elizabeth was unable to control her anger and Darcy was easily able to see the fury behind her reply, and he regretted it the moment "that smile" left her face and her eyes turned into dark pools of fury.

Sternly, through clenched jaw and gritted teeth Elizabeth replied. "No, Mr. Darcy YOU must be hard of hearing, I said only that I am expected to marry and leave so that there is one less mouth to feed and one less body to worry about. Although I am sure you have heard my mother's effusions" - the word was said with a bit of disdain - "on the topic of matrimony for her daughters, what you do not know is my feelings on the subject. Before you dare assume..." Elizabeth practically spit out the words "too much, remember that I have grown up in said household with said mother and been every day witness to that which a match without love, esteem and respect can do to a person. Regardless of anyone's sentiments I have my own plans for matrimony and no matter the situation, those plans include love." The last word was no more than a whisper as Elizabeth's fury mounted, but her not wanting to draw the attention of others. Elizabeth scowled and walked quickly towards the door, leaving Mr. Darcy on the dance floor alone and gaping at her hastily retreating figure. What no one witnessed was the tear that Elizabeth wiped from her eye as she realized Mr. Darcy was just another proud and disagreeable man from the ton just like the others supposed him to be. Her mind was glad she had discovered this before making a fool of herself, but could someone please tell the same to her heart, which had began to already be touched by the handsome Mr. Darcy.

Colonel Fitzwilliam and Charlotte Lucas had been dancing near Mr. Darcy and Elizabeth and to the mortification of each they had overheard every word. Charlotte was distressed for her friend and Colonel Fitzwilliam wanted nothing more than to help Darcy from the dance floor before more embarrassment occurred to him and so it was done with a slight look and nod at each other, Charlotte took off after Elizabeth and the Colonel took hold of Darcy's arm and led him to Sir William's library.

The Colonel had never seen Darcy in this state. He was at a loss to know what to do, he desperately wanted to help, but it took everything in him to keep from laughing once the realization of the situation finally set in. Never had anyone, much less a country lady from an obscure county like Hertfordshire, put Mr. Fitzwilliam Darcy, Master of Pemberley, in his place in such a way. He was just about to start to speak when it dawned on him... *Darcy likes this country lass more than I originally suspected. Oh, how I wish he had overhead what I did this very night, he would have saved himself some heartache and embarrassment.* Having received that knowledge before he began to speak he started in an entirely different manner.

"Darcy, old chap, I saw what happened out there, and perhaps you should lay low here in the library for a bit. Do you have any objection?"

Darcy said not a word; he just stared at the wall in front of him with a blank look on his face.

"Well man, are you going to answer me?"

Darcy was silent, the colonel was at a loss, the two had always been easy telling each other everything and this was not going well, Darcy was staring into a void, non-responsive and un-communicative.

Fitzwilliam turned to Darcy and stated "Darcy, I will leave you to your own devices for the time being, but rest assured that we will be discussing this later. I have intelligence from that lady that may be of some use to you. I will call for you when it is time to return to Netherfield. Until then I recommend that you stay here and think through your rudeness to beautiful ladies."

Darcy grimaced at the comment, but still said nothing as he sunk into a nearby chair.

The Colonel returned to look for Charlotte. He surprisingly had enjoyed dancing with her, despite knowing her perception of marriage and was concerned over Miss Elizabeth.

Charlotte had caught up with Elizabeth at the gate leaving Lucas Lodge; however she would not talk more than to request that Charlotte inform Mr. Bennet that Elizabeth had walked home, as she needed some fresh air. Charlotte did not miss the sound of tears in Elizabeth's voice.

The Colonel found Miss Lucas as she was relating the news to Mr. Bennet. Mr. Bennet thanked her and went in search of some privacy; already he had been forced to talk to too many people. He would have preferred Lizzy to tell him herself so that he could have escorted her home, but it was not to be.

The Colonel asked Charlotte for another dance to replace their last. As they waited for the next dance to begin the Colonel was desperately trying to think of a way change Miss Elizabeth's current perception of Darcy. But how was that to be done? He had insulted her to her face.

Chapter 3
The Library at Lucas Lodge

Mr. Bennet had decided he was through with the frivolity that accompanied a gathering and headed for Sir William Lucas's library for a bit of privacy. This was the first gathering Mr. Bennet had accompanied his wife and daughters to in the past two months and already he was regretting it. He had stayed on the outskirts of the room but it was not far enough, some of his acquaintances had detected his presence and required conversation, something Mr. Bennet was loathe to give in general. Sir Lucas had once told him that he had an open invitation to that room whenever a gathering occurred if he would just agree to bring his lovely family out into the neighborhood society.

Mr. Bennet walked in grabbed the book he had been reading at the last gathering he attended, a little over six months ago, from the same place that he had left it. It was not hard to find as Sir Williams library was used rarely, the only library in the neighborhood being used less being that of Netherfield. Mr. Bennet sat down in his favorite one of Sir William's chairs by the fire. He was too occupied with his own current distresses to notice the other man already in the library.

Thus Darcy and Mr. Bennet stayed for close to ten minutes, each lost in his own preoccupations until Mr. Bennet became cognizant of someone mumbling to himself. Turning he noticed the gentleman for the first time, yet sat where he was, knowing he would not want to be bothered, and further he did not want to be bothered with inquiring himself.

He knew the gentleman from his wife pointing him out, however he had never received a formal introduction. Propriety demanded that the man of greater worth initiate the introductions, therefore he was confident that he would not be disturbed as that man was unlikely to initiate conversation.

As Mr. Bennet continued reading he could not help but be annoyed that the gentleman's mumblings turned into more loudly proclaimed exclamations and was beginning to interrupt him.

"What have I done? What does she think of me? Why did I treat her so? Will she ever forgive me? What can I do to make amends? Do I want to make amends? Of course I do, she is the best lady I have yet to encounter. What of her family? They have absolutely nothing and no connections. Do I need a lady of fortune? No, I have plenty of wealth for the both of us and any future children I ever have. Do I need the connections that a good match would bring? No, I have plenty of connections for myself, and of those I care nothing for more than half of them. Why am I even considering all of this, it is much too soon to be considering a match, I barely even know her. Do I though, consider her as a possible match for me, a potential wife and Mistress of Pemberley? Yes, perhaps I do."

Mr. Bennet had only been half hearing Mr. Darcy, but here the mumblings began to arrest his attention.

"What of her mother and numerous sisters? The mother." He shuddered and shook his head, no comment seemed appropriate to describe the woman. "The three younger sisters are nothing. Oh, the way the one plays," again another shudder, "and the other two are such flirts, but what of Jane?"

Mr. Bennet was all awareness now for he was sure that the gentleman was not only talking of his family but that his interest was in his dearest Lizzy.

"How are Miss Jane and Miss Elizabeth so different from the others in the family? I guess I shall never know as she now hates me so. I must escape from here, out of Meryton, away from Netherfield, away from her, I must go now." Mr. Darcy turned to leave and as he did he saw a gentleman staring at him strangely. Mr. Darcy could not help but be offended that someone had listened to his private ruminations and stated to the gentleman in the same cold manner previously used on Elizabeth "Sir!"

Mr. Bennet did nothing but stare at the gentleman. Mr. Darcy began to feel uncomfortable and headed towards the door with long strides. Mr. Bennet stopped him as he was halfway across the room.

"Mr. Darcy?" It was said as a question making the gentleman stop in his tracks. "Do I know you, sir?"

"No, we have never been properly introduced and I do not believe now is a proper time, as you are in quite a state; however if you will sit Mr. Darcy I would speak with you." This was said more as a demand and with a bite to the words.

Mr. Darcy did not know what to think. The gentleman had as much as demanded that he would stay to be spoken to yet refused introductions. This irritated yet intrigued Darcy, he sat in the chair across from the stately gentleman.

Mr. Bennet did nothing but look at Mr. Darcy for what seemed an eternity. Mr. Darcy had never in his life been observed in such a fashion, he was generally the one to do the observing, and it did not put him at ease to be under such scrutiny at this time. The scrutiny of matchmaking Mama's was nothing to this. Darcy felt his very soul was being evaluated. He did not know this gentleman but was sure that despite the fact that he was a gentleman he must be beneath Darcy since they were not already acquainted.

As Darcy was reaching the height of anxiety Mr. Bennet began with "I could not help, as much as I tried to avoid it, but overhear your mutterings and mumblings. It appears as if you have gotten yourself into quite a fix, young man." Darcy did nothing but nod at this, slightly offended at being told he had been muttering and mumbling.

"If I am to properly understand you have taken an interest in a young lady of the neighborhood and if I am not too presumptuous in interpreting the description of her and her family it is none other than Miss Elizabeth Bennet. Am I correct?" Darcy nodded hesitantly. He did not like where this conversation was going with this unknown gentleman.

"If I may say so sir, you have good taste." Darcy smiled slightly here as Mr. Bennet continued "If I am also correct I take it you offended her and now interpret her actions towards you as unfavorable?"

Mr. Darcy was worried that this man had interpreted so much but again nodded his head in the affirmative.

"So what do you propose to do about it, sir?"

Darcy was incredulous and spitefully stated "Do about it, why sir you overheard this much did you miss the fact that I am to leave and forget about her and her unfortunate family."

Mr. Darcy did not see Mr. Bennet's offense that flashed across his face for a split second.

Mr. Darcy stood and began to leave the room though at a slower pace this time.

"Well, Mr. Darcy, if this is your reaction then you do not deserve a woman as perfect as Miss Lizzy Bennet." This statement made Darcy stop and turn around to look at the gentleman as he continued. "I have been in this neighborhood for many years, may I say more years than I have not, and have known each member of that particular family since infancy. In my opinion the lady you have just referenced is by far the best woman that ever graced Hertfordshire, maybe even the whole of England and quite possible the earth. If I were not so closely connected to that family, and she were not many years younger she would be just the sort of lady I would feel blessed to invite into my life and my home. She deserves the best man, which you obviously are not."

The last was said in such a way that Darcy could not miss the insult and he just stood and gaped at the gentleman with his mouth open. How could anyone presume to tell him, Fitzwilliam Darcy, Master of Pemberley with wealth amounting to most likely more than ten thousand pounds a year that he is not good enough for some country lass with no connections or fortune?

Mr. Bennet saw the emotions of shock, anger, fury, and rage flash across the face of Mr. Darcy as he stood stiff and proud. After a few minutes passed Mr. Bennet continued "If you have a minute and would like to attempt to become a better man, one that may someday attain the hand of some **other** lady, I ask you to stay and talk for a few minutes." Darcy did not miss the fact that the gentleman implied he could not attain the lady in question.

Mr. Darcy hesitantly sat next to Mr. Bennet and raised his eyebrows indicating that he was listening.

"I would tell you about that family." Darcy nodded and Mr. Bennet continued, "The late Mr. Bennet, grandfather to said lady, was an honest and caring man. He had two sons, Mr. Matthew Bennet and Mr. Thomas Bennet, the father of the lady we currently speak of. Mr. Matthew Bennet was the older of the two and had been groomed to take the estate since infancy. The elder Mr. Bennet was very stout in his devotion to propriety and order of birth. As Mr. Matthew Bennet aged it became evident to everyone that in his heart he wanted to be a clergyman; however knowing the family as everyone did there was never a doubt that Mr. Matthew Bennet would do his duty to his family and the estate that so many relied on and forsake his own desires to assume his position as oldest son and Master of Longbourn.

Unfortunately it was not to be; however he waited until the estate was near ruin. Upon the death of Mr. Bennet, he assumed the position of master of the estate; however he neglected it and his duties. Mr. Thomas Bennet had gone to Oxford, excelled in his studies and although young became a leader in the education of others' sons. He was very content and pleased in the occupation he had chosen. He vowed never to marry anything but his books. Thomas had long known his brother, not himself, was to inherit and never had any thought of running the estate, or any formal training. He was content with his books."

"Mr. Matthew Bennet had become engaged to Miss Frances Gardiner who was overjoyed at becoming the wife to a country gentleman. You see, her family was in trade in London and this was her chance to advance in society and no one was to take that from her. It was commonly known at that time that the Longbourn Estate was one of the more prosperous estates in the county; no one was yet aware that Matthew was running it into ruin. She was pleased to be marrying into such a wealthy family."

"The afternoon of August 18th, 1788 was the coldest for Mr. Thomas Bennet, despite the fact that the temperature outside was reaching unprecedented heights. Mr. Matthew Bennet stood in the doorway of his brother's room at Oxford and informed him that he had accepted a living and would be abandoning the estate in one week's time. Either Thomas would assume responsibility or it would be sold to the first person who offered for it, regardless of price, leaving their mother and sister destitute. Matthew cared not for any of it; he only wanted to serve a flock even if he abandoned others, including his family in the process."

Mr. Darcy could see and hear distress in the voice and face of this long time family friend of the Bennet's, but the gentleman continued.

"The two fought for many hours about familial duty and such. It ended with Mr. Thomas Bennet leaving for Longbourn and Mr. Matthew Bennet nursing several facial wounds, each vowing never to see the other again."

"Miss Frances Gardiner was horrified and claimed that the Bennet family had vowed she would become the Mistress of Longbourn Estate and she would have it no other way. She no longer loved her "Dear Matthew", but insisted that she would have none other than her "Dear Thomas". Thomas Bennet had no interest in being married, but also knew the estate needed an heir and now that he was master of said estate it was his responsibility to provide the heir as well. It mattered not to him who he married, Miss Gardiner was prettier than most and would be just fine. Since it was obvious that she did not love him, she only wanted to advance her status he was not made to feel guilty for not loving her."

Mr. Bennet looked up here and could see that he still had Darcy's attention so he continued.

"Thomas Bennet knew he had no interest in a family but he also knew that the estate needed an heir. He also knew that despite his loathing for his brother Matthew, Matthew was one to want a family, and Thomas knew he would eventually marry and produce a strong brood. All in all Thomas was still not resigned to taking Longbourn and hoped his brother would regret forsaking it and return to claim it at a later point of time, so he made an agreement with his brother through a series of letters. First, Matthew could come and take over Longbourn at any point in the future and secondly that if he never took it over it would pass back to his line if Thomas did not have a son and Matthew did. Despite the fact that Mr. Thomas Bennet took over the estate and Matthew never did come to claim it, he always resented his brother for resigning it and taking orders, thus not allowing him to marry his books and become a professor."

Here Mr. Bennet paused to collect his thoughts, but continued shortly after. "It was not many years later that Thomas regretted that hasty decision made in his youth, for if he had not made it the estate would not be entailed away from the current ladies of Longbourn, however it was made, and before Thomas could regret it, Mr. Matthew Bennet died. He was happily married with not only one, but two strong and healthy yet very young sons."

"Matthew's wife, left with two small children and little money, remarried a whiney groveling caricature of a man, named Collins, who adopted her sons when he could not have any himself."

"So as you see Mr. Darcy, the Bennet estate is entailed on heirs male and Mr. William Bennet Collins is who is to inherit instead of the ladies Bennet. He is no longer the small strong child, but was altered into a mirror image of his step-father, a whiney groveling man."

Mr. Darcy stated, "So that is how the entail came about and I have heard that the Bennet parents are indifferent to each other."

Mr. Bennet inwardly cringed that his and his wife's indifference was so noted by society in general, but also knew that Mr. Darcy did not require a response so he went on.

"Do you want to know more of the family or are you tired of hearing an old man drudge on about his dearest, oldest friends."

Mr. Darcy eagerly said he wished to know more of the family if he had the time. He was beginning to understand a lot.

Mr. Bennet continued, "For three years everyone was content at Longbourn. Mr. Bennet worked hard to learn what it took to run an estate and bring it back from the brink of ruin. Mrs. Bennet was now a gentleman's wife and was free to go here and there visiting and gossiping. There were no children and no plan for any and both Mr. Bennet and his lady were content with that; however, one day the entail became known to Mrs. Bennet. She had not been informed of it upon her marriage, you see."

"I laugh when I remember the day. I was myself there that day, sitting in Mr. Bennet's library reading his books and drinking his port. Mrs. Bennet came running in, lace and satin blowing behind her... Mr. Bennet, Mr. Bennet, I am all in an uproar, you must come here and speak to me at once."

"What my dear, what can you want at such a time of day?"

Mr. Bennet was playing out the discussion for Mr. Darcy amusing both of them in the process.

"I must know, is this estate entailed on heirs male? For I have just had it from my sister Phillips, you know my sister, the one who married the attorney in Meryton... Well she said that she was visiting her "dear husband" when he got called away and so she decided to straighten the files in his desk so that they would be orderly and neat. She is such a good wife is she not... Would you like me to straighten your files? Well, never mind, what I want to say is that she saw a file labeled Bennet and knowing I, her dear sister, am a Bennet decided she must know all so that she could ensure I knew of all of my dear family's dealings. Well you can imagine her shock and horror and mine upon her telling me that Longbourn is entailed to heirs male. What have you to say? Were you never to tell me of this tragedy? And on whom is it entailed? It is entailed to none other than my dear Matthew, the one who I so tragically lost due to him abandoning me in my greatest time of need."

Mr. Bennet looked up here, crooking his eyebrows at Mr. Darcy as he continued. "It was then that she collapsed on the settee waving her fan ferociously and calling for her maid."

"No response was necessary; the maids helped her to her room and she was not seen for a few days."

"Prepare yourself, Mr. Darcy, for the next is quite shocking. I was again at the Bennet household in the library enjoying Mr. Bennet's books and port a few days later when Mrs. Bennet walked into the room scantily clad and demanded Mr. Bennet's presence above stairs to, I quote, begin working on the removal of the entail."

Darcy could not resist an outright smile and gasping laugh as Mr. Bennet continued. "Thus the Bennet family began."

"First, the angelic Jane was born into the family, then the feisty Elizabeth, then the solemn Mary." His story continued, but in a different vein now "Mrs. Bennet's brother Mr. Edward Gardiner had just married a wonderful lady from Lambton, in Derbyshire."

Mr. Darcy looked straight at his storyteller slight amazement registering on his features at the mention of Lambton but said nothing.

Mr. Bennet noticed and asked "Are you familiar with Lambton, Mr. Darcy?"

"Indeed I am sir; it is but five miles from my estate of Pemberley."

Mr. Bennet continued, "Mrs. Madeline Gardiner would be pleased to meet you, she enjoys meeting anyone from Lambton or the surrounding area and often says how she misses the people there. You see, since her parents passed away she rarely returns for visits, I think nothing more than once a year, although her sister is married to a local tradesman, but where was I, oh yes... Mrs. Bennet dearly wanted a son and said that her nerves were too much with all the girls running around to entice a son to the family so she sent the two eldest to live with her brother and sister-in-law for what I thought was too long and the baby Mary was turned over to the nursemaid and ignored. Two more daughters were born and no one else. The family finally returned together after the Gardiners had begun their own family. Let's see, Jane must have been thirteen or fourteen and Elizabeth twelve or so."

Mr. Darcy was shocked to learn that the girls had been practically raised by the Gardiners, living with them for nine or ten years.

"Yes, Mr. Darcy, now you know where Miss Jane and Elizabeth get their manners, it is not because of any instruction of their parents, for they were only here for but a few short years and then nothing more than a monthly visit. Although Mr. Bennet went to them frequently their mother never did."

"For years Mrs. Bennet said a son would come, but it all came to naught. It was but another few years when Jane and Elizabeth came out into society that their mother turned her energy to finding them husbands, and what better place for that than London. So the two ladies were once again sent to London each year after the Christmas celebrations and would stay until near the end of the season, returning in late May. Each year that the ladies returned unattached Mrs. Bennet became sillier."

"Mrs. Bennet has been beside herself for years trying to marry them off, but the girls are quite content to sit at home and enjoy the company of each other and now their father. You see, despite Mr. Thomas Bennet's original aversion to a family, he took more than a father's fancy to the two eldest girls. He adored them and particularly doted on them when they were home. He paid particular attention to their education as he would have to that of others' sons if he had stayed at Oxford. Jane for many years studied and improved herself but eventually her tranquility and goodness took her education to more feminine pursuits, but you see, Miss Lizzy, to this day studies with her father. I think she would have made the perfect son to any gentleman."

Mr. Bennet laughed at his own remark as he sat back in the chair and looked again at Mr. Darcy.

"What say you, Mr. Darcy, do you approve of Mr. Bennet's improvements of Miss Elizabeth?"

The way it was stated made Mr. Darcy blush as he said "I do!"

"Well, the stubbornness of both ladies is further presented as the ladies even defy their mother. The past two seasons the ladies have refused to go to town. I will admit that I believe Miss Lizzy instigates the revolt as Miss Jane is too kind and complacent to defy her mother on her own."

Mr. Bennet was repositioning himself in his chair and Mr. Darcy was worried that he was to leave and anxiously asked if he was uncomfortable and if he would like to stretch his legs a bit by walking about the room or, if sir preferred, they could even take their conversation to another venue, perhaps the nearby gardens. Mr. Bennet declined and said that a moment to make himself more comfortable in the chair was all that an old man with old bones needed.

"I have a request of you, sir. It seems you are quite intimate with the Bennet family and I was wondering if you might help me. You are correct in surmising that I have an interest in the lovely second Miss Bennet. You have indeed provided me a great deal of information about her family and a few tidbits about the lady herself, however I would like to meet with you again to learn more of the lady so that I may determine how to apologize for my recent behavior and see if she will allow me to get to know her better. Would you be willing to meet with me, sir, and provide me additional insights about the lady and her family, particularly the lady?" Mr. Darcy was apprehensive since this very man had insulted him not an hour before, but waited patiently for the gentleman to respond.

Mr. Bennet thought a moment. He did not like getting involved too much in affairs of the heart and knew his Lizzy would be quite irate with him if she ever knew, but something inside of him said to give this gentleman a chance. Mr. Bennet, however, was not going to give in easily. "Well I would, sir; however you have yet to prove your worth to me from your earlier display and then you vowed to leave the place directly. I have not the time, energy or patience to wait for you to develop into a good man and I have no intention of traveling at this juncture."

Mr. Darcy grimaced at the reference to the gentlemen's perception of him and then smiled at the second reference and said "I hope that I am not as bad as you currently believe. I believe you are only judging me from my actions here today, which I admit were juvenile and in poor taste; however I would be pleased to stay in the country a little longer if it will aid me to learn more of Miss Bennet and her family and let you get to know my true character a little better. I believe I will postpone my departure for a few days at least."

Mr. Darcy and Mr. Bennet agreed to meet on the morrow for a morning ride. As they were dismissing themselves Mr. Darcy again tried to receive a proper introduction but got nothing but a laugh from the gentleman in return. "Oh no, son, if the Bennet family ever heard of my telling you any of this I would be denied admittance into their most pleasing home, I dare not do anything to compromise my admittance at Longbourn. I think it best if you wait to learn who I am until you are surer of what you want."

With that Mr. Darcy left Mr. Bennet to his book in the library. The remaining hours of the gathering had quickly passed and everyone was in the process of leaving when Darcy exited the library. Colonel Fitzwilliam saw him leave in a pleasant manner and figured that Darcy had at least for now internally resolved what to do about his predicament.

Chapter 4
The Gentlemen's First Meeting

The party at Lucas Lodge the evening before had revealed to the Bennet ladies that a regiment of militia had just arrived and was stationed in Meryton for the entire winter. Catherine and Lydia frequently went into Meryton to visit their Aunt, Mrs. Phillips, to hear all of the latest gossip. Mrs. Phillips was known in the neighborhood to always have the latest news. Every trip to visit their aunt added to their pleasure since they also loved nothing more than a good gossip.

That morning Mr. Bennet was listening to their effusions of the subject of officers when he observed: "From all that I can collect by your manner of talking, you must be two of the silliest girls in the country. I have suspected it some time, but I am now convinced." With that he stood and stated that he was going for a morning ride before he retired to his library.

No one noticed how unusual this was except for Lizzy who knew that this was not the day that he made the rounds to the tenants and wondered at her father's going on a ride. Her thoughts ceased though as a letter arrived for Jane from Netherfield and a servant was awaiting the reply.

Mrs. Bennet's eyes sparkled with pleasure, and she was eagerly calling out, while her daughter read, "Well, Jane, who is it from? What is it about? What does he say? Well, Jane, make haste and tell us; make haste, my love."

"It is from Miss Bingley," said Jane, and then read it aloud.

> *"MY DEAR FRIEND, --*
>
> *"If you are not so compassionate as to dine to-day with Louisa and me, we shall be in danger of hating each other for the rest of our lives, for a whole day's tête-à-tête between two women can never end without a quarrel. Come as soon as you can on receipt of this. My brother and the gentlemen are to dine with the officers. –*
> *Yours ever,*
> *"CAROLINE BINGLEY"*

"With the officers!" cried Lydia. "I wonder my aunt did not tell us of THAT."

"Dining out," said Mrs. Bennet, "that is very unlucky."

"Can I have the carriage?" said Jane.

"No, my dear, you had better go on horseback, because it seems likely to rain; and then you must stay all night."

"That would be a good scheme," said Elizabeth, "if you were sure that they would not offer to send her home."

"Oh! But the gentlemen will have Mr. Bingley's chaise to go to Meryton, and the Hursts' have no horses to theirs."

"I had much rather go in the coach."

"But, my dear, your father already took one of the horses, I am sure."

Jane was obliged to go on horseback and true to the surmise; it began to rain not ten minutes after she left.

Her sisters were uneasy for her, but her mother was delighted. The rain continued the whole day without intermission; Jane certainly could not come back.

Mr. Bennet and Mr. Darcy had just met up when the rains began. Mr. Darcy had feigned an excuse of needing to write to his steward and cried off the militia engagement; only Mr. Bingley and Colonel Fitzwilliam had attended. Mr. Bennet began to state that they should meet at another time; however Mr. Darcy was eager to continue their talks and in no hurry to return to Netherfield and the clutches of Miss Caroline Bingley and asked if there was anywhere dry that "sir" knew about where they could talk. Mr. Bennet smiled at the invitation.

Darcy and Mr. Bennet had met a scarce quarter-mile from Mr. Bennet's own fishing lodge. He replied to Mr. Darcy that he knew of a place and off they headed in search of it.

It had been many years since the lodge had been used, but Mr. Bennet always had it attended to so it was clean and comfortable.

Upon arrival Mr. Darcy stated, "Is this your lodge, sir?"

Mr. Bennet was not ready to disclose his identity but also knew there were likenesses of Lizzy and Jane in the place and he would be shortly discovered if he did not come up with an ingenious answer. Therefore he quickly thought and replied "It is Mr. Bennet's retreat; however, he and I are quite close and he allows me access at any time. See, he has even provided me a permanent key." With that he withdrew his key chain from his pocket and after holding it up for the other gentleman's observation he unlatched the door.

The two entered and Mr. Bennet gathered wood as Mr. Darcy started the fire. While Darcy continued to stoke the fire to a raging point Mr. Bennet got some water and prepared tea and brandy to warm them up.

Once they were warmly situated in the two chairs by the fire Mr. Bennet asked Mr. Darcy if he had determined an action to take towards beginning to earn the love of Miss Elizabeth. Darcy not quite ready to admit all to this still unknown gentleman said, "Not love sir, as of now I just want to earn her forgiveness, respect and maybe even trust. Let us begin there; I am not willing on such a short acquaintance to jump to love. I also have family obligations and responsibilities that I cannot set aside."

That was just the opening Mr. Bennet desired to also fulfill his wish of knowing more of the gentleman before he aided him to win his Lizzy. Although Mr. Darcy did not know it yet Mr. Bennet was sure he would want Lizzy's love before the end of all their meetings, but did he want him to obtain it? That was the question. If he left things as they were Lizzy would be his longer than if he aided Mr. Darcy in obtaining her forgiveness and them in finding happiness with each other.

"So, what are your family obligations and responsibilities, sir, and how would an association with Miss Lizzy make you set them aside?" Mr. Bennet opened.

Mr. Darcy shrugged, sighed, and began. "I am the only son of Mr. George Darcy. My good father died five years ago, just as I had come of age. My mother died in childbirth many years before that. I along with my cousin am the guardian of my only sibling, a sister; Georgiana is but sixteen years old. I am also the master of a large estate; it is a full ten miles around. Pemberley is in Derbyshire, which makes me responsible for many others and thus I must make an alliance that will secure the stability of my estate and the future livelihood of many under my care."

At this point Darcy stopped and looked as if he had no intention of proceeding.

Mr. Bennet looked at him and dully said, "Is that all? If it is why would you pursue a penniless Bennet? Although she is bound to make her future husband the happiest of men it will not be because she brought a fortune to their marriage along with her beauty, charm, and wit."

"What do you mean sir, is that all?" Darcy said as he totally disregarded the second half of the question, or thought he did.

"I mean just that, you are responsible for an estate with many who are dependent on you and your sister but so are many others Mr. Darcy. There are many large estates and parentless children sprinkled all over England. I want to know who you are. What are your responsibilities, characteristics, virtues, strengths and weaknesses?"

Mr. Darcy, not used to talking about himself, added a little more. "As I said, my estate is a full ten miles around. I have many tenants and servants that are under my care. I try to be honest and fair with all yet I am strict and demand that each fulfill their duties to their best abilities. When they do so I reward them in return, however when they fail I reprimand them accordingly and stress the importance of succeeding."

With this Mr. Bennet laughed. "Why son, no wonder Miss Elizabeth did not respond favorably to you, she is all spirit and liveliness and you are quite dull. I suggest you give up now and save yourself the trouble. You are destined to fail if this is all YOU are."

Mr. Darcy was slightly offended, but swallowed his pride and tried again. "Sir, I was born at Pemberley and lived with my parents as an only child for more than twelve years. I began life observing a couple that had a deep love and regard for each other. They preferred to be with each other and me more than anything else in the world. I thoroughly enjoyed going to the orangery with my mother to smell the flowers and have her read to me. I also loved to follow my father around the estate mimicking and copying him in all that he did. I would move as he moved and talk as he talked as I desperately tried to be just like him. My mother became very sick while she was pregnant with Georgiana. I stayed by her daily begging my father to end her illness. One day my father came to me in tears and said my mother wanted me. When I went to her she was dressed in the most beautiful ball gown I had ever seen. It was a deep red, which was brilliant against her pale white skin. She had on the family jewels and had her hair done in a most exquisite design. I sat by her for many hours talking. She told me many things that she said she hoped to wait until I was older to tell but was afraid if she did not say them now then she would not be able to later. I did not know what she meant but I listened to all she said, especially about the things that she encouraged me many times over and over, almost begging me to repeat each thing she said to ingrain it into me. The one she dwelled on most was that she wanted me to marry for love and only the love she had for my father. She was almost desperate to make me understand at such a young age what true love was. Although I was unable to tell her, I knew what it was when I looked at my father who was standing beside the door crying. Once I completed all of my talk with mother, father escorted me to the housekeeper Mrs. Reynolds to be put to bed for the night. That was the last time I saw my mother alive. The next morning Mrs. Reynolds came in to me carrying the most beautiful doll I have ever seen. She looked as if she had been crying but told me that the doll was my angel from heaven to watch over and guard for the rest of my days. She said my mother especially wanted me to have her and protect her. From that day forward my sister Georgiana became my angel for me to guard with my life. My father told me that Georgiana was named in honor of love, for she carried the name of two people who loved each other more than life itself, George for my father and Anne for my mother. My mother had given her life that night in childbirth, giving life to my angel Georgiana. My father was never the same after that. He was withdrawn and distant from both Georgiana and I. He died years later from grief that started that horrible night that he was never able to recover from."

There was a pause here, but Mr. Bennet knew nothing was required to be said, "I laugh when I think that it was almost since that day, when I was but just over twelve, that I began the management of Pemberley and care for my infant sister. Though my father's steward did most of the work on the estate for years he trained me as he did it and handled all as I went to Cambridge. In addition, Mrs. Reynolds took over the care of Georgiana always appearing as if she allowed the decisions to me, that was so long as the decision coincided with her own. I think she must have even taken over the raising of me as well. She is to this day as a mother to both Georgiana and me. The day my father passed away was but a few months after I came of age to formally assume responsibility of Pemberley. Many of our family's acquaintances from ton said he would have died sooner had I come of age quicker. I moved easily into the position of master and joint guardian with my cousin of my dearest angel Georgiana." Here Darcy paused again.

Mr. Bennet just continued to listen.

"From my mother's death I had to grow and learn faster than any young boy of twelve or any gentleman should ever have to. I missed out on many assemblies, evenings at my clubs and theater showings. Georgiana was now over ten years old and I was beginning to see that she was going to require more than just a brothers presence, a housekeeper's devotion and a child's governess and nurse to ensure she was clean, dressed, fed and loved. She required a lady's education. With the help of

Lady Matlock, one of my aunts, I was persuaded to take Georgiana to London and engaged a ladies' governess and companion to oversee her education and return with her to Pemberley. At the age of fifteen her studies had greatly progressed and much of her education was done on her own as she was already outstripping her educator. Her governess resigned and I decided to hire a companion and tutors instead. It was at this point that I decided to step back and begin spending time with my friends that I had neglected for many years. Unfortunately at this point an event occurred that I would rather choose not to share. Since then I have tried to trust and have feeling around others, but to be honest I have felt nothing for anyone besides my dear Georgiana, my closest family, and my truest friend Mr. Charles Bingley. I have never been easy in company and am even less so now. I have never before wanted to have the respect and esteem of anyone before Miss Elizabeth Bennet and this is a very new sensation to me."

Mr. Bennet was beginning to understand this gentleman and decided he had said enough for the evening and that he would provide him information about his family and said daughter.

"Well, now I am beginning to know the true man behind the stature of Mr. Fitzwilliam Darcy, Master of Pemberley, guardian of Miss Darcy and devoted cousin and friend. It is evident that you have had much responsibility from an earlier age than any other that I know. I think that your life's events would make the wildest youth somber; as it appears you were never wild to begin with, it is evident why you appear to be so reserved. I also take it back that you have no liveliness and passion; you just keep it to yourself not allowing just anyone to see it. With the right inducement in your life, that passion will break free and you will be very happy."

Inside himself Mr. Darcy was thinking *dare I hope?*

With that nod Mr. Bennet proceeded. "Sir, I could tell you much about the Bennet family, however I rather think that your interest lies with one in particular of that household, therefore let us dedicate today to discussing her. Does that suit your plans?"

Darcy readily assented that it did and asked his new friend to proceed.

Mr. Bennet began as thus: "First of all before I begin I should tell you that letting Miss Lizzy see a glimpse of the passion that you just showed me would get you a lot farther than anything else you could do. She loves to see passion and purpose in others because she has so much herself. You must be careful though, Miss Elizabeth Bennet is quick to see right through falseness and insincerity. She is one that cannot be rushed and if you try, she will only resist more."

"Thank you sir, I shall look for an opportunity to teach her all there is to know about me and my passions." This was said with a smile by Mr. Darcy. Mr. Bennet was happy that he should do so but as a father hesitant that Mr. Darcy should show Elizabeth too much of his *passions*.

"Good then, Miss Elizabeth Bennet was a very active child. I have already mentioned to you that as a particular favorite of her father's she was allowed to attend to his estate business with him, but what I have yet to relate is the fact that she was also allowed many additional liberties that most daughters of a gentleman are not allowed."

Darcy inwardly smiled at this and Mr. Bennet continued.

"As I mentioned before the two eldest Bennet daughters lived apart from the family for extended amounts of time. When they would return from the "stifling town", as Elizabeth called it, she would take every opportunity to ramble about the countryside unattended. She began this about as early as I can remember, in fact I can barely remember her ever not doing so. In so saying, I can also not remember a time that Miss Elizabeth Bennet has not had an avid interest in tree climbing since it also developed at this time."

Darcy's eyebrows rose at this comment and Mr. Bennet began to laugh, "Yes indeed Mr. Darcy, you heard me correctly. Miss Bennet **has** an interest in countryside rambling and climbing trees. I see you are laughing even harder at that comment, but you heard and interpreted it correctly, she has had and still does have an affinity in climbing trees, particularly at Oakham Mount." The last was said with a bit of emphasis as it was obvious that the gentleman intended Mr. Darcy to remember the location.

Oakham Mount did not sound familiar to Darcy; however he noted it as a place of import and stored it in his mind for future retrieval.

"As a young child she would climb to the highest point possible and then sit on the branch and sing. Oh how her mother would get angry with her. Frequently I would be enjoying the evening, of course in the Longbourn library, and I would be entertained with the ranting of Mrs. Bennet on the lady we were just speaking of. Can you imagine a nine-year-old being scolded that if she did not present herself in the fashion of a lady that she would never catch a husband?"

Mr. Darcy could not help but laugh at this, what a sight that would have been.

"You laugh, so you must not realize that the ranting of how to catch an eligible husband began at the ripe age of about four and two for the Misses Jane and Elizabeth, I believe it was about the time they were sent to town to stay with Mr. and Mrs. Gardiner. To top it off I fear that it has only increased as Mrs. Bennet gave up on having a son and as the girl's age increased each year without having secured a husband. As an intimate friend of the family I have been acquainted with many such speeches. Sir, as a gentleman you can imagine that I never would have dreamed such speeches would accost my ears. Never would I have assumed my ears would hear them as frequently as they have over the years as I visited Longbourn. Where was I? Oh yes... Miss Lizzy and her tree climbing escapades. I know for a fact, in fact I am so sure I would bet my own life on it, that Miss Lizzy still climbs trees, however by the age of twelve she had perfected the art of disguise from her mother and so she still does so, but with peace. Why just last week as I was riding at Oakham Mount my ears were accosted with a most delightful melody. As I rode under the largest tree at the mount the sound increased and as I looked up I saw far above me the pretty lady perched on a branch singing melodies from the "Marriage of Figaro" at the top of her most delightful voice."

Darcy smiled at all that Mr. Bennet said.

"Have you had the opportunity to hear Miss Bennet sing, Mr. Darcy?"

"I have not sir, however I doubt anything would be more delightful, especially if I was permitted to hear the melody while Miss Elizabeth was thus engaged in a tree."

"Have you yet seen Oakham Mount Mr. Darcy?"

"I have not sir," and with a slight smile in the older gentleman's direction he added, "Though I assure you I shall be visiting there very soon, to take in the beauty of the Mount of course."

Had Mr. Darcy known who his informant truly was he would never have been so upfront with him.

Mr. Bennet inwardly smiled at Mr. Darcy's comment, but he was also unnerved by it. Yet he was not done.

Earlier Mr. Darcy had avoided answering a question and Mr. Bennet wanted to know the answer, as it would most assuredly affect Lizzy's happiness. "Mr. Darcy, I am afraid it is getting late, but I beg to ask you to answer my question from earlier that was avoided. Why would an association with Miss Lizzy make you put aside your family obligation? I would assume your family obligation would be to marry and produce an heir to carry on the Darcy legacy and as you said your own mother practically begged you to marry for love. If you fell in love with Miss Lizzy what would there be to stop you? Is there more to this?" Mr. Bennet had learned a lot from his new friend today and knew that his Lizzy would soon be lost to him. Mr. Bennet had expected that Mr. Darcy was a good man and as he got to know him his expectation was not disappointed, in fact it was exceeded. If Mr. Darcy was successful at showing a little of his true self and Elizabeth was able to discover it then it would not be long, Mr. Bennet was sure, before the two would unite their happy lives.

Mr. Darcy rubbed his hand across his brow and leaned forward, head in hands, thinking of how to phrase his answer to the question. "Sir, that is a great question, one that I have asked myself many times since meeting Miss Elizabeth. I have two answers. First is an off the cuff answer that stems from discussions with extended family members who know not of my parents wishes for me to find love. It has long been assumed that I would make an alliance with my cousin thus combining our estates and fortunes. Even if I do not marry her, my family assumes I will marry wealth and consequence, thus furthering my position in society. But then I think of the other side of my family, my long dead precious parents. They would want me to marry only to secure my happiness. They wanted me to marry for love, for happiness and joy, but unfortunately they are the only ones who know they told me this. Many times I have argued with the Fitzwilliam's, which includes the Earl and Lady Matlock and Lady Catherine de Bourgh about my intentions surrounding the topic of marriage. My aunts and uncle feel I am remembering only what I want and they believe my parents would want me to marry for love as long as it was within my own sphere of wealth and importance. They, Lady Catherine most of all, believe that two people outside of social spheres could never be compatible because of their vast differences in upbringing, and without compatibility, regardless of love, a breach would form. I however feel that they meant it regardless of sphere and that if two people have love, their unity will see them through anything; as their love matures so does their learning and compatibility. What do you think?" Darcy looked up at the gentleman expectantly as he stopped rubbing his head. He desperately wanted someone to agree with him, because he could feel himself becoming lost each time he heard more about Miss Elizabeth Bennet, a lady of no wealth and not in that sphere with which he was identifying himself.

"I agree that your parents would want you to marry for love, respect, esteem, and joy regardless of sphere or wealth. I know that is what I would want for my children. In saying that, I would also want them to be comfortable and not jeopardize their own situation and forget that the future must be planned for." Mr. Bennet was now positive he would lose his Lizzy and he was beginning to be more comfortable with who he knew would be her choice.

"Sir, I do not need the wealth of a wife to secure my future. My income is more than enough to sustain myself and Georgiana and any future family I may have for quite some time regardless of anything else. I could marry someone who comes with nothing but the dress she wears if that is my wish. I just wish that if I choose someone in such a situation that my family would accept her as I do, unfortunately I fear if I do not choose someone that meets with their approval she may never be accepted or mentioned by any of them except in order to pain her. I have begun to think about this recently and believe that regardless of how Miss Elizabeth was raised that she could easily feel comfortable in the "sphere" in which I associate; indeed she would be comfortable in any sphere, because that is her natural way. All that she requires is a chance. That may seem simple, but that is what worries me. What if I give her a chance but my peers never do? Will she be content to be shunned by society and left with no one but her family and me?" The question hung in the air unanswered.

Mr. Bennet could see Mr. Darcy's pain and knew why he was reluctant to chase after his feelings, he already cared for her enough that he would rather harm his own feelings by not having her than have his family injure her.

Mr. Darcy and Mr. Bennet agreed that it was getting late and since the rain had let up slightly to just a drizzle they decided that now would be the perfect time to head home. Each agreed that they should meet the day after tomorrow at this same location. It had been determined throughout the stay that this was an ideal location to pass the time in discussion.

With one last entreaty from Mr. Darcy to learn who his informant was and the other again denying him the knowledge, the two men departed with a quick bow to each other.

Mr. Bennet arrived home and went straight to his library. Mrs. Bennet was still congratulating herself that she had devised such a plan to keep Jane at Netherfield since the rain had begun again and Jane had not returned while it had subsided. Upon hearing the commotion, Mr. Bennet asked Elizabeth into his library to learn the situation.

Mr. Bennet was not pleased; however, he resolved that nothing could be done about it at present. Likewise Elizabeth was upset about the occurrences; however, like her father she could do nothing but hope her sister was well until Jane came home on the morrow.

When Mr. Bingley and Colonel Fitzwilliam returned to Netherfield after dining with the officers, they were met by Mr. Bingley's man who informed them that Miss Jane Bennet had taken ill while visiting for tea and was thus occupying the last guest room on the second floor. Mr. Bingley was confused by the pronouncement, but hurried to his sisters for an explanation.

Miss Bingley and Mrs. Hurst were sitting on the settee discussing Pemberley and the alterations that Miss Bingley planned to make once she became its mistress when Mr. Bingley came hurrying in with Colonel Fitzwilliam right behind him.

The two were then forced to explain that they had invited Miss Jane for tea and she had shown up on horseback during the rain. During tea she had become ill and been taken to the guest quarters to recover. Miss Bingley ensured Mr. Bingley that it was a trifling cold and that she would be well enough in the morning to head home.

Mr. Bingley truly hoped she would be well in the morning so that he would not need to worry about his sweet angel and spent the rest of the evening ordering the servants to make Miss Bennet as comfortable as possible and provide her with everything that she could possibly want or need. Everyone was to give her their utmost care and attention.

Colonel Fitzwilliam sat back smiling, and when Darcy returned he accompanied him to the library and related all of the events to him. Mr. Darcy voiced his concerns and hopes that she would quickly recover and the two spent the rest of the evening in quiet discussion. Throughout their discussion it became evident to the Colonel that this was the moment when he should approach the subject of the party at Lucas Lodge and the occurrences between Darcy and Miss Bennet.

Hesitantly the colonel began… "Darcy, I see that you are well now and that upon leaving the library at Lucas Lodge last night you were significantly better than when I took you in there, but still, I must ask, are you well?"

Darcy had all but forgotten the mood he had been in when he entered the library at Lucas Lodge the night before and slightly smiled to himself as he began to remember all that the anonymous gentleman had told him. His only statement to his cousin was "I am quite well, Fitzwilliam, think no more of it."

The Colonel was glad to hear it but by no means was he satisfied with the answer. "Darcy, come man, we have always been candid with each other and you know I will accept nothing except the full truth. I was dancing next to you and overheard the whole of it. Come man there is no way a man of your feeling and character is quite well after such a setting down."

Darcy sighed, but Fitzwilliam knew that meant he was wearing down and one more push and he would have his information.

"Darcy, tell me, maybe I can help."

To no surprise of the colonel Darcy pursed his lips and began. "Well you already admitted that you heard the whole of the conversation so you are fully aware of what occurred between the two of us, am I correct?"

41

With that the colonel nodded.

"What you are not aware of is what occurred in the library subsequent to your departure. I was berating Miss Bennet and myself under my breath. When I turned around to leave I became aware that I was not alone in the library. I was at first upset at the man for invading on my privacy; however he was unapologetic and intrigued me. Come to think of it he was downright rude to me. The two of us began to talk and I determined that he is a close friend to the Bennet family. He talked to me of that family and a bit about Miss Elizabeth. I began to understand them better. I have hope and must believe that Miss Bennet will not stay mad at me forever and therefore I am quite well and looking forward to meeting her again and apologizing."

With that Darcy stopped talking and looked at the Colonel waiting a reply.

Admit it, man you like this Miss Bennet, do you not?"

Darcy hesitated and looked straight at the Colonel, he knew not whether he should answer because he knew that the Fitzwilliam family had no secrets. This would surely be known by the whole of the family in less than a week's time. Despite his inner struggle of whether or not to answer he decided that the colonel knew him well and the statement was not truly a question, it was just phrased as such for the benefit of conversation. With that knowledge Darcy began. "I do, however, know this, Fitzwilliam, that I am aware that you are unable to keep your mouth closed. I may like the lady, but what man could ignore such a pretty face? I have no present intentions towards the lady and so would advise you to keep your counsel instead of informing the family in the morning post that I am head over heels in love."

Fitzwilliam laughed and said "Darcy, man, I of all people understands what a pretty face can do to a man, but I did not realize they affected you as such." The last was said with a sly grin. "My perception is that as long as they have soft delicate voices, long eyelashes, and wear beautiful flowing dresses that cling to their delicate figures…" here Fitzwilliam raised the pitch of his voice and batted his eyelashes as he moved his hands mimicking the figure of a well-endowed lady, "I will pay them attention. I do confess however, that Miss Elizabeth Bennet has a rare beauty that is not easily matched; perhaps I should pursue her myself. Or not…, I suppose…, since I need a lady of fortune and it appears as she has none unless the neighborhood gossip is not accurate."

"No, I am afraid the gossip is accurate." For one Darcy was relieved that ladies gossiped.

As the last was said Colonel Fitzwilliam stood and prepared to leave the room. Fitzwilliam smiled broadly clasped Darcy on the shoulder and said in a conspiring voice. "I will tell you a secret, cousin. I had many over-hearings yesterday and my earlier one would have been to your advantage to know sooner."

Darcy was very interested and raised his brow as a signal for the Colonel to continue.

"I overheard Miss Bennet in conversation with her friend Miss Lucas as they extolled the virtues and their views of love and marriage. I must say that Miss Lucas is not worthy of being pursued due to her view of a match solely to be well-situated, but Miss Bennet, now she freely and spiritedly explained how she would only marry for love, respect and esteem of her partner. Do you not think a woman like that is worthy? I believe I have often heard you spouting much of the same, cousin, perhaps she is your soul mate." With the last said the Colonel did not wait for a response, he unclasped Darcy's shoulder and left the room in a few long smooth strides before Darcy could begin to deny everything as Fitzwilliam knew he was sure to do.

Chapter 5
Off To Netherfield

The morning following the rain dawned on a beautiful sunny day and breakfast was scarcely over when a servant from Netherfield brought the following note for Elizabeth:

> *"MY DEAREST LIZZY, --*
>
> *"I find myself very unwell this morning, which, I suppose, is to be imputed to my getting wet through yesterday. My kind friends will not hear of my returning till I am better. They insist also on my seeing Mr. Jones—therefore do not be alarmed if you should hear of his having been to me – and, excepting a sore throat and headache, there is not much the matter with me. –Yours, etc. JANE"*

"Well, Mrs. Bennet," said Mr. Bennet, when Elizabeth had read the note aloud, "if your daughter should have a dangerous fit of illness—if she should die, it would be a comfort to know that it was all in pursuit of Mr. Bingley, and under your orders."

"Oh! I am not afraid of her dying. People do not die of little trifling colds. She will be taken good care of. As long as she stays there, it is all very well. I would go and see her if I could have the carriage."

Elizabeth, feeling really anxious, was determined to go to her, though it was declared to her mother that the carriage was not to be had; and as she was no horsewoman, walking was her only alternative. She declared her resolution.

"How you can be so silly," cried her mother, "as to think of such a thing, in all this dirt! You will not be fit to be seen when you get there."

"I shall be very fit to see Jane, which is all I want."

Elizabeth set out on her walk crossing field after field at a quick pace, jumping over stiles and springing over puddles with impatient activity, and finding herself at last within view of the house, with weary ankles, dirty stockings, and a face glowing with the warmth of exercise.

Upon reaching the edge of Netherfield's lawn Elizabeth came face to face with Mr. Darcy. Mr. Darcy was so stunned by the appearance of the one he had just been meditating that he could not determine whether or not she was real and so just stood there gaping at her.

Elizabeth was not sure he was going to say anything or not and so once her curtsy had been completed she thus began, "Mr. Darcy, I am come to see my sister."

When no response was given she continued, "Would you be so good as to take me to her?"

With that Mr. Darcy came to his senses, agreed and began walking towards the house. Half way to the house Mr. Darcy remembered himself and his manners and offered Elizabeth his arm. Elizabeth who had been wondering how many faults was running through Mr. Darcy's head on her person to make him this out of sorts was determined not to accept. This was the first time they had seen each other since the unfortunate dance together at Lucas Lodge and Elizabeth was still angry at his manner.

Mr. Darcy was disappointed that she had not accepted his arm. His disappointment was even more acute as it was a sure indication that she was still upset at him for his comments during the dance at Lucas Lodge. He decided he must remedy the situation soon before Miss Bennet became more upset at him. With the decision to take action firm in his mind he thus began "Miss Bennet, before I show you to your sister could I bother you for a few minutes of your time to discuss something with you?"

Elizabeth was unsure whether she wanted to take time away from her visit with her sister to listen. Yet she was slightly curious as to what he could possibly have to say to her. So she nodded in agreement. Darcy noticed a large stone-crafted bench along the gravel walk and indicated it for Elizabeth to seat herself. Elizabeth and Darcy both sat down and Darcy began. "Miss Bennet, I want to apologize to you for my behavior at the party at Lucas Lodge. I in no way meant what I said to be taken as an insult to you or your family, I simply spoke without thinking."

He paused there for Elizabeth to reply. Elizabeth was thoughtful, but did not respond immediately. Darcy who was on edge already was even more disheartened by her silence and so quickly continued. "Miss Bennet, I will be honest with you, and please do not take offense at anything I tell you now. I am sure you are aware of my worth, since I have heard your own mother mention it. Well, in town I frequently hear it mentioned by ladies and their mothers; however, their intentions are in no way honorable, they are generally mercenary. Thus it puts me on edge in society whenever I hear it mentioned. The fact that I have heard your mother discuss the worth of myself and my friends, and then you yourself mentioned marriage I automatically jumped to a conclusion that I now see was not accurate. I again apologize for my cold manner and offense: I ought not to have said anything no matter what your intentions. But because I did, I am glad that it had a positive result in that you were able to clarify your position for me so that I did not misunderstand your views on the subject."

With that Darcy stood and stated "Thank you for your time, I will now show you to your sister."

Elizabeth did not stand immediately, but remained seated and said "Mr. Darcy, I appreciate your honesty and apology. I confess you were wrong when you assumed I had mercenary intentions in telling you I am expected to marry and leave home, however I give you credit for your observations. I have often tried to limit the vocalizations of my mother while in company about the fortunes of gentlemen in the neighborhood or the eligibility of her daughters; however, it is not to be. I recommend that you ignore her as the rest of the neighborhood does. You will in time determine that she is harmless and only has the best interest of her daughters in mind. As for myself I should not have been so forthright in my admissions or so bitter in my response to you. My frankness often gets me in trouble, yet no matter how I try I cannot curb it. I suppose that is because I truly do not wish to."

Darcy smiled at the description and again offered her his arm to escort her to the house. This time Elizabeth took his arm as they walked towards Netherfield. Darcy was pleased that since she had accepted his arm, it was a sure sign that she was mending in her opinion of him. All Elizabeth could think about was how unexpected, honest, artless, and open his apology was. All the feelings she had felt for Mr. Darcy before came back full force, as did a few new ones. Elizabeth scarcely recalled being upset at him.

Elizabeth was shown into the breakfast-parlor by Mr. Darcy, where all but Jane was assembled, and where her appearance created a great deal of surprise. It was incredible to Mrs. Hurst and Miss Bingley that she had walked three miles after such a bad rain. Mr. Bingley was overjoyed to have her visit her sister and was all that politeness could be. Colonel Fitzwilliam was admiring her strength and stamina at walking the distance without so much as one heavy breath and Darcy was admiring her person and the effects that the vigorous walk had on her complexion. Mr. Hurst said nothing at all, only attending to his breakfast.

Her inquiries after her sister were not very favorably answered. Miss Bennet had slept ill, and though up, was very feverish, and not well enough to leave her room. Elizabeth was glad to be taken to her immediately; and Jane, who had only been withheld by the fear of giving alarm or inconvenience from expressing in her note how much she longed for such a visit, was delighted at her entrance. She was not equal, however, to much conversation, and when Miss Bingley left them together, could attempt little besides expressions of gratitude for the extraordinary kindness she was treated with. Elizabeth silently attended her.

When breakfast was over the sisters joined them; and Elizabeth decided to take the opportunity to get a book from the Netherfield library to entertain her while she attend Jane. No one was in the library, so Elizabeth took a few minutes to browse the collection at her leisure. She noticed that although the room was large the selection was more limited than someone of Mr. Bingley's status normally is, but it had a few books that she was not familiar with. She continued to look and as she was preparing to leave she spotted an interesting-looking tome on the top shelf. Unfortunately she was just short enough that she could not reach it. Elizabeth began to stretch and lean in all unusual manners trying to gain some height and become tall enough to reach the book. It was at this time that Mr. Darcy entered the room where the lovely sight arrested him. As Elizabeth had her back to Darcy she did not notice him enter and stop to admire her. After a few moments Elizabeth decided she would not be able to reach the book without assistance and quickly grabbed the small chair next to the shelf, slid it over and jumped on it to reach the tome. It was now that Darcy decided to announce himself to her and try to help.

"Miss Elizabeth, please let me be of service to you." He walked over to her, but was too late; she had grabbed the book and was already studying its pages as she remained standing on the chair. From here, she was a little taller than Mr. Darcy.

Elizabeth blushed slightly and said "Mr. Darcy, sir, I did not see you there. I am just come to get a book to occupy my time with my sister above stairs. This one looked particularly interesting and since it was too high I decided…" Elizabeth was blushing more at the realization that he knew exactly what she had done and had no need to retell it.

Mr. Darcy took the book from her, offered her his hand and helped her off of the chair. He then turned the book over to inspect its title, already knowing full well what it was since he had set the book there himself just the night before and was at that very moment going to retrieve it. "Oh what a good choice, Miss Bennet, though this is not a title that ladies normally delight in. I have read it myself and highly recommend it."

Elizabeth colored again and stated "I know that it is not one that ladies normally read Mr. Darcy, but as I told you at the party at Lucas Lodge I am my father's son. Not only have I been permitted to attend to the estate with him, but also as he is rather fond of education and reading he has allowed me to read any literature that I see fit. Including those not generally read by fashionable ladies of society. If you do not mind I will just take the book and return to Jane's room to attend to her." With that said Elizabeth snatched the book from Darcy's hands and began to walk from the room.

Mr. Darcy thought quickly and decided to make a comment before she left again just to ensure that there was no way she could construe a misunderstanding or think that he disapproved of something about her. "Miss Bennet, I am glad that your father has attended your education so thoroughly. I also believe it is appropriate for a lady to improve her mind by extensive reading of all forms of literature and have thus encouraged my sister to do the same. Although she is younger than you and most likely has not read as much as you have her reading has been extensive and I am sure that the two of you would be able to have enjoyable conversation discussing literature that is not in fashion for most ladies of society."

"Thank you Mr. Darcy; if I ever have the pleasure of meeting Miss Darcy I would be delighted to discuss literature with her." Elizabeth turned and left to attend Jane.

Mr. Darcy smiled, content that he had just shown Miss Elizabeth that he approved of her reading habits. One part of him hoped he was now on track to show her that he approved of her. The other part of him was telling himself to slow down as he himself did not know how far his intentions were running and did not want to give hope where he was not sure he wanted to go.

The apothecary arrived as Elizabeth returned, and having examined his patient, said, as might be supposed, that she had caught a violent cold, and that they must endeavor to get the better of it; advised her to stay in bed, and promised her some draughts. The advice was followed readily, for the feverish symptoms increased, and her head ached acutely. Elizabeth did not quit her room for a moment; and upon hearing the apothecary's diagnosis Mrs. Hurst and Miss Bingley did not return once, saying they had no desire to get sick themselves.

When the clock struck three, Elizabeth felt that she must go, and very unwillingly said so. Elizabeth demanded no less than a promise from Miss Bingley that she would personally attend to Jane. When Miss Bingley could not provide her the promise, she instead offered an invitation to remain at Netherfield for the present. Elizabeth most thankfully consented, and a servant was dispatched to Longbourn to acquaint the family with her stay and bring back a supply of clothes.

When Elizabeth was summoned to dinner Jane was by no means better. Mr. Bingley was all solicitude and demanded that all attention be paid to Jane. His sisters, on hearing this, repeated three or four times how much they were grieved, how shocking it was to have a bad cold, and how excessively they disliked being ill themselves; and then thought no more of the matter: and their indifference towards Jane made Elizabeth dislike them even more.

During dinner Elizabeth was interested in watching Miss Bingley's attentions to Mr. Darcy and wondering at their unusual relationship. It was obvious that Miss Bingley wanted Mr. Darcy's attentions fully on herself, yet it was obvious to Elizabeth that Mr. Darcy was disgusted with her advances and wanted nothing of them or her. Elizabeth could also tell that Miss Bingley was not pleased with her although she could not fathom why since the two had barley spoken to each other. But since Elizabeth cared not for her opinion she thought no more on the matter.

When dinner was over, Elizabeth returned directly to Jane and sat with her until late in the evening. When she had the pleasure of seeing Jane sleeping peacefully she decided that it was rather rude of her not to attend to the party downstairs, so gathering the book she had borrowed from Mr. Bingley's library she joined the party downstairs.

On entering the drawing-room she found the whole party playing at loo, and was immediately invited to join them, but suspecting them to be playing high she declined it, and making her sister the excuse, said she would amuse herself for the short time she could stay below with a book.

Mr. Hurst looked at her with astonishment. "Do you prefer reading to cards?" said he, "that is rather singular."

"Miss Eliza Bennet," said Miss Bingley "despises cards. She is a great reader, and has no pleasure in anything else." She laughed at the conclusion of her statement.

"I deserve neither such praise nor such censure," cried Elizabeth; "I am NOT a great reader, and I have great pleasure in many things."

"In nursing your sister back to health I am sure you have pleasure," said Bingley; "and I hope it will be soon increased by seeing her quite well."

Elizabeth thanked him, and then went back to reading her book.

"What is it that you are reading Miss Bennet?" asked Colonel Fitzwilliam.

Elizabeth responded and looked quickly at each person in the room. Darcy was smiling to himself and the ladies and Mr. Bingley had a look as if they knew not what she was talking about. Mr. Hurst had no look at all. She then went on speaking to the Colonel, "I found it this morning in the library and took the liberty of borrowing it during my stay while I am with Jane. I hope you do not mind Mr. Bingley."

"Very well, you have nothing to fear, you may borrow any book you like. Although the collection is small I have more than I look into, which is evident because I do not even recognize the name of that book."

Miss Bingley began to say "I am astonished, that my father should have left so small a collection of books. What a delightful library you have at Pemberley, Mr. Darcy!"

"It ought to be good," he replied, "it has been the work of many generations."

"And then you have added so much to it yourself, you are always buying books."

"I cannot comprehend the neglect of a family library in such days as these."

"Neglect! I am sure you neglect nothing that can add to the beauties of that noble place. Charles, when you build YOUR house, I wish it may be half as delightful as Pemberley."

It was here that the Colonel interrupted with a mischievous smile. "Say Darcy is that not the same book you have been reading and placed up on the upper shelf in the library for safe keeping?"

Darcy gave the Colonel a pointed look to not say anything more but the Colonel was bent on having some fun. The fact was that the Colonel feared that Darcy would get nowhere with the lady without some intervention. The Colonel thought that a good step in laying the foundation for her to like his cousin would be to let her know that they shared an interest in the same book. The Colonel had seen Darcy smile when she mentioned the book and knew that he was pleased that she had selected his book out of those that were in the library.

"Oh, Mr. Darcy, I am so sorry, have I taken the book you have been reading, this place marker here must be yours then?" asked Elizabeth as she held up a stiff piece of brown leather and began to close the book and hand it to Darcy. "Why did you not say something earlier when we met in the library?"

Here the Colonel raised his brows in Darcy's direction. So he had already made some discussion on the book with Miss Bennet. *Well done, Darcy, I would never have guessed,* the Colonel thought to himself.

Darcy waved his hand "No, No, I was not reading it. I was just using it as a reference resource. In my last letter from Georgiana she was inquiring about another book that was similar to this one and since she and I have read them both she was seeking a point of clarification. You may read it for as long as you desire. The reason Bingley does not recognize it is because it is a book from Pemberley, not Netherfield."

"Thank you, I assure you I will not crease or ruin it. Mr. Darcy, does your sister often seek clarification from you while reading?"

"She does." Darcy continued "Georgiana no longer has a governess and so she and I frequently chose a book to read together and then discuss our opinion and thoughts on the topic. It always provides intelligent conversation between us and further increases her education."

"I frequently do the same with my father."

"If you have any particular opinions you would like to discuss about this book or any other which I have read I would be honored to discuss them with you at any time." Elizabeth smiled and Darcy felt emboldened. "Also, if you have suggestions of books that you wish to discuss that I have not read I would just have you mention them and I would also be honored to read them and discuss them as well. I am always looking to further my knowledge by reading new material. Once you have completed this one you need only ask and I may be of additional service to you in providing a few more titles that you may enjoy." Darcy was out of breath and his heart was racing. This was the longest speech he had made in some time and it was obvious to him that Colonel Fitzwilliam was enjoying it a bit too much.

Elizabeth smile and said "Thank you, I will remember that."

Miss Bingley felt that she was losing Darcy's attention and was furious. It was her intention to get it back. "Mr. Darcy, I would also enjoy discussing book opinions with you. As I was saying earlier, you have never neglected your library and I have often commented on how splendid it is. Why I think it is the finest room in all of Pemberley. Charles, when you take your house you must have a library as fine as Pemberley."

"I wish I may, Caroline."

"But I would really advise you to make your purchase in that neighborhood, and take Pemberley for a kind of model. There is not a finer county in England than Derbyshire." said Caroline quickly.

"With all my heart; I will buy Pemberley itself if Darcy will sell it."

"I am talking of possibilities, Charles."

"Upon my word, Caroline, I should think it more possible to get Pemberley by purchase than by imitation."

Caroline was not pleased with this answer and decided to try a new topic to draw Mr. Darcy back to the conversation.

"Is Miss Darcy much grown since the spring?" said Miss Bingley; "Will she be as tall as I am?"

"She is now about Miss Elizabeth Bennet's height, or rather taller." said Darcy as he looked out the corner of his eye for Elizabeth's reaction.

The colonel could not lose an opportunity to tease Darcy and here he said "Are you sure Darcy, upon my honor I think she is a bit taller. Maybe you should stand up with Miss Elizabeth again to properly assess her height. You may not be able to accurately tell unless you are standing close."

Both Elizabeth and Darcy blushed as if on cue.

Miss Bingley most assuredly did not want Darcy to do such a thing and hurriedly continued on as if nothing had been mentioned. "How I long to see her again! I never met with anybody who delighted me so much. Such a countenance, such manners! And so extremely accomplished for her age! Her performance on the pianoforte is exquisite."

"It is amazing to me," said Bingley, "how young ladies can have patience to be so very accomplished as they all are."

"All young ladies accomplished! Charles, what do you mean?"

"Yes, all of them, I think. They all paint tables, cover screens, and net purses. I scarcely know anyone who cannot do all this, and I am sure I never heard a young lady spoken of for the first time, without being informed that she was very accomplished."

"Your list of the common extent of accomplishments," said the Colonel "has too much truth. The word is applied to many a woman who deserves it no otherwise than by netting a purse or covering a screen. But I am very far from agreeing with you in your estimation of ladies in general. I cannot boast of knowing more than half-a-dozen, in the whole range of my acquaintance, that are really accomplished."

"Nor I, I am sure," said Miss Bingley.

"Then," observed Elizabeth, "you must comprehend a great deal in your idea of an accomplished woman?"

"Yes, I do comprehend a great deal in it."

Miss Bingley thought this was the perfect opportunity to point out her accomplishments to Mr. Darcy and so she began. "No one can be really esteemed accomplished who does not greatly surpass what is usually met with. A woman must have a thorough knowledge of music, singing, drawing, dancing, and the modern languages, to deserve the word; and besides all this, she must possess a certain something in her air and manner of walking, the tone of her voice, her address and expressions, or the word will be but half-deserved."

"All this, she must possess," added Darcy, "and to all this she must yet add something more substantial, in the improvement of her mind by extensive reading."

The colonel smiled, this was not one of his requirements of an accomplished woman, but it was one of Darcy's and knowing Miss Bingley most certainly did not match the description yet Miss Elizabeth did made him smile.

"I am no longer surprised at your knowing ONLY six accomplished women. I rather wonder now at your knowing ANY." This was said in jest as Elizabeth had heard this from Darcy earlier in the day and that she realized that Miss Bingley was listing the qualities she thought she herself had and it appeared as if the Colonel had all but dropped out of the conversation, although those who knew him knew he was still intently listening. Elizabeth was also cognizant of the fact that there she sat with an open book on her lap and was a bit embarrassed. She decided she had heard enough and stated that she must check on Jane. With that she stood and went upstairs.

"Elizabeth Bennet," said Miss Bingley, when the door was closed on her, "is one of those young ladies who seek to recommend themselves to the other sex by undervaluing their own; and with many men, I dare say, it succeeds. But, in my opinion, it is a paltry device, a very mean art."

"Undoubtedly," replied the Colonel and Darcy in unison and the Colonel continued "there is meanness in all the arts which ladies sometimes condescend to employ for captivation. Whatever bears affinity to cunning is despicable."

Miss Bingley was not so entirely satisfied and even a bit affronted with this reply and thus discontinued the subject.

Elizabeth joined them again only to say that her sister was worse, and that she could not leave her. Bingley urged Mr. Jones being sent for immediately; while his sisters, convinced that no country advice could be of any service, recommended an express to town for one of the most eminent physicians. Elizabeth declined the ladies' offer but she was not so unwilling to comply with their brother's proposal, and it was settled that Mr. Jones should be sent for early in the morning, if Jane were not decidedly better.

Chapter 6
The Gentlemen's Second Meeting

Elizabeth passed the chief part of the night in her sister's room, and in the morning had the pleasure of being able to send a tolerable answer to the inquiries which she very early received from Mr. Bingley through a housemaid, and some time afterwards from the two elegant ladies who waited on his sisters. In spite of this amendment, however, she requested to have a note sent to Longbourn, desiring her father to visit Jane, and form his own judgment of her situation. The note was immediately dispatched, and soon enough her mother arrived. Mr. Bennet received the note, however did not want to attend for the fear of meeting Mr. Darcy and allowing his secret to be known. Despite knowing that his favorite daughter would be upset, he sent his wife to attend Netherfield in his stead.

Mrs. Bennet accompanied by her two youngest girls, reached Netherfield soon after the family breakfast. Elizabeth was surprised her father did not come, but understood when her mother explained that her father had business to attend to this morning. Had she found Jane in any apparent danger, Mrs. Bennet would have been very miserable; but being satisfied on seeing her that her illness was not alarming, she had no wish of her recovering immediately, as her restoration to health would probably remove her from Netherfield. She would not listen, therefore, to her daughter's proposal of being carried home. To top it off, the apothecary, who arrived about the same time, did not think it at all advisable for Miss Bennet to travel in her ill state.

Seeing that Jane's illness was not dangerous Mrs. Bennet was ready to leave Jane here at Netherfield in the hands of a nursemaid and Lizzy. Lizzy, her mother, and her younger sisters were attended by a housemaid to the breakfast parlor, where the Netherfield party was gathered. Bingley met them with hopes that Mrs. Bennet had not found Miss Bennet worse than she expected. "Indeed I have, sir," was her answer. "She is a great deal too ill to be moved. Mr. Jones says we must not think of moving her. We must trespass a little longer on your kindness."

"Removed!" cried Bingley. "It must not be thought of. My sister, I am sure, will not hear of her removal."

"You may depend upon it, Madam," said Miss Bingley, with cold civility, "that Miss Bennet will receive every possible attention while she remains with us."

Mrs. Bennet was profuse in her acknowledgments. "I am sure," she added, "if it was not for such good friends I do not know what would become of her, for she is very ill indeed, and suffers a vast deal, though with the greatest patience in the world, which is always the way with her, for she has, without exception, the sweetest temper I have ever met with. I often tell my other girls they are nothing to dearest Jane." The Bingley sisters could not help but roll their eyes in derision at the coarseness of

Mrs. Bennet. The colonel however gave them a scolding look and they sat back in a harrumph properly chastised as Mrs. Bennet continued. "You have a sweet room here, Mr. Bingley, and a charming prospect over the gravel walk. I do not know a place in the country that is equal to Netherfield. You will not think of quitting it in a hurry, I hope, though you have but a short lease."

"Whatever I do is done in a hurry," replied he; "and therefore if I should resolve to quit Netherfield, I should probably be off in five minutes. At present, however, I consider myself as quite fixed here."

"That is exactly what I should have supposed of you," said Elizabeth.

The colonel could not refrain from commenting either. "Bingley does have a bit of wistfulness to his actions, but it does his happy disposition credit and those who know him well know it suits."

"You begin to comprehend me, do you?" cried he, turning towards Elizabeth and the Colonel.

"Oh, yes – I understand you perfectly." stated Elizabeth.

"As do I, my friend." the Colonel said as he smiled.

"I wish I might take this for a compliment; but to be so easily seen through, I am afraid, is pitiful."

The Colonel just laughed at such a statement but Elizabeth replied. "That is as it happens. It does not follow that a deep, intricate character is more or less estimable than such a one as yours."

"Lizzy," cried her mother, "remember where you are, and do not run on in the wild manner that your father suffers you to do at home."

"I did not know before," continued Bingley immediately, "that you are a studier of character. It must be an amusing study."

"Yes, but intricate characters are the MOST amusing. They have at least that advantage."

"The country," said Darcy, who desperately wanted to be part of the conversation, "can in general supply but a few subjects for such a study. In a country neighborhood you move in a very confined and unvarying society."

"But people themselves alter so much, that there is something new to be observed in them forever."

"Yes, indeed," cried Mrs. Bennet, offended by his manner of mentioning a country neighborhood. "I assure you there is quite as much of THAT going on in the country as in town."

Everybody was surprised, and Darcy, after looking at her for a moment, turned silently away. Mrs. Bennet, who fancied she had gained a complete victory over him, continued her triumph. "I cannot see that London has any great advantage over the country, for my part, except the shops and public places. The country is a vast deal pleasanter, is it not, Mr. Bingley?"

"When I am in the country," he replied, "I never wish to leave it; and when I am in town it is pretty much the same. They have each their advantages, and I can be equally happy in either."

"Aye – that is because you have the right disposition. But that gentleman," looking at Darcy, "seemed to think the country was nothing at all."

"Indeed, Mama, you are mistaken," said Elizabeth, blushing for her mother. "You quite mistook Mr. Darcy. He only meant that there was not such a variety of people to be met with in the country as in the town, which you must acknowledge to be true."

The conversation had turned bad and everyone, except Mrs. Bennet noticed it. Darcy had completely withdrawn, the Bingley sisters were laughing behind their handkerchiefs and Mr. Bingley and Elizabeth were trying to repair the damage. The Colonel tried to help them. "Madam, I agree with Miss Bennet, you certainly mistake the matter. My cousin, Mr. Darcy's estate is also in the country, near a town not to dissimilar from Meryton. I personally know that he enjoys the country and country society very much."

Mr. Darcy turned from the window towards the group gathered, slightly nodding his thanks to his cousin. Mrs. Bennet was not to be deterred however.

"Certainly, sir, nobody could deny your superior knowledge of your cousin. But as to not meeting with many people in this neighborhood, I believe there are few neighborhoods larger. I know we dine with four-and-twenty families."

No one said anything after the comment; Darcy was pleased that Elizabeth and his cousin had defended him, but dared not speak further. Elizabeth began to feel the awkwardness of the situation and decided to change the subject by asking "Has Charlotte Lucas been at Longbourn since my going away?"

"Yes, she called yesterday with her father. What an agreeable man Sir William is, Mr. Bingley is he not? So much the man of fashion! So genteel and easy! He had always something to say to everybody. That is my idea of good breeding, and those persons who fancy themselves very important, and never open their mouths, quite mistake the matter."

Elizabeth was furious at her mother but determined to maintain conversation and so biting her lower lip in aggravation she continued. "Did Charlotte dine with you?"

"No, she would go home. I fancy she was wanted about the mince pies. For my part, Mr. Bingley, I always keep servants that can do their own work; MY daughters are brought up very differently. But everybody is to judge for themselves, and the Lucas's are a very good sort of girls, I assure you. It is a pity they are not handsome! Not that I think Charlotte so VERY plain – but then she is our particular friend."

"MOTHER!" Elizabeth exclaimed and walking quickly over to her grabbed her arm and stated to the room. "I apologize, but I think it is time that my mother and sisters return to the house as I think they said Mrs. Phillips is coming to tea today. Come, Mother, I would not want you late." With that Elizabeth turned on her heels, hand still grasped to her mother's arm and quickly strode to the front door, practically dragging her mother.

Mrs. Bennet began repeating her thanks to Mr. Bingley for his kindness to Jane, with an apology for troubling him also with Lizzy. Mr. Bingley was unaffectedly civil in his answer, and forced his sisters to be civil also, and say what the occasion required.

Mrs. Bennet then boarded her carriage and departed. Elizabeth all but ran back to Jane's room in mortification.

Darcy looked at his timepiece and decided it was time for him to go and meet his ally in his quest to succeed at improving Miss Elizabeth's opinion of himself. He called for his horse to be readied and quickly went to change into his riding attire.

Fifteen minutes later he was on his way to meet the newfound friend at the Bennet cottage. Mr. Darcy was prompt in his arrival but his friend was already there sitting next to the fire with a book.

Mr. Bennet had wanted to escape Longbourn before the ladies of the house returned from visiting Jane and Lizzy and so he came early to wait for Mr. Darcy.

Mr. Darcy entered, sat down and sighed a heavy sigh. The sigh was enough to make Mr. Bennet put down his book and face the gentleman questions in his eyes. "What was that for Mr. Darcy?"

"For the endurance of a very trying morning sir."

"Come now, it cannot be that bad. What could have possible occurred this early in the day to be that trying for a young man of your age?"

"Well sir, Miss Jane and Miss Elizabeth Bennet are currently in residence at Netherfield."

"Based on our earlier discussions I would have thought you pleased with that more so than considering it a trial." The last was said with a smile.

"Oh indeed, sir, you must let me finish. Miss Jane became ill while visiting Mr. Bingley's sisters. She was assigned a guest room and the following morning her sister came to check on her. The invitation to stay was offered to Miss Elizabeth as well. Those events are not trying; in fact it is close to Heaven itself, which I will relate to you later. The trying part is the fact that this morning Mrs. Bennet came accompanied by her two youngest daughters. It seemed at every turn they were misinterpreting my statements and finding fault with me. Miss Elizabeth was mortified and in the end roughly escorted her mother to the carriage and all but forced her to leave, afterwards hurrying off in quite a state, not to be seen again this morning."

Mr. Bennet did not like hearing the episode that Mrs. Bennet caused, but he was not unaccustomed to it. To put Mr. Darcy at ease he decided to joke about it a bit. "I can just imagine it, sir. Mrs. Bennet was probably waving her handkerchief as she fluttered here and there, Miss Kitty and Lydia standing behind her smiling and laughing and Miss Elizabeth looking at her shoes while biting her lower lip trying not to explode, yet mortified at the occurrences."

"Yes that pretty well sums it up and quite well, if I do say so, right down to the adorableness of biting her lower lip."

Mr. Bennet chuckled at the last comment. "Worry not; it is a common event at the Bennet household. Miss Elizabeth will laugh herself out of it as soon as she gets a chance to go on a walk and reminisce about it. She may be mortified for a few minutes, but she is used to it and never takes it to heart. She has too much sense for that. So now tell me about the Bennet girls being in residence there. You said sweet Jane has taken ill. Is it very serious?"

"I have not seen her myself sir, but her sister says that she is a little better. She has had a sore throat, a cough, and a headache. The apothecary has been to see her twice each day. He says she should stay abed and not venture out for a few days at least. Her sister, who is very concerned, watches over her constantly."

"Yes, Miss Elizabeth and Miss Jane are very close and take such care of each other. If Miss Elizabeth says she is on the mend then it must be so. She knows her sister better than anyone else and would know when she was feeling better. Have you been able to see Miss Elizabeth at all or has she kept to herself?"

Mr. Darcy was pleased to relate to his friend that he had seen her and was able to give her a successful apology. He then related all of the events and conversations that had occurred in the library and sitting rooms. In the end stating "I am most pleased with how quickly the apology was able to be made and all that I have been able to learn of Miss Bennet, though I would wish they had occurred elsewhere since that would mean that Miss Jane was not ill."

Mr. Bennet smiled at his sincerity and began to talk of Georgiana. "So, sir you, like Mr. Bennet, encourage your sister to read all literature whether intended for ladies or gentlemen?"

"Yes, I do. In fact as I stated before, my sister and I often select a book to read together and then discuss it. What I did not mention is that I usually choose one and then Georgiana does, and so on and so forth. In the end I must confess that not only has Georgiana read those books intended for gentleman, but I have read my fare share of novels intended for ladies."

Mr. Bennet could not help but laugh. "I believe you have, sir."

"I know Miss Bennet may have only been agreeing out of politeness; however I am planning on offering to read a book of her choosing simultaneously so that we may discuss it. What think you of this idea, sir?"

"I think that if Miss Bennet agreed to read a book with you in the first place she was not agreeing just to be polite, that is not her way. So if she agreed, I think it is a novel idea." Mr. Bennet laughed at his own joke. "Do you have additional plans for conversing with Miss Elizabeth or are you going to stick to books forever?"

"Well, thus far I have failed dismally. So far the only common grounds I know of are literature and walking, any suggestions?"

Mr. Bennet thought about it for a minute and said "People."

"People?" Darcy asked in a questioning voice.

"Yes, Mr. Darcy, people, Miss Lizzy enjoys observing and discussing people. Not in the gossiping manner that most ladies discuss, but in a thoughtful, insightful manner, about their persons and personalities."

"Yes, I think she indicated as much this morning, anything else?"

"She also enjoys the theatre, particularly plays by Shakespeare. Oh yes, and the opera, I think her favorite opera is "The Marriage of Figaro" by Wolfgang Amadeus Mozart. Elizabeth is also fond of flowers and nature in general. Lastly, I would have to say that Lizzy likes to think."

"To think?"

"Yes, to think. She likes to just sit down and think about anything and everything. Where she will be and what she will be doing tomorrow or next year or in ten years. To think about her family, friends, and neighbor's or just about anything really."

"Interesting, that is not a hobby I generally would have thought of, but I see what you mean. I shall have to remember these things as I meet her in the future."

"Sounds good, young man, what say you to chess?"

"Why, I like it very much."

"Very good then, reach around that table there and pull out the board from that old trunk."

The two began a game as they continued talking. The conversation and day progressed amiably for both gentlemen. As the game was coming to a close Mr. Darcy paused to address Mr. Bennet.

"May I make a request of you sir?"

"Yes, anything."

"I am hoping, sir, that you will keep an open ear on your visits to Longbourn as to my present failure or success with the young lady we speak about. I fear that in my past with Miss Elizabeth I have inaccurately made conclusions about her comments. I fear that I may do so again and I seek confirmation that I am correct, that I have indeed been forgiven for my rudeness and that her opinion of me is now more favorable. I realize that you cannot reveal any words spoken in confidence, that is, if you are in her confidence, however if there is any opinion that you discover that you can share with me I would appreciate it."

"I shall think on it and let you know next time that we meet if I have heard any opinions voiced by that person whose opinion you seek."

"Wonderful, sir, when shall we meet again?"

"What say you to three days from now during the morning tea hour?"

"Very well, sir, see you then. Shall we enjoy another game of chess?"

"Yes, I believe we shall."

Darcy was pleased as he mounted his horse and headed back to Netherfield. He had gleaned additional insight into Elizabeth's hobbies and interests and was impatient to meet with her to attempt another discussion. The remainder of the day was spent dodging Caroline and trying to cross paths accidentally with Miss Elizabeth.

Chapter 7
Drawing Room Discussions

The morning for Miss Bingley and Mrs. Hurst was spent as all mornings were for them, talking and discussing Pemberley and the alterations that would be made as soon as Caroline was mistress of the great estate, and criticizing Miss Elizabeth and the entire set of Bennet relations.

Mr. Bingley and Colonel Fitzwilliam went on a ride throughout the estate looking over the property and taking note of improvements that Mr. Darcy had suggested to them after one of his morning rides. Bingley was glad to have Mr. Darcy's advice, since he would not have noticed half of the items that he had pointed out. He was also pleased to have the company of his good friend the Colonel but wondered at the recent absence of Darcy from their morning party and other social engagements. This was most unlike him to not be as solicitous to his host.

Upon the departure of Mrs. Bennet and her daughters for Longbourn Elizabeth went to Jane's room and related to her the catastrophe that had taken place below stairs. Jane was very distressed by what Lizzy related and upon seeing this Lizzy discontinued the conversation, not wanting to upset her sister and inhibit her recovery. The rest of the day passed with relative ease as Miss Elizabeth read while her sister rested. That evening, Elizabeth again joined the Netherfield party in the drawing room. The evening passed much the same as the night before had, however the loo table did not appear. Mr. Darcy was writing a letter to his sister, and Miss Bingley, seated near him, was watching the progress and repeatedly calling off his attention by messages to his sister. Mr. Hurst and Mr. Bingley were at piquet, and Mrs. Hurst was observing their game. Colonel Fitzwilliam had gone to town to visit Colonel Forster. Elizabeth took up some needlework and was sufficiently amused in attending to what passed between Darcy and his companion. The perpetual commendations of the lady on his handwriting, or on the evenness of his lines, or on the length of his letter, combined with the perfect unconcern with which her praises were received, formed a curious dialogue and was exactly in union with her opinion of each.

"How delighted Miss Darcy will be to receive such a letter!"

He made no answer.

"You write uncommonly fast."

"You are mistaken. I write rather slowly."

"How many letters you must have occasioned to write in the course of a year! Letters of business, too! How odious I should think them!"

"It is fortunate, then, that they fall to my lot instead of yours."

"Pray tell your sister that I long to see her."

"I have already told her so once, by your desire."

"I am afraid you do not like your pen. Let me mend it for you. I mend pens remarkably well."

"Thank you – but I always mend my own."

"How can you contrive to write so even?"

He was silent.

"Tell your sister I am delighted to hear of her improvement on the harp; and pray let her know that I am quite in raptures with her beautiful little design for a table, and I think it infinitely superior to Miss Grantley's."

"Will you give me leave to defer your raptures till I write again? At present I have not room to do them justice."

Elizabeth could not help but interject at this point. "Miss Bingley, if you want to relay so many messages to Miss Darcy why do you not write her a letter yourself. I am sure there is sufficient writing paper available here at Netherfield."

"Oh no, I never write, it is so boring compared to first hand discussion! It is of no consequence. I shall see her in January. I only write to those who I know have not the resources to come and visit me."

Elizabeth was not insulted by Miss Bingley, for she felt too little of her opinion as a whole. Darcy however felt the insult that she had just leveled at Miss Bennet and her sister and was angered by it.

Caroline continued, "Mr. Darcy, do you always write such charming long letters to Miss Darcy?"

Darcy was beginning to get irritated and it could be heard in his voice. "They are generally long, but whether always charming it is not for me to determine."

"It is a rule with me that a person who can write a long letter with ease, cannot write ill."

"That will not do for a compliment to Darcy, Caroline," cried her brother, "because he does not write with ease. He studies too much for words of four syllables. Do you not, Darcy?"

"My style of writing is very different from yours."

"Oh!" cried Miss Bingley, "Charles writes in the most careless way imaginable. He leaves out half his words and blots the rest."

"I suppose those friends who receive Mr. Bingley's correspondence feel so fortunate to receive a letter from their friend that they care not what the letter looks like upon receipt of it," said Elizabeth.

"My ideas flow so rapidly that I have not time to express them—by which means my letters sometimes convey no ideas at all to my correspondents."

The entire room laughed at this accurate portrayal of Mr. Bingley's writing abilities. It was at this point that Colonel Fitzwilliam returned and joined everyone in the drawing room. He sat on the opposite end of the sofa from Elizabeth with a glass of brandy in one hand and the latest newspaper about the current war in the other.

Mr. Darcy wanted Elizabeth to expound on her writing and asked "Do you enjoy writing letters, Miss Elizabeth?"

"I suppose I do, Mr. Darcy. I have a most beloved aunt who is almost a second mother to me in London, to whom both Jane and I write quite frequently."

Caroline could not pass up the opportunity to slander the family and replied "Oh, good heavens, another Mrs. Bennet."

The entire room felt the rudeness of her comment and she thought she had succeeded in silencing any dialogue between Miss Bennet and her Mr. Darcy until Elizabeth stated "Indeed, you mistake me Miss Bingley. Mrs. Gardiner, who is my aunt through marriage, and my mother are quite the opposite in temperaments, I only say she is as a second mother because I have frequently stayed with her and my uncle growing up and am so fond of her."

Mr. Darcy was pleased that Miss Bennet had revealed this piece of information about her past and was determined to keep her talking. He turned his attentions away from his letter to Georgiana and towards Elizabeth. "Where in London do Mr. and Mrs. Gardiner reside?" The question was asked innocently on the side of Mr. Darcy, but as soon as Miss Bingley spit out "Cheapside" before Lizzy could respond he knew he must remedy the situation before Miss Bennet thought he shared Caroline's opinions.

"Yes, you are correct Miss Bingley, my Aunt and Uncle Gardiner live at Gracechurch Street in Cheapside in London. My uncle feels it is best to be within a short distance from his warehouses."

"Your uncle is in trade then Miss Bennet? What merchandise does he trade?" said Mr. Darcy desperately trying to redeem the conversation that was going further awry with every comment made.

"Yes, his primary merchandise and what his warehouse is most known for is manufactured textiles, in the form of both fabrics and readily confectioned clothing, however he also trades wool along with coffee, furs, and arms. He may have traded other merchandise, but those are the ones with which I am familiar."

"He has traded wool then. Do you know if he has ever traded in wool from Derbyshire?"

Colonel Fitzwilliam's attention was aroused at this point as he was beginning to see Darcy's direction of thought as he asked questions to Miss Bennet.

"I am not sure where his suppliers are from. I do know who his past supplier was, however the gentleman passed from this life and I am not familiar with his replacement. It happened a few years ago; however I am not in residence as frequently with my aunt and uncle as I was when I was younger."

"What was his name, if you do not mind me asking?"

"Wickham."

With this Colonel Fitzwilliam was all attention and although he said nothing, Darcy and Fitzwilliam looked at each other in caution and then quickly looked away before anyone noticed.

Elizabeth had noticed though, being the quick studier that she was. She saw what passed between the two, but was not sure what to make of it.

Mr. Darcy was all curiosity now "Would you recognize the new supplier's name if you heard it?"

"Yes, most likely."

"Is it Mr. Jenkins?"

"Why yes, I believe it is. How do you know that, sir?" Elizabeth dismissed the curious looks she had just seen between the colonel and Mr. Darcy, now understanding that they both were aware of the connection.

"I am familiar with the wool that Mr. Jenkins sells. It is thought to be some of the best in England. Your uncle must be an excellent tradesman and businessman to secure Mr. Jenkins' business; he only sells his goods to the best tradesmen who come with the highest recommendations."

Elizabeth did not miss the fact that Mr. Darcy did not answer her question, was pleased that the praise he gave her uncle and replied "Thank you, I am sure Mr. Gardiner will be pleased to know he is regarded highly by the trade community. I know he has worked hard to obtain a reputation for the highest quality of merchandise, honor, and hard work."

Elizabeth went back to her needlework. As the evening's activities resumed she frequently felt Mr. Darcy's gaze on her. His gaze confused yet excited her. A few days ago she would have regarded it as contempt and ridicule, but now her opinion was changing. He had apologized for his behavior, joined her in a few conversations and now was praising her family. The more Elizabeth learned about Mr. Darcy the more she enjoyed his company and conversation. Part of her was thrilled with this knowledge, finally meeting a man who may be worthy of getting to know a bit better. On the other hand though she was also saddened, he was clearly from a sphere of society that she was not, and allowing herself to get to know him better may in return cause her a broken heart when he did not return the stronger feelings that she imagined could develop. The thoughts were beginning to cause a headache in Elizabeth so shortly thereafter she expressed her intention of checking on Jane and excused herself for the evening.

Within the next half hour Colonel Fitzwilliam invited Darcy to the library with the pretence of informing him of some business that he wanted to discuss with him. The rest of the party retired to their separate rooms for the night.

When Darcy and Fitzwilliam entered the library it did not take the Colonel long to get to his point; "Darcy I assume you heard all that I did there in the drawing room from Miss Bennet?"

"I did."

"What do you think we should do?"

"Do, why nothing, what do you mean?"

Darcy, if you are saying this then I must assume that you are not aware?"

"Aware of what Fitzwilliam? You are making no sense at all."

"Aware of the fact that even now George Wickham is a member of the militia stationed here in Meryton."

"He is what? You say he is here in Meryton."

"Yes, that was my reason for meeting with Colonel Forster tonight. I heard a Lieutenant Saunderson mentioning him to another of his friends and decided to find out when he would be arriving with the regiment. I discovered that he arrived this very evening. Without providing any information or details I indicated to him that he should be watched closely until his full character is known and said he should not be deceived by his appearance of amiability. I believe Colonel Forster listened and will keep a close eye on him."

Darcy sat contemplating and the colonel continued. "It sounds as if Miss Bennet is familiar with his father. I know not whether she knows the son, yet if her family trusts the father then they will be more disposed to trust the son than any others on a first acquaintance. This could be very bad for a family of five beautiful daughters, with a dowry or without one."

Darcy recognized that what the colonel said was true and responded. "I have recently become acquainted with a close friend of the Bennet family. I meet with him in three days time, and at that point I will provide him enough information to warn the Bennet's of his true character."

The colonel was satisfied that the Bennet's would be warned, but was again curious about his new acquaintance and so he asked "Who is this new acquaintance of yours, Darcy? Is it the same person you met in Sir Lucas's library?"

"It is."

"Have you discovered the gentleman's identity yet?"

"I have not."

"Does it not seem odd to you, Darcy, that you meet this gentleman and discuss a family in the neighborhood without the knowledge of who he is?"

"Somewhat, however he has given no indication of being untrustworthy or disrespectful in his discussions and so has given me no reason as to not trust him. I fully intend to engage in future conversations with him and in fact look forward to them."

"Very well, I hope your conversations are successful, I will see you tomorrow," and with one last swallow of his drink he departed for his room.

Chapter 8
Up a Tree

The following morning dawned bright and beautiful. Elizabeth took breakfast in her room early and then went on a morning walk around the Netherfield Park East Gardens wandering in and out of the various paths and walkways. The East Gardens were the most remote gardens of the estate. They were wild and had oversized pathways. She was relishing in the fact that she had escaped unnoticed from the house and wondered how long she could stay away before she was missed when she spotted it. One of the most fabulous climbing trees she had ever seen, one that rivaled even those at Oakham Mount and there it was at the edge of the gardens. Quickly looking around Elizabeth assessed that she was truly alone and ran to the tree. As she approached she slowed to a walk and gazed into the branches above her. To her delight she was quickly able to determine a safe and stable route of limbs that would lead her all the way to the top with very little difficulty. Without any hesitation upon reaching the tree Elizabeth began to climb. She only stopped once she had reached the highest limb so far above the ground. She situated herself comfortably upon a crook in the limb leaning her back against the trunk for support and gazed over the countryside below. She loved being in the treetops; she could see for miles without a care in the world. She felt as if she were a bird ready to soar at any moment. This feeling always made her giddy with excitement and frequently she would burst into song. Being as she was at Netherfield and not Oakham Mount, where persons were rarely met with, Elizabeth did not feel comfortable singing out her joys, however, she could not refrain herself from humming. Elizabeth was content with this situation for nigh on a half hour when she realized she was no longer alone in the gardens and forced herself to be quiet and calm until the intruders departed. She was content in watching the passing clouds until her ears arrested her as she realized those in the garden below her were speaking of her.

Mr. Darcy searched the house all morning without a clue as to the location of Miss Elizabeth. She had not come down to breakfast, which he assumed was not in her energetic nature and was set on learning why. He assured himself that it was just to be sure she had not taken ill from tending her sister, but the truth be known, he missed her intelligent conversation and wit. Darcy had just come to the conclusion that she was not in the house when he overheard Miss Bingley talking to her maid.

"Walking in the East Gardens since before anyone else arose. Why would anyone do such a thing?"

"Perhaps she enjoys the outdoors, madam". The maid shyly said as she looked at the ground in front of her toes.

"Whatever for? Oh well I suppose someone as plain and unsightly as her has no hope even for beauty sleep to aid her. You are dismissed." That said, Caroline turned on her heel and departed from the maid's presence. She had learned Elizabeth was outside, so now all she needed to do was keep Darcy indoors.

Darcy overheard her location and instantly headed to his room for his other jacket and boots. Once properly attired for a walk outdoors, Darcy headed out of his room and ran straight into Miss Bingley.

"Oh Mr. Darcy, I see you are already dressed. I cannot thank you enough for wanting to accompany me into town and assist with my errands." Caroline purred to Darcy.

"Oh…, Miss Bingley…, I had not intended…, that is…, I have no intention of going to town. I am just on my way out to walk in the gardens for some air and exercise."

"That would be delightful Mr. Darcy; I think I will join you."

"What of your errands Miss Bingley?"

"Oh, I daresay they can wait. I find I am also very much in need of some air. I would love to go and see the West Rose Gardens."

"The West Rose Gardens you say, well I apologize that I will not be able to accompany you since my route consisted of a different direction and a different garden area. If you will excuse me I must be going."

"It matters not, I can visit the other garden later, I will accompany you Mr. Darcy."

With that Caroline linked her arm in Darcy's and he could do nothing but lead her out on a walk in the gardens.

Upon reaching the East Gardens Darcy's eyes quickly scanned the expanse looking for signs of Elizabeth's whereabouts. He did not see her and his mood was significantly deflated in a moment's notice as he realized he would not have her company as soon as he had anticipated. In such a dampened state of mind Darcy proceeded to block out all that Caroline had to say and walked in his stiff and stoic manner. Luckily for him, Caroline's conversations did not require him to pay attention. In that way she very much resembled Aunt Catherine.

"Darcy, I still cannot believe you think she has fine eyes and a very pretty smile. I see nothing so extraordinary about them. She is not at all pretty; she dresses so plain and has no fashion whatsoever. Can you believe her family… the youngest two are such reckless and unruly flits. They are completely ridiculous…"

Darcy had tuned Caroline completely out of his mind all he heard from her was blah-blah-blah, but amongst the blah-blah-blah's he heard it, the most amazing humming that had ever graced his ears. Darcy knew instantly that it was Elizabeth but where was it coming from? It sounded like it was coming from the heavens. Then the memory arrested him, *yes indeed Mr. Darcy, you heard me correctly Miss Bennet has an interest in climbing trees.* That was it, Elizabeth was in a tree and it appeared as if she was humming. Just then it stopped. *Oh how am I to find her now* Darcy thought. *Listen, listen very hard.* All he could hear was Caroline.

65

"I hope," said she, "you will give your mother-in-law a few hints, when this desirable event takes place, as to the advantage of holding her tongue; and if you can compass it, do cure the younger girls of running after the officers. And, if I may mention so delicate a subject, endeavor to check that little something, bordering on conceit and impertinence, which your lady possesses."

All Darcy could think of was *Oh no, if I could hear her humming she is quite close and most definitely overhearing all that is said. Does she think that I agree with Miss Bingley? That will not do, I must let her know that these sentiments are not my own so she does not hate me. Yet I cannot let on that I like her and definitely not that I have other feelings and desires. At least I will make an effort.*

"Miss Bingley," stated Darcy rather abruptly, "Have you anything else to propose for my domestic felicity?"

Not realizing Darcy's anger, Caroline continued. "Oh, Yes! Do let the portraits of your Uncle and Aunt Philips be placed in the gallery at Pemberley. Put them next to your great-uncle the judge. They are in the same profession, you know; only in different lines. As for your Elizabeth's picture, you must not attempt to have it taken, for what painter could do justice to those beautiful eyes?"

"It would not be easy, indeed, to catch their expression, but their color and shape, and the eye-lashes, so remarkably fine, might be copied. In addition, I would be delighted to add the portraits of my wife's family to those already residing in Pemberley gallery. If they are her family they are dear to her and if she is my wife she is dear to me, therefore her family would be dear to me as well, notwithstanding their professions. Therefore, someday when the happy event arrives and I take a wife I would be honored if she would allow me to meld her family's portraits into mine, thus melding us into one as well."

Well said, Mr. Darcy, Elizabeth thought *a very diplomatic answer.*

Caroline instantly took him to mean that he was speaking of herself and instantly tightened her grip on Darcy's arm.

Darcy cringed at the sensation, desperately hoping that his speech was heard by Elizabeth and that she was not angry with him.

At that moment they were met from another walk by Mr. and Mrs. Hurst. "Oh Caroline, Mr. Darcy, I did not know that you intended to walk," said Mrs. Hurst coming straight over and taking Mr. Darcy's other arm as she released her husband's.

"You used us abominably ill," answered Mr. Hurst, "running away without telling us that you were coming out. I was thus forced to leave my bed and accompany my wife instead. Now that Mrs. Hurst has found other walking partners, though, I must be off." With that said, he fled back to the house for more solitude before anyone could even answer.

Darcy desperately wanted to leave as well and knew if he did not do it now he would be stuck with them for the remainder of the morning. "Dear me, look at the time, I was supposed to meet Mr. Bingley's steward to go over the improvements for the watering system a quarter hour ago. If you will excuse me ladies, I must also depart." He turned and quickly fled from the gardens, though he did not flee far. As soon as Darcy was out of sight from the ladies he redirected himself and backtracked his way around the garden and came in from the back to return to his previous location. As he arrived at his position he was pleased to see the retreating figures of Mrs. Hurst and Miss Bingley heading back to the house.

"You may come down now Miss Bennet, the garden is clear."

Darcy did not hear a response, but he did hear a gasp and movement in the tree above him. Darcy realized it would be a few minutes before she reached the bottom so he stepped away from the tree a bit too where he could still easily assess her progress and be near enough should she need assistance, but not to unduly embarrass her with his presence directly below her person. Darcy was fascinated with her agility and adeptness within the tree.

Elizabeth was mortified that she had been found out by one of the Netherfield party, particularly because it was Mr. Darcy. As she was approaching the bottom limb of the tree she remembered the fact that she had had to jump to reach it and then struggle to pull herself up to begin her climb to the top. How was she to get out of the tree gracefully in front of Mr. Darcy? If she had been alone she would have merely jumped. When Elizabeth reached the last branch she sat down upon it and hesitated with her legs hanging eyeing Mr. Darcy as she decided whether she should jump or not.

Darcy quickly rose to his feet and began to move towards Elizabeth to aid her final descent from the tree when he saw her jump and land directly in front of him. He was stunned by her and stood there motionless for a moment.

Elizabeth took his silence as contempt, curtsied and quickly began to leave without as much as a word.

The last thing Darcy wanted was for Elizabeth to leave after he had spent all morning searching for her and even put up with Miss Bingley.

"Miss Bennet" Darcy cried as he reached out for her. He stopped with his arm in mid-air stretched towards her, not actually making contact with her person. "If you have a moment, I would invite you to take a stroll through the gardens with me."

Elizabeth stuttered over her words. She could not believe that Mr. Darcy wanted to be near such a lady as herself after witnessing her tree-climbing indiscretions. "Thank you Mr. Darcy, I would be pleased to accompany you if you are indeed seeking my presence despite my recent unladylike display."

Darcy chuckled at her response "Yes, I am indeed seeking your presence after your unladylike display. In fact it is that unladylike display I would speak to you about."

Elizabeth cringed "Mr. Darcy, I apologize that you were made to witness…"

"Miss Bennet"

"The inappropriate manner in which…"

"Miss Bennet"

"I conducted myself just now, it is just that…"

"Miss Bennet" Darcy practically shouted to make her stop. Then returning to his calm manner with a smile upon his face he continued. "Please put yourself at ease, I in no way want to censure you for your 'unladylike display' as you put it, I only want to talk to you of the view from your perch and whether this is the best tree in the area, or should I try another for my own tree-climbing enjoyment?"

Mr. Darcy's face broke into a huge grin as he saw shock register across Elizabeth's face. She could not respond as she contemplated whether he was mocking her or not. A request for tree-climbing advice from her was the last thing she would ever have imagined to come out of Mr. Darcy's mouth. Once her senses were under her command again she said "Mr. Darcy, do you mean to inquire as to the best climbing trees in the neighborhood?"

"I do indeed, Miss Bennet, for it has been many years since I have climbed, but upon seeing you in the tree it has revived my desire to do so and so once I know the best tree I shall plan an outing of tree climbing." Darcy flashed a brilliant smile and Elizabeth could not help but smile back, which warmed his heart and assured him that she understood him to be sincere.

"Well, Mr. Darcy, I must admit that this is an exquisite tree for climbing in the direct vicinity. However, if you would prefer to do your climbing in solitude I can recommend a few other trees, since as you yourself can see one can easily be found out in this tree."

"If you do not mind Miss Bennet, I would like to hear of all the best trees so that I can assess each myself and determine which would suit me best."

Elizabeth was enjoying this playful banter between the two and indulged him with the locations of a few others, including those at Oakham Mount. "As you see Mr. Darcy the country is covered with marvelous climbing trees, but there is but one more location which I feel possesses the best trees. The place is Oakham Mount. There you will find the BEST climbing trees."

Darcy had wondered whether she was going to tell him of the location, since he was already aware from his new friend that this was one of her favorites. He was pleased that she did. "Thank you so much for revealing the best locations, I will most assuredly try them soon and if it is not too much, once I have tried them would you be willing to discuss the views and suitability of each tree with me?"

"It would be my pleasure Mr. Darcy."

"Thank you, now we have two topics to discuss. We already know that we have a common interest in books, and now tree climbing." With a glint of mischief in his eye Mr. Darcy continued. "Perhaps we should discuss books while sitting in the treetops. Would that not be agreeable Miss Bennet?"

Elizabeth gave a hearty laugh at his comment and replied "Indeed it would be, Mr. Darcy, indeed it would."

Darcy and Elizabeth wandered through the gardens for close to an hour talking about various topics and enjoying each other's company. Darcy was just beginning to wonder whether she would realize the time when she stated that Jane was most likely awake now and that she should check on her. Darcy walked her back to the house and departed from her presence in the foyer.

Chapter 9
Wickham Revealed

Elizabeth was pleased that Jane was doing so well and asked her whether she felt up to joining them downstairs after dinner. Jane said she would like that, and Elizabeth sought out Miss Bingley to have her informed.

As Elizabeth walked past the billiards room on her way to talk with Miss Bingley she again was arrested by the sound of her name.

Elizabeth knew not what to do. In no way did she want to overhear yet another conversation at Netherfield, but she was curious and definitely wanted to know why she was being mentioned, so she abandoned propriety and listened to another private conversation.

"…Miss Elizabeth's Uncle must know of him, or at least of his father."

"You are right Richard, but that is also what worries me, if her Uncle trusts the father they may be more inclined to trust the son though he is not worthy of any person's trust. If they trust him it may bring them to some sort of harm or ruin."

Elizabeth was amazed by the conversation and continued to listen.

"Well Darcy, after our conversation in the library last night I went to my room thinking. I know prior to coming here we had told Georgiana she may join us in December until we return to London for Christmas. However it was to be next week when you were to go and retrieve her. Under the present circumstances have you considered what you are to do?"

"Yes, yes, Richard I thought it through last night and I cannot risk her being here while Wickham is in the neighborhood."

Darcy continued "When we left I was still under the impression that she has not fully recovered from this summer's events with him. Why she even confided in me that she could not believe that he tried to hurt her. She still remembers him as the amiable boy that accompanied his honored father around the grounds. She brought up that our own father died trusting his entire family and she was so disappointed that he did not live up to his own father's goodness." Darcy became very distressed as he continued. "Oh, how could I have been so careless? I almost lost her and she is all that I have left."

"Do not distress yourself, cousin, I believe you are correct in that she is not recovered enough to meet him; however, I think you need to give each of you a little more credit that you do. Your brotherly instincts made you visit her the very day that you did and her sisterly love and respect for you made her confide in you that she was to elope with him the next day. Although it hurt her deeply, I feel that most of her hurt now stems from her self-recrimination, not from the loss of George Wickham. She would indeed hurt much more if she had eloped with him."

"So do you then agree with me that she should not come into the area?"

"Well, I do, for the time being. I think you should write to her and say her visit is going to need to be delayed until the first week of December. That gives us a few weeks to observe Wickham and make our decision."

Elizabeth was aghast at this point but could do nothing more than think about all they had said. It appeared as if Darcy's father had employed a Mr. Wickham, who had a son that tried to elope with Darcy's younger sister. Could it by chance be the same family of Wickham's that Mr. Gardiner did business with? That would explain why Mr. Darcy had avoided her questions the day before and how he knew the name of the present supplier, Mr. Jenkins. Elizabeth continued listening as she thought.

"You are correct, I shall write to her again this very afternoon. She will be very disappointed but there is nothing else we can do at the present."

"You are correct, she may be disappointed; however, I think she will recover quickly. She is never overly eager to be in Miss Bingley's company." Here the Colonel laughed in spite of himself.

Darcy could not help but chuckle a bit to himself as he replied "You are correct; however, I have also written to her about my enjoyment at the local assemblies, especially when I have been honored with the hand of one of the local ladies as a dance partner. I have never written to Georgiana about any lady before. I fear that by doing so now I have raised an expectation for her."

Here the Colonel outright laughed. "Say, now Darcy, I think you are a little more than interested if you wrote to your sister about the lady, but I promise not to question you any further as I am fully aware of your present state of mind and your recent scolding of me."

"Thank you, Fitzwilliam. I appreciate that you do not ask, because until I know more of the lady I cannot know more myself."

"So Darcy, I hear from Smith that you were looking at some new horseflesh…"

Elizabeth realized that they had permanently changed the subject and she retreated to Jane's room with her mind in a jumble and without finding Miss Bingley.

Jane realized Lizzy seemed a bit out of sorts since returning, but she was unable to get her to say anything and in the end gave up trying. Jane rested and Lizzy's thoughts began to invade her mind. In the end she determined that it could not be denied that Mr. Darcy admired her, for he had only danced with Bingley's sisters and herself and it was evident that she was the only local lady he had danced with. These thoughts led her to others, and in the end she had to ask herself. *Do I care for Mr. Darcy? Does Mr. Darcy care for me?*

When the ladies removed after dinner, Elizabeth ran up to her sister, and seeing her well guarded from cold, attended her into the drawing-room, where she was welcomed by her two friends with many professions of pleasure. Elizabeth had never seen them as agreeable as they were during the hour which passed before the gentlemen appeared. Their powers of conversation were considerable. They could describe an entertainment with accuracy, relate an anecdote with humor, and laugh at their acquaintance with spirit.

But when the gentlemen entered, Jane was no longer the first object; Miss Bingley's eyes were instantly turned toward Mr. Darcy, and she had something to say to him before he had advanced many steps. He addressed himself to Miss Bennet, with a polite congratulation on her mending health.

The Colonel bowed and smiled, wishing her good health and a speedy recovery; Mr. Hurst also made her a slight bow, and said he was "very glad;" but diffuseness and warmth remained for Bingley's salutation. He was full of joy and attention. The first half-hour was spent in piling up the fire, lest she should suffer from the change of room; and she removed at his desire to the other side of the fireplace, that she might be further from the door. He then sat down by her, and talked scarcely to anyone else. Elizabeth, at work in the opposite corner, saw it all with great delight. When tea was over, Mr. Hurst reminded his sister-in-law of the card table, but in vain. She had obtained private intelligence that Mr. Darcy did not wish for cards; and Mr. Hurst soon found even his open petition rejected. She assured him that no one intended to play, and the silence of the whole party on the subject seemed to justify her. Mr. Hurst had therefore nothing to do but to stretch himself on one of the sofas and go to sleep. The Colonel was reading the paper and Mrs. Hurst was playing with her bracelets. Darcy was writing another letter to his sister and Miss Bingley began in the same manner as she had the day before.

"So, Mr. Darcy, you write again to your lovely sister. Much must have happened today, for you just wrote to her yesterday and even Miss Darcy could not expect so many letters from you in such a short period of time."

"You are correct, much has happened and I must tell Georgiana."

"Pray, tell us all your splendid news, I am sure we all wish to rejoice with you."

"I fear it is not a matter of rejoicing as my business will not allow me to claim Georgiana next week for her visit, therefore she is to remain in London at the present."

Darcy knew that they would stop asking after his business with such news and he was correct. The following half hour was spent by Miss Bingley and Mrs. Hurst exclaiming at the loss to their party and trying to persuade the Colonel to fetch her instead.

Colonel Fitzwilliam exclaimed that he also had business as there is a regiment encamped in Meryton and they had asked for his assistance on several matters; therefore, he would be unable to escort her as well.

The discussions soon ended and went another course as Miss Bingley heard her brother mentioning a ball to Miss Bennet, she turned suddenly towards him and said: "By the by, Charles, are you really serious in meditating a dance at Netherfield? I would advise you, before you determine on it, to consult the wishes of the present party. As you know, I will be responsible for organizing such an event," she grumbled, "should you not consult me upon this decision first? Organizing a ball is not as easy as you think Charles, I cannot just snap my fingers and have guest lists, menus and decorations drawn up and completed." Then looking slyly at Mr. Darcy she continued in a way she expected would please him and make her increase in his esteem. "Also, if I am not much mistaken, there are some among us to whom a ball would be rather a punishment than a pleasure."

"If you mean Darcy," cried her brother, "he may go to bed, if he chooses, before it begins, but as for the ball, it is quite a settled thing; and as soon as the alterations to the ballroom are complete and Nicholls has made white soup enough, I shall send round my cards."

Darcy interrupted, "Bingley, you are too quick to judge me, I have thoroughly enjoyed the local gatherings here despite that I am not considered as lively as you. I look forward to your ball with pleasure." After making his statement he offered up a look at Elizabeth that did not escape the notice of Miss Bingley.

"I should like balls infinitely better," she replied, "if they were carried on in a different manner; but there is something insufferably tedious in the usual process of such a meeting. It would surely be much more rational if conversation, instead of dancing, were made the order of the day."

Colonel Fitzwilliam could not help but laugh here. "Much more rational, Miss Bingley I dare say, but it would not be near so much like a ball. I think it a grand idea Charles, count me in. I do love a good ball."

Miss Bingley was furious; she had been contradicted by her brother, the colonel and even worse by Mr. Darcy himself. She made no answer to the colonel, and soon afterwards she got up and walked about the room. Her figure was elegant, and she walked well; but Darcy, at whom it was all aimed, was still inflexibly studious in his attention to his letter. In the desperation of her feelings, she resolved on one effort more, and, turning to Elizabeth, said: "Miss Eliza Bennet, let me persuade you to follow my example, and take a turn about the room. I assure you it is very refreshing after sitting so long in one attitude."

Elizabeth was surprised, but agreed to it immediately. Miss Bingley succeeded no less in the real object of her civility; Mr. Darcy looked up. He was as much awake to the novelty of attention in that quarter as Elizabeth herself could be, and unconsciously laid down his writing instrument atop his letter. He was directly invited to join their party, but he declined it, observing that he could imagine but two motives for their choosing to walk up and down the room together, with either of which motives his joining them would interfere. Caroline interjected "What could he mean? I am dying to know what his meaning could be." and asked Elizabeth whether she could at all understand him.

"Not at all," was her answer; "but depend upon it; he means to be severe on us, and our surest way of disappointing him will be to ask nothing about it."

Miss Bingley, however, was incapable of disappointing Mr. Darcy in anything, and persevered therefore in requiring an explanation of his two motives.

"I have not the smallest objection to explaining them," said he, as soon as she allowed him to speak. "You either choose this method of passing the evening because you are in each other's confidence, and have secret affairs to discuss, or because you are conscious that your figures appear to the greatest advantage in walking; if the first, I would be completely in your way, and if the second, I can admire you much better as I sit by the fire."

The colonel laughed outright at his statement, proud of his cousin's response.

"Oh! Shocking!" cried Miss Bingley. "I never heard anything so abominable. How shall we punish him for such a speech?"

"Nothing so easy, if you have but the inclination," said Elizabeth as she looked around nervously. Jane, Bingley, and Mrs. Hurst were enjoying the amusement; Mr. Hurst still slept, but the Colonel was looking at Darcy with archness. "We can all plague and punish one another. Tease him, laugh at him. Intimate as you are, you must know how it is to be done."

"But upon my honor, I do not. I do assure you that my intimacy has not yet taught me that. Tease calmness of manner and presence of mind! No, no, I feel he may defy us there. And as to laughter, we will not expose ourselves, if you please, by attempting to laugh without a subject. Mr. Darcy may hug himself."

The colonel raised his eyebrows at the thought of his cousin hugging himself. What a sight that would be.

"Mr. Darcy is not to be laughed at!" cried Elizabeth. "That is an uncommon advantage, and uncommon I hope it will continue, for it would be a great loss to me to have many such acquaintances. I dearly love a laugh."

"Fear not Miss Elizabeth, you shall not lose many such acquaintances for I could enlighten you about Mr. Darcy. I assure you he is not exempt from the follies of man." Then giving a quick look towards Darcy in a threatening smile he continued. "I could tell you a story or two where Mr. Darcy is definitely to be laughed at."

Mr. Darcy gave his cousin a sharp and threatening look as he interrupted. "Miss Bingley," said he "has given me more credit than can be. I have frequently been the object of laughter and in fact enjoy being the object, depending on who is doing the laughing."

Elizabeth colored here and instantly returned to her seat. Knowing now as she did that Mr. Darcy admired her made her blush when normally she would not. It seemed now that everything that he said was in some way a compliment to her.

"Do let us have a little music," cried Miss Bingley, fully aware of where the conversation had turned. "Louisa, you will not mind my waking Mr. Hurst?"

Her sister had not the smallest objection, and the pianoforte was opened.

Chapter 10
Jane and Elizabeth Return Home

In consequence of an agreement between the sisters, Elizabeth wrote the next morning to their mother, to beg that the carriage might be sent for them in the course of the day. But Mrs. Bennet sent them word that they could not possibly have the carriage before Tuesday. Against staying longer, however, Elizabeth was positively resolved; and fearful, on the contrary, as being considered as intruding themselves needlessly long, she urged Jane to borrow Mr. Bingley's carriage immediately, and at length it was settled that their original design of leaving Netherfield that morning should be mentioned, and the request made.

The master of the house heard with real sorrow that they were to go so soon, and repeatedly tried to persuade Miss Bennet that it would not be safe for her, that she was not enough recovered; but Jane was firm where she felt herself to be right and Mr. Bingley relented and let her use his carriage.

Therefore that very day after tea, the separation, took place. Miss Bingley's civility to Elizabeth increased at last very rapidly, as well as her affection for Jane; and when they parted, after assuring the latter of the pleasure it would always give her to see her either at Longbourn or Netherfield, and embracing her most tenderly, she even shook hands with the former. Mr. Bingley handed Jane into the carriage and made every effort to see to her comforts that propriety allowed. Then Darcy took the opportunity to hand in Elizabeth bowing to her and saying he looked forward to their future meetings. The colonel expressed his delight at Jane's speedy recovery, his satisfaction in getting to know them both a little better and then waved and wished a safe journey to their home as the carriage began to move forward

Miss Bingley turned and entered the house before the carriage wheels had made even a full rotation to leave Netherfield. Mr. Bingley, Mr. Darcy and the Colonel all stayed to watch the carriage depart. Mr. Bingley was contemplating how soon it would be before he would meet Jane again. Colonel Fitzwilliam was wondering how dull the conversation would be without Miss Elizabeth to liven it up and Mr. Darcy was kicking himself mentally for not obtaining permission to call upon Miss Elizabeth.

Jane and Elizabeth were not welcomed home very cordially by their mother. Mrs. Bennet wondered at their coming, and thought them very wrong to give so much trouble, and was sure Jane would have caught cold again. But their father, though very laconic in his expressions of pleasure, was really glad to see them; he had felt their importance in the family circle. The evening conversation, when they were all assembled, had lost much of its animation, and almost all its sense by the absence of Jane and Elizabeth.

They found Mary, as usual, deep in the study of topics that no one thought worthwhile except herself and they listened as she informed them of all of the extracts she had come upon of interest during the days that they were away from Longbourn. Catherine and Lydia had information for them of a different sort. Much had been done and much had been said in the regiment since the preceding Wednesday; some new extremely handsome officers had arrived, several of them had dined lately with their uncle, a private had been flogged, and it had actually been hinted that Colonel Forster was going to be married to a young girl near Lydia's age. Lydia was positive they would become the "dearest friends" and that she would introduce her and Kitty to all of the officers.

Elizabeth listened with interest, but was relieved when her father called her to his library.

"Lizzy, my dear, come and join me."

Lizzy got up and joined Mr. Bennet in his library.

"So, Lizzy, you have finally returned to save your poor father. I thought the week would never end."

"As did I, father."

"Well Lizzy, it sounds as if you did not enjoy your stay at Netherfield. Do you care to share it with me?"

"Well father, as you know Jane was sick this week. How could I enjoy myself when my dearest sister is suffering?"

"Yes, my dear, I see what you mean. Despite Jane's illness did you enjoy yourself?"

"I did sir. I was very pleased to see Mr. Bingley's attentions to Jane strengthen, not wither, with her in residence in his home. Her preference is growing and I do not wish her to have her heart broken. Although I was pleased with Mr. Bingley, I was a bit disappointed with another of the household."

Mr. Bennet was all curiosity and probed her to continue. "Do you mean that gentleman's friends?"

"No sir, I mean his sister. I have never met with a more disagreeable woman than Miss Bingley in all of my life. She thinks not of others, only of herself and is mean and spiteful. I could easily imagine her nose scraping the ceiling with how proud she is. "

"Can that be so, my dear? I think that would be hard to accomplish."

"I assure you, father, she could. Her sister, Mrs. Hurst is nothing out of the ordinary. She follows her younger sister such the same way as Kitty does Lydia."

Mr. Bennet just laughed and inquired further into what he truly wanted to know. "So what are your opinions of Mr. Bingley's friends now that I have heard your opinion of everyone else?"

"Well, about Mr. Hurst there is very little to say. He drinks more than he ought and sleeps a great deal. When he does say something it is pointless and often without any topic at all. The Colonel is pleasant enough by nature but I saw very little of him as he is frequently engaged with the militia group that is in town. He is not part of their regiment, but apparently they have asked his assistance on some matters."

Mr. Bennet continued to listen and was not unaware that she changed the subject before mentioning the final gentleman.

"Say, father, do you remember my Uncle Gardiner mentioning his supplier of wool?"

Mr. Bennet was curious to the change of topic and decided to pursue it with her before he inquired about Mr. Darcy. "I do indeed, a Mr. Jenkins, I have met him myself and must say that he is a very respectable man and only supplies the best wool to your uncle. It is because of his business that your uncle has been so successful these past years."

"Was there not a different man prior to him, sir?"

"There was, a Mr. Wickham, though he died a few years back."

"Do you know much of Mr. Wickham's family, father?"

"A little and mind you, it was heard third hand and I am not sure as to the reliability of the source. Why do you ask?"

"I promise to tell you, father, after you have informed me. Please go on and trust me for a few minutes."

Mr. Bennet sighed and continued: "It is said that Mr. Wickham was the steward of a very large estate in the North Country. The master of the estate trusted his steward exclusively. The master's wife had died and he did not care as much as he had in the past, therefore all of his business was left to the steward and solicitor to run and ensure the estate did not fall into ruin. The master had a son that aided from a young age; however he was very young and still much away at school that he could not do much. Mr. Wickham heard of your Uncle Gardiner and sought him out because he was aware that Mr. Gardiner was respectable and did not require a lot of oversight; therefore the steward could concentrate on other estate business." As Mr. Bennet was saying the words aloud, recognition of them being so close to those spoken by another was dawning and his curiosity began to be piqued.

"That is great father, but what do you know of the steward's family?" Elizabeth was curious; as she was sure the estate owner was Mr. Darcy, though she wanted to know if what the Colonel and Darcy talked of could indeed be true based on the character of the person in question.

"Calm yourself Lizzy, I am getting there. Mr. Wickham seemed to be held in high esteem, however at one point I heard that the remainder of his family was not. You are aware that your Aunt Gardiner hails from Lambton, a small village in the north and was acquainted with Mr. Wickham's wife when she was younger. It seems the late Mrs. Wickham was an extravagant woman who spent more than her husband earned and frequently slandered the family that employed him. Her son was just like her in every way and frequently got in trouble with merchants because of his debts and other deeds. It seems that the master of the estate never knew these things because of his inattentiveness to matters once his own wife died. Mr. Wickham died an extremely poor and sorrowful man."

"What was Mr. Wickham's son's other deeds father?"

"Now Lizzy, why would you care of such things? They are not anything your young ears need to hear, my dear; suffice it to say they were not honorable."

"Father, I ask these things because I am to understand that there is a new officer in the regiment by the name of Mr. George Wickham. I believe that Colonel Fitzwilliam's business with the regiment is to look after him. It seems he has past knowledge of the man as does his cousin Mr. Darcy. Mr. Darcy is the master of a very large estate named Pemberley which is in the northern county of Derbyshire. My understanding, though it is pieced together, is that Mr. Wickham's father was the late Mr. Darcy's steward. There has been some falling-out with the family and the current Mr. Wickham is not held in high regard by Mr. Darcy."

Awareness had already dawned with Mr. Bennet, but concern as to how his daughter could know all of this was surfacing. He was resolved to discuss it with Mr. Darcy tomorrow at their meeting.

"I see my dear, well though we do not know the particulars I think it would be wise of you to stay clear of Mr. Wickham and any officers he associates with. I would also ask your assistance in keeping your sisters from him as well. Until we are certain that he is one and the same person there is no use risking anything. Say Lizzy, how came you to all of this information?"

"Father, as you are well aware I am an observer of persons and Mr. Darcy and his cousin have lively conversations."

"So you enjoy watching Mr. Darcy and his cousin, do you?"

Lizzy was well aware of her father's meaning and a deep blush rose upon her. She had to clear her throat before she replied. "You mistake me father, I enjoyed listening and watching all of the Netherfield party, and it is just that the two of them have more lively and intelligent conversation than the rest of the persons in residence. Colonel Fitzwilliam is a lively and congenial person, but he has made it clear that he is a second born son and must marry a woman of wealth. Therefore I interpret that as meaning that the Bennet girls are free from his designs and that we should set our sights elsewhere."

"Well Lizzy, did you set your sights elsewhere?" Mr. Bennet said with a glint in his eyes and a smile upon his lips.

"I have not father, all I did while at Netherfield was what I have already told you, nursed Jane to health and observed everyone."

"Lizzy dear, you have told me about everyone except the one that the neighborhood most speculates about. I want a direct answer and no more beating around the subject. What is your opinion of Mr. Darcy?" Mr. Bennet had hoped she would volunteer the information because he knew her heart would be less engaged if she did. However, she would not; therefore Mr. Bennet knew his favorite must have some feeling for Mr. Darcy.

"Father, I know not what to tell you, there is nothing really, I had several intelligent conversations with Mr. Darcy. He happened upon me on my various walks about the Netherfield grounds and we seem to be on friendly terms." Elizabeth could not look at her father and so she looked out the window to his right as she continued "I had many lively and intelligent conversations with him. He challenged my knowledge and wit and overall I enjoyed talking with him and getting to know him a little better."

Mr. Bennet had seen and heard enough, he was sure that his favorite's heart was well on its way to another. He dismissed her with a kiss on the forehead.

Chapter 11
The Gentlemen's Third Meeting

Mr. Bennet worried that this would be the morning in which his identity would be discovered as the family attended church. Mr. Bennet knew that the Netherfield party would be in attendance and so as the last carriage pulled up and the party began to descend the carriage Mr. Bennet looked towards them searching out Mr. Darcy to see his reaction. His mind raced to determine if the man would approach and speak with him or if he would somehow be able to stretch the truth far enough without one of his daughters or wife blowing his disguise. The thoughts were making him distressed and his ever perceptive Lizzy recognized it, inquiring to him as they walked towards their family pew.

"Father, are you well? You look distressed. Is there something I can do to relieve you?"

"No Lizzy, I am fine, I am just a little out of sorts at the moment. This morning I received a message from some of the tenants that I thought could wait until later in the day, however the more I think on it the more urgent it sounds and I worry that my waiting may indeed cause more harm."

"Father you are of the opinion that some harm could come."

"Perhaps, Lizzy, I am not entirely sure. I will not know for sure until I ride out and discover for myself but I am beginning to question whether it was prudent of me to wait."

"Father, you must go this instant. The tenants and their families depend upon you. I would not have them suffer so that you can be spiritually edified. I will tell mother; you go now. In fact there, go and use the side door. No one will even notice your departure."

This was just the opportunity that Mr. Bennet could not resist. He truly was distressed at the idea of Mr. Darcy learning his identity as he did not want the association to end, and he needed to be sure for his Lizzy's sake that when his identity became known that Mr. Darcy would be so much engaged with her that he would overlook the father's indiscretions.

Mr. Bennet was able to slip out the side door as Mr. Darcy was walking into the chapel.

Mr. Bennet congratulated himself on his escape to the house. He retired to the library to wait until the completion of church services.

The Bingley pew was on the opposite side of the chapel as the Bennet's, but afforded a direct view with very little more than a turn of the head, which Mr. Darcy did frequently during the service. Not only did his vision turn with pleasure towards the Bennet pew and a certain lady with chestnut hair, but it also searched the rest of the congregation for his friend. Mr. Darcy had expected to see him with, or at the least very near, the Bennet's and hoped to meet him after the services. Mr. Darcy had hoped by seeing his friend at church he would be near him as he was addressed, thus enabling him to learn his identity, but unfortunately he could not locate his friend anywhere. Resolved that his friend was not in attendance Mr. Bennet sought out the Bennet family again to catch a glimpse of the father whom he had never met, but who he had heard so much about. Again Mr. Darcy was disappointed as he could not distinguish any male figure amongst the ladies. He considered it slightly unusual but did not dwell upon it until the service was over.

At the completion of the sermon all of the parishioners lingered a few minutes speaking amiably to one another. Mr. Bingley and Mr. Darcy moved almost in unison towards the Bennet ladies as the Colonel, Hurst's and Miss Bingley also followed, though at a slower pace.

Mr. Bingley addressed Mrs. Bennet as they approached. "What a fine Sunday sermon that was, was it not?"

"Indeed it was, sir, we are pleased to see you here today."

"Thank you, it is a pleasure to see you as well, may I inquire as to Miss Bennet's health?" Mr. Bingley said as he turned towards Jane.

Jane smiled sweetly as her mother boisterously answered "Oh Mr. Bingley you do honor us with your concern. As you can see she is well recovered."

"Indeed madam, I can see it, and I am well pleased."

Jane and Mr. Bingley continued to speak with Mrs. Bennet and Mr. Darcy addressed Elizabeth.

"Miss Elizabeth, I hope that you enjoyed the services today."

"I did yes, thank you Mr. Darcy."

"What was your favorite part?"

"I generally enjoy singing best." Mr. Darcy smiled at her reply and his remembrance of being able to clearly decipher her soprano voice amongst the entire congregation while they were in song.

"Yes, today's songs were well chosen. I enjoyed them as well." Then looking around him he asked. "Is not your father with you? I hope to meet him one day soon."

"Father was called away on some tenant business that I fear was unable to wait this morning. Whenever we are next in company with him I will be sure to introduce you."

Mrs. Bennet had begun to lead the group out of the chapel and soon the entire party dismissed.

With the arrived time of the completion of Sunday services and before the ladies of the house returned Mr. Bennet headed out to meet Mr. Darcy.

Mr. Bennet had arrived before Mr. Darcy and was sitting in a chair near an already blazing fire with the chess board set-up nearby.

"Good day, sir, I hope I have not kept you long." Mr. Darcy said as he entered the room.

"Not at all."

"Very good, may I join you?"

"Yes, have a seat. Shall we begin a game of chess?" Mr. Bennet said as he indicated with his hand towards the chess board next to him.

"Yes, that sounds enjoyable." said Mr. Darcy as he nodded. "I missed you in church today. I had hoped to meet you there, perhaps have you introduce me to Mr. Bennet."

"Um, yes, well Mr. Bennet had some pressing estate business to attend to this morning and since we share some property boundaries he invited me to attend with him so that we could settle the business to the best advantage for both of us."

"Very well, I hope to meet you there in the future."

"Yes son, you shall." Mr. Bennet continued with a glint in his eye, "I was lucky enough to be admitted to Longbourn last night. I saw that the ladies returned from Netherfield in good health. I must say the nursemaid there must be good if the glow upon the ladies' faces were any indication."

"Indeed, she is good, sir, although she rarely saw Miss Bennet. If you must know the only nursemaid who saw Miss Bennet regularly was her sister. Miss Elizabeth would rarely allow anyone else to wait on her sister."

"Very good, she knows Miss Jane best. I must say that generally having the two eldest home calms the household down, but not last night. There is a new regiment of officers in the area and I must say, to Mr. Bennet's consternation they have caused quite a stir amongst the ladies of the house. It is interesting how each lady of the household is reacting to the news. Each of their reactions is so different from that of another sister."

Darcy could not believe that his opportunity was presenting itself so well "I bet it has, sir. I am sure the arrival of many men in the area would cause a stir in any household, especially one with such an abundance of femininity."

"The actual arrival of the regiment is not the part that worries Mr. Bennet, but the arrival of a particular gentleman of the regiment. It seems Mr. Bennet's family has a long time, yet rather distant acquaintance with the family of one of the officers. From what I gather, the officer is not an honorable person. May I be bold enough to ask if your estate was the past employer of Mr. Wickham?"

Mr. Darcy started and Mr. Bennet did not miss it and so quickly continued. "I do not mean to alarm you, however Mr. Bennet has heard that a Mr. George Wickham has joined the militia and is in the neighborhood. His brother-in-law knows of his past through his good wife, who is from Lambton. I am aware that Lambton is in Derbyshire where I believe you said your estate Pemberley is located. It appears as if Miss Elizabeth Bennet somehow became aware of his presence in the neighborhood and was asking questions to her father. The two had a long talk and now are endeavoring to keep him from the remaining Bennet sisters. I have been tasked with keeping an eye out and learning all I can to ensure the safety of the Bennet ladies and any other ladies of the neighborhood. I apologize if I am presuming too much in assuming you must know of him due to the location of your estate."

Darcy let out his breath that he was holding and began "Sir, you are correct, I know of him. Nothing pleasant, I am afraid. To own the truth I am a bit relieved by how informed you already are, one of the things I wanted to discuss today was this very topic and to have you warn Mr. Bennet of him, thus ensuring the ladies safety. I am glad to know that it is not necessary, though I will tell you all I know and if there is additional information that you feel important then you may relate it to Mr. Bennet. I must extract a promise of secrecy for some parts, though, as they could hurt my sister. I will not withhold anything, but you will be able to know what to hold in confidence when relating it beyond the two of us."

Here Mr. Darcy related the entirety of his acquaintance with Mr. Wickham withholding nothing from his friend. He told him of all young Mr. Wickham's doings, his petty thefts from shops in the neighborhoods and the sums that he borrowed from many people and never repaid. He continued to tell of the young Mr. Wickham's dallying with both serving maids and ladies of stature all across the country. Mr. Darcy was on the verge of emotion as he spoke of his sister and her near ruin as she trusted her long time childhood friend.

When Darcy finished Mr. Bennet thanked him for the information, promised to never betray his confidences and said he would only relay what was absolutely necessary to protect not only the Bennet ladies but the other families with daughters and merchants in the area. As of now it appeared as if Mr. Bennet had the situation well in hand.

The conversation had finally calmed in intensity and the two could concentrate a little better on their chess game and enjoy lighter conversation.

Mr. Darcy began "Sir, how did you say Miss Bennet became aware of Mr. Wickham's presence in the neighborhood?"

"I did not say."

"Oh did you not, well, could you enlighten me?" Mr. Darcy had begun to understand his friends mind and knew that he was teasing him.

"I suppose I could if I wanted to."

"Do you want to?"

"Why yes, I believe I do. Miss Elizabeth became aware of the information because she is an astute observer."

Mr. Darcy looked at his friend blankly and stated "An observer? Did she meet him recently then?"

"No, I do not believe that they have ever met before, she knows him only by name."

"How did she observe him then?"

"I did not say she observed him, I merely said she observed."

"Oh I see, who would it be that she observed, then, to learn this information?'

"Why, she observed you and your cousin Mr. Darcy!"

"But I do not remember discussing any such subject in her presence so that she could observe us. In fact, I only remember discussing this with my cousin once or maybe twice and we were segregated from everyone; she was not present."

"I do not know, Mr. Darcy. She did not say when or where she observed, just that she did observe."

"Interesting, if I remember right, in the conversation where we discussed Wickham we also had a discussion of some other topics as well. I wonder if she heard them as well?"

"I am sure she did, for if she heard one she was bound to hear them all."

Darcy shifted uncomfortably.

"Does that concern you, Mr. Darcy?"

"Concern me…, no, it does not concern me, it just makes me concerned that I may have said something that would lessen my chances with the lady."

"Oh, and what would that be?"

"Well I told my cousin of my interest in a local lady that I had danced with."

"Why would that concern her? She must know that she is the lady since you have danced with no other local lady."

"Well it was that I also told my cousin that I was concerned that I had raised my sister's hopes in mentioning the lady in a letter. My sister now knows I like her, and I told my cousin that it concerns me because I myself am not sure how engaged my heart is. I was not ready to admit it at the time. Do you think she will think ill of me for the comments?"

"No, I do not think so; she is a sensible girl with good judgment, if anything it let her know your possible interest and therefore she also asked herself some questions about you to ensure she would match your affection if you wanted to give it or to be able to discourage you better if she did not."

"That sounds reasonable, sir, and since you know her best I will rely on your assessment."

"Good, my boy, I must say that it also appears as if your friend Mr. Bingley has made a very good impression on the neighborhood."

"Yes I believe he has, sir. Bingley is always making good impressions wherever he goes. He has an easy and friendly disposition that is always well liked."

"Is he also a frequent favorite of the ladies wherever he goes?"

"Generally, yes."

"It appears as if he is quickly becoming a favorite of a particular Bennet lady, if my ears did not deceive me last night."

"Is that so, sir, do you mind if I ask which lady of the party in particular?" Darcy really did not need confirmation but he thought he may as well get it.

"Well mostly the mother," here he laughed as Darcy cringed "but I must admit that the more that she mentioned Mr. Bingley the more rosy the complexion of Miss Jane became. She is a dear sweet girl who frequently receives the attentions of gentlemen in the neighborhood, but from my prior observations she never returns them. I must admit, though, it appears as if her heart has been touched this time around. Mr. Bennet fears that she will have her heart broken. Would you mind doing me a favor, as I have been doing some for you?" Darcy nodded his agreement. "If you do not think that your friend's attentions to the lady are steadfast, make him discontinue his attentions to her immediately. Jane is angelic in nature and if her heart is broken she will not quickly recover as her sister would and the more he provides attention to her the more attached she will become. I do not wish to see her hurt."

"I will, sir. I must say that Mr. Bingley seems more inclined towards her than any other lady in the past, though I admit that I have not watched him as I normally have because I have been preoccupied with my own musings. I will observe, inquire, and act accordingly. Thank you for the information. What small observances I have had of the lady made me think that her heart would not be easily touched, I must presume then that she is like me in that she just does not lay out her feelings for everyone to see."

"You are correct in that, but I ask you, would you, in such a household as she comes from? I believe neither Miss Jane nor Miss Elizabeth do, however Miss Jane is easier to read and comprehend once you know her temperament."

Here Darcy did nothing but smile and nod in agreement.

Mr. Bennet continued to relate various pieces of information he had gleaned from Elizabeth about everyone at Netherfield. That is, everyone but Mr. Darcy. Mr. Bennet could see he was becoming impatient, but in spite of himself made the young man suffer.

"I must say Mr. Darcy, I can tell you are adept in the art of chess despite that fact that your mind has been wandering here and there. I think I shall enjoy playing you in the future. Mr. Bennet and I have each other's moves figured out so well that we are no longer much competition to each other; I often think that we are one mind and whenever Miss Elizabeth plays me she refers to the rooks as castles and the knights as horsies. You can imagine how those games proceed."

Darcy laughed in spite of himself. He was anxious to learn what Elizabeth thought of him but at the fear of seeming desperate withheld his inquiry and continued in a different vein instead. "So Miss Elizabeth plays chess, does she?"

"Yes, though she is very bad at it. It is not because she does not have the mind for it, because there is none sharper or that has a keener sense of strategies. She just has a tendency to tell you what those strategies are so that you can plot against her easily."

Darcy smiled and their game continued in silence. Mr. Bennet was enjoying torturing Darcy and was impressed at the gentleman's ability to withhold his desire to know. After hearing a few deep breaths of exasperation Mr. Bennet decided on a few more minutes of torture, and then he would tell him.

"What are those heaving's for, Mr. Darcy, I am not that poor of a chess partner, am I?"

"Oh no, sir, you are a very skilled player. I am just realizing how my mind has not been in the game and it is certain that I am to lose this one as I do not think my mind will return."

"I hope I have not upset you, sir, by our discussions today."

"No, not at all I am almost fully pleased."

"Almost?"

"Yes, almost."

"Why are you not fully pleased, have I not been open and told you almost everything that you requested from our last meeting?" Darcy was so disquieted that he missed the almost that Mr. Bennet said and continued.

In a frustrated yet quiet voice Mr. Darcy responded, "You have been most open, sir, however you have related no information about the one subject I most want to know even though we talked of her for some time earlier. All of the discussion revolved around me and my perceptions and blunders, not her perceptions. I presume as you have information of everyone at Netherfield thus far that you also have some about me." It then dawned on Darcy "almost." "Oh, I see sir, you are being coy with me, were you trying to see how much I could endure without asking? Were you going to see if you could make a grown man beg?"

"Well now, it is about time you came to the point. I thought you would leave today without making me tell you." Here Mr. Bennet laughed and began. "Well my boy, Miss Elizabeth is a hard one to crack and if you do not know her well, you may think that what I am going to relate is not encouraging, however if you took the opportunity at Netherfield to get to know her at all you may be pleased by what I have to relate. Miss Elizabeth would not reveal anything to me at first. She told me of every person at Netherfield except you." Here Darcy's face cracked and a slight smile spread across his lips. "As much as I could figure out was that she enjoyed watching the interaction of everyone at Netherfield, particularly the interactions between yourself and your cousin. When questioned she admitted she is aware that your cousin must seek an attachment to a lady of worth and therefore she would enjoy his friendship and expect nothing more. She tried to end the conversation there. When questioned directly about you she colored, blushed, looked out the window or down at the floor and spoke in the quietest voice saying you are an intelligent conversationalist. She admitted to happening upon you on some walks and that you and she had pleasant, lively, and knowledgeable conversations. Then she said she enjoys talking and spending time with you. After completing her stuttered speech and being dismissed she practically ran from the room in embarrassment. Her father thinks that her behavior is most strange and that it definitely implies that her heart is engaged." By the end of Mr. Bennet's recitation Darcy was sporting a smile to rival any child being given a treat.

Mr. Bennet looked at Darcy, who was grinning like a schoolboy. Mr. Bennet laughed a hearty laugh and said "Your smile lets me know that you have learned enough to be encouraged; am I correct, Mr. Darcy?"

"You are sir, I am very pleased. I believe Mr. Bingley is going to have a ball at Netherfield and I plan on using the opportunity to the best of my advantage with Miss Elizabeth."

"Well sir, I can now honestly wish you all the luck in the world. Before last night I wished you well, however I believe Miss Bennet is also partial to you and I think she deserves to be happier than any other woman on this earth. From the times we have spent together and allowing my understanding of you to grow further, I believe you would make her happy and therefore I wish you luck."

"Thank you sir, I am thankful to have that luck, for this far I have needed it and most likely will need it again. Although I have come to know you well I have yet to either meet or make a good impression on Miss Bennet's parents. I fear her mother despises me and her father is quite elusive. I have never caught a glimpse of him. I fear the first time we will meet will be the day I blind sight him with a request to marry his daughter." Mr. Darcy nervously laughed. "I fear that if Miss Elizabeth is his favorite as you say that the interview would not turn out well for me."

Mr. Bennet replied with his secret understanding. "You may be pleasantly surprised Mr. Darcy. Mr. Bennet is a keen observer of everything that involves his daughters, most particularly the eldest two, and although you do not yet know him he has made his inquiries and knows you very well."

Mr. Bennet noticed Mr. Darcy turn thoughtful as he searched his mind for what the gentleman could think of him. He was not entirely at ease for if he believed the opinion of Mrs. Bennet or perhaps anything Miss Elizabeth may have originally related upon their initial acquaintance he may have an unfavorable opinion.

Mr. Bennet could sense the unease of his friend. Their meetings together had brought him to a decent understanding of Mr. Darcy's mind, so it was easy for him to comprehend where it had wandered. He was able to put Mr. Darcy entirely at ease with one final comment. "Mr. Darcy, Mr. Bennet is not a man to listen to the gossip about town, he bases all of his opinions and resolutions upon his own opinion and when in doubt he seeks mine. I assure you son, he does not have an unfavorable opinion of you."

Mr. Darcy looked up with gratitude towards his friend who with one sentence was able to conquer the very fear that had enveloped his mind.

The two finished their game and were preparing to leave. Darcy wanted to meet again, however Mr. Bennet could not fix a date due to business. Mr. Bennet told Darcy that he would send a note confirming a day if he could.

Just as the two were separating to go to their own residences Mr. Bennet began. "Mr. Darcy, I would have you know who I am prior to the Netherfield Ball."

"Certainly sir, I would know it now if you would tell me."

"No, not today sir, I enjoy this too much and am still afraid it would be spoiled with the knowledge of who I am."

"Sir, why would you think that? Nothing would change with the knowledge of a name?"

"We shall see Mr. Darcy, I am afraid that you are wrong. I am sure it will change with that knowledge although I hope it will not. It will surprise you to learn who I am and truly how close of a friend of that family I am."

"I am sure it will not, sir."

"Well we best not argue over it now, we will know soon enough, though not today. I am not ready as of yet to tell you, perhaps at our next meeting."

The two separated each to their own residences. Mr. Darcy had never really tried to discover who his friend and informant was, but now it appeared as if he should. He was enjoying the companionship of the gentleman and was beginning to think of him as a father, something he had not had for many years. He truly hoped that the camaraderie would not be changed by the knowledge of a name.

That night as Darcy, Bingley, and the Colonel all talked in the library Darcy inquired after Bingley's affections and intentions in regard to Miss Jane Bennet. Upon hearing a favorable response Darcy was satisfied that his friend would not hurt the lady and would indeed be happy with his choice. Colonel Fitzwilliam thought this the perfect opening to update Bingley on his overhearing at the party at Lucas Lodge about the lady's views on matrimony. Bingley was so happy to receive all of the information that he broke out his finest bottle of Wine to toast the ladies.

Chapter 12
The Odious Mr. Collins

"I hope, my dear," said Mr. Bennet to his wife, as they were at breakfast Monday morning, "that you have ordered a good dinner to-day, because I have reason to expect an addition to our family party."

"Who do you mean, my dear? I know of nobody that is coming, I am sure, unless Charlotte Lucas should happen to call in and I hope my dinners are good enough for her. I do not believe she often sees such at home."

"The person of whom I speak is a gentleman, and a stranger."

Mrs. Bennet's eyes sparkled. "A gentleman, and a stranger! It is Mr. Bingley, I am sure! Well, I am sure I shall be extremely glad to see Mr. Bingley. But good Lord! How unlucky! There is not a bit of fish to be got today. Lydia, my love, ring the bell I must speak to Hill this moment."

"It is NOT Mr. Bingley," said her husband; "As we have the good fortune of being acquainted with him already. The man is most definitely not a stranger. As I said, the gentleman whom I refer to is a stranger, a person whom I never set my eyes upon in the whole course of my life."

This roused a general astonishment; and he had the pleasure of being eagerly questioned by his wife and his five daughters at once. After amusing himself some time with their curiosity, he thus explained: "About a month ago I received this letter; and about a fortnight ago I answered it, for I thought it a case of some delicacy, requiring early attention. It is from my nephew, Mr. Collins, who, when I am dead, may turn you all out of this house as soon as he pleases."

"Oh! My dear," cried his wife, "I cannot bear to hear that mentioned. Pray do not talk of that odious man. I do think it is the hardest thing in the world that your estate should be entailed away from your own poor children; and I am sure, if I had been you, I should have tried long ago to do something or other about it."

"It certainly is a most iniquitous affair," said Mr. Bennet, "and nothing can clear Mr. Collins from the guilt of inheriting Longbourn. But if you will listen to his letter, you may perhaps be a little softened by his manner of expressing himself."

"No, I am sure I shall not; and I think it is very impertinent of him to write to you at all, and very hypocritical. I hate such false friends. Why could he not keep on quarreling with you, as his father did before him?"

"Why, indeed; he does seem to have had some filial scruples on that head, as you will hear."

"Hunsford, near Westerham, Kent, 15ᵗʰ October.

"DEAR SIR,--

"The disagreement subsisting between yourself and my late honored father always gave me much uneasiness, and since I have long ago had the misfortune to lose him, I have frequently wished to heal the breach; but for some time I was kept back by my youth and my own doubts, fearing lest it might seem disrespectful to his memory for me to be on good terms with anyone with whom it had always pleased him to be at variance. My mind, however, is now made up on the subject, for having received ordination at Easter, I have been so fortunate as to be distinguished by the patronage of the Right Honorable Lady Catherine de Bourgh, widow of Sir Lewis de Bourgh, whose bounty and beneficence has preferred me to the valuable rectory of this parish, where it shall be my earnest endeavor to demean myself with grateful respect towards her ladyship, and be ever ready to perform those rights and ceremonies which are instituted by the Church of England.

"As a clergyman, moreover, I feel it my duty to promote and establish the blessing of peace in all families within in the reach of my influence; and on these grounds I flatter myself that my present overtures are highly commendable, and that the circumstance of my being next in the entail of Longbourn estate will be kindly overlooked on your side, and not lead you to reject the offered olive-branch. I cannot be otherwise than concerned at being the means of injuring your amiable daughters, and beg leave to apologize for it, as well as to assure you of my readiness to make them every possible amends—but of this hereafter.

If you should have no objection to receive me into your house, I propose myself the satisfaction of waiting on you and your family, on Monday, November 18ᵗʰ, by four o'clock, and shall probably trespass on your hospitality till the Saturday se'ennight following, which I can do without any inconvenience, as Lady Catherine is far from objecting to my occasional absence on a Sunday, provided that some other clergyman is engaged to do the duty of the day.—I remain, dear sir, with respectful compliments to your lady and daughters, your well-wisher and friend,

"WILLIAM BENNET COLLINS"

"At four o'clock, therefore, we may expect this peace-making gentleman," said Mr. Bennet, as he folded up the letter. "He seems to be a most conscientious and polite young man, upon my word, and I doubt not will prove a valuable acquaintance, especially if Lady Catherine should be so indulgent as to let him come to us again."

"There is some sense in what he says about the girls, however, and if he is disposed to make them any amends, I shall not be the person to discourage him." declared Mrs. Bennet.

"Though it is difficult," said Jane, "to guess in what way he can mean to make us the atonement he thinks our due, the wish is certainly to his credit."

Elizabeth was chiefly struck by his extraordinary deference for Lady Catherine, and his kind intention of christening, marrying, and burying his parishioners whenever it was required.

"He must be an oddity, I think," said she. "I cannot make him out. There is something very pompous in his style and what can he mean by apologizing for being next in the entail? We cannot suppose he would help it if he could. Could he be a sensible man, sir?"

"No, my dear, I think not. I have great hopes of finding him quite the reverse."

Mr. Collins was punctual to his time, and was received with great politeness by the whole family. Mr. Bennet indeed said little; but the ladies were ready enough to talk, and Mr. Collins seemed neither in need of encouragement, nor inclined to be silent himself. He was a tall, heavy-looking young man of five and twenty. His air was grave and stately, and his manners were very formal. He had not been long seated before he complimented Mrs. Bennet on having so fine a family of daughters, said he had heard much of their beauty, but that in this instance fame had fallen short of the truth; and added, that he did not doubt her seeing them all in due time disposed of in marriage. This gallantry was not much to the taste of some of his hearers; but Mrs. Bennet, who quarreled with no compliments, answered most readily.

"You are very kind, I am sure; and I wish with all my heart it may prove so, for else they will be destitute enough. Things are settled so oddly."

"You allude, perhaps, to the entail of this estate."

"Ah! Sir, I do indeed. It is a grievous affair to my poor girls, you must confess. Not that I mean to find fault with you, for such things I know are all chance in this world. There is no knowing how estates will go when once they come to be entailed."

"I am very sensible, madam, of the hardship to my fair cousins, and could say much on the subject, but that I am cautious of appearing forward and precipitate. But I can assure the young ladies that I come prepared to admire them. At present I will not say more, but, perhaps, when we are better acquainted."

He was interrupted by a summons to dinner; and the girls smiled on each other. They were not the only objects of Mr. Collins' admiration. The hall, the dining room, and all its furniture, were examined and praised; and his commendation of everything would have touched Mrs. Bennet's heart, but for the mortifying supposition of his viewing it all as his own future property. The dinner too in its turn was highly admired; and he begged to know to which of his fair cousins the excellence of its cooking he owed. But he was set right by Mrs. Bennet, who assured him with some asperity that they were very well able to keep a good cook, and that her daughters had nothing to do in the kitchen. He begged pardon for having displeased her. In a softened tone she declared herself not at all offended; but he continued to apologize for about a quarter of an hour.

During dinner, Mr. Bennet scarcely spoke at all; but when the servants were withdrawn, he thought it time to have some conversation with his guest, and therefore started a subject in which he expected him to shine, Lady Catherine de Bourgh. He was not disappointed and they were able to learn more about her ladyship, daughter, and estate than any of them wanted. Mr. Bennet also determined that Mr. Collins was ridiculous in the fact that he actually studied and planned compliments to the ladies.

By tea time, however, the dose had been enough, and Mr. Bennet was glad to take his guest into the drawing room again, and, when tea was over, glad to invite him to read aloud to the ladies as he retired to the corner by the fire. Mr. Collins readily assented, and many books were produced. After some deliberation he chose Fordyce's Sermons. Lydia gaped as he opened the volume, and before he had, with very monotonous solemnity, read three pages, she interrupted him with: "Do you know, Mamma that my uncle Phillips talks of turning away Richard; and if he does, Colonel Forster will hire him. My aunt told me so herself on Saturday. I shall walk to Meryton tomorrow to hear more about it, and to ask when Mr. Denny comes back from town with Mr. Wickham, what a handsome man he is, I saw him yesterday, just you wait Lizzy I am sure you are to like him."

Lydia was bid by her two eldest sisters to hold her tongue and Mr. Bennet stood up and came to stand over Miss Lydia and began. "Did I hear correctly that you have been in contact with Mr. George Wickham and think him agreeable?"

Lydia was amazed that her father knew the man but took that as a good sign towards the gentleman and continued to expand on his amiability, handsomeness and all the good qualities she could think of.

This did nothing but raise Mr. Bennet's anger especially now that he knew even more of the truth of the man's character and after two minutes of Lydia's chatter exploded. "Lydia, you listen to me, I forbid you to go anywhere near that man or any of his acquaintances; if I hear that you have conversed with any one of them you will be forbidden to go into town or attend any assemblies and will remain on the ground of Longbourn until the entire regiment has left the area. Do I make myself perfectly clear?" then, looking around, he said "and that goes for all of you." With that pronouncement he turned on his heel and went to his library.

Mr. Collins stated that he would no longer importune his young cousins and retired with Mr. Bennet to the library. He shortly returned to converse with the ladies, as Mr. Bennet was in no humor for company. Lizzy was in no mood to listen to him, and so she went to the library to calm her father.

Lizzy could not get her father into any sort of conversation and ended up retiring to her room with a book.

Mr. Collins was not a sensible man; the greatest part of his life having been spent under the strict confines of first his father's and then his stepfather's parish without having received any duties to expand his knowledge or compassion, and though he belonged to one of the universities, he had merely kept the necessary terms, without forming at it any useful acquaintance.

It quickly became known to Mrs. Bennet that Mr. Collins had a good house and a sufficient income and that he intended to marry, and in seeking reconciliation with the Bennet family he had a wife in view, as he meant to choose one of the daughters, especially if they were as beautiful as they were generally reported to be. His plan did not vary on seeing them. By the end of the evening with a few hints from Mrs. Bennet away from Jane he had made his choice of Elizabeth.

Chapter 13
Mr. Bennet Revealed

The following morning dawned bright and clear and after breakfast it was decided that all but Mr. and Mrs. Bennet should walk into town. Mrs. Bennet was not a good walker and Mr. Bennet was anxious to have his library to himself.

The walk passed quickly enough and soon the group reached Meryton. The attention of Lydia and Kitty was immediately wandering up in the street in quest of the officers, their father's threat gone from their minds, and nothing less than a very smart bonnet indeed, or new muslin in a shop window, could recall them.

The attention of Elizabeth was soon caught by a young man, whom she had never seen before, of most gentleman-like appearance, walking with another officer on the other side of the way. The officer was the very Mr. Denny concerning whose return from London Lydia came to inquire, and he bowed as they passed. Lydia and Kitty suddenly seemed quiet, but Elizabeth was struck with the stranger's air, she wondered who he could be; and Kitty and Lydia, determined if possible not to let Lizzy and Jane find out, led the way across the street, under pretense of wanting something in an opposite shop, and fortunately had just gained the pavement when the two gentlemen, turning back, had reached the same spot.

Mr. Denny addressed them directly, and entreated permission to introduce his friend when Lydia cut him off inquiring about his trip to London. He answered the questions and again tried to introduce his friend. It was here that the sound of horses drew their notice, and Mr. Darcy, Colonel Fitzwilliam, and Mr. Bingley were seen riding down the street. On distinguishing the ladies of the group, the gentlemen came directly towards them, and began the usual civilities. Mr. Bingley was the principal spokesman, and Miss Bennet the principal object. He was then, he said, on his way to Longbourn on purpose to inquire after her. Mr. Darcy corroborated it with a bow, and was beginning to determine not to fix his eyes on Elizabeth, when they were suddenly arrested by the sight of the stranger, and Elizabeth, happening to see the countenance of both as they looked at each other, was instantly aware that the man that they had yet to be introduced to was Mr. Wickham. Not wanting to appear as if she was accepting his introductions, Elizabeth began. Gentlemen, I would like to introduce you to our cousin, Mr. William Collins. He is to stay with us for a fortnight, and then turning to the others she introduced Mr. Denny and then said, "I apologize, but the other gentleman must be introduced by Mr. Denny for we are just meeting him ourselves."

With that introduction Mr. Denny introduced his friend Mr. Wickham.

The Colonel and Darcy looked at each other uneasily, but not wanting to draw undue speculation and attention bowed to the gentleman; "We are pleased to make your acquaintance." The Colonel and Mr. Darcy both then stood to the side without talking.

Elizabeth was watching all that occurred, Mr. Darcy and the Colonel were visibly mad; their posture easily portrayed it. In looking at Mr. Wickham, Lizzy could see that he was scared. All of the gentlemen began to walk with the ladies but Mr. Wickham quickly dismissed himself on some pretense of business. Mr. Denny soon also departed and the Netherfield gentlemen were free to walk on with the Longbourn ladies and their cousin conversing comfortably towards the center of Meryton where the shops and public places were laid out. The younger girls wished to view bonnets and lace and so quickly departed while Jane, Elizabeth and Mary went with the gentlemen to the bookshop. Elizabeth wished to inquire after the latest work of Sir Walter Scott.

"Ah, Miss Elizabeth you have come." Said the bookstore owner very excitedly as Elizabeth walked through the door. "I have a surprise for you."

The entire party had looked at Elizabeth as he spoke. She had a huge grin on her face, one of longing, yet knowing, hoping, yet apprehensive.

"Is it here Mr. Richards, did you finally receive copies?"

"I did, just this very morning. As I opened the shipment I put two aside, one for myself and one for you. If I did not see you this very morning I was to send it to Longbourn by messenger boy so that you would no longer have to wait."

Elizabeth laughed as she accepted the book he handed to her "If you would please place the cost of the book on the Longbourn account and send the bill to my father, he will clear it with you as soon as possible. I had hoped, although I did not really expect that this would be in today and therefore I did not bring sufficient funds."

"As you wish Miss Elizabeth. I must say that I have been occasionally reading a page here and there as I arrange books today and I am sure you will be most pleased, as I am." Mr. Richards walked away to place the cost of the book on Mr. Bennet's account.

By now just about everyone had dispersed from watching Elizabeth and Mr. Richards. They realized the excitement was over a book and went to their own amusements. Mr. Darcy, however, lingered with Elizabeth.

"Miss Bennet, what masterpiece has brought about this excitement between you and Mr. Richards?"

"Well Mr. Darcy, it is the newest bit of poetry, I daresay a bit of love poetry. Although I have yet to read it, it is my understanding that the poem encompasses six days and has three story lines. There are reported to be three men vying for the love of one woman."

"Ah, I have heard of this work, *The Lady of the Lake* by Sir Walter Scott".

"You are correct, Mr. Darcy, have you read it?"

"I have not, however I intend to. I see Mr. Richards has additional copies there by the desk, I think I shall also purchase a copy."

"Mr. Darcy, you once asked me if I cared to read and discuss a book with you. If you are still interested in such a scheme I believe I have the perfect book for us to begin with."

Darcy was joyful that she had not only remembered but asked him. "I would be delighted and honored, Miss Bennet. If you will excuse me I will go and make my purchase.

"Mr. Richards, I would like to make a purchase."

"Of course, sir, will there be anything else?" He asked as he began to wrap the book for Mr. Darcy.

"Nothing for me, however I would like to clear the debt owed on Miss Bennet's book as well if you please."

Mr. Richards looked at Mr. Darcy and began to say something but changed his mind. "As you wish sir, it is done." Mr. Darcy paid the man and shortly after the entire party left the bookseller's.

Jane looked at her timepiece and declared that much time had passed and they needed to return home. Lydia and Kitty were recovered and the whole party, escorted by the gentlemen, walked back to Longbourn.

Upon entering the house Miss Jane called for tea, called her mother to the drawing room and informed her father that Mr. Bingley was visiting. The following time was spent in quiet and easy conversation.

After a quarter of an hour Mr. Bennet decided he had better join the party and get to know Mr. Bingley a bit better. If Mr. Darcy was correct, then in the future he may be welcoming this young man into his family. He determined that he should waste no time in getting to know him. Mr. Bennet entered at the back of the room surveying all around him.

The moment Mr. Bennet walked into the drawing room his heart sunk. No one at first noticed him, his mind was racing for a way to retreat and just as he was about to attempt leaving unnoticed he heard, "There you are sir, I thought you were not to join us and leave our guests without a word from you."

Everyone looked up at him except Lizzy and Mr. Darcy; they were sitting near each other, each of them engrossed in a book, which appeared upon first glance to be the same book.

His face became despondent as he comprehended that this was it, the moment that Mr. Darcy would learn who he was. He felt sorrow and regret. He had really enjoyed his meetings with Mr. Darcy; he felt it was close to what might have been had he had a son. Mr. Bennet began to be concerned how Mr. Darcy would react there in his home. He has every reason to call him out as a liar and accuse him of deceit. Mr. Bennet knew that this would change their relationship forever. Quite likely Mr. Darcy would leave Longbourn and never return. Mr. Bennet felt regret over this. Not just because he would miss his friendship, but Mr. Bennet also feared he would break his own daughter's heart with his thoughtlessness for he was sure Elizabeth was well on her way to losing her heart to him. All of the emotions played across his face as he walked towards Lizzy and Mr. Darcy to take a seat near them.

It was now that Elizabeth looked up from her book at the sadness and regret on the face of her father. She instantly became concerned and her voice betrayed it. "Are you well, Father? You look as if something has occurred that saddens you deeply. Would you like me to fetch you a cup of tea, or some wine, or perhaps something stronger?"

It was now that Mr. Darcy looked up as well. Shock instantly registered on his face, his jaw dropped, and he was unable to say anything.

Knowing very well that Lizzy would interpret his response as rude and unfeeling, and not knowing how Mr. Darcy would react, but knowing full well that he would understand, Mr. Bennet began with clear anxiety in his voice.

"No, no, my dear, it is nothing. I suppose I am concerned that I joined the party. I did not know who was in attendance today. I was only informed of Mr. Bingley's being here. Had I known that Mr. Darcy was here as well I would not have joined the party and let my cover down as of yet." The entire speech was said as Mr. Bennet looked intently at an extremely shocked Mr. Darcy.

Elizabeth did not understand but thought that Mr. Darcy's shocked look was because of her father's insulting comments. She became anxious herself at the rudeness of her father and was quickly thinking of how to recover. She was not quick enough, though, because Mr. Darcy began first.

"I wish you had known sir so that your cover could have been spared, if that was your wish. However, I do not see that anything has changed for my part, though to say that I am utterly and completely surprised would be an understatement."

Mr. Bennet smiled the relief evident to both Mr. Darcy and Elizabeth.

Elizabeth did not understand, but as she tried to ask both men interrupted her. It was evident that neither would share their knowledge. In the end she quit asking, just glad that the sadness in her father's face was gone. The exchange had lightened both, however, and the three were able to pass the remainder of the time until the gentlemen left in pleasant conversation.

"So, my dear, what are you reading?"

"*The Lady of the Lake*, Father, it was just arrived today and Mr. Robinson saved me a copy. Father, I placed the cost of the book on our account and so a bill shall be sent soon. I did not have my allowance with me today. I hope you do not mind?"

"It matters not Lizzy; I shall pay it as soon as the bill arrives, thank you for letting me know. I must say, although you have waited a long time for this book, it is very rude of you to be reading and ignoring your guests." This was said with such a smile that everyone knew he was saying it in jest. Mr. Darcy took the opportunity to respond now.

"I assure you, sir, that she is being the perfect hostess, for you see, I am reading as well."

"Yes, I do indeed see that. Is it your practice to bring literature to read at all of your social visits, Mr. Darcy, or just when you visit Longbourn?"

Concern was again seen upon Elizabeth's face as she wondered how her father could so pointedly speak in jest to this relative stranger. So many who knew her father rarely understood his teasing; how Mr. Darcy, who had only met him just now could understand his statements were teasing was beyond her. She was surprised when Mr. Darcy did just that, understand him. Things just did not make sense.

"Just Longbourn, sir; my friends and I happened upon Miss Bennet and her sisters while they were in town today and we accompanied them in their shopping and then their return to Longbourn. I also purchased a copy of Sir Walter Scott's *The Lady of the Lake* and so Miss Bennet and I are perusing it and in discussion about the anticipation of a very fine read."

Mr. Bennet's eyebrows rose knowingly at Mr. Darcy, a small smile beginning at the corner of his mouth. "Very well, I see, so you have each purchased a copy of the same book entirely by chance today have you?"

Elizabeth blushed and cast her eyes down "Perhaps not entirely by chance father. When Mr. Darcy saw what I was purchasing he declared that he had yet to read it and also purchased a copy for himself. I have proposed that we read it and discuss our views together."

"That was rather bold of you Lizzy, what if your friend Mr. Darcy does not want to discuss the book with you? Perhaps you should have let him make the suggestion, my dear." Mr. Bennet was having fun teasing Elizabeth, for he already knew Mr. Darcy had proposed the idea while Elizabeth was in residence at Netherfield.

Elizabeth was scarlet red now and ashamed that her father was ridiculing her in front of Mr. Darcy. Mr. Darcy came to her rescue.

"You are mistaken sir, I assure you that Miss Bennet would never overstep the bounds of propriety and suggest such a thing; however, she was already assured of my willingness and acceptance. While she and her sister were in residence at Netherfield, I made the suggestion after noticing our similar interest in a particular book."

"Well then, I agree, read away, I hope you both have many long and happy discussions on the merits of Sir Walter Scott."

Elizabeth was bright red by now, "Thank you, Father."

"Sir, while we are here and everything is out in the open I hope you will overlook a little liberty I myself took today."

With his curiosity piqued, Mr. Bennet turned to look at Mr. Darcy "What would that be, Mr. Darcy?"

"I have reason to believe that you will not be receiving a bill for Miss Bennet's book today."

"Oh… and why would you believe this? Mr. Robinson is not in the habit of giving books away for free, no matter how much he likes the person receiving it."

Elizabeth was very interested and listened intently to the two.

"I believe it because I took the liberty to pay for the book when I purchased my own copy."

Elizabeth gasped at the indelicacy of his behavior, her face betraying hurt at his disregard for her reputation. It would have been bad enough for him to make a purchase and then present it to her, but to have paid for something that she had already charged and alerted Mr. Robinson of the event was very indelicate indeed.

They had no connection what so ever, no relation, no engagement, nothing. Thankfully Mr. Robinson was not a gossip and had a very high regard for her. She felt safe that he would say nothing, but still felt betrayed nonetheless.

"Well, Mr. Darcy, I believe that you are correct, I will not receive a bill for the book; however from the look on Elizabeth's face she was not aware of your actions."

"No sir, she was not, I did it all of my own choice." In looking at Elizabeth, Darcy began to get a feeling of dread from his actions.

"Very well, in the future you may want to leave the cost of the books to my lot and just purchase some other pretty trinket for the lady. She will be less offended."

"Father!" With but a small statement all of Elizabeth's ire transferred to her father. After their initial greeting Elizabeth had begun to believe that there was more to the relationship of her father and Mr. Darcy than they were saying. The more they talked, the more evident it became. Now they were jesting at her expense and she was mortified.

Mr. Darcy was getting more and more nervous with Mr. Bennet's forward comments. He was becoming worried for Elizabeth and needed her to understand he was not laughing at her and saw no inappropriateness in anything that she did.

"What, my dear, I am only making a statement so that Mr. Darcy understands you to know that his presumption in paying for your book has raised your ire and that if he wants to avoid that in the near future he should make his purchase of gifts for you a little more discretely."

Elizabeth was now furious. She stood, clenched her teeth and replied to the gentlemen coarsely as she departed the room. "Father that is quite enough. Mr. Darcy, good day!"

Darcy was frantic; she could not leave in this state. He feared that she would never speak to him again. What was her father doing, driving her away from him just as he was beginning to make progress? "Miss Bennet, wait, please wait."

Elizabeth stopped and looked at Mr. Darcy, anger and humiliation written all over her face.

"I apologize if my thoughtlessness has placed you in an awkward or even compromised position. I had not thought that purchasing the book for you would be so controversial. I will ensure that you are not affected by it in any way."

"You are very kind Mr. Darcy, but I am not concerned about your purchase sir, for Mr. Robinson is a trustworthy and honest man, my concern is with my father." She turned her fiery gaze to her father. "He seems to find amusement in these proceedings, which are of a serious nature. I generally participate in his jests when they are of a harmless nature, but this. Father, how could you, and in front of our guests? I am ashamed."

Mr. Bennet began to regret his actions "I am sorry, Lizzy, I had not thought you would be offended, we generally find amusement in these things together. I was sure you could laugh about it as I do."

"Not this time, father. You have gone too far."

"Very well Lizzy, off with you, go and rest but come see me tonight. I will see our guests off with a proper apology. Will that suit you, Mr. Darcy?"

"Yes, sir, it shall. Good afternoon, Miss Bennet, I hope that you enjoy your book and that we can begin discussing it next time we meet."

"Very well, Mr. Darcy, until we next meet."

With that, each bowed and Elizabeth left the room.

"Mr. Darcy, would you join me in my library for a drink?"

"Yes sir, I believe I shall. Just let me tell Mr. Bingley and Colonel Fitzwilliam that I shall meet him at Netherfield if they need to leave before we conclude our discussion."

The two arose and Mr. Bennet headed towards the library while Mr. Darcy addressed Mr. Bingley and Colonel Fitzwilliam.

"Bingley, Fitzwilliam, I shall be joining Mr. Bennet in a discussion about estate business. I know not how long I shall be. You may depart without me and I will meet you at Netherfield later this evening."

"Estate business, gall, Darcy, you are a bore, aren't you. I saw Miss Bennet leave; you truly must have been a poor companion for her to run as she did. Very well, we are nearing the end of our visit; we will meet you at Netherfield."

"Thank you, Bingley, I shall meet you there."

Mr. Darcy left to join Mr. Bennet in the library. He entered and sat down and accepted the drink that Mr. Bennet handed him without a word. Each sat in silence for a few minutes until finally Mr. Bennet began.

"Well, I daresay the drawing room did not go as smooth as I would have liked, though you handled yourself well, my boy. I daresay that she likes you."

"I think she is furious with me and a far cry from having any emotion other than anger at this moment."

Mr. Bennet chuckled at Mr. Darcy's response before continuing. "I think you need to rethink the discussion or rethink your knowledge of the lady sir, for the way she reacted affirms her opinion to me."

Mr. Darcy sat in thought a moment. "No, regardless of what I know about her or how I reassess what occurred I still think she is furious. I truly hope that I have not lost her good opinion because of our..." Darcy paused to rethink the correct word to say "thoughtlessness."

Mr. Bennet laughed, "You are being nice, my boy. You truly do not mean to include yourself in that thoughtlessness. You are just saying that to spare an old man. You as well as I know that you mean to say my thoughtlessness."

Mr. Darcy said nothing, which acknowledged his opinion of the truthfulness of the statement.

"Touché, Mr. Darcy, touché. I will tell you something in hopes that I can improve your opinion of me and we can continue as friends. I would not have you leave with a sour taste in your mouth because of my conduct."

Mr. Darcy nodded in assent.

"My perceptions are not in line with yours and so they may cheer you a bit if you believe me. I believe that Elizabeth is only mad at me. She and I have always had a like mind and teased at the absurdity of our neighbors, using each other's conduct as a basis for a laugh, however we have never until today cared one stitch what those persons thought of us in return. Today's manner in which Elizabeth reacted was so altered because she cares for your opinion. There could be no other reason she would react so."

"I am not sure, sir; she did not appreciate you calling into question the possibility of her acting in an inappropriate manner. She holds herself and her conduct to high standards and to have those standards questioned did not sit well, but to have those standards questioned in front of a guest was upsetting. Might I add that if you are correct, and I hope that you are, and she does have a sentiment for me then it would have only made your mentioning them even more angering? Due to the fact that I participated in the conversation her ire cannot be limited only to you, it extends to me out of association at the very least, possibly, which I dread, but agreement as well."

"You are correct in a few items, but not all. I think that her ire is focused solely on me. She may be embarrassed next time you see her, but she will not hold it against you as she will with me. Also, Mr. Darcy, you supported her, which I must say was in very good form. Well done, man."

"I hope you are correct, sir, but unfortunately only time will tell. As you know I have not made it secret from you what my intentions toward Miss Bennet are. As I have gotten to know her, these past weeks, those intentions have not wavered; they have only become more reinforced in my mind. If this lessens my chances with her, I will truly be despondent, possibly angered. I am a gentleman and so I would never be able to do anything about it, but you must know how I will feel. Is that honest and fair enough?"

"Fair enough, Mr. Darcy, fair enough. Let us hope that it does not occur. I will apologize to her again tonight and she will act angry for awhile, but if it is as all occasions in the past, she will forgive me and all will be back as it was."

"I hope so, Mr. Bennet."

The gentlemen broke up and Mr. Darcy returned to Netherfield.

That night Darcy related to his cousin the identity of his informant and watched as the Colonel had a hearty laugh. His laugh altered, though, as Darcy told him the extent of the discussions the two had in the past and again today.

"Think, Darcy, you have been baring your soul to an acquaintance with the sole intention of wooing a lady... there, Darcy, no denying it" the Colonel said sternly as Darcy tried to interrupt. "I know you are trying to woo the lady, leave it at that. Anyways back to what I was saying. Here you are baring your soul and talking of this lady and what you want from her and all this time it was to her father." The Colonel let out a strangled laugh "Does that not make you uneasy? You are as much honor bound to her now as you could ever imagine. Her own father knows you want to marry her. You told him as much today, not to mention your past discussions. What of it man, now you must marry the lady, whether you want to or not. Her father will see to that."

"I do not agree, Fitzwilliam. You do not know him as I do. He is not that sort of man."

"He is a father, one with an entailed estate and five unmarried and penniless daughters. You are a rich and handsome gentleman of the upper gentry; you have all but proposed marriage. He will make you honor your implied intentions, mark my word, Darcy."

"Fitzwilliam, I can admit to you alone that I am so lost to her already that I hope he does. It would save me from having to explain to the family that I have chosen her of my own free will."

Fitzwilliam genuinely laughed and the two continued talking comfortably for a few additional minutes the Colonel told Darcy that he must return to his regiment as early as tomorrow.

"I am sorry, Darcy, but you are going to have to deal with this Wickham situation on your own."

Darcy shrugged and related to his cousin, Mr. Bennet's, knowledge of the man and that he had related his dealings to him, therefore assuring him of an ally that was well known and respected in the area.

The colonel was pleased though nervous that Georgiana's tale had been told but if Darcy trusted the man then there was nothing to it he was also to be trusted by the Colonel. Darcy's judgment was unquestionably good and the colonel retired at ease knowing his cousin would be well assisted.

After supper Elizabeth directly followed her father to the library. "Father, I must speak with you."

"Yes Lizzy, I imagine you must!"

"Father, I have two things to discuss with you. We will come to what occurred in the drawing room in a minute. First I must inform you that we met Mr. Wickham in Meryton today. Lydia and Kitty tried to hide his identity from us so as to associate with him, however when the Netherfield party arrived he soon dismissed himself."

"Thank you Lizzy, I shall know how to act. Now what about you second item?"

"Yes, I must know what that was all about in the drawing room today. How could you act that way in front of our guests?"

Mr. Bennet sighed unsure of whether to tell Elizabeth or not. His head said not to tell her. He would then ensure that she would make her own decisions and not be biased off of his or any other's opinion. On the other side his heart was dying to tell her all that he knew of the man's goodness and that he knew that Mr. Darcy was just the man to make her happy for all of her days. In the end his head won out and he told her that he had a mere slight acquaintance, giving her nothing but vague details. He desperately wanted to tell her, rationalizing that she deserved to know his opinion of the man. Perhaps she would open up to him more if she knew the man himself had. Yet despite all, he could not tell her everything and left her with but a brief understanding, more confusion than anything else really.

"Lizzy, my dear, Mr. Darcy and I have a prior acquaintance that you need not worry yourself about. Through this acquaintance we knew each other by sight alone, or at least he knew me by sight, I had the fortune of knowing his name. Today we were revealed to each other and I was afraid our acquaintance would change once he knew my identity. I am honored to know that our knowledge of each other has not changed Mr. Darcy's intentions or opinions. Our knowledge of each other has extended to our understanding of personality. Mr. Darcy knew I was jesting with him and he was not offended. I had no idea you would become so defensive. You normally react with calmness and jest when we tease, even when we tease ourselves."

"Father I do not understand, how do you know Mr. Darcy? Why would an acquaintance change by knowing your name?"

"No, Lizzy, it is not your place to ask such things and I will not tell you. There are some things in this world that you must be content in being ignorant about. But do not distress yourself my dear; I can only imagine that there is one reason that you would do so."

"Oh, and what would that be, father?"

"Why, that you like Mr. Darcy and that you do not want him to know of anything that may make you appear in a less than perfect light."

"Father, I cannot believe your audacity today. What has gotten into you?"

"Nothing my dear, I am the same as ever, it is you who is beginning to change. For the first time you have found someone who you care what they think of you."

Lizzy paused to think *is father correct, do I care what Mr. Darcy thinks of me?*

Mr. Bennet just smiled at her during her pause for thoughts. As she began to speak again he rose and walked over to kiss her forehead. "Now off with you, my dear, I hope you and your Mr. Darcy have many long and happy discussions on the merits of Sir Walter Scott."

"He is not my Mr. Darcy, father."

"Oh is he not... well I have the highest regard for OUR Mr. Darcy." This time the word was emphasized even more and he continued. "And if he is not YOUR Mr. Darcy, already then he certainly shall be very soon." With that said Mr. Bennet dismissed a shocked Elizabeth with a wave of his hand.

Just as she was to exit the door he said one last time. "I truly am sorry, Lizzy, if today's conversation upset you. You must know that Mr. Darcy knew we were in jest and has not lessened his high opinion of you in the least. You shall see him again, worry not, daughter."

Lizzy left the room no longer angered at her father or Mr. Darcy and thought only of her Mr. Darcy and what their future discussions of Sir Walter Scott would bring.

It had been over a week since Jane and Elizabeth met to talk. Jane came to Elizabeth's room and they situated themselves upon her bed. Elizabeth related to Jane what she had witnessed pass between Mr. Wickham, Mr. Darcy and the Colonel and the knowledge that she knew of each. When Jane asked her source she said much of it was from their father and uncle, but some of it had been gleaned from Mr. Darcy and his cousin. Today's looks between them and father's scolding the day before had confirmed it all.

After they talked of Mr. Wickham they moved to more pleasant conversations, what each thought of the gentleman inhabitants of Netherfield. It soon became apparent to each that their sister was falling, if not already, in love.

Chapter 14
A Songbird at Oakham Mount

The following morning Bingley, Darcy, and Fitzwilliam met in the breakfast room and Darcy and Bingley bid the Colonel farewell. The meeting with Bingley was short, as he was engaged to offer invitations to the Netherfield Ball with his sisters. The Colonel and Darcy, however, had a nice long discussion that ended with the Colonel promising to check on Georgiana that very evening and personally explaining to her why she could not come into Hertfordshire. They departed each other's company with best wishes for safe travels and a quick brotherly like embrace.

Mr. Bingley and his sisters came to give their personal invitation for the long expected ball at Netherfield, which was fixed for the following Tuesday. Mr. Bingley was excited to be hosting a ball and all but declared that it was in honor of Miss Bennet. He was fortunate enough to claim her hand for the first set of the evening and the supper set, thus opening the evening and eating supper with his angel. Jane was very pleased to accept the dances.

The prospect of the Netherfield ball was extremely agreeable to every female of the family. Mrs. Bennet chose to consider the ball as given in compliment to her eldest daughter, and was particularly flattered by receiving the invitation from Mr. Bingley himself, instead of a ceremonious card. Jane pictured to herself a happy evening in the society of Mr. Bingley, and Elizabeth thought with pleasure of dancing a great deal with Mr. Darcy.

Elizabeth's spirits were so high on this occasion, that though she did not often speak unnecessarily to Mr. Collins, she could not help asking him whether he intended to accept Mr. Bingley's invitation, and if he did, whether he would think it proper to join in the evening's amusement, and she was rather surprised to find that he entertained no scruple whatever on that head, and was very far from dreading a rebuke either from the Archbishop, or Lady Catherine de Bourgh, by venturing to dance.

"I am by no means of the opinion, I assure you," said he, "that a ball of this kind, given by a young man of character, to respectable people, can have any evil tendency; and I am so far from objecting to dancing myself, that I shall hope to be honored with the hands of all my fair cousins in the course of the evening, and I take this opportunity of soliciting yours, Miss Elizabeth, for the two first dances especially, a preference which I trust my cousin Jane will attribute to the right cause, and not to any disrespect for her."

Elizabeth felt herself completely taken in. She had fully hoped to be engaged by Mr. Darcy for those very dances, at the very least engaged with someone more agreeable, and to have Mr. Collins instead! Her liveliness had never been worse timed. There was no help for it, however. Mr. Darcy's happiness and her own were perforce delayed a little longer, and Mr. Collins' dances accepted with as good a grace as she could.

Elizabeth felt as if she must flee the house at this point and abruptly turned and left the room in search of her bonnet, spencer, gloves, and book to go out on a walk. She was not the better pleased with Mr. Collins' gallantry from the idea it suggested to her of his expectation of something more. It now first struck her that she was selected from among her sisters as worthy of being mistress of Hunsford Parsonage.

Elizabeth walked towards Oakham Mount determined not to go home until she absolutely must and thus avoid Mr. Collins for the majority of the afternoon.

Upon reaching the mount Elizabeth sat down on her favorite rock to admire the beauty surrounding her and tried to read. She quickly found that reading was useless: her mind was too active. She thought about all that had occurred over the past few weeks, and frequently caught herself frowning at the thought of Mr. Collins and smiling whenever a memory happened upon Mr. Darcy. Although she was trying primarily to think of only Mr. Darcy, the events of the morning kept recurring in her mind and in the end she could scarcely think of anyone except the horrible Mr. Collins. Elizabeth determined that mental exercise was not enough to purge her of Mr. Collins and instead she indulged herself in physical. Elizabeth stood, discarded her bonnet and book on the rock and walked to her favorite climbing tree and climbed to her preferred branch at the very top. Once situated, Elizabeth began one of her favorite tree climbing pastimes, she began to sing. Elizabeth did not come down from her perch or cease singing for nigh on an hour.

Mr. Darcy was concerned that his cousin had been called back to his regiment early but happy that the Colonel would be able to look in on Georgiana without requiring Darcy to leave the area. His mind was occupied with many familiar items that he constantly thought of each day of his life, including Pemberley and London business dealings, Georgiana, his cousin and other family relations, Mr. Bingley taking on the task of Netherfield, Miss Bingley not leaving him alone, and now one more, Miss Elizabeth Bennet. In addition to it all, Darcy had slept ill last evening, having dreams that he would never dare mention to anyone and scarcely even admitted to himself. He desperately needed air and exercise, yes, that would help to clear his head. Now more than ever he needed a clear head to combat Miss Bingley. With the Colonel departed he would no longer have anyone to save him and he would require all of his senses at their top performance in order to constantly dissuade her.

Darcy called for his horse and asked the stable boy directions to Oakham Mount, which were given thoroughly as he presented him a sixpence. Darcy mounted his horse, offered a thank you to the boy in the form of a coin, and galloped in the direction of Oakham Mount.

Mr. Bennet had mentioned that Oakham Mount was Elizabeth's favorite place; it was time that he saw it for himself. He had no expectation of meeting Elizabeth there; he only wanted to behold the place that she held dear. As he drew closer he could hear singing. Although he had heard her singing voice but a few times he recognized it as Elizabeth's immediately. Darcy turned and rode his horse to the edge of the mount. Far enough away that it would not be seen or heard. He dismounted and let his horse graze while he walked towards the lovely sound. He was easily able to locate the tree in which she was perched. Not wanting to disturb her, he looked around and saw a large rock, not far away, that would be perfect for him to sit and wait unseen in silence. Upon approaching the rock Darcy saw Elizabeth's bonnet and book haphazardly discarded. He picked them up and held them as he seated himself upon the rock and listened for above half an hour to the most beautiful, enchanting singing that he had ever heard. He recognized all of the songs as being from the "Marriage of Figaro" or "Romeo and Juliet," which reaffirmed to him that Miss Elizabeth did in fact love the opera and theater. Darcy was becoming enchanted with the sound of her voice, even wondering so far as which tree at Pemberley she would label her favorite when she arrived, for he was ever more sure she would someday go there, for a visit at the very least. As the minutes passed Darcy convinced himself that Elizabeth should join him at Pemberley, making it her home forever.

Elizabeth finally tired of singing and feeling more at ease after her distressing morning decided to remove herself from the tree; she descended easily. Once she reached the final limb she jumped from the tree with grace then turned to it and lovingly placed her hand on it saying "Well my dear friend, I must thank you again for allowing me solitude, peace and tranquility in your strong and sturdy arms. I am a selfish creature for demanding your comforting embrace and depressing you with my tales of woes, but I cannot help it. I have no one else whom I can talk to. Jane is of course always willing to listen, but she currently has much on her own mind to keep her occupied and as you are well aware, I cannot speak to any others of my family. I suppose as we are the dearest of friends and dearest friends listen to each other unconditionally that you do not mind; I truly appreciate it. I hope my songs rejuvenated your spirits as they have mine and made you forget all of my troubles just as I have. Until I come again, dear friend, farewell and stand strong in the winds of nature as I stand strong in the winds of society." With her speech concluded Elizabeth kissed the palm of her hand and blew the kiss towards her friend and then turned to retrieve her belongings only to be standing face to face with Mr. Darcy.

Elizabeth was embarrassed and could say nothing.

"Good afternoon Miss Bennet." Darcy said, his voice portraying that he was slightly distressed. When he first sat to listen he thought nothing of it, it was harmless, but as Elizabeth descended the tree and poured out her heart to her friend he realized he had interrupted her solitude and peace. Would she be offended at his interruption and audacity to stay unannounced for so long? It seemed each meeting with her was determined to upset their emerging friendship.

"Mr. Darcy" Elizabeth said blushing from head to toe as she realized he had again witnessed her climbing habits and now also her fondness to talking to trees.

"I believe these are yours," he said as he quickly but gently handed her bonnet and book to her.

Darcy could tell that she was embarrassed and quickly tried to put her more at ease. "You mentioned this was a fine walk and that you frequently come here. I thought I should discover it for myself. I hope that I have not engaged in an unwelcome intrusion upon your time of solitude?"

"Whether it was intruding or not does not mean that it must be unwelcome. You are correct that I came for solitude, however that time is past and I am at present happy with company. Did you come only to walk or did you also come in mind to select a tree for yourself this fine morning?"

Mr. Darcy was relieved that her distress at seeing him here had left her features for the most part, but could tell that she was still not entirely at ease. "I will indeed if you will walk with me and tell me of each of your favorites."

"It would be my pleasure, sir."

Mr. Darcy offered Lizzy his arm and they began to walk slowly around the mount.

"Mr. Darcy, the tree you witnessed me in today is the best climbing tree at the mount. It has long been my friend, its strong branches are well positioned and a good space apart, ideal for climbing. The view is spectacular from the third branch from the top as the smaller branches are positioned in such a way to create an opening that can be seen through as one sits with their back to the trunk of the tree." A sly mocking grin replaced her soft smile as she added. "As I have admitted that it is the very best and my personal favorite I prefer to come to this mount and have it available at my every whim. I would be most seriously displeased if I arrived here to find it occupied and not available to me on the schedule that I demand".

Darcy loved watching Elizabeth as her face lit up during her speech. He found himself laughing by the end of her it and grateful that she was finally comfortable displaying her teasing nature to him.

"Miss Bennet, I agree, this particular tree appears as if it is most fine, however is it strong enough to accommodate a man such as myself or does it prefer delicate ladies seeking solitude, peace, and tranquility?" Darcy glanced at her out of the corner of his eye.

Elizabeth recognized the repetition of her own words by Mr. Darcy and stopping turned to address him, she began softly and solemnly "Mr. Darcy, this tree has stood proud, tall, and strong in this location for many years longer than either you or I have experienced. I have faith that it could withstand the stress of a man of your stature, I daresay if we wanted to test, it would prove itself by withstanding the stress of a man of your stature and a lady of my delicateness simultaneously. I am sure that my friend would be honored to prove its strength to you."

"Do you believe it would like to prove its strength to us?"

Elizabeth blushed and replied "Yes, no, I mean… well that is Mr. Darcy, this marvelous tree has already proved its strength to me and I need not question its abilities, but if you do not take my word for it and continue to doubt then it would be prudent of me to join you in the tree and let it prove its strength to you."

"I would like that Miss Bennet."

Mr. Darcy turned to walk back to the tree.

"Where are we going?" Elizabeth inquired.

"To let this tree of yours prove its strength to me."

"Now?"

"Yes, that is unless you revoke your willingness just after you agreed to it?" Darcy looked at her slyly.

"Hardly, as you have seen, I am an adept climber and I need not concern myself with a second climb today."

"Very well, shall we?"

"Yes, I believe we shall. Would you prefer me to go first and show you the best path for climbing or would you like to prove your nimbleness and climb ahead of me?" This was said as a challenge, which Darcy eagerly took.

"I shall go ahead of you and if you require assistance be at the ready to pull you up."

"I daresay Mr. Darcy that I will be able to reach the top with no assistance."

Mr. Darcy reached for the bottom limb, pulled himself up and began to climb; Elizabeth was right behind him. Quite quickly both reached the top and situated themselves in the branches, Elizabeth claiming her favorite and Darcy taking one next to her.

"Well I must agree, Miss Elizabeth, that this is a magnificent tree for climbing. As you said the branches are just the right distance apart for smooth climbing and situated just so to make a spectacular view of the countryside as we sit here. I must also admit that this tree is very strong and sturdy and its branches easily able to accommodate both of us."

"I am glad you approve, Mr. Darcy."

The two then sat in silence for some time both looking at each other shyly. Darcy was the first to break the silence.

"Miss Bennet, I admit that I happened upon you long before you descended the tree and was able to sit and listen to your sweet melodies for above half an hour. I then heard your parting words to the tree. I cannot help but be aware that you have a woe pressing upon you. I dearly hope it had nothing to do with yesterday. Would you… could you, share it with me?"

"Mr. Darcy, I assure you this particular woe is not about yesterday. I daresay that I am over my anger towards my father from that unfortunate episode. I am afraid this woe is that of a personal nature. As much as I have enjoyed our frequent conversations I do not believe that our acquaintance is at a level that I am comfortable divulging that which has troubled me today. Let us instead talk of better things."

Darcy was disappointed that she did not feel ready to confide in him, but pleased at the opportunity she was giving him to get to know her better so that some day she would permit him to calm her troubled mind and perhaps hold and comfort her in his arms and she allowed this tree to do.

"Very well Miss Bennet, I see you have Sir Walter Scott with you. Have you also been indulging yourself in a bit of reading this morning?"

"I did want to try however my mind unfortunately was a little pre-occupied; I have gotten no further than where I ended last night."

"How far was that, Miss Bennet?"

"I was able to complete through the first Canto, 'The Chase', after talking half the night with Jane. And you, Mr. Darcy, were you able to read much last evening or did particular persons at Netherfield occupy your attention most of the evening?" The last was said in such a playful way that Darcy had no doubt about whom she meant and he chuckled lightly.

"No, Miss Bennet, particular persons of the Netherfield Party retired early last evening as I had earlier mentioned that all well bred young ladies must always get their beauty sleep. My cousin, however, is as conversational as any attentive female so I suppose, yes, I was up late in conversation."

Elizabeth laughed at this "Mr. Darcy, considering that statement and the knowledge that I stayed up half the night talking before I even began the book I must admit that I am not a well-bred young lady."

"I am glad to hear it, Miss Bennet, for I much prefer a nimble nymph who sings in the trees to a well bred young lady."

Elizabeth colored and quickly continued "So if certain person retired early, but your cousin proceeded to talk too long you also were unable to read any of our book?"

"Indeed not, I was able to escape my cousin and spent the evening engrossed in Sir Walter Scott. In fact I was able to read the entire first canto as well and even whetted my appetite a bit by a few pages into the second, 'The Island'."

"What think you thus far, Mr. Darcy? Do you enjoy *The Lady of the Lake*?"

"I do indeed, although I think it is reckless that the man would push his mount to the point of death by exhaustion."

"I agree, Mr. Darcy, however maybe a man such as James Fitz-James, who you must have realized was none other than King James V of Scotland traveling incognito, does not care what happens to his mounts as he has many and can spare one now and again."

"As you say, Miss Bennet, I did also realize that James Fitz-James was the King of Scotland, however being who you are does not give you any more right than another to disregard the welfare of an animal or person in your charge. What think you of him traveling incognito?"

The conversation of the two pleasantly continued on close to an hour as they sat reclined in the tree branches. At length Darcy reminded them both of the time and they descended from the tree. Mr. Darcy offered to escort Elizabeth home. Their conversation on the way to Longbourn continued, but it was on a different subject.

"Did Mr. Bingley arrive at Longbourn before your departure this morning?"

"Indeed he did, sir; he brought an invitation for his ball at Netherfield."

"And was the invitation accepted by Longbourn?"

Elizabeth let out a hearty laugh at this "Indeed it was, if you ask that question I fear you do not know my family well. I think it would be safe to say that nothing could keep the Bennet family away." Here Elizabeth's voice changed to one that sounded very much like her shrill matriarch "Why, girls, Mr. Bingley himself came to offer his personal invitation. He is such a handsome and eligible gentleman, how could we not go? What a fine thing for our girls is it not, Mr. Bennet, a personal invitation?"

With such an interpretation of the happenings at Longbourn Darcy was beginning to get an idea of why her mind was troubled and he said nothing in response.

Elizabeth recalled herself and replied almost sadly, "Yes, Mr. Darcy, we are to attend the Netherfield Ball. In fact I believe the other ladies of the house are home right now planning their gowns and hair despite the lapse of almost a week before the ball."

Darcy smiled at the thought of it all "So the ball has caused a bit of excitement with the ladies then, has it?"

"Yes sir, as I am sure you are aware, ladies in general enjoy dancing, and so this ball has brought happiness to many hearts among my family."

"You enjoy dancing do you not, Miss Bennet?"

"I do indeed sir, you can ease your mind knowing that I am also one in anticipation of certain parts of the evening."

Darcy could tell she was hiding something but he did not know what.

"I hope one of those parts would be a dance with me." Darcy said as he turned to Elizabeth and looked into her eyes.

"I believe it will be when you ask me."

"Well then let us make it official, may I have a place on your dance card, Miss Bennet?"

"You may, sir, is there any particular dance that you request?" Elizabeth did not think Darcy was bold enough to claim the opening set due to the speculation that would be excited and therefore thought she was safe from having to explain. Little did she know how wrong she was.

"I will claim the first set if that is agreeable to you."

Elizabeth's smile left her features and her face went pale as she choked back a cry; her wish could have been fulfilled if only her impertinence had been in check earlier in the day. Darcy saw her look and heard her efforts to hold back, he realized he had just hit on her woes from the morning. He was afraid he had said too much and started to make up excuses when Elizabeth stopped him and said in a disappointed manner, "Mr. Darcy, it would be an honor to have you claim that very set, but unfortunately I must decline, sir, for I have already been claimed for those dances by my cousin, Mr. Collins this very afternoon shortly after Mr. Bingley issued the invitation and just before I left the house."

"I see that your dance card fills fast Miss Bennet. I should have learned it from my first experience, even this time I am late, but I will learn from my mistake and now claim you for the second set."

Elizabeth looked up at him and smiled "I would like that, Mr. Darcy, I will be sure to be waiting for you then."

"If I may be so bold, may I also claim you for the supper set and the final set of the evening."

"Three sets, Mr. Darcy!" Elizabeth exclaimed surprised.

"Indeed you are correct, I believe if I count them here on my fingers that would be three."

Elizabeth could not help but laugh aloud at his statement. "But Mr. Darcy, I am not sure how such a, how shall I say this, declaration would be received in London, however you are in Meryton, which is but a small county society. If you dance three dances, particularly the three dances you have chosen, with the same lady in one evening, speculation and talk will most certainly begin. Are you sure you want to excite such behavior in the neighborhood, especially after meeting my mother?"

"If you mean that I want to declare to everyone that I am interested in a particular lady by dancing the first set, that I would prefer to get to know her better by eating supper with her and having extended conversation and that I want to leave the dance with her on my mind in order to have pleasant dreams then yes, I suppose I know what gossiping I will excite and what position I am getting myself into. And I consider myself warned about your mother, what say you, will you reserve the dances for me?"

Elizabeth turned scarlet with each word of his recitation but readily agreed to it, it appeared as if this dance was going to be monumental in her life and she was very excited for it.

"You honor me, Mr. Darcy, with your request. I am indeed pleased to accept and I hope that you are not disappointed come Tuesday. I also hope that you are not foiled in your plans because your declaration of intent to dance must be foiled by it being the second instead of the first."

"It will not be foiled; my intent shall be known by other means if I intend it. In addition, you must know that I could not be disappointed knowing that I share three dances with you."

Elizabeth had been extremely embarrassed throughout the entire conversation and Darcy knew it; however, he wanted her to know how he felt and did not want to hide his feelings from her. He knew he stood the chance of frightening her with his boldness, yet felt deep down that she was willing to hear it. After such an agreeable day today, no longer would he hide himself, he was ready to declare to all that she was his, or at least that he wanted her to be. He was ready to earn her trust and have her confide in him, let him comfort her and most of all ready to sweep her off to Pemberley. Now all he needed was the right moment to ask her.

"I know I shall be looking forward to Tuesday evening with more enjoyment than I originally could have imagined." Then shyly, and with a lot of hesitation she continued "Perhaps I will break an elastic on my shoe or make the entire family late for the first set of the evening and then although it would be the second set of the night it would be my first set when I was to dance with you."

Elizabeth was amazed at her own boldness regardless at how shyly and hesitantly it was stated. Never before had she been so candid with anyone other than Jane on such a topic, and definitely never had she been so with a man.

Darcy could not be more pleased with her statement.

"Anything, Miss Bennet, except making the family late, for I daresay Mr. Bingley would never forgive you for making him stand up with anyone other than your sister, Miss Jane, at his own ball."

Elizabeth beamed at him after he made this declaration and said "Oh, I could never endure it if Mr. Bingley were upset with me. Perhaps I shall just stub my toe and need a short rest before the second set."

"I prefer you breaking your elastic on your shoe; that way you are in no way injured or in pain, for I could not bear to see you hurt."

"Elastic it is, Mr. Darcy, I propose you having some sort of a replacement available at Netherfield, for if I came prepared it would look a little premeditated."

"As you wish, Miss Bennet."

They were nearing Longbourn and the closer they got the more Elizabeth became visibly distressed. As they approached the drive both could hear the commotion inside. Elizabeth looked at Darcy in concern saying, "I thank you for accompanying me home, Mr. Darcy, would you like to come in for tea?" Each knew that the invitation had only been offered out of politeness and although Darcy would have very much enjoyed being with Elizabeth longer, no matter the commotion going on inside, he could see the distress on her face and therefore he declined and made ready to leave.

As his declination was made Darcy could see the relief portrayed on Elizabeth's face. He reached for her hand, kissed it with a bow, mounted his horse and left to return to Netherfield.

Elizabeth stood watching him until he reached the end of the lane. Just before he was to exit the lane he slowed his horse, turned to look behind him and seeing her standing there tipped his hat to her as he again kicked his horse onward.

Darcy was elated that she had stayed to watch him depart. He was more than satisfied with the day's events; in fact he was downright pleased. Elizabeth's heart jumped and her pulse quickened as he turned and saw her standing there; he tipped his hat to her and she returned to the house happier than she ever imagined she could be. Nothing Mr. Collins or her mother did could dampen her attitude towards this day now.

Mr. Bennet had been watching from his library window. He had begun to worry about Elizabeth and was watching the window often awaiting her return. He saw the entire exchange and smiled despite the pang in his heart that he was sure to lose his favorite very soon. It appeared to him upon witnessing the exchange of the couple that Mr. Darcy had indeed made a lot of positive progress.

Chapter 15
The Days Pass So Slowly

Colonel Fitzwilliam's return to London was smooth and uneventful. He stopped first at the Darcy townhouse where Georgiana was currently in residence.

"Georgie, my sweetling, how are you?" Richard said as he entered her sitting room.

Georgiana leapt to her feet and rushed to him giving him a hug. Before he could say another word she had accosted him with many questions about Meryton, Netherfield, her brother, and most of all, the lady he had written about.

"Who is she, Richard? Is she lovely? Is her family nice? Will she like me for a sister?"

Richard Fitzwilliam could easily see that Darcy's information to his sister had made her jump to every possible conclusion and the next hour was spent in conversation.

"First of all, sweetling, let me apologize for my attire, I have not returned to my own lodgings to change, I came here first."

"Oh Richard you know I care not for travel dust and much prefer you to come straight to see me."

"I am glad, but before I answer the happy questions that you have, let me speak of a more serious topic first." Georgiana nodded her agreement and each of them took a seat near the warm fire.

"Your brother and I both apologize that you are not to go to Hertfordshire right now…"

"What, not go, but I must, I need to…" Georgiana began to protest her unhappiness at the decision but was cut off, "Now before you become too upset let me speak. We made the decision together, although it was hard because he would dearly like you to meet a certain lady." Here the Colonel smiled and again held up his hand to silence Georgie. "Our reason is a sound one and I will tell you now. Mr. George Wickham is presently stationed in Meryton in the militia and we thought it best to keep you here until he has departed."

The Colonel saw Georgiana go pale and thought she was going to cry as he told her but was surprised by what followed. She took a deep breath, her color began to come back and she said "Richard I thank you for being honest with me, but now I must be honest with you. I appreciate all that you and Fitzwilliam do to try and protect me, but I am no longer a child. I cannot go around hiding for the remainder of my life hiding, missing out on the remainder of my life because someone tried to hurt me when I was young. I have grown and learned from the experience this past year and would appreciate it if in the future you each sought my opinion before making up your minds."

Richard was surprised and said so. "Oh dear, sweetling, I have missed your blossoming. It is evident to me that you have learned and grown much from the experience, more so than either of us has given you credit for. Please be patient with us Georgie, we will come around sooner or later."

Georgiana smiled radiantly at him, glad that she had finally been able to tell Richard what she felt. "Now, Richard, tell me all about Netherfield and this lady that William has met."

"Well my dear, Netherfield is a pretty enough estate though it is nothing to Pemberley. The neighborhood is average, but not anything spectacular, though one family caught our interest, your brother and Mr. Bingley's most especially." Georgie raised her eyebrows with interest towards Richard who continued. "The family has five daughters, two of which are particular beauties, Miss Jane and Elizabeth Bennet. Your brother took an active interest in the later and Charles in the former."

"Oh Richard, you must tell me all."

Richard related the events of the Meryton Assembly as Georgie laughed at the ridiculous situation her brother was in asking Miss Elizabeth for a dance when her card was full. She was grieved at the discovery that he had made many blunders and foolish remarks towards her and her family and was relieved and curious to hear of Darcy's friend who told him all about the family. She was horrified for her brother when she heard from Richard that the friend turned out to be the lady's father but pleased to know that things were well on their way to being right when the Colonel left Netherfield.

Georgie was equally pleased to hear that Bingley had also met a wonderful lady and laughed at the fact that it was a sister of William's lady. "Poor Miss Bingley," Georgie said with a bit of a laugh in her voice. "I am truly pleased with all that you have told me, Richard."

"Well, I am sure I would please even the most proficient gossiper in town with all that I have related, but now it is getting late and I must return to my regiment on the morrow so I must depart, but you must remember, Georgie, all of this was told to you in confidence. I promised your brother I would not breathe a word to a soul. So you must be surprised when next he writes or you see him." With that he stood, gave Georgie a quick hug and departed.

Georgiana sat and thought about all that Richard had said. The more she thought the more she was determined to write to her brother for him to expect her tomorrow.

Georgiana quickly found the housekeeper and asked her to send the post express immediately and to have the carriage ready the next morning; she then went in search of Mrs. Annesley to inform her that tomorrow they would be departing for Netherfield.

The following day passed slowly for the inhabitants of Longbourn and Netherfield. Longbourn was buzzing with talk of the ball as little else could be done with such a succession of bad weather. The planning was underway for which dress and gloves to wear and how each lady's hair was to be done to best flatter her features.

Mr. Collins continued his attentions to Elizabeth and she tried to avoid him at all costs, which required her to stay in her room more than she would have otherwise. Jane tried to sooth her, but Elizabeth was restless and anxious for the ball where she was to share not one, not two, but three dances with Mr. Darcy. Elizabeth told no one, not even Jane, but being the loving and caring sister that she was, Jane could tell that Elizabeth held a secret but decided not to press her, since her own mind was well occupied with thoughts of her two dances with Mr. Bingley.

Netherfield was likewise humming with activity. The Bingleys' were busy planning the ball, which left Mr. Darcy much to his own devices.

"Mr. Darcy, I apologize, sir, it seems this letter arrived for you express from London House last evening but just now was given to me for you."

"Thank you, John"

Mr. Darcy accepted the letter, expecting it to be from Colonel Fitzwilliam, but was distressed upon opening it by its contents.

Wednesday Evening, November 20, 1811
London House
DEAREST BROTHER,

> *I am pleased to receive your letters and to know that you are enjoying yourself in Hertfordshire society.*
>
> *Richard came to see me upon his return to his regiment this very night. He told me of Mr. Wickham joining the regiment and being in Meryton. He also told me that I am not to join you as soon as I was due to the aforementioned.*
>
> *I will tell you what I told him. I appreciate your being honest with me but now I must be honest with you. I recognize all that you do to try to protect me, but I am no longer a child. I cannot go around hiding for the remainder of my life hiding, missing out on the remainder of my life because someone tried to hurt me when I was young. I have grown and learned from the experience and would appreciate it if in the future you each sought my opinion before making up your minds on matters concerning me.*

> *Now with that said, I would like to inform you*
> *that you may expect Mrs. Annesley and me at*
> *Netherfield tomorrow afternoon.*
> *Your Loving and Almost Obedient Sister,*
> *GEORGIANA DARCY"*

Darcy did not know what to do other then fret and await his sister, praying for her safe arrival after such weather. By the time the note had reached him it was early afternoon and if he was accurate in her departure time she would reach him within a few hours. If he were to leave for London to accompany her they would pass in route. All that was left for him to do was ensure that a room was prepared for her arrival and then wait for her.

Georgiana was determined to leave London despite the threat of bad weather. She and Mrs. Annesley were not an hour away from the house when the heavens opened and rain poured down. They continued for approximately an hour before the carriage was required to stop at the Inn to seek shelter from the elements. Georgiana soon discovered they were close to halfway to Netherfield and seeing that the rains had let up enough for a rider, though not for a carriage, sent a servant to deliver a message to her brother.

Darcy had been out of sorts ever since receiving Georgiana's post. He was worried about her traveling in such weather. When the express rider arrived with a post announcing her delay he was miserable but relieved that she was safe. He would be off on the morrow to fetch her, rain or no rain.

Friday dawned gray skies that promised rain, though presently there was none. Darcy took the opportunity to pen a quick note to Bingley and set out for Georgiana. He reached her in good time, although not before the rain had started.

Upon discussion with her both decided that they would wait at the inn for the time being to see if the rain would let up; they had plenty of catching up to do in the meantime and so Darcy procured the room next to Georgiana's and accompanied his sister to the sitting room to talk. The whole of Saturday was spent in discussion first with Darcy scolding her for coming, questioning her about the frankness in her letter, and finally they settled in and Darcy told her in his own words all about Miss Bennet and the neighborhood. The more he spoke, the more it became evident to Georgiana that her dear brother's heart belonged to another and she could not be happier. Darcy had told her even more than Richard had and Georgiana was pleased that she had defied them and come, especially since Darcy had relented and said she could attend the Netherfield Ball if she promised to watch and not dance. In the end though, Georgiana had extracted a promise that he would ask her for one dance near the end and when Bingley requested a dance, as he was sure he would, she could accept. Georgiana looked to Tuesday with as much anticipation as any other lady.

Sunday morning again dawned gray and rainy, and Darcy and Georgiana continued their stay at the inn not wanting to brave the weather to return to Netherfield, especially as it was Sunday and one should not travel on the Lord's Day if at all possible. Sunday was spent much like Saturday, with the addition of reading and Georgiana sewing. Monday dawned more gray skies but no additional rain, at least for the moment and early travelers were reporting clear roads towards Meryton the Darcy siblings were determined to make it to Netherfield. They entered the coach and set out for Netherfield as early as they could, hoping to arrive before more rain. Luckily, they made it to Netherfield as the first raindrops were spotted.

Upon their arrival at Netherfield Darcy, Georgiana, and Mrs. Annesley departed to their rooms to bath and warm up, not returning below stairs until supper. Bingley was happy that they had arrived safe and very quickly began to tell Georgiana everything he knew about the coming ball to be held on the morrow. He was pleased that she had made it in time, earnestly offered an invitation, which was just as earnestly accepted, and led her to the drawing room with Darcy trailing behind them.

The entire Netherfield party spent an enjoyable evening talking and Georgiana was even more pleased as Bingley openly and fervently discussed his angel, Jane Bennet. Because of the openness of Mr. Bingley's personality, Georgiana was able to glean even more knowledge of Elizabeth, which pleased her greatly.

Through it all Georgiana saw that Miss Bingley and Mrs. Hurst were not pleased with their brother's attentions to the lady. Caroline and Louise constantly ridiculed the family's relations in trade, the mother's boisterous nature and the younger girls' habit at running after the officers. It was evident that Caroline most especially despised Miss Elizabeth, but Georgiana had already heard so much about the Bennet ladies that she was disposed to like them and could not help but want to meet them very soon and so she looked to tomorrow with great anticipation.

Chapter 16
The Netherfield Ball

Darcy was in eager anticipation as Tuesday arrived and sunshine poured into his room. He anxiously called his man.

"Wilkins!"

"Yes, Mr. Darcy, Sir."

"Have you prepared my attire for the evening?"

"I have, sir."

"Have you performed my other request in addition to obtaining elastic for a ladies slipper?"

"I have, sir."

"Good, good!"

Wilkins could tell the master wanted to ask more, but did not, so Wilkins, contrary to normal practice, offered the information.

"Sir, so you are aware of the manner of delivery I should relate to you that I did not deliver the item directly to the lady sir. I delivered it to Mr. Bennet and let him arrange delivery to the lady. You requested that it be done using discretion, and no one was to know except Mr. Bennet himself if need be. Upon arrival, it became evident that discretion would not occur without Mr. Bennet's assistance. Prior to arriving, I had them wrapped for concealment, so with Mr. Bennet's assistance everything was accomplished as you requested. Will there be anything else, sir?"

"Yes, I shall require a bath prior to the ball this evening and I wish to dress with care and add this to my attire." Darcy held out his hand and gave the delicate object to Wilkins.

"As you wish, sir, is there anything else, sir?"

"Thank you, no, that shall be all."

Wilkins left Mr. Darcy with a smile knowing that this evening was very important to the master that he had served for more than ten years. If all went as Wilkins believed it would, then it would not be long before there were some significant changes to his master's life.

Mr. Bennet headed upstairs and knocked upon Elizabeth's bedroom door. He was still smiling as he remembered the occurrences from twenty minutes prior. A Mr. Wilkins had arrived with a wrapped box under his arm requesting an interview. When he was shown into Mr. Bennet's library he left no time in getting straight to the point.

"Mr. Bennet, I presume?"

"Yes."

"My name is Wilkins and I am in the service of Mr. Darcy of Pemberley. He has requested that I use discretion in making this delivery to a lady of your house prior to this evening ball. Could you be of assistance to me in this?"

"I am afraid if discretion is your charge, you have discarded it in seeking my assistance."

"Sir, I was told that you were the only one I was allowed to let know my business."

"In that case I can be of great assistance to you. If you leave your parcel in my care I assure you it will make it to Miss Elizabeth with haste and secrecy." Mr. Bennet smiled as he saw shock register on Mr. Wilkins face for he had not imparted the lady's identity; however Wilkins handed over the parcel.

"Thank you Mr. Bennet, I shall leave you now and tell Mr. Darcy that I have fulfilled his request with success. One last thing sir, there is no indication of who this is from in the box and Mr. Darcy would prefer it that way until tonight."

"I understand, I will not tell her who it is from, although he must be aware that she may guess it."

"Sir, if I may be so bold to say I can only think that he hopes she will. It would make him very happy to know she thinks well enough of him to receive such a gift."

Mr. Bennet only smiled, speculating what was in the parcel.

"Enter." Elizabeth called as she rose to see who was at her door.

"Oh father, what do you do here, am I needed below stairs?"

"No my dear, I come to bring you this parcel that has just arrived for you by special courier."

"What could this be, I wonder? I have not sent away for anything, especially something to come by special courier."

"No, my dear, this appears to be more of a local delivery."

Elizabeth gently took the box from her father and began to open it with him there. It was obvious to her that he intended to stay to see what it was, and since it appeared as he knew more than she did, she had no objection.

As Elizabeth began to open the wrapping her father imparted more. "Lizzy dear, not only did this arrive by special delivery but the courier had instruction for it to be delivered using discretion, only you and I are to know of this."

"Why father, what could...?" Elizabeth stopped as her breath unexpectedly released at the sight of the most perfect red rose buds delicately laid upon white silk within the black box wrapped in plain brown paper.

Elizabeth had dressed with more than usual care, and prepared in the highest spirits for the evening. She had a pretty good idea of who the rose buds were from and was pleased that he was thinking of her. It was her goal to look her best, specifically for him. She had selected her most flattering and elegant gown for the evening. The deep scarlet colored played off the softness of her skin and the darkness of her hair and eyes. She had not worn it frequently, never for Mr. Darcy to see, but when she did she was sure to turn the heads of many men. To top it off Elizabeth had Martha, her maid weave the rose buds into her hair, making the most exquisite crown.

"Martha, how many rose buds are there?"

"Eleven miss."

"Eleven, do you suppose there is supposed to be twelve and I have misplaced one?"

"I think not miss, only eleven were sent. We have been very careful, one was not misplaced. I am sure it was just an oversight."

"Oh well, I shall just hope no one counts and notices that one is missing."

"No one will notice miss, your beauty will make them forget to count the roses."

"One last think Martha, I need you to break the elastic on my shoe rose for this evening."

"Why miss, that would cause you to be unable to dance."

"Only the first Martha, for I have it on good authority that I will spend the first dance replacing the elastic and be as good as new to resume dancing the second set of the evening."

"Very well, miss, shall I locate a replacement?" Martha asked as she broke the elastic on Elizabeth's slipper.

"No, there shall be another awaiting me at Netherfield."

As Elizabeth descended the stairs everyone was attuned to the sight she made and the younger girls crowed that she would draw too much attention from them tonight.

Mr. Collins thought it was for him and Mrs. Bennet was sure it must be. Jane, Mary, Kitty and Lydia questioned her about where she had found roses in November and after such a rain, since not even one trip to Meryton was made, let alone a trip to London from where such flowers would have had to come. Everyone was disappointed as no information was revealed. Mr. Bennet smiled, as he only was assured of the truth. Although Elizabeth had not asked he knew that she was also aware of whom the roses were from. Mr. Bennet took a moment to help Elizabeth into her cape before they left the foyer for the carriage, leaning close and whispering to her "I think your young man will be very well pleased tonight, Elizabeth."

Elizabeth blushed and smiled prettily at her father.

The Bennet family all loaded into the one family carriage and upon arrival at Netherfield disembarked less than elegantly. Lydia and Kitty both were demanding to disembark first and as a result toppled out of the carriage with little grace or elegance. Mrs. Bennet followed after them trilling about what fun the night would bring and demanding that Jane stand straight and Elizabeth not offend any young men with her pert opinions. The sight was enough to gather the attention of everyone near the Netherfield entrance.

As Elizabeth stepped out of the carriage she eagerly looked around her, drinking in each sight and smell of the evening that was sure to be a highlight of her life. She saw movement from the upper window and upon looking up, she noticed a young lady standing at the window. She did not recognize her, but thought her quite lovely.

Upon entering the ballroom, Elizabeth instantly scanned the room for Mr. Darcy. She was slightly disappointed when she could not locate him around all of the magnificent decorations and people, so she went to the far corner of the room to her dear friend Charlotte Lucas. Elizabeth had just finished complaining about having to dance the first with Mr. Collins when the music began and he came to claim her.

Elizabeth turned to him and as she did feigned tripping, grasping the chair next to her. "Oh dear, I believe I just broke the elastic on my slipper. I apologize, Mr. Collins, I cannot dance in such a state, you must allow me to go and see if I can find a replacement."

"Of course, Cousin Elizabeth, it will not do to have broken elastic for the whole of the evening; you would not be able to enjoy the dance festivities."

"Thank you, Mr. Collins." Elizabeth curtsied and left him to Charlotte in search of Mr. Darcy and her replacement elastic.

Mr. Darcy and his sister had been watching the arrival of the guests from an upper window, specifically waiting for the Bennet carriage to arrive. When the carriage arrived Darcy's eyes instantly sought it out. He stepped slightly behind the curtain wanting to watch for Elizabeth, but not wanting to be seen by anyone in the family. He watched each person depart the carriage and walk into Netherfield, telling Georgiana who each was. Elizabeth was the last to leave the carriage and Darcy most particularly pointed her out to Georgiana. She paused upon exiting the carriage with her father's help and briefly looked up at the window from underneath the hood of her black cape, her eyes settling on Georgiana but not seeing Darcy. Georgiana was at first amazed at the beauty she could perceive from under the hood of her head to toe cape, but then thought that nothing less than the best could be right for her brother. She could tell that Elizabeth had fair yet extremely healthy skin, soft and sturdy features that hinted at a soft delicateness, and that her eyes sparkled like diamonds under bright sunlight. Georgiana instantly wanted to go down and meet the lady, but Darcy asked her to allow him to meet her first and have their dance. Georgiana was welcome to come down and watch at any point; however Darcy would not introduce her until after their dance.

Georgiana was resigned to wait, a small price to pay considering her brother's happiness. She knew her brother had his reasons for wanting to approach Elizabeth on his own and that he would not answer her if she inquired, so she patiently waited for the moment when her brother would bring the lady to her to be introduced.

Darcy left Georgiana upstairs and went to the ballroom, entering just as the music for the first dance was commencing and Elizabeth was standing up from inspecting her slipper. She has done it, her slipper has a broken strap, and she will now search me out for a replacement, Darcy thought. He was pleased and smiled at the thought of her thinking of him and searching for him.

Darcy took a few steps backwards into the hallway, not wanting their meeting to be in the public room.

Elizabeth exited the ballroom into the hallway and instantly she saw him. Mr. Darcy was standing in the far corner slightly to the right of the staircase leaning on the wall with his shoulder. His arms were crossed across his chest with all of his weight resting on one leg as the other crossed at his ankle. He was intently watching the door where she was exiting the ballroom.

As soon as she appeared he straightened himself and dropped his arms to his sides. His eyes widened at the sight before him. Never had he seen so much beauty in one place.

"Miss Bennet," here he paused "You look exquisite this evening. I doubt heaven itself could produce such a sight as you make this evening."

Elizabeth blushed at his compliment and walked towards him with her eyes lowered to the floor. This gave him more of an opportunity to openly admire her.

As she approached, she began to raise her eyes to his. As she did she took in his entire appearance. Here stood the most handsome man she had ever seen. As she reached his chest the pocket of his jacket instantly arrested her and an enormous smile spread across her face as she saw the twelfth of her delicate red rose buds. She was now exceedingly happy that she had worn the flowers in her hair. Anyone who looked at the two could not doubt the attachment forming between them.

Instantly her mind was overcome with the statement he had made to her as they sat in the tree at Oakham Mount. *"It will not be foiled; my intent shall be known by other means if I intend it..."*

Her current happiness was only transcended when she was brave enough to smile shyly as she looked into his eyes and heard him whisper in a deep throaty voice her name, her Christian name, "Elizabeth!"

Darcy indeed had remembered the elastic for Elizabeth's slipper. He produced it from his vest pocket and with very little effort they had her shoe repaired. With the shoe elastic repaired and a few words of readiness exchanged, Darcy offered Elizabeth his arm and the two together walked into the ballroom as the first chords of the second set began. The two approached their place in the set and Darcy squeezed the hand that was currently resting on his arm and then released it. Both of them were well aware of the talk that began the second they appeared at the door together. It seemed that everyone realized the rose buds in her hair matched the one pinned on his lapel and if they had not noticed they soon looked closer, as the news was being spread around the room at a very rapid rate and both realized the second it made it to Mrs. Bennet for she loudly announced "Lizzy, why my Lizzy and Mr. Darcy, they have matching roses, what is this that everyone is speaking of, I must know it. Lizzy, Lizzy, oh, where are you girl?"

Darcy and Elizabeth both ignored Mrs. Bennet as they were each too caught up in the emotion of being together and able to touch as they passed throughout the dance. At the end of the first dance of their set Darcy returned her arm to the crook of his and walked to an unoccupied location of the room.

"Miss Elizabeth, I must thank you for the pleasure of this dance. Would you like some refreshment during this small break in the set?"

"I am fine Mr. Darcy, thank you for offering, however if you require refreshment I would be happy to accompany you to the refreshment table."

"Thank you, but I am fine."

The two stood at the side of the room in silence, yet lost in the emotion of what they were feeling. Elizabeth dared herself to look up at him. When she did her eyes arrested his.

Darcy drew in a breath and began, "Eliz…, Miss Bennet, you look beautiful this evening. That shade of red suits you and I must say that your hair is also adorned in the most beautiful fashion this evening." Darcy blushed as he said this.

"Thank you Mr. Darcy, I must admit that you too are quite handsome this evening. I particularly like this beautiful rose bud that is pinned to your jacket. Wherever did you find such a gorgeous flower specimen?"

"Why Miss Bennet, I am afraid I must ask you the same thing as you have far more than I, surely you must be knowledgeable about the location." This was said with laughter in his eyes. He was teasing her and she loved it.

Elizabeth leaned into Darcy as if to impart a secret and he had to catch his breath as she did so. "Well Mr. Darcy if you must know, I have a secret admirer. I know it shocks you, but I know not where my roses come from as they arrived by special courier just this morning. But I must beg you not to tell anyone as we must use complete discretion."

Elizabeth gave him a slight wink as she said the last and Darcy also leaned in and said, "I am afraid your admirer is no secret, Elizabeth." Once said he quickly stood upright and led her back to the floor for the second dance of their first set together. This dance had a bit more conversation than the last. Elizabeth asked Darcy of his week of rain and he was pleased to be able to tell her of Georgiana's safe arrival. Elizabeth was confused as she thought the Colonel and Darcy would not bring Georgiana into the area with Wickham being here but she also knew Darcy to be very protective of her and realized he must have determined that there was no further threat and sent for her.

Darcy told her of Georgie traveling in the storm and Elizabeth's fear for Georgiana's safety was written plainly across her face. Darcy was pleased to see the genuine concern as he related to her the fact that she had stopped when the storm got too bad and that he rode to fetch her personally to ensure her safety as soon as he had heard. Elizabeth was touched by his love and concern for her and told Darcy how she admired him for it and was glad that he returned safely so that she could be enjoying this dance with him.

Elizabeth decided she would try to get some information about why Darcy changed his mind about bringing Georgiana to the neighborhood and she inquired. "I thought that Miss Darcy was not going to be able to come due to a lack of escort from you and your cousin. I remember you saying as much at Netherfield."

Darcy was well aware of the conversation she referred to and also aware that she was acquainted with Mr. Wickham's character, and wanting to be completely honest with her even if it reflected badly on Georgiana he began. "Miss Bennet, I remember the conversation that you refer to very well. Georgiana was not supposed to come; in fact I can only say that Georgiana came without permission. She defied the Colonel and myself and took it upon herself to come when we told her she was not to."

Elizabeth laughed at the aghast look upon Darcy's face as he continued to tell her what Georgiana did.

"Georgiana came to Netherfield with her companion without my knowledge until she was already on her way and in the middle of a storm. She knows full well why we wanted her kept from the area and cares not, I think she has really matured and grown this past half year. She very particularly wishes to be known to you. Will you allow me, or do I ask too much, to introduce my sister to your acquaintance this evening?"

"I would like that very much, Mr. Darcy."

The dance came to an end and Darcy led Elizabeth off of the dance floor towards Georgiana.

Georgiana had been watching from a small alcove and was amazed at the beauty of the lady dancing with her brother. She saw the beautiful rose buds woven through her hair. The very same rose buds that were even now pinned to her brother's jacket, and she smiled knowing that her brother was truly smitten. As Georgiana watched the dance progress she saw that not only was her brother in love with the lady but it was evident that the lady was also in love with him. Georgiana treasured the thought that she was soon to have a sister and anxiously awaited her introduction, very eager and anxious to please.

Elizabeth knew not what to expect of Georgiana prior to the introduction. She had gleaned much of the lady's talents and accomplishments but nothing of her personality. She had just learned that Georgiana defied her brother's wishes of her remaining in town, so she must be very brave and confident. Elizabeth could not be more wrong and her astonishment upon meeting her shy new acquaintance could not be beaten.

Miss Darcy was tall, on a larger scale than Elizabeth; and, though little more than sixteen, her figure was formed, and her appearance womanly and graceful. She was less handsome than her brother; but there was sense and good humor in her face, and her manners were perfectly unassuming and gentle.

They had not long been introduced before Mr. Darcy offered to fetch them refreshment. It was accepted and he left. The ladies settled in for a nice chat about music and dancing while he was gone. Elizabeth began "I hear you are fond of music and play very well."

"No... that is I am very fond of music, however I do not play very well."

"Your brother thinks you do, as do others of your acquaintance."

"Well I am very fond of it and do try my best. Do you play and sing?"

"A little, but very ill indeed; I would not wish to excite your anticipation."

"My brother says that you sing very well and that there are none that he would prefer to hear."

Elizabeth blushed with embarrassed, but was secretly well pleased and changed the topic to literature. "Do you enjoy reading, Miss Darcy?"

"Yes I do, in fact William and I often read together; that way we can each see a variety of interpretations of the same book, it often expands my knowledge to a greater capacity than if I were to read the book alone."

"William? Is that your brother's name?"

"William is what I call him, though his full name is Fitzwilliam. He frequently calls me Georgie instead of Georgiana."

"I see, well now, back to books. Although I have no brother, only four sisters, my father and I frequently read a book together and discuss it just as you and Mr. Darcy do."

"I should have liked to have a sister; did you enjoy growing up with so many sisters?"

"Oh let me see, you lose a dress because one says it looks better on her, another likes your new bonnet and so they take it from you. Yet another likes the rose buckles that you selected for your shoes and complains until your mother relents and makes you take them off and give them to her. Oh, yes, I should say that I dearly love having four sisters."

Georgiana could not refrain herself from letting out a laugh. It was this sight that Darcy returned to, his lovely Elizabeth and his darling sister enjoying a laugh together. Laughing was not something his sister did frequently, especially in recent months, and so the sight filled him with more joy than he could possibly imagine.

Mr. Bennet saw his chance to speak with Darcy and proceeded to intercept him before he reached the refreshment table. "Mr. Darcy, sir, may I have a word with you?"

This was the first time that the two had met since discovering who Mr. Bennet was. Each was filled with a bit of trepidation. "Certainly, Mr. Bennet, would the ballroom suffice or would you prefer somewhere a little more private?"

"We do not need solitude sir, just a more secure spot than this." With that said Mr. Bennet led Darcy to the edge of the room next to the wall.

"Mr. Darcy, I want to thank you for not being upset at me for not letting you know who I was. You must understand, sir, the night we met you were in no position to talk to the father of Elizabeth and the dreadful sisters and the husband to the horrible mother." All of this was said with a smile and a bit of exaggeration.

"You're welcome sir, I believe you are correct, I would have run out of the library very quickly, never to return, and if I did I would have never known the joy I have received from getting to know you and your daughter."

"Correct, my boy; I am glad that you stayed to see beyond the surface. I think you have learned a great deal the past few weeks. I am very glad that you wish to continue our friendship because I have looked forward to the days that we meet and converse. It is very nice to be able to converse with another intelligent gentleman. I have come to respect you and your views."

Darcy was pleased because he had come to feel the same way. "I am also glad sir, because I too have enjoyed getting to know you and learning different views. I believe you opened my eyes to seeing beyond the surface of people. I fear that by losing my father at a young age I missed out on the larger outlooks of things by not having him there to guide me as a father normally does. I have appreciated our meetings and discussions and hope that they continue for a very long time."

"As do I, what say you to tomorrow? I am sure I will have all sorts of information to relate after tonight." This was said with a sly wink towards Mr. Darcy.

"Yes sir, I think tomorrow afternoon would be perfect. I have promised my sister Georgiana a ride through the neighborhood in the morning but would like to meet you, say two o'clock."

"Yes, two o'clock would be good. So that is your sister, I am surprised you let her join you here under the circumstances."

"Well sir, I had little choice, she came without my consent or knowledge, a story I will save until tomorrow. Would you allow me to stop by with her tomorrow morning to introduce her to the rest of your family?"

"Yes that would be fine. Mr. Darcy, before you go I must ask, do you realize the level of speculation that has accompanied your name and Miss Elizabeth's this evening?"

"I do sir."

"I am sure you are aware, but Elizabeth was most pleased to receive your parcel today and if you are not already aware I will inform you that just tonight has Mrs. Bennet come into the knowledge that you admire Lizzy, you had best be prepared tomorrow. Does this bother you Mr. Darcy?"

"It does not sir."

"I see, well get along with you I know you have more important things to do than sit around talking to me all night."

Darcy smiled at Mr. Bennet and departed to pick up refreshment, once obtained he returned directly to the ladies.

The sight that Darcy returned to was more beautiful than he could ever have imagined lovely Elizabeth and his darling sister enjoying a laugh together.

"What could possibly be so funny ladies?" Darcy said as he walked up and handed them each some lemonade.

"Sisters!" That was the only reply he got as each of them started laughing again.

"Well I see that this must be a joke only for the ladies, as I do not understand what is so funny about sisters."

Georgiana chimed in here "And you never will, dear William, because you have not more than one. I only understand because I am a woman and can imagine."

Darcy smiled coyly at Georgiana and Elizabeth and said "I only have one sister at present, however someday I may have a few more." Elizabeth blushed and Georgiana smiled, never had her brother been so bold; to her it seemed as if that was almost a proposal of marriage. She surely hoped so: she really liked Elizabeth and was sure she could easily love her as a sister. She hoped Elizabeth would not be upset at receiving another sister and no brothers.

Chapter 17
A Satisfying Evening

A couple of dance sets had passed as the three talked and Darcy realized Elizabeth had not been claimed for any of them. "Miss Bennet, I fear we have been monopolizing you this evening and you have been unable to enjoy the ball. Do you have other dance partners to attend to?"

"I do have other dances reserved this evening Mr. Darcy, when those sets arrive I am sure my partner will claim me. Fear not, I am enjoying myself more sitting here and talking with the two of you then ever I could having to stand up with a disagreeable dance partner."

"Very well, Miss Bennet, I know most ladies are fond of dancing and I have been assured on more than one occasion that your dance card fills fast. I just want to make sure that you do not leave the ball feeling less than satisfied with the evening."

"I assure you, Mr. Darcy, I am most satisfied with the ball's proceedings."

The supper set arrived and after whispering something to Georgiana, at which she smiled and nodded, Darcy took Elizabeth's hand and with a bow helped her up and led her to their spot in the dance set. All Elizabeth could think about was how well her hand fit inside of his, how strong his forearm and shoulders were, how straight and tall he stood, how handsome he was and most of all how she loved being the one for whom he reserved his dances. Elizabeth was very aware of all the eyes on them and the talking that was going on. It seemed as if more than one person had noticed that Elizabeth had only danced with Mr. Darcy and that the exquisite crown of rose buds suspiciously matched the one affixed to his lapel. The thought pleased Elizabeth; in fact she was very glad that thus far no one had dared to ask her to dance and hoped no one else would either. It was more than evident to all in attendance that she and Darcy were closer than anyone had ever before presumed. Elizabeth was pleased and she hoped that Darcy was as well. She did not have to wonder long before Darcy broached the subject.

"Miss Bennet, I hope I have not placed you in an awkward situation." Elizabeth looked at him curiously and he knew she did not know what he meant, which pleased him because it proved she was not uncomfortable by it. "What I mean to say is that, it appears as if I have selfishly occupied all of your attention, with my sister that is. No other gentlemen have been able to ask you to dance because of me standing guard around you and I fear that by doing so we have give rise to a bit of gossip about the two of us."

"Indeed we have, Mr. Darcy, though I care not what any of them think about me. If it has made you uncomfortable or if we are placing dear Miss Darcy in a bad situation I will refrain myself from your company and visit with my sister Jane or my friend Charlotte, but if you do not mind, I have very much enjoyed your company and would continue it. If I had been uncomfortable I would not have stayed with you all evening, I would have departed on some pretense or another."

"I would be most pleased to have you stay in my company forever; I care not what anyone here, except you, thinks of me."

"Do you really care what I think of you Mr. Darcy?"

"Yes, more than you will ever know."

Elizabeth blushed; she was unable to respond other than to squeeze his hand tighter as they went down the set. Darcy took this as a positive sign and decided to change the subject.

"Tomorrow morning I am to take Georgiana on a tour of the countryside. I am hoping that upon its completion I may stop by Longbourn and introduce her to the rest of your family. Would that be all right with you?"

"Yes Mr. Darcy, I am sure they would all enjoy meeting Miss Darcy."

"Very good; then, we shall be around between ten and eleven in the morning."

The rest of the dance was spent in a very companionable silence. The only communication between them was unspoken as they squeezed hands and gazed at each other throughout the dance. Towards the end of the two dances Darcy began caressing Elizabeth's palm with his fingertips when they came together again and Elizabeth lightly brushed the skin above Darcy's cravat and jacket as she moved her hand from his shoulder into another pose of the dance. This small act of bravery on Elizabeth's part sent sparks of fire all through Darcy and he could not help but hold her a little closer the next time they came together in the set.

The dance set came to an end and everyone began moving into the Dining Room. Darcy asked Elizabeth if he could escort her to dinner, to which she very quickly said yes. They then went to find Georgiana and once she was located, the three of them entered to find a seat. Darcy saw a small circular table off in the corner, which seated only six instead of twelve as the rest, was set. He led Elizabeth and Georgiana to it. At first Darcy was distressed with how to seat their party, he knew how he wanted to place the seating, with him in the middle and a lady on each side, but that would not allow them an easy flow of conversation. He desperately wanted to sit next to Elizabeth but propriety said he should sit his sister next to Elizabeth with him on the far side. By chance as he paused to consider his options Jane and Bingley approached and Elizabeth introduced Jane to Georgiana. In the end, the ladies all chose to sit together with Georgiana between the two of them. This arrangement was perfect for it allowed Darcy to sit by Elizabeth and Bingley to sit by Jane. Darcy had never been so happy for the arrival of his friend in his life.

Supper passed remarkably well, much of the Bennet family theatrics were missed by the well-situated table. There had been one seat that remained empty at the table during dinner, and towards the end Mr. Collins claimed it exclaiming "I have found out by a singular accident, that there are now in the room two near relations of my patroness. I happened to overhear the lady of this house talking of them as being her brother's dearest friends. My methods of deduction have led me here to introduce myself to you. How wonderfully these sorts of things occur. Who would have thought of my meeting with, perhaps, a nephew and niece of Lady

Catherine de Bourgh in this assembly? I am most thankful that the discovery is made in time for me to pay my respects to you, which I am now going to do. I trust you will excuse my not having done it before when we met on our walk in Meryton. My total ignorance of the connection must plead my apology."

Without allowing Mr. Darcy or his sister to respond Mr. Collins continued.

"I am pleased to report to you that her Ladyship and her daughter were in the best of health Saturday se'nnight before and I shall be equally pleased to relay to her ladyship upon my return the report of your health and happiness."

Mr. Darcy gave his thanks and Mr. Collins then continued on about his excellent parsonage, the improvements her ladyship had suggested, and that he had been invited twice to tea. Elizabeth was becoming visibly distressed and Darcy felt he needed to calm her. Despite all rules of society he reached for her hand under the table and grasped it trying to give her support. It was then that Mr. Collins began in a vein that Darcy did not like.

"How honored you must be to be engaged to such a lovely lady as Miss Anne, Mr. Darcy, I know no one with her beauty and talents as her own mother says."

Darcy could feel Elizabeth stiffen and her hand go limp in his. All he could do was squeeze it a few times trying to reassure her.

Mr. Collins continued "What a glorious day your wedding shall be. The heavens will burst forth with trumpets heralding the day as a great one."

Georgiana sat pale and stunned, fearful Elizabeth would not know that her own cousin was lying to her. Georgiana knew the truth and wanted to stop Mr. Collins, but knew not how.

As Mr. Collins continued and Elizabeth became more and more distressed she forcefully withdrew her hand from Mr. Darcy's despite him trying to retain her grip under the table and looked at her lap almost in tears. Darcy knew not what to do but he had to stop the man and fast. He had to let Elizabeth know the truth.

"Mr. Collins…, Mr. Collins…" The man did not stop and then he said something that arrested Darcy's ears.

"And I do hope that you shall be as happy as my dear Elizabeth and I shall be." Elizabeth's head snapped up in shock, her face that had just a minute before been pale went red with fury as he continued. "I took the liberty of speaking with her mother this afternoon and have been assured the family's support in our suit. I think we shall be the second happiest of couples, only second to you and Miss de Bourgh."

With that Elizabeth could take no more she quickly got up, knocking her chair over and ran from the room, tears bursting out as she passed the door. Darcy did not take long to follow her. Mr. Bennet had heard it all, as his table was nearby and Mr. Collins did not speak in hushed tones and was becoming furious at his wife and nephew. He also went to follow Elizabeth and Mr. Darcy.

Elizabeth made it into the Netherfield gardens before Darcy could catch her. "It is a lie, it is all a lie, and I shall never marry that toad." Elizabeth sobbed as she collapsed on a bench in tears. "Please say he lied about you too," she sobbed as Darcy laid his hand on her shoulder. She did not acknowledge his touch, instead she continued on. "Please say you are not engaged to your cousin Anne. I knew I should never have allowed my heart to fall in love with you. What am I ever to do now? My father always says that a woman likes to be crossed in love, but I assure you we do not. Where did he ever come up with such a ridiculous notion?"

Darcy sat down next to Elizabeth and raised her chin with his hand to look at him. He was happy to know that she loved him although it was not really her intention to tell him. He was smiling as he began to say. "Listen carefully, Miss Elizabeth Bennet, I am not now nor have I ever been engaged to another, neither am I honor bound to anyone because of the dictates of society. You know as well as I do that your cousin is an oaf." Elizabeth tried to look down so he could not see all of the tears on her face as he held it in his hand, but he did not let go and allow her to, so she closed her eyes against him instead. He beseeched her to open her eyes and look at him. "Please look at me and listen though; Lady Catherine de Bourgh, my aunt, has said from the day of my parent's death that I am to marry my cousin Anne. As she says 'It was your mother's dearest wish as well as mine that you two should marry, from your birth you have each been planned for one another, a union of titles and riches.' That is what she wants, but that is not what I want. Do you understand? I want a woman who can be carefree and lively climbing trees and singing to the wind, I want a woman whose mind will challenge me and not agree just because she is supposed to agree with her husband. I want someone who I can go on long walks with, read with, dance with and most of all love. My cousin Anne is not that lady, but I believe you are. What I am saying, my dearest, loveliest Elizabeth is that if you will have me as your husband I would love to make you my wife, forever by my side at Pemberley."

Elizabeth had been locked in his gaze since he had asked her to look at him, unable to move her eyes from his. All she could see was love and support. As he completed his proposal she melted into his arms saying "Oh yes, Fitzwilliam, I want to marry you more than anything else in this world. I was so scared when my cousin said you were to marry another because I thought that meant I could never have you. Then I was mad that you had paid attention to me when you were thus attached. It was only when he said I was to marry him that I was scared that my family would make me marry him. I know my father respects you and he would never make me marry someone I do not want to, so I know my tears are all for nothing, but I cannot help it, they come uninvited."

Darcy held Elizabeth close and kissed the top of her head. He then turned her face to look at him again and very gently laid the softest, most delightful kiss upon her lips. He had wanted to kiss those lips since he had first seen them and was completely lost in her. His kiss gradually became stronger and he held her tighter.

Elizabeth was surprised by the kiss. She had often wondered over the years what it would be like to kiss a man, especially the past few days as she considered what it would be like to kiss him and now that it was happening it was better than she could have imagined. It felt as if her lips were on fire, then the kiss deepened and his arms held her tight; she had never felt anything like it in all of her life. Elizabeth had just lost herself to headiness when she felt yet another sensation. No longer was Mr. Darcy just kissing her lips but he was pressing them with his. Elizabeth could not resist; instinct was leading her to slightly part her lips and be taught what it was to truly kiss a man. It did not take long before she was returning his kiss with equal passion, copying his every action. The kiss lasted a few minutes at least, both participants completely lost to anything beyond their own pleasures.

"Miss Elizabeth Bennet, Mr. Darcy, what do you think you are doing?" came the voice of a stern Mr. Bennet as a hand was placed on each of them and pulled them apart. Elizabeth could do nothing but lick her lips and look at her hands as she laid them in her lap mortified at being caught out.

The ever-blunt and slightly annoyed Mr. Darcy replied "Kissing!"

Mr. Bennet could not help but laugh, but he quickly checked himself. "Mr. Darcy I would appreciate it if you would accompany me on a stroll in the garden. Elizabeth you will wait here, do you understand me?"

Elizabeth nodded and as her father began to walk away anxiously said "Father…, please know that Mr. Darcy is a gentleman and was not trying to take advantage of me. He is honorable and the fault is mine, he was trying to comfort me after I had been upset."

Darcy began to defend Elizabeth and take part of the blame, which only amused Mr. Bennet further.

"Well my dear, I thank you for your contribution, however as your father I shall know how to act and we will not stand here and quarrel about who is to blame. As I said, wait here for me, I shall return after I have a private word with Mr. Darcy about his methods of comforting and the ramifications of such methods."

Mr. Bennet sternly led Mr. Darcy to the furthest point of the garden and asked him to sit. Darcy sat down and tried to begin to apologize for his action but Mr. Bennet would not have any of it.

"Mr. Darcy, please hear me out without a word and then I will hear you." Mr. Darcy nodded.

"First of all, I was privy to the conversation that took place in the Dining Room. I was sitting not five feet away to the left and know that each of you has full right to be mad and offended by Mr. Collins. I also followed both of you out to the garden and heard everything from the very beginning. Yes, I see recognition forming on your face; yes, I was here when each of you made your declarations. I was behind the shrubbery out of sight. I was also here as your kiss began and as it progressed. What have you to say for yourself?"

"Why did you not stop us sooner?" Darcy blurted it out before he even thought about what he was saying.

Mr. Bennet laughed and just shook his head "Well, my boy, that is for me to know and you to find out…later. Maybe tomorrow when we meet I shall enlighten you. I think we shall have a lot to discuss tomorrow, perhaps engagement ground rules will be a topic."

"Yes sir, perhaps you are correct. Now may be as good of a time as ever for me to ask your permission to marry Miss Elizabeth."

"Ask my permission Mr. Darcy, I think now may be a little late for that, you will now be walking down the aisle to her at the end of my hunting rifle." Mr. Bennet and Mr. Darcy laughed.

"That will not be necessary, sir; I would walk down the aisle to marry her even if you had that rifle aimed at my front trying to keep me from her."

"Yes, I believe you would. Now before we go over to relieve Elizabeth of her stress, let me tell you that I could not be more pleased to invite you into our family and call you, son, remember that here in a moment when I reprimand you both." With that Mr. Bennet clasped his hand and then he and Darcy began walking back to Elizabeth.

"Mr. Darcy, as Elizabeth is still my unwed daughter and I am still her protective father, please put up at least a little of a façade that I am in charge. I do not wish to lose credit in her mind."

"Yes sir."

With that said, the two arrived back where Elizabeth was waiting. They found her standing and pacing the ground in front of the bench with quick strides biting one of her fingernails. Darcy thought she had never been more beautiful and Mr. Bennet laughed.

Elizabeth heard them and stopped. She turned to look at them, directly facing her father.

"Elizabeth my dear, it is incumbent on me to let you know that whether you agree or not, you will be marrying Mr. Darcy." Elizabeth started to talk when her father cut her off. "You have each placed yourself in a precarious situation that demands nothing less, what if it had been someone other than me to detect the two of you? Your reputations would be utterly destroyed. Mr. Darcy informed me that he has already asked for your hand and been accepted; well I am glad of it because if that is true then you need not be distraught over the engagement. In addition, I must admonish you that this is never to be mentioned among anyone until after you are married. I will not have you destroying the reputations of the family with your weakness to Mr. Darcy."

Elizabeth could do nothing but smile and say "Thank you, father" as she ran to him and kissed him on the cheek. She knew her father well enough to know that his speech was nothing more than a show and most likely for the benefit of Mr. Darcy.

"Very well child, now off with you. I will not have you out here missing the ball and raising more talk than the two of you already have. I will escort you inside and Mr. Darcy if you would please follow in a minute or two."

Darcy nodded his agreement and stood as Mr. Bennet led Elizabeth by the elbow back into the ballroom. As they turned the corner Elizabeth looked back at him lovingly and he blew her a kiss. He could never be happier than he was at that moment.

Mr. Bennet led Elizabeth to Jane and left her with a kiss on the forehead. He whispered to her, "Lizzy, my dear, I believe you will be a very happy woman." He then turned and walked away. Jane instantly inquired about Lizzy's health and with a small smile and a promise to tell all tonight before they went to bed the subject was dropped.

Elizabeth was happy that Georgiana was still with Jane because it would be easy for Mr. Darcy to rejoin them without causing a scene, and come he did. Elizabeth had been watching the door for his arrival and when he appeared a smile diffused so rapidly across her face that anyone who observed her would know the truth instantly. Luckily no one had observed her but Georgiana and Mr. Bennet, who was intent on watching her for the rest of the night. Georgiana leaned in close to Elizabeth and began talking before her brother had time to reach them.

"William told me at supper that we are to visit your family after our ride through the countryside tomorrow. I shall be so happy to meet all of them, especially if they are all like you and your sister Jane."

Darcy heard Georgiana's statement as he arrived. Elizabeth glanced at him from the corner of her eye as she responded. "I hope you are not disappointed then, I fear Jane and I are quite different from the rest of our family, however tomorrow you shall judge for yourself."

Darcy joined the conversation as he sat down, "Dearest Georgiana, would you be too upset if we invited a third on our little outing tomorrow. I fear since I do not know the area as well as the local populace we may get lost. What say you to having Miss Bennet join us? That is if you would like." The last was said as he turned to smile at Elizabeth.

"Why yes, I would be honored to join you, however I must first ask my father." Darcy knew why Elizabeth must seek permission and Georgiana thought nothing more of it than the fact that Elizabeth was required to clear all of her outings with her parents. "If you will excuse me I will go to him now and seek his consent."

"I will attend you, Miss Bennet." Darcy said as the two walked away, again leaving Georgiana with Jane and Mr. Bingley.

Mr. Bennet saw them coming over to him and smiled inwardly what could this be all about. He was almost sure they would avoid him for the rest of the evening.

"Father, I have a request to make of you. Mr. and Miss Darcy have invited me to help guide them on a tour of the area tomorrow. May I be allowed to go?"

Mr. Bennet smiled in spite of himself. "Guide them, eh. Is that true Mr. Darcy? You require a guide to take your sister on a drive tomorrow and Elizabeth here just happens to be available." Elizabeth was mortified but Darcy was not intimidated.

"Your speculations are correct, sir, I do not require a guide to take my sister on a tour of the neighborhood, however both Georgiana and I would be pleased to have Miss Bennet accompany us for no other purpose than the one you are intimating. Rest assured sir, that Georgiana will accompany us and as her guardian, I, like you, am responsible for her protection. You need not fear that anything inappropriate will occur on our outing. I promise to be the perfect gentleman. If you wish sir, you may even send along another of Miss Bennet's sisters as a chaperone."

The discussion was taking place in hushed tones and beginning to draw attention. Mr. Bennet wished to complete it quickly. "Fear not, Mr. Darcy,

Elizabeth may go if she wishes and one of her sisters only need accompany her if she chooses. I believe our previous discussion this evening made my point to you."

"Thank you sir." was all that was said and Mr. Darcy and Elizabeth returned to Georgiana.

"Miss Darcy, I am pleased to say that my father has agreed that I may go on the outing with you and Mr. Darcy."

Georgiana was so happy she began to lightly bounce up and down with joy as she grabbed Elizabeth's hands and smiled from ear to ear. Darcy was amazed at the transformation in his young sister, back to her playful self that he had not seen in the past few years, since their father's death required both siblings to grow up faster than they would have otherwise. Elizabeth would indeed be a perfect addition to the Darcy family.

The remainder of the evening passed pleasantly enough. Elizabeth was only asked to dance by one other person, Mr. Bingley. It was at this time that Darcy and Georgiana had their dance. Georgie was so happy at the progression of the evening she could not help but say so to her brother "William, I am pleased that I arrived in the neighborhood and you allowed me to come tonight. I cannot imagine an evening more wonderful than tonight has been. I very much like Miss Bennet and am happy that we have already become good friends."

Darcy was pleased with what she said and told her so. "Georgie my dear, although I do not approve of you disobeying Richard and myself, I am also glad that you were able to come and meet Miss Bennet. Do you truly like her?"

"Yes, brother, I do."

"Could you like her as more than just a friend and acquaintance?"

"Yes, brother, in fact I already think of her as my sister. I hope that pleases you?"

"Yes my dear it does, if you will allow me a few minutes tonight I should like to talk to you privately after all the guests have departed and the rest of our party has retired. I know that will require you to stay awake longer; however I ask it of you nonetheless. Please will you stay up to talk with me?"

"I am honored, brother; it will not be a trial for me to stay awake to talk to you as I am most anxious for you to tell me your and Miss Bennet's news formally."

"Is it that obvious?"

"It is to those who know you as I do, but since no one else here knows you like that I will say your secret is safe with me. As for Miss Bennet, if anyone paid any attention to anyone other than themselves it is written all over her face. I knew the instant you walked in the door from the gardens just by looking at her face upon seeing you, and I am happy to say nothing could bring me more joy."

Their dance was coming to an end. Darcy thanked his sister with a kiss on the cheek and said "Even though you have guessed my motive I still wish to talk to you tonight and I know you will not object, so I end this dance saying we shall talk more at length tonight."

Bingley and Darcy brought Elizabeth and Georgie back together after the dance. Darcy excused himself, saying he had to attend to something before the conclusion of the dance and left Elizabeth and Georgiana to talk.

By the time he returned they were no longer Miss Bennet and Miss Darcy or even Elizabeth and Georgiana. They had endeared themselves to each another as only sisters could; now addressing one another as Lizzy and Georgie.

The only thing Darcy had to attend to was the setting straight of Mr. Collins. Darcy finally found him at the refreshment table with a large plate of cakes, tarts, and fruit in one hand and a glass of wine in the other. "Mr. Collins, sir, may I have the honor of your company in the library sir?"

"Certainly, I could not deny the nephew of my esteemed patroness anything."

Mr. Collins followed Mr. Darcy to the library spouting praises and flattery the entire way as he juggled his plate and drink, trying not to spill but leaving a trail behind him. When they reached the library they stepped inside the door and Mr. Darcy closed it. He did not offer a seat but instantly began his discourse. "Mr. Collins, you can be at no loss to know why I have asked you here."

"Indeed sir, you must want me to convey a message to your honored aunt and cousin." With that Darcy cut him off.

"No, sir that is not why I asked you here; I asked you here to make it known to you that I am seriously displeased with the manner you sought to recommend yourself at supper tonight. It is not proper to discuss things in which you know nothing about. I am not nor will I ever be engaged to my Cousin Anne de Bourgh. She could never make me a proper wife and I have no intention of marrying her."

Mr. Collins tried to interrupt but Darcy would not let him. "It was most presumptuous of you to make such a declaration in company without my consent. It was also presumptuous of you to declare yourself to Miss Bennet in company even if you had already spoken to her mother. What woman would accept such a man? Certainly no lady that I know, including Miss Bennet, I am afraid I must tell you that you have spoiled all chances of her favor and should move to another lady. In addition, you should be more particular in your selection of a wife if you do not want to displease Lady Catherine. I know for a fact that Miss Bennet's lively and outspoken disposition would not be looked upon in a parson's wife with a friendly eye. I encourage you to think on these things before declaring yourself. Good day Mr. Collins." With his piece said Mr. Darcy turned and quitted the room smiling.

Mr. Darcy returned to Elizabeth and Georgiana just in time to claim her for the final dance. As Mr. Darcy took her hand and placed it on his arm he leaned into her and said, "Dearest Elizabeth, if I am not mistaken you no longer need to fear the attentions of Mr. Collins."

Elizabeth looked up at him questioningly but he refused to say another word about it. The final dance of the evening was spent much as the last one that they shared with caressing and grasped hands, the tingle of touching each other's skin and closer dancing than deemed entirely appropriate.

When the dance ended each was disappointed, however tomorrow was another day, the first full day of their engagement and they were already guaranteed to spend some of it together.

Chapter 18
Poor Ending to a Most Perfect Evening

The Bennets' were among the last to depart, which was not complained about by the majority of those in attendance. Miss Bingley and Mrs. Hurst were the only exception; Miss Bingley especially. Darcy had not asked her to dance yet he had danced three dances, and all of them principal dances with that upstart Miss Eliza Bennet. Not to mention that she had somehow trapped him into wearing that rose and occupied all of Georgiana's attention, thus making it impossible for her to even come near them. She was made furious by the gossip she had been hearing, but was too tired to think more of it. She would consider it tomorrow. She cared not what the country nobodies thought of her, and so even though they had not all left for the evening she departed to her room for the night, followed closely by the Hursts'. This allowed Bingley and Darcy to escort the entire family to their carriage, and while no one was looking Darcy bestowed another kiss on Elizabeth. That is while Darcy thought no one was looking. Mr. Bennet had seen the kiss, though, and would talk with Mr. Darcy about it tomorrow.

The Bennet family departed and Bingley went to his room; Darcy then escorted Georgiana to the library.

Once they were situated comfortable Darcy began, "Well, dearest, how was your evening?"

"William, brother, we both know that we did not come here to discuss my enjoyment of the evening. I will flatter you and tell you I enjoyed it immensely and in return ask you how you enjoyed it."

Darcy laughed, "Georgie, when did you grow up? You are correct; I did not come here to inquire about your evening and you well know what I asked you in here for. I have asked Miss Elizabeth to become my wife and she has accepted. We are to marry and you are to have a sister. I hope you are pleased?" The last was asked out of politeness but Darcy knew his answer, the look on Georgiana's face said it all.

"Oh, William, I am so happy for you." Georgiana jumped up and crossed to his seat and reached over to give him a sisterly embrace. "You must tell me all. Did it happen when you both left supper? How did you ask her? Did you stand or kneel? What did she say? Did she cry or laugh? Have you asked her father? When shall it be announced? When is the wedding going to be?"

Darcy stopped Georgiana and told her all even about the kiss, the scolding from Mr. Bennet and the threat of a shotgun wedding. Georgiana was humiliated for her brother but laughed at the entire story as he related it to her. He then revealed to her his discussion with Mr. Collins and with that tale complete sent her to bed with a wish for sweet dreams.

"Brother, I am so proud of you, you have not only made yourself the happiest of men but by doing so have made me the happiest of sisters. I think tomorrow shall be spent quite pleasantly for our new little family." Georgiana blew him a kiss and skipped out of the room.

Darcy remained awhile longer sitting in his chair reliving every touch, caress and most of all kiss that he had shared with Elizabeth. It was evident to him that Elizabeth loved him as much as he did her. So far she had been his equal in passion and he hoped that would continue. He went up to his room with the sweetest thoughts on his mind. He hoped that they would be married soon and that his days of retiring alone were shortly numbered. Darcy planned to sleep well that night as he let loose his dreams of Elizabeth and the life that they would share together. Little did he know what other events were unfolding that would make the night end anything but perfectly.

The carriage ride home from Netherfield began as a noisy affair. Lydia and Kitty were trying to over talk themselves and relate to the rest of the group about each of their dance partners. No one paid them much mind except Mrs. Bennet, until Lydia mentioned Mr. Wickham. "It seems like he was purposefully excluded from tonight's ball at the request of Mr. Darcy. It seems that man was abominably cruel to him, denying him a living that had been granted in his father's will." Lizzy scolded Lydia with a look and a stern command but she went on regardless. "It seems that based on the lies that Mr. Darcy and that rotten cousin of his have been telling, the man can barely do anything without being watched. Most of the officers have been aiding him to get out into the neighborhood without guard, but no matter how he tried he would not be admitted to the ball. I also heard he knows Miss Darcy very well and knows she is here at Netherfield. It is his dearest wish to see her. He and some of the other officers are planning to run into her as soon as he can. It sounds like they know some of the Netherfield servants and will be having some help from the inside. Wouldn't that be such a sight! I am sure her brother would be furious." Lydia laughed and laughed at the thought until she saw the look on her father's face as the moonlight passed over it, bringing her to silence instantly.

Mr. Bennet's voice began in nothing more than a strained stern whisper "Lydia, you are from this day forward confined to Longbourn until I have changed my mind. You are to have no visitors and attend no teas, assemblies, or balls." As Lydia began to protest his voice became louder and gruffer, "Once I relent and let you back into society it will be under my guarded hand. You will be reintroduced into society at a later date. I can see that you are not mature enough to be out yet and therefore you are again considered a child." Lydia continued to protest; not taking the hint that it was in her best interest to be silent. That was it, Mr. Bennet snapped as he growled out in a harsh voice, "In addition, I will never hear you speak another unkind word about Mr. Darcy or his sister unless you have confirmed the lies told to you by the officers with written documentation in hand to prove it to me. You have disobeyed me and from this day forward you will know that when I have told you to stay away from someone and anyone associated with them that you will obey or you will be severely punished. Do I make myself clear?"

Lydia was in tears and unable to control her sobbing. Kitty was hiding as best she could with her hands clasped and her head down.

Mr. Bennet was not finished however, "Kitty, I know that you follow wherever Lydia leads. You had best learn to follow in the footsteps of Jane and Elizabeth or you will also suffer the consequences. This is to be your last warning: next time you will suffer the same fate as Lydia, am I understood?"

"Yes, Papa." Was all Kitty could say.

Elizabeth was pleased with her father and proud of him for the manner that he defended Mr. Darcy, yet she was distressed by the other news. Somehow she must speak to Mr. Darcy about his sister's safety, and soon. The remainder of the carriage ride home was silent and when they reached Longbourn all of the ladies headed for their rooms except Lizzy, who waited in the vestibule for her father to enter after talking with Mr. Hill, and then followed him into the library.

"Father, what are we to do? Please you must help me get a message to Mr. Darcy this very evening. What if Miss Darcy is in danger?"

"You are correct my dear, in fact I have already ordered my horse prepared and Mr. Hill is already on his way to Netherfield to alert Mr. Darcy of my returning instantly. I must prepare you my dear that Mr. Darcy and his sister will most likely be leaving the area in the morning."

"I know, father, and I want it, for if they are away from here they will be safe. Father, you must know that as she is the sister of Mr. Darcy I already love her as one of my own sisters."

"I know, my dear, now off to bed with you. I will go and talk to Mr. Darcy."

"Please, father, when you return come directly and tell me. I must know the outcome; you know I will not be able to sleep."

"Very well, my dear, off with you or you will not have finished telling Jane the tale of your engagement by the time that I return."

Elizabeth had just returned to her room when Jane knocked lightly on Lizzy's door. "Lizzy, may I come in?"

"Yes, Jane, please do."

Jane entered the room and began turning down the bed for Lizzy.

"Jane, dearest, I am bursting with both happiness and anxiety, Mr. Darcy loves me and we are to be married. He asked me in the garden this evening and has already asked father's permission. I am so happy."

Jane beamed and hugged her sister. "Oh Lizzy you must tell me all, but what of this anxiety? Surely it cannot be from your engagement."

"No, sweet Jane, it is from Lydia's disclosure. I fear Miss Darcy is not safe. Father is returning to Netherfield to speak with Mr. Darcy even now."

Lizzy told Jane everything, of the proposal, being caught kissing by father, their dancing together, and their slight caresses. Jane was mortified for Lizzy to be caught in such a situation but when Elizabeth said she would gladly endure anything if Fitzwilliam, as he now was to her, would just kiss her that way again. Jane blushed and thought how amazing it must be to be kissed by the one you love. After Lizzy was done telling Jane all, it was Jane's turn to tell Lizzy her news. Though she was not engaged Mr. Bingley had asked to call on her tomorrow. "He was very particular in that he wanted to be able to have a moment alone with me. I consented and tomorrow, if I am not mistaken, I shall have some news of my own."

"Oh, Jane, this is so wonderful we shall not only be best friends and sisters, but we shall be making best friends brothers."

They spent another hour discussing their dreams for the future and then very reluctantly Jane declared she must have some sleep and Elizabeth agreed that she must look her best for tomorrow. They parted with the best of intentions and the best of dreams that night, yet Lizzy could not sleep, not yet, for her father had not returned.

Mr. Bennet arrived at the steps of Netherfield but a few minutes after Georgiana retired to bed. Mr. Darcy was still sitting up remembering the pleasant events of the evening when a servant arrived to tell him that a Mr. Hill had arrived with a message from Mr. Bennet. Mr. Darcy allowed him to be brought in and heard that Mr. Bennet was to be returning to Netherfield this very night to speak on a most urgent matter. Mr. Darcy said he would remain prepared to see the man when he arrived and allowed Mr. Hill to return to Longbourn. It was not long before a tired Mr. Bennet arrived.

"Mr. Darcy sir, I apologize at the hour and that we have barely left your doorstep when I return uninvited, but I hope that you can spare me a minute, sir, for I have some distressing news."

"Surely, Mr. Bennet, please join me in the library."

Mr. Bennet followed Mr. Darcy to the library.

Mr. Darcy performed the proper functions of host and offered a seat and a drink, but Mr. Bennet declined and instead began directly.

"Mr. Darcy on our way home this evening it was brought to my attention by my silly youngest daughter, Lydia, that Mr. Wickham is aware of Miss Darcy's presence in the neighborhood."

"I am sure he is, sir, for we have not tried to keep it a secret."

"Very well, would it concern you to know that he and a few other officers are planning on trying to see her while she is here?"

"It does, however knowing now what they plan I will be careful to always accompany her and talk to her to ensure Mrs. Annesley is always around as well."

"I do not mean to distress you, sir, however it has also come to my attention from same said daughter that there is at least one servant, perhaps more here at Netherfield that have agreed to assist them in their plans."

"Are you saying Mr. Bennet that they are not just trying to run into her by chance, but are plotting and strategizing a method to do so, perhaps going as far as abduction?"

"It appears as if you are correct, Mr. Darcy. I came here this evening to advise you to leave the county. I have talked with Elizabeth, and although she is very distressed for you and your sister and may I add, a little upset for herself as well, she agrees with me that you should leave as soon as you can."

"What about Miss Elizabeth?"

"What do you mean, sir, as I said she is upset, but she will be more at ease knowing you and Miss Darcy are safe?"

"You miss my meaning, sir. As you are well aware my attention to her tonight has caused gossip to arise. Knowing, Mr. Wickham, as I do I now fear for her safety as well, I will not leave her here without my protection. My sister and I will stay and you and I together can protect the both of them."

Mr. Bennet smiled, knowing that Mr. Darcy would do anything to protect Elizabeth. "I feel she is safe, sir, no one knows of your engagement and we shall keep it secret for the time being until it is safe to make it publicly known."

"Mr. Bennet, I will respect your wishes, sir, but I had hoped for it to be announced soon so that I could obtain a special license and we could be married soon, perhaps by Christmas."

"Christmas, why, Mr. Darcy, that is scarcely a month away."

Darcy smiled "I know, sir, but I need to return to Pemberley and now that I am determined to marry her I do not want to be away for any length of time. A trip to Pemberley would most assuredly take me a few weeks to a month; I am determined not to return there until I can do so with Elizabeth at my side as my wife."

Mr. Bennet was pleased at his sentiments, yet concerned at the timeline considering the present situation.

"Mr. Bennet, if we announce the engagement in the morning and set the date a few days before Christmas it would be natural that Miss Bennet should go to London to purchase her trousseau. Being the bridegroom I naturally could not leave her side and therefore must return as well, taking my unmarried and dependent sister with me. This would be the best method of departing without causing Mr. Wickham to wonder, yet still foiling any plans of his."

Mr. Bennet worried at the short notice to the Gardiners, but knew they would understand when they read his letter. He could not refuse Mr. Darcy's plan and it was determined that Mr. and Miss Darcy would attend breakfast with a carriage ready for London and the announcement would be made.

Mr. Bennet departed for home and Mr. Darcy informed Wilkins and his sister's maid to have the trunks ready early, for they were to depart for London on the morrow. Darcy then wrote a quick letter to the Colonel and ordered it sent express first thing tomorrow morning and settled in for a short night's rest.

Mr. Bennet returned home and went directly to Mrs. Hill. "Hill, please instruct Martha to wake Miss Elizabeth early and have her trunks ready for London after breakfast."

Mrs. Hill said she would, and Mr. Bennet climbed the stairs to Lizzy's room.

"Lizzy, dear, are you awake?"

"Yes, father, please come in."

Mr. Bennet entered, shut the door and sat on the edge of Lizzy's bed.

"It appears as if Mr. Darcy and his sister will be leaving the neighborhood after breakfast in the morning."

Lizzy knew it would be happening, but having her father confirm it made tears well up in her eyes and she could not stop herself from sniffling.

"Yes, father, I assumed it would be so."

"Do not cry my dear, at least not for the loss of Mr. Darcy's company, for you shall not lose it."

"What do you mean, father?"

"I mean do not cry for the loss of Mr. Darcy, cry for the loss of me, for you shall also be heading to London. I will write to my brother Gardiner, for you shall be going to Gracechurch Street."

Elizabeth could not keep the smile from her face as she inquired, "Why father, why must I leave as well?"

"Lizzy, I see you are pleased to be going and I do not mean to distress you, however Mr. Darcy made a good point. He showed you much attention this evening and much speculation has been arisen in the neighborhood. From what I know of this Mr. Wickham and his history with Mr. Darcy, his motive may be revenge and knowing Darcy loves you would now make you a target as well."

Mr. Bennet could see the distress beginning on Elizabeth's face. "Fear not, my dear Mr. Darcy and I will not let any harm come to you. He and his sister are to come to breakfast in the morning and then you are all to depart for London straightaway."

"After breakfast, father, so soon, how are we to explain this?"

"Wait Lizzy, hear me out. Mr. Darcy has expressed a wish for the two of you to marry soon. He needs to return to Pemberley as he has been away for a long while. He wants you to return with him. He plans to return by Christmas, so you are to go to London and with the assistance of your Aunt Gardiner, purchase your trousseau while your mother remains here to plan your wedding."

"Before Christmas, but, father, that is less than a month away."

"Yes it is, does that suit you, or should I speak with Mr. Darcy about it being too soon.

"No, it pleases me, father."

"Very well, my dear, now get some sleep as Mrs. Hill and Martha are to wake you early in order to pack your trunks. We will tell everyone at breakfast."

Chapter 19
Preparations for London

Elizabeth did not sleep well: she was excited to be engaged, but distressed that someone would want to harm Mr. Darcy, Georgiana or possibly even herself.

Mr. Darcy put everything into motion for an early departure as soon as Mr. Bennet left to return to Longbourn. He spent the rest of the night trying to sleep but not succeeding. His first wish and desire had just been granted this very evening and now, not two hours later, his greatest nightmare began to take form. Mr. Wickham, his worst enemy, inserting himself to cause problems in his life once again. How could anyone sleep with such conflicting emotions?

Dawn arrived and Mr. Darcy gave up trying to rest and finished preparations for departure. It was likely everyone would sleep in after a long night at the ball, but Darcy hoped that Bingley would awake at a reasonable time, as he wanted to speak with him. Darcy sent him a note, which upon awaking he would receive. Darcy then turned to the window to assess the weather. He could see the trunks being loaded onto the carriage and was pleased at the efficiency of his own and the Netherfield staff. It appeared as if Bingley had made a good choice in leasing Netherfield.

After all was accomplished, Darcy decided it was time to awaken Georgiana. Darcy knocked on her door and when no one answered he stepped in quietly. He silently approached Georgiana's bed and smiled as he looked at her sleeping peacefully. She truly had grown into a beautiful woman and he was pleased at how she had turned out. He knew what he was to tell her would distress her, but he hoped that she would bear it well and not be too upset.

"Georgiana, dearest."

"Hmmmm.... " Georgiana rolled over to her other side.

"Georgie dear, please wake up, I need to speak with you."

"William, what time is it." Georgiana whispered as she began to open her eyes.

"It is not yet seven o'clock."

"What is the matter? Why are you up so early after such a..." Georgiana's eyes were opened and becoming accustomed to the candlelight from the candle Darcy was carrying. As she saw her brother she stopped mid sentence and exclaimed "William, why are you dressed for traveling? Are you leaving Netherfield?"

"Yes dearest, we are leaving."

"We? I did not know we were to leave, why did you not tell me?"

"I did not tell you because I did not plan it so until late last night after you retired for the night."

"Why are we to go, William, and where?"

"We are to London."

"London, why?"

"Georgiana, I do not want to distress you but as you yourself have declared that you are no longer a child and wish me to discuss things with you I will tell you all, but first you must ready yourself. We leave to collect Miss Bennet in an hour and a half."

"Lizzy, is she to go to London with us?"

Darcy smiled at his sister already calling Elizabeth by a cherished family name. "Yes, we shall deliver her to her aunt and uncle's home in London where she is to stay until we return here for the wedding."

"William I think you had best start from the beginning. I can get ready quickly; I would prefer to hear all now." Georgiana sat up, ready to listen. She straightened the duvet around her, making a point to her brother that she was not moving until she had heard what he had to say.

Darcy had not time to argue with her, especially as he was learning that she had a bit of a stubborn streak. Fitzwilliam quickly told her all. "Georgie, on the way home from the ball last night Miss Lydia Bennet brought to her family's attention that Mr. Wickham, his friends, as well as some Netherfield servants may be plotting something against you now that he knows that you are in the neighborhood. Mr. Bennet was concerned enough that he returned here late last night and we discussed the best action to be taken. He feels that we should leave the area. Further discussion made him realize that although it is not yet known that I am to marry Elizabeth, it was quite evident last night that I admire her. My attention to her has now made her a target as well as you my dear. Her father agrees and is sending her with us to town, although she will be staying with her aunt and uncle there. We will return to Meryton before Christmas where we will be wed and then almost immediately return to Pemberley."

Georgiana sat calmly throughout Darcy's narrative. "Brother, I thank you for telling me the truth. You are correct; it is not safe here for us while he is in the neighborhood. We must return to London. If you will excuse me I shall ready myself for departure, I have much packing to do and little time to do it in."

"I shall leave you now. When you are ready please call for me and we shall depart. We are breakfasting at the Bennet's this morning. I believe your maid packed your trunks for you. You should have plenty of time to ready yourself."

Darcy left Georgiana to ready herself and walked to the library to await Bingley.

Mr. Bingley had not slept well either. Miss Jane Bennet was on his mind or in his dreams all night; all he could currently think about was planning how he would propose to her this very day. He was already awake when his man entered with a note from Darcy requesting an audience as soon as he was awake. He quickly readied himself and went down to the library where he knew he would find Darcy.

"Darcy, man, why are you awake so early? I know why I am but you man, I was sure nothing bothered your sleep."

"Good morning Charles, indeed I did not sleep well."

"Why is that Darcy and why are you dressed for travel? Are you leaving?"

"Yes Charles, I believe we must. Georgiana and I are off to London this very morning. Sit down I will tell you all."

"Surely you do not mean it. Is there someone ill or injured? What can I do to help, man?"

"Please Bingley, sit, I have quite a story to tell but first you must congratulate me. I am to be married."

"Married, to whom? Though I bet if last night's performance is any indication I am sure that I can guess."

"You are correct, Miss Elizabeth Bennet has accepted my offer of marriage and it is last night's performance along with a prior history with a particular acquaintance in the neighborhood that causes our departure. In fact Miss Elizabeth will be traveling with us as far as her aunt and uncles home in London."

"No, you are joking, why must you leave due to being engaged. Would not her family want her and you here to celebrate?"

"Indeed Charles, however Mr. Wickham would not." Darcy proceeded to tell Bingley all, just as he did with Mr. Bennet.

"I agree Darcy, you must leave, Georgiana and Miss Elizabeth are not safe here. You say one of the men may be a member of my own staff. Did Mr. Bennet tell you who the man was?"

"No he did not."

"Well I must accompany you to breakfast in order to talk to the man myself. Any less action would be unpardonable."

"It would indeed Bingley; we leave in an hour. Bingley, if I may offer up some friendly advice. Being engaged is about the best feeling I have ever felt in my life as of today. I highly recommend it to all young men who know a special lady. As you have informed me earlier that you intend to talk with Miss Jane today I say you should take all advantages of private conversation to become most happy yourself."

"Thank you, Darcy, I believe I shall."

An hour later saw off the Darcy carriage and Mr. Bingley on horseback, fifteen minutes after that they arrived at the gate to Longbourn for breakfast.

Caroline Bingley woke in a decent mood, however it lasted about as long as it took her maid to detail that the Darcys' and her brother were breakfasting at Longbourn and that the Darcys' were departing for London this very morning.

Her anger was escalating with each piece of information related to her. It was rumored that Mr. Darcy was to London for the purpose of announcing his marriage, that he had only made his sister travel all the way here to meet and approve of the lady before the news was made public.

Caroline was furious and thus determined to foil their happiness. If she could not have her desires fulfilled she was certainly not going to stand by while some country upstart would steal her perfect life at Pemberley.

She went to the drawing room and penned a quick note.

> *Wednesday November 27ᵗʰ, 1811*
> *G.W.,*
>   *I write to inform you of the Darcys' plans as agreed upon previously. Contrary to my first note to inform you of Georgiana's arrival and intended stay at Netherfield, it appears as if their plans have changed and they will be returning to London today.*
>   *If gossip is to be believed, then Mr. Darcy has gotten himself engaged to none other than Miss. Elizabeth Bennet.*
>   *As we both know, this engagement must be stopped at all costs. I trust that you will know what to do.*
> *C.B.*

Caroline read her short note with an eye on revenge. Miss Elizabeth Bennet was stealing her Pemberley and she would not have it. Upon overhearing Mr. Wickham telling his tale of woe to an innocent lady at the habadasher's a few days previous she introduced herself as someone who could help him and told him of Mr. Darcy's possible attraction to a lady in the area, so much so that he had brought his sister here to meet her. Recognizing the equal glint of revenge in his eyes she realized she had an ally in her quest to separate the two.

Elizabeth had hardly closed her eyes all night; her mind was too occupied with other thoughts to rest so at dawn, when Martha came in to assist her she was already awake.

Elizabeth, with Martha's help, was quickly made ready for travelling.

"Thank you Martha, I daresay I could not have accomplished this so fast this morning without your assistance."

"You're welcome Miss Elizabeth. Will there be anything else or should I begin to pack your trunks?"

"We shall pack my trunks, I will help you."

"Yes, miss."

"Martha, have you been told where I am traveling to?"

"No miss, Mrs. Hill informed me just to ensure that your trunks were packed for a few weeks at least."

"You are correct Martha; I am off to London to stay with the Gardiners until just before Christmas."

"Wonderful miss, I know how much you love Mr. and Mrs. Gardiner that should be an enjoyable journey for you."

"Yes, Martha, it shall." This was said with a bit more warmth than necessary for such a statement, but Martha did not notice.

"Miss Elizabeth, may I inquire about your evening? Did you enjoy yourself at the Netherfield Ball?"

"Oh yes, it was the most spectacular ball of my life, I daresay life-changing."

Martha raised her eyebrows as she stood up to look at Miss Elizabeth. She usually reported the follies and nonsense of the evening; never did she state that it was good, and most definitely never did she describe it as spectacular. The balls were generally survivable or tolerable at best. Martha was beginning to wonder at Miss Elizabeth's current mood.

"Life-changing miss, a ball being life-changing, I do not understand."

"Martha, I am dying to tell someone besides Papa and Jane. I am to be married."

"Married, what excellent news, Miss Elizabeth, I am so happy for you. Who are you to marry?"

"I am to marry Mr. Darcy, Martha."

"Mr. Darcy, why he is a handsome one, I have seen him a few times as he visits with Mr. Bingley."

"Yes, I daresay he is extremely handsome. He is the one who sent the roses last evening, you know, and when I arrived at the ball I found my twelfth rose. It was pinned on his coat."

"How romantic, I wish I could have seen you and the look on your mother's face of course."

Both girls had to stifle a laugh here.

"Yes, Martha, mother made quite a fuss the rest of the night. I must say she instantly took a fancy to him and now he is among her favorites, but now, we must complete the packing. I definitely want to take this, it is now my favorite." This was said as Elizabeth held up her red dress from the night before.

"Also, you must know Martha; it is Mr. Darcy who is transporting me to London. I am to go with him and his sister."

Martha smiled at Elizabeth "You shall have a wonderful time, miss, I am sure you will arrive comfortably and in good time."

Martha finished packing Elizabeth's wardrobe while the lady prepared her trinkets and belongings. The roses that adorned her hair the night before were attached to the lid of her keepsake box to hang inside for drying. Elizabeth then lightly kissed the box as she laid it atop the clothing just before the trunk was closed and locked in preparation for the arrival of Mr. Darcy's carriage.

Mr. Hill came up for the trunk at half past eight, just as Lizzy went down to join her family for breakfast. Only Jane and Mr. Bennet were there, though Elizabeth could hear everyone else in their morning preparations.

"Ahhh Lizzy, you are ready I presume?"

"Yes, father, I am ready, my trunk has just been taken down by Mr. Hill."

"Trunk, but Lizzy where are you to go?" Jane inquired with a hint of worry in her voice.

"I am to London, Jane, to stay with Aunt and Uncle Gardiner."

"Why, is something the matter?" Jane looked around expectantly and Elizabeth glanced at her father as she quickly answered. She did not want her family to be worried and the only way to make that so was to not tell the entire truth.

"Jane dearest, do not fret, nothing so dreadful. Mr. Darcy has business in town and has also expressed a wish to marry early, as he needs to return to Pemberley. With that being the case we need to expedite the purchase of my wedding clothes. What better ways than for me to accompany Mr. and Miss Darcy to London and have Aunt Gardiner take me shopping?"

"But why did you not tell me last night?"

"Because I did not know, Mr. Darcy had indicated as much, however the note was just received this morning."

"Oh!" Jane looked a bit distressed but said no more.

"In fact, dear Jane," began Mr. Bennet "We are expecting Mr. and Miss Darcy for breakfast this morning. The announcement of the engagement and Lizzy to London will be made shortly."

"What will be done shortly Mr. Bennet, I did not hear you?" Mrs. Bennet said as she walked into the breakfast room trailing the remainder of the household and Mr. Collins.

"You shall soon find out, why don't you all sit down, we are expecting visitors this morning."

"Visitors at breakfast, why, who should dare to visit so early on the morning after such a long night? I should think they would leave us alone."

Before anyone could respond Mr. Collins stood and began to leave the room.

"Mr. Collins" inquired Mr. Bennet.

"Sir"

"Where do you go just as we are to eat?"

"I am to go out; I fear I have no appetite this morning."

"No appetite, I can scarcely believe that. Thus far in your stay you have displayed an ample appetite for our cook's creations."

"I have sir, however I think last night's activities put stress on me and I have no desire to be in company this morning. I shall walk towards town and see if I meet any of my newest and dearest friends from last night." He rose and departed from the room leaving many astonished looks at his back.

Just then the bell was heard and Mrs. Hill came in trailing Mr. Bingley and Mr. and Miss Darcy.

"Mr. Bingley, Mr. Darcy, and Miss Darcy, Ma'am."

"Why sirs, we did not expect you this morning, how delightful. Why did you not tell me last evening you were to visit this morning? Come in and sit, we are just to begin breakfast."

No reply was made, as one was not truly needed. The three sat down and Mr. Darcy introduced his sister. Once introductions were complete Mr. Bennet began.

"Mrs. Bennet, my dear, I have a bit of an announcement to make. Shall I tell you now or would you prefer to eat and hear the news later?"

"Mr. Bennet, tell me now, for I must know. We cannot stand to wait, can we girls? And I am sure our company would like to hear also, do you not?"

Everyone nodded and Mr. Bennet began. "Well my dear it appears as if Lizzy must leave us for some time."

Mrs. Bennet interrupted confused and a little distressed.

"Leave us, why Lizzy my dear, where must you go and why? I am sure you would like to stay here with your dear family."

"Please, Mama, listen to Papa."

Deciding to sport a little with everyone, Mr. Bennet continued "Is that true Lizzy, would you prefer to stay with your dear family over your present planned adventures? I had thought your actions last night in the gardens indicated that your decision was pretty well established."

Elizabeth turned bright red, Jane shifted slightly with distress for her sister and Mr. Darcy hardly knew what to do as he stared straight ahead, not daring to look at anyone.

"It is, Papa; I have not changed my decision." Elizabeth whispered.

"Very well, it appears as if Lizzy does indeed leave us." Mr. Bennet took a drink of his coffee preparing himself for the next onslaught.

"Well are you to tell us, Mr. Bennet, or do we have to drag it from you?"

"I am getting there Mrs. Bennet. If you must know Lizzy is to London to stay with Mr. and Mrs. Gardiner. She will return the week before Christmas."

"Why Mr. Bennet, what a lovely idea, perhaps we should all go. What a nice trip it shall be. I do so miss my brother Gardiner and London this time of year is so perfect with the theater and shops and public places."

"No, Mrs. Bennet, we are not all to go for you must stay here to plan."

"Plan, Mr. Bennet, of what do you speak? Surely I do not know of anything that must be planned."

"Well, my dear, if you will listen I will tell you. You must plan a wedding for it appears that shortly after Lizzy returns she is to marry."

Mrs. Bennet sat stunned, recognition beginning to dawn on her as she looked at Mr. Darcy and then back to Mr. Bennet as if inquiring if he was the man.

Mr. Bennet did not leave her in suspense long. "Elizabeth and Mr. Darcy have decided to marry just before Christmas."

Now that the man was confirmed the date became more important. "Christmas, why that is less than a month away, no it cannot be done. I will not allow it."

A worried look crossed Mr. Darcy's face but was soon relieved as Mr. Bennet interjected.

"Mrs. Bennet, have you any thought that it might be necessary for a speedy wedding to take place in order for Mr. Darcy to return to Pemberley with Elizabeth?"

"No I have not, and I will not. One month is simply not long enough to sufficiently prepare a wedding for my daughter, and there is no way that it possibly could become so under any circumstances. No matter the business Mr. Darcy has or where he has it. Mr. Darcy may return to Pemberley for his business and we shall have a wedding once it is completed and he returns. That should give us enough time to plan."

"If you feel as such Mrs. Bennet then I shall ask Mrs. Gardiner to plan the wedding with Lizzy while she is in London, I am assured that she would be able to plan such an affair as necessary under the timeline that I have presented. Then we shall all travel to London and see Lizzy marry from London, or perhaps you prefer Pemberley, Mr. Darcy?" Mr. Darcy smiled at such an idea, knowing it would not actually happen, but smiling none the less as he replied.

"Certainly, sir."

Mrs. Bennet became distressed and continued; "But Mr. Bennet, you would presume to allow the first Bennet daughter to marry from London or some far-off unknown place and not her home, it is unheard of. I will not stand for it. She must marry from Longbourn, where all of her sisters can stand up with her."

"But Mrs. Bennet you just said it cannot be done, perhaps if you called upon other more experienced mothers of the neighborhood such as Mrs. Robinson or Mrs. Andrews, you could get sufficient assistance. Each of those ladies has ample experience planning as they have each married off their daughters. They may assist you in preparing under such a short amount of time."

"Mr. Bennet! You dare presume that I need the assistance of Mrs. Robinson or Mrs. Andrews to plan a wedding! I shall forgive you for the comment since I am sure you are distressed as I am about the short notice, However, I assure you that I am perfectly able to plan a wedding in any amount of time without the assistance of them. Lizzy, my dear, you go to London and purchase your wedding clothes with Mrs. Gardiner and when you return you will have a spectacular wedding. I am sure under the tighter constraints of time your father has provided ample funds to compensate and therefore I shall accomplish it. Come to think of it, Mr. Darcy, if Mr. Bennet has not provided ample funds I am sure you will."

"Yes, ma'am, if there is anything that is needed, please have Mr. Bennet write to me and I will ensure it is taken care of quickly."

"Mr. Bennet write, no, I shall write to you myself. Mr. Bennet is such a negligent correspondent it shall not reach you in time. I do hope that you are not negligent in your correspondence as well, Mr. Darcy, or else I will not be able to accomplish this in time."

"I am not, ma'am; I assure you my speedy response will be made to all of your letters."

Finally, all was settled to everyone's satisfaction and breakfast commenced.

Upon completion of breakfast, Mr. Darcy went to oversee that Elizabeth's trunks were properly loaded on the carriage and Mr. Bingley asked for an audience with Mr. Bennet.

"Mr. Bennet sir, if you have a moment could I speak with you privately?"

"Yes Mr. Bingley, let us go to my library."

Both men went to the library and upon closing the door Mr. Bennet began.

"I believe I know why you are here this morning and unfortunately I have no further information for you. I do not know what man of yours was to assist Mr. Wickham."

"Thank you, Mr. Bennet, that is what I came to inquire about. I am afraid I have troubled you for no reason sir."

"'Tis' no trouble, Mr. Bingley."

"Mr. Bennet, sir, before I return to my home this fine morning would you allow me an audience with Miss Jane Bennet?" Mr. Bingley broke into a huge grin.

"I will sir, if it is what you wish. Perhaps after your audience you would like to join me back here in the library for a drink, sir?"

Mr. Bingley eagerly answered, "I would like that sir, thank you. I shall seek out Miss Jane even now, if you will excuse me." This was said as Mr. Bingley moved towards the library door and exited.

Mrs. Hill was walking past the library towards the drawing room carrying a tray of tea as Mr. Bingley exited. She stopped and curtsied to Mr. Bingley "May I help you, sir?"

"Yes, I am looking for Miss Jane; do you know where I can find her?"

"Yes sir, if you will follow me, sir, she is in the drawing room."

Mrs. Hill opened the door and entered with the tray of tea, Mr. Bingley right behind her.

"Mr. Bingley, ma'am."

"Mr. Bingley, we are so glad that you have joined us, may we offer you some tea, sir?"

"No thank you ma'am, I have just inquired and been granted by Mr. Bennet an audience with Miss Jane. If she is not needed I would request a short stroll in the gardens. I believe it is not too cold this morning if she has a warm wrap."

Jane had already stood to get her outer clothing as Mrs. Bennet continued, "You do honor us, sir. Jane, do run and fetch your things. You do not want to keep Mr. Bingley waiting, do you?"

Jane left the room with Bingley right behind her. Bingley stood waiting in the vestibule while Jane was assisted into her wrap by Mrs. Hill.

The two left the house for the gardens and walked about a few minutes in silence until Mr. Bingley began.

"Miss Bennet, are you warm enough?"

"Yes sir, I am, thank you for asking, and you, how are you, sir?"

"Yes, yes I am quite fine. I hope you are happy for your sister's news?"

"Yes, I am. Elizabeth is so happy; I assume Mr. Darcy is as well?"

"Oh, I daresay he is. He has spoken of her fine attributes quite openly, which is so unlike Darcy you know. He is generally a quiet and reserved man, but recently he is open and unassuming. I am sure we owe it all to Miss Elizabeth."

"Yes, Lizzy does have a way of making everyone open up, doesn't she?"

"Yes she does, in fact Darcy and I had quite a discussion about his present happy situation and he provided me a bit of advice, though I am pleased to say that I did not need his advice as I had already come to the same conclusion beforehand."

"Indeed, and what was this advice Mr. Bingley? I hope it was not to hie away to London this morning."

"No it was not, though if I succeed then I may need to do just that, however so may you."

"Really Mr. Bingley I cannot think of what you mean, I have no idea of what may need me in London."

"Do you not? You can think of no reason that you would be needed in London presently?"

"No I cannot." Jane said very shyly. She could barely talk, as affected as she was.

"I can!"

"Can you?"

"Yes, would you like to know what it is?"

"If you wish to tell me."

"Then you shall hear it because I wish to tell you." Jane looked at him shyly but encouragingly. "I believe you could go to London if you were in need of purchasing wedding clothes yourself."

"Yes, that would be a good reason if I were engaged, but since I am not I doubt it could be done."

"You could become engaged."

"Well sir, I am sure that is easy enough for an amiable man such as you, but for a woman I must sit and home and wait for a proper proposal."

"If a proper proposal were to come soon would you go to London?"

"Yes, I believe I would."

"Well then I suppose you need a proposal. Jane, my Angel, would you do me the greatest honor of becoming my wife?"

"I will, oh yes, I will."

"Will you allow me to accompany you to London to purchase wedding clothes?"

"I will."

"Will you also allow a short engagement such as Mr. Darcy and Elizabeth are embarking on?"

"Why sir, they are marrying in a month because he must return to Pemberley, what excuse can we provide for marrying that soon?"

154

"Let us see if they require one or if we can simply try to get by without an explanation. If one is needed I am sure I can think of something. Or perhaps we could cause a scene and then be made to marry quickly?"

Bingley laughed at the shocked look on Jane's face. He offered her his arm and started towards the house. "I believe I have another appointment with your father. Do you think that you can be ready to travel to London on Friday?"

"Friday, that is so soon, why it is only the day after tomorrow."

"I daresay your sister was prepared with just this morning's notice, is not two days enough time, Jane?"

Bingley was almost pleading with her to consent.

"Yes, Charles, I shall be ready."

Bingley leaned down and pressed his lips to hers with unrepentant passion. Jane was instantly overcome with desire and matched his passion equally.

"Bingley, Miss Jane..." came the voice of Mr. Darcy as he came around the corner of the hedgerow. "Ah, there you are, I apologize if I am interrupting, however we are to leave soon and Miss Elizabeth would like to speak with her sister."

"Well Darcy, we were just returning to the house, I have an appointment with Mr. Bennet straightaway."

"I presume if the smile on your face, the blush on the lady's cheeks and the wonderful position I just caught the two of you in, which I must apologize for, are any indication that I am to wish you much joy and happiness. I will be most pleased to have you as a brother, Charles."

Jane was blushing furiously and could but whisper, "Thank you, I will go to Elizabeth."

"Darcy, you must allow me to go as well. I will see you off in a few minutes." He headed straight for Mr. Bennet's library.

"Enter!" Mr. Bennet responded to Mr. Bingley's knock.

Once the door was closed he continued. "So it is done, is it? Well you made short work of that, son. I presume you now come to seek my consent?"

"I do, sir, will you give it?"

"I see you come to the point directly."

"I do, sir, I indicated when I left what my intent upon returning would be and you properly deciphered it. You had that time to consider, and I presume you know what your answer will be. There is no point in beating around the bush since I have additional items to discuss with you once I obtain your consent."

"Well, I am intrigued about the other items, therefore I will quickly tell you that I will support your marriage to Jane and now I would like to hear your other items."

"Like Elizabeth, I request that Jane be allowed to go to London to purchase wedding clothes."

"I suppose as the wedding approaches that can be arranged." Mr. Bennet smiled wryly at Mr. Bingley, knowing exactly what the young man had in mind.

Mr. Bingley fidgeted and began again. "Mr. Bennet, sir, we also wish to marry soon, perhaps shortly after Mr. Darcy and Miss Elizabeth, and I wish Miss Bennet to travel to London on Friday to being her purchases. I must be in town as well and it would be a perfect opportunity that we should take advantage of. Miss Elizabeth will be shopping with her aunt and Miss Jane could go with them, saving the time and effort of having to shop two times."

"Yes, I am sure you, thought only of the time and effort it would save, didn't you?"

Mr. Bingley smiled but made no comment.

"Well, I suppose when you put it that way it sounds reasonable. Jane shall be ready Friday morning. Will your sisters be traveling with you, or does Miss Jane require an escort?"

"I do not know, sir, I will send word."

"Very well, shall we make the announcement to the family?"

Mr. Bennet and Mr. Bingley left in pursuit of the drawing room. As they passed Mrs. Hill he told her to summon everyone there for a meeting prior to Elizabeth's departure.

When Jane left Bingley and Darcy she went directly to Elizabeth. The happiness that overflowed in Jane was easily read by Elizabeth and congratulations were quickly made. The two were instantly in deep conversation about their happy situations, each unable to say enough good about her future husband. It was shortly decided between the two that as long as their intendeds agreed nothing would please them more then sharing the most special days of their lives. They were finishing their decision when Mrs. Hill summoned them to the drawing room.

Upon entering Jane and Elizabeth saw that everyone was there. Lydia and Kitty were entertaining an increasingly open Georgiana, Mary was reading in the corner, near then window. Mr. Bennet was sitting by the fire, while Mrs. Bennet accosted Darcy about wedding plans and Mr. Bingley eagerly listened to their conversation.

Jane and Elizabeth went straight to the gentlemen and asked their mother for tea prior to Elizabeth's departure. Mrs. Bennet left to ring for tea and Jane and Elizabeth quickly informed Bingley and Darcy of their ideas about a double wedding. The arrangement was to the satisfaction of all, so they quickly informed Mr. Bennet before the arrival of tea.

As tea arrived and was poured out everyone was attending to his or her own conversations until Mr. Bennet began "Well I must say this has been an eventful morning with Elizabeth leaving for London, and now Jane informs me that she also must hie to London on Friday for a bit of shopping. Is that not right, Jane?"

"It is, father."

"No Jane, you must stay here to aide me in wedding preparations. I assure you that you shall have a new gown, however, not from London, we will have one made in Meryton." Mrs. Bennet said.

"Why, Mrs. Bennet I would presume that you would want your daughter's wedding dress made in London, but if you think the Meryton seamstresses are just as good perhaps she should stay here."

"Wedding dress, what do you speak of Mr. Bennet, are you confused. You said it was Lizzy that was marrying Mr. Darcy. Unless you mean to say…" here she fell silent, stunned that she could be so lucky as to have two daughters engaged in the same day and to such splendid gentlemen.

"Yes my dear, today Mr. Bingley has requested and been granted the hand in marriage of our eldest daughter Jane. To top it off, Mrs. Bennet, they are to marry the same day as Mr. Darcy and Elizabeth in a double wedding."

"A double wedding, sir, you cannot be serious."

"I am indeed, Mrs. Bennet; I have just been informed of it by all of the intendeds." In order to stop Mrs. Bennet before her tirade started he continued. "I am prepared to provide the normal sums for wedding preparations for both girls, so think my dear you shall have double the allowance to plan one affair. Such splendor you shall be able to procure."

"Indeed, you are correct and since Mr. Darcy has already assured me of his assistance I am sure Mr. Bingley shall do so also, shall you not, sir?"

"I shall indeed, ma'am; however I am as negligent of a correspondent as Mr. Bennet, so I suggest if you have any requests of me then write them in your letters to Darcy and he shall inform me and correspond back in a single missive from both of us."

"Thank you, sir, I shall do that."

"Well now that it is all arranged we need to get Elizabeth and the Darcys' on their way. If not, it will be too late for them to arrive unexpected on the Gardiners' doorstep. Go get ready, my dear." Mr. Bennet gestured towards Elizabeth and she went to fetch her coat and bonnet.

"Mr. Darcy, will you accompany me to my library before embark on your journey?"

"Yes, sir."

Both men arose and left for the library.

"Mr. Darcy, I am entrusting my dearest child into your care. Please take care of her and keep her safe. I depend on you."

"You have my word, sir. You must know by now the depth of my love for her. I would do anything in my power to keep her safe. Have no fear; I will take care of her."

"Very well, Mr. Darcy I know you will. Let us go out now."

"Yes, sir."

Mr. Darcy stood to follow Mr. Bennet to the door. With his hand upon it Mr. Bennet turned and said, "Oh yes, I almost forgot. Mr. Darcy, be assured that I saw last evenings display of affection upon Miss Elizabeth as we left Netherfield. I should advise you that Mr. Gardiner has small children in his home and will not tolerate such behavior. If you wish to visit Elizabeth on a regular basis you had better learn to control yourself. Be assured, we will have a wedding in less than a month, I am sure you can regulate yourself that long. Am I understood, sir."

"Yes you are, perfectly."

"Very good, let us go out then."

Mr. Bennet led the way to the drawing room where everyone was gathered wishing congratulations to Jane and Mr. Bingley and saying some goodbyes to Elizabeth and their newest acquaintance, Miss Darcy.

"Elizabeth, Miss Darcy, are you both prepared for departure? Mr. Darcy wishes to get on the road to London, already you are departing far later than originally anticipated."

"Yes, papa, we are."

Elizabeth gave everyone a final hug goodbye and took the arm that Mr. Darcy offered her as he escorted her to the carriage and helped her in. He also handed in Georgiana and gave each of them warming blocks and blankets and then entered himself and sat across from them on the other seat. The footman closed the carriage door and almost instantly they were off.

Elizabeth looked out the window waving furiously at her family as a tear rolled down her cheek.

"Sister, why do you cry? Are you not happy to be going to London with us?"

"Oh, Georgie, I am very happy to be going to London with you and Mr. Darcy, however, upon thinking about it this is to be my last time leaving Longbourn as a single woman. Upon my return, Mr. Darcy and I will be married and when I leave it will be as his wife and your sister."

"Oh, Lizzy, I am sorry I had not thought about that."

"Do not be sorry, Georgie, for I am not, I am just slightly affected. I am so happy to be spending some time in London with the Gardiners. They practically raised me, you know. Mrs. Gardiner is a second mother to me. I love her dearly and could not ask for a better person to aid me in preparing to marry your brother."

Elizabeth looked shyly at Mr. Darcy, who was openly admiring her.

As they approached Meryton to pass through, the coach slowed to a steady pace. Each of the travelers was looking out at the passing scenes, content that they were on their way without any mishaps or interference. Georgiana was about to comment on a bonnet she saw in a shop window that they were passing when her eyes caught sight of the last man she would ever want to see again. She drew in a deep breath and placed her hand at her throat.

Both Elizabeth and Darcy saw it happen. Darcy recognized her concern exactly, but Elizabeth did not. She leaned forward to look out the window that Georgiana had just turned from. Her eyes were instantly arrested by none other than Mr. George Wickham.

Mr. Wickham was distressed when he was excluded from the ball at Netherfield, for it thwarted his plans with Georgiana Darcy. He was calmed, however, knowing that the Darcys' were in the neighborhood for an extended stay and he would have another chance to extract some funds from Mr. Darcy with threats against his sister.

He was further calmed when he began to hear the rumors of Darcy's attention to Miss Elizabeth Bennet. One thing Wickham knew was the Darcys', and if Fitzwilliam Darcy displayed even a quarter of the attention that was currently being gossiped around Meryton then he was in a fair way to being engaged. Mr. Wickham smiled an evil smile at his thoughts, even better, the Darcy men are known for their attachments to their women. Just look at the poor Mr. George Darcy, when his beloved Anne died he no longer had the will to live, even for his children. It took years and was agonizing, but happened nonetheless and Fitzwilliam Darcy would be no different. He is a Darcy after all. Wickham knew that he could wound Darcy to the core of his very soul; a wound that he was not likely to recover from for a very long time, if at all. Wickham was beginning to thank his lucky stars, thinking that things could not get better. Not only could he hurt the sister, but now he had another source to injure Darcy; his heart.

The note delivered at breakfast had made him uneasy. What could he do if the Darcys' departed town? He needed them here so that he could stir things up a bit. If he left Meryton he would risk his militia post, something he could not afford to do at present. The thought of not knowing was driving Wickham near distraction; he had to know for himself, so he got ready and set off for the main thoroughfare through Meryton. If the Darcys' left Meryton he would be there to see it.

Seeing the Darcy carriage roll over the ruts and stones on the road through Meryton towards him made Wickham's pulse race. The closer the carriage came the more uneasy Wickham became, it appeared as if the carriage would not stop but instead head onward towards the London road. As the carriage passed, Wickham caught a glimpse of Georgiana as she quickly leaned back behind the curtain, distress written all over her face. His eyes stayed glued to the spot and he was glad that they had for if not he would be late in knowing that the carriage held not only Georgiana but also Miss Bennet. If the two were there then undoubtedly the carriage held a third, which was confirmed as George saw Darcy's horse being tethered behind the second carriage that had joined them carrying the Darcy's luggage and paid help to town.

George Wickham, despite failing university, was not senseless. He had lived around Fitzwilliam Darcy his entire life and knew that what you saw was exactly what you would get with him. Seeing a loaded carriage rolling towards London meant just that, a departure for London. George swore under his breath, which made Mr. Denny look at him strangely. Denny was about to say something when Mr. Wickham interrupted him.

"Denny, man, I just realized that I have business in Kent. It cannot be delayed; it is of a most urgent nature. Will you cover for me with Colonel Forster if he realizes I am gone and inquires about me? I will return no later than tomorrow night if I leave straightaway."

"Surely Wickham, if you must go, but wouldn't it be safer to take a moment and go speak with Colonel Forster yourself, he will undoubtedly grant you leave and then you will not have to suffer the consequences of being caught."

"No, no, he will inquire as to my business, which is personal and it will be hours before I can speak with him; he may even deny me leave. If I leave now I can be in Kent by late tonight and about my business first thing in the morning. I can then be on the road and back here by tomorrow evening. If I am lucky I will not even be missed and no one will know the difference."

"Very well Wickham, off with you then."

Wickham bowed slightly without noticing the letter that slipped from his pocket as he took off towards his quarters to grab some things and then to the stables for his horse. In less than an half an hour he was on his way to Kent, more precisely to Rosings Park, the estate of the estimable Lady Catherine de Bourgh.

Chapter 20
The Darcy-Wickham History

Elizabeth quickly leaned back in the seat again after coming face to face with George Wickham. The look she had seen on his face made her glad for her departure. Perhaps her father and Mr. Darcy were correct in assuming he would try something against her as well. Instincts made Elizabeth drop her hand and pick up Georgiana's; they were to be sisters, they may as well act as sisters do and calm each other when distressed. Elizabeth knew that there had been some falling-out with Mr. Wickham and the Darcys' though she knew not what. Whatever it was obviously pained Georgiana and Elizabeth's instinct was to provide comfort. Mr. Darcy saw it and decided it was time for Elizabeth to know all so that she could protect herself and Georgiana better if he was not close by.

"Georgie, dear, I think we had best tell Elizabeth everything, as a member of our family she needs to know."

Georgiana looked distressed and Elizabeth confused, but Mr. Darcy continued.

"I know it pains you, Georgiana, but she needs to know. She must know what she is up against in order to keep herself safe. I would not want Elizabeth endangered because of ignorance."

Georgiana nodded slightly and both she and Darcy turned towards Elizabeth.

"Elizabeth, what I am going to tell you will distress you greatly, I am sure, but please know that we have been dealing with him for years and thus far we are safe and have every intention of remaining so. I originally felt it my duty to keep all to myself and handle him, but my thoughtlessness left Georgiana susceptible to harm. We are now able to remain safe, the both of us because we keep each other and ourselves informed and aware. I ask you to do the same." Elizabeth nodded her agreement for him to begin.

"Mr. Wickham is the son of a very respectable man, who had for many years the management of all the Pemberley estates, and whose good conduct in the discharge of his trust naturally inclined my father to be of service to him; and on George Wickham, who was his godson; his kindness was therefore liberally bestowed. My father supported him at school, and afterwards at Cambridge – a most important assistance, as his own father, always poor from the extravagance of his wife, would have been unable to give him a gentleman's education."

"My father was not only fond of this young man's society, whose manners were always engaging; he had also the highest opinion of him, and hoping the church would be his profession, intended to provide for him in it."

"As for me, it is many, many years since I first began to think of him in a very different manner. The vicious propensities – the want of principle, which he was careful to guard from the knowledge of his best friend, could not escape the observation of a young man of nearly the same age with himself, and who had opportunities of seeing him in unguarded moments, which my father could not have."

"My excellent father died about five years ago; and his attachment to Mr. Wickham was to the last so steady, that in his will he particularly recommended it to me, to promote his advancement in the best manner that his profession might allow – and if he took orders, desired that a valuable family living might be his as soon as it became vacant. There was also a legacy of one thousand pounds."

"Wickham's own father did not long survive mine, and within half a year from these events, Mr. Wickham wrote to inform me that, having finally resolved against taking orders, he hoped I should not think it unreasonable for him to expect some more immediate pecuniary advantage, in lieu of the preferment, by which he could not be benefited. He had some intention, he added, of studying law, and I must be aware that the interest of one thousand pounds would be a very insufficient support therein. I rather wished, than believed him to be sincere; but, at any rate, was perfectly ready to accede to his proposal. I knew that Mr. Wickham ought not to be a clergyman; the business was therefore soon settled – he resigned all claim to assistance in the church, were it possible that he could ever be in a situation to receive it, and accepted in return three thousand pounds. All connection between us seemed now dissolved. I thought too ill of him to invite him to Pemberley, or admit his society in town. In town, I believe, he chiefly lived, but his studying the law was a mere pretence, and being now free from all restraint, his life was a life of idleness and dissipation."

"For about three years I heard little of him; but on the decease of the incumbent of the living which had been designed for him, he applied to me again by letter for the presentation. His circumstances, he assured me, and I had no difficulty in believing it, were exceedingly bad. He had found the law a most unprofitable study, and was now absolutely resolved on being ordained, if I would present him to the living in question – of which he trusted there could be little doubt, as he was well assured that I had no other person to provide for, and I could not have forgotten my revered father's intentions. You will hardly blame me for refusing to comply with this entreaty, or for resisting every repetition to it. His resentment was in proportion to the distress of his circumstances – and he was doubtless as violent in his abuse of me to others as in his reproaches to me. After this period every appearance of acquaintance was dropped. How he lived, I know not. But last summer he was again most painfully obtruded on my notice."

Georgiana was fully crying, Elizabeth gripping her hand for support through the whole recitation. It was evident that something more dreadful was coming she could tell by Georgiana's beginning to shake as the recitation progressed and the concerned look on Mr. Darcy's face.

"I must now mention a circumstance which Georgiana and I would wish to forget and in which no obligation less than the present should induce me or her to unfold to any human being. As you well know, Georgiana is more than ten years my junior and after our parents death she has been under my and our Cousin, Colonel Fitzwilliam's, guardianship.

"About eight months ago, she was taken from school, and an establishment formed for her in London; and last summer she went with the lady who presided over it, a Mrs. Younge, to Ramsgate."

Despite Georgiana's distress she interrupted. "Brother, let me tell it. It was my foolishness and it is mine to tell. I must let Lizzy know this myself."

Georgiana turned further on the seat towards Elizabeth, grasped both of her hands for support and began.

"Mrs. Younge and I traveled there on a Monday. We spent Tuesday and Wednesday morning unpacking and resting and then after afternoon tea on Wednesday we decided to take a walk along the seashore. It was a beautiful sunny day and I was so excited to be there on holiday. This was the first trip I had ever been on without Fitzwilliam and I wanted to show him how grown up I was to be able to handle myself away from him and my cousin."

"As we were walking along the seashore there was a group coming towards us. We paused to let them pass and just as we were beginning to walk again I heard my name called "Miss Darcy, is that you?" I turned to look and there before me was Mr. Wickham. At that time I knew nothing of his past with my brother, I only remembered him as being a kind and loving person, one who my father loved and was almost another brother to me. Little did I know that he and Mrs. Younge had formed designs upon me."

"Mr. Wickham and Mrs. Younge had a prior acquaintance, which my brother knew nothing about. She encouraged us to walk together when we met that day, which we did for almost an hour. She then promoted to me to ask him for tea the following day, which I did and in which he came to. She then continued to promote him to me all of the next week, encouraging us to walk and talk together and when he was not there, telling me all of her nicest impressions of him."

"Mrs. Younge knew of my fear of coming out, I am dreadfully shy and do not want all of the attention pushed upon me. She began to tell me that if I already had a suitor that my coming out could be a lessened affair and then a few days later began to say that it could be done away with altogether if I was to marry soon."

"Between his attentions and her persuasion I thought myself in love with him and I am afraid to admit that I agreed to an elopement. I dearly wanted to tell Fitzwilliam but she told me that he would insist that I have a proper coming out, allowing my aunts to plan it as a grand affair. My fear of the event overpowered me and I did not tell him."

Georgiana took a deep breath and looked at Elizabeth, she could see the concern and fear written all over her face yet she could also tell that Elizabeth was not judging her; she was instead distressed as any sister would be, which gave her the strength to go on.

"Somehow though, most assuredly by fate, Fitzwilliam came to surprise me with a visit. It was but the day before we were to elope. I was so excited that he had come. I just knew that he would be as excited as me and would go with us to see my wedding that I could not keep it from him. He is after all more to me than just a brother; he is all that I have and is almost a father to me. I did not even give him time to change; I instantly took him into the drawing room and told him all. I became afraid as I saw his face, tight and red with anger, looking as if he was about to explode. He was just about to speak when the door opened to admit Mr. Wickham. He instantly stood and without saying a word to me demanded that Mr. Wickham follow him into the library where they were for over an hour. Mrs. Younge came down to me and as the time passed her own features became white and pale. She became agitated and nervous. When the door finally opened and the two came out Mr. Wickham went towards the door and exited without looking back. My brother came to stand before me and without looking at Mrs. Younge he said to her "You have fifteen minutes to gather your things and depart from this house before I call the constable and have you arrested." She all but flew to the stairs and not ten minutes later she had all of her things packed and departed from the house."

"I did not understand what had just happened, all of my happiness had been shattered and I was very angry with Fitzwilliam. I began to scream at him that he did not love me if he was sending away the man I love and that loved me in return. I told him that I hated him for removing the one woman who actually understood me and did not try to make me into something that I never wanted to be."

Georgiana was in so many tears that she could barely get each sentence out. Mr. Darcy began to tell the story for her.

"Georgiana yelled at me for close to ten minutes before she collapsed into my arms in tears. She cried for another hour and during that time I knew that she needed to know what Mr. Wickham truly was. I was finally able to calm her and asked her if she would come to the library to inspect some things. She followed me more out of curiosity than willingness. When we entered the library I sat her down and told her that Mr. Wickham had admitted to me that his chief object was unquestionably Georgiana's fortune, which is thirty thousand pounds; but I cannot help supposing that the hope of revenging himself on me was a strong inducement. His revenge would have been complete indeed. She was shocked and denied it but then I told her that I had offered to let them marry if he would sign a waiver that denied him all claim and access to her funds except those required for day to day living and that they must be married from Pemberley. She knew that I told the truth for we have never lied to one another, she also knew he had denied it. I believe the knowledge of the seriousness was beginning to sink in. Georgiana began to ask about her reputation and what he would say about her. It was then that I showed her my bankroll ledger, the most recent entry being that of Mr. George Wickham in the amount of five thousand pounds. I paid him for his silence. Today is the first time Georgiana has seen him since he walked out the door at Ramsgate."

Georgiana was crying and Elizabeth had moved from holding her hand to embracing her as she cried. She had a question, but was not sure if she wanted the answer that she was sure she already knew, but it needed to be asked.

"My father told me that you were afraid for our safety though he would not tell me why, I presume he knows all of this?"

Mr. Darcy nodded in affirmative.

"You believe that he will continue to try to injure yourself and Georgiana and now me?"

Mr. Darcy nodded again.

"My father agrees that he may try it and so he is sending me with you away from where Mr. Wickham is, in hopes to keep me safe?"

Mr. Darcy nodded a third time.

"Are we to run from his evilness our entire lives?"

There was no response from Mr. Darcy.

"What is to happen when we have children, an heir to your estate? Will our child be hunted his entire life by a man who wants vengeance for something he did to himself? Are you to continue paying a worthless scoundrel all of your honest and hard-earned fortune in order to do what, wait for it to happen again and have to pay him even more?"

Georgiana had stopped crying and was sitting up looking in awe at Elizabeth. No one had ever dared question her brother in such a manner. Georgiana could easily see the sense in what Elizabeth was saying. Instinctively Georgiana had thought similar thoughts over the past year, but had not once said them aloud. Saying these things out loud it became clear to everyone that a different form of action must be taken against this vile and evil man, or he would plague their family forever.

"Brother, what Elizabeth says makes sense. If God is so willing there is more Darcys' to come, I do not want my nephews and nieces to live in fear of what he will do as we do. We must act somehow."

"Georgiana, do you know what you are saying? I paid him to help you, to keep you safe. If his lying tongue was to flag around town your reputation could be damaged or even worse yet ruined. I could stand anything for myself, but not for you. I paid him to keep you safe, dearest, and I will do it again for either you, or Elizabeth or any future Darcy's in an instant. Do you understand?"

"Yes, I do, however Elizabeth is right we must do something and if it requires knowledge of my folly to become commonly known then so be it. We must not live in fear, changing our actions because of him. I do not worry; someday I will also find an honorable man to love as you have found Elizabeth, one who will not blanche at my past, who will trust our family and me despite this episode. I will know then that I have truly found a man worthy of my love."

"Very well Georgiana, we will await the proper time and when next he tries to interfere we will utilize the proper methods to ensure it is finished forever."

All looked at each other in acknowledgment and that was the end of it, at least for the moment.

Darcy and Elizabeth continued their discussion of *The Lady of the Lake* and Georgiana, after realizing how tired the conversation had made her, turned to rest her head upon a pillow propped against the carriage window. She was asleep within a few minutes.

Chapter 21
London

"Colonel Fitzwilliam, you have just received this express, sir."

"Thank you."

Instantly noticing his cousin's hand he opened the letter to read, first smiling and then frowning.

> *Tuesday November 26th, 1811*
> COUSIN,
>
> *I write this in great haste late in the evening. I must first demand your congratulations for I am the happiest of men. Miss Elizabeth Bennet has agreed to be my wife. We are to marry in one month's time. I know I have become an impulsive man under her expert tutelage, but the story shall be saved for another time.*
>
> *I also write this to inform you of our whereabouts. First thing in the morning I return to London with Georgiana and Miss Elizabeth. Yes Georgiana is here, yet another story that I shall not currently entertain you with. We come because it has been brought to my attention that Wickham may be trying to cause his usual mischief and this time may have an accomplice at Netherfield.*
>
> *We must return to London for everyone's safety.*
> COUSIN F. DARCY

The Colonel knew that Darcy was capable of protecting the ladies and trusted his judgment in removing them from Meryton. He would have to visit in a few days to ensure all was right, hear a few stories, and offer his heartfelt congratulations in person.

Martha, the maid at Longbourn, did not know how to read in general, but she did know a few words and one of them was Bennet. When she looked at the note she saw laying on the ground next to the butchers the name jumped out at her. For that reason she picked it up and returned it to Longbourn where she was sure it belonged.

"Mr. Bennet sir, while I was in town today running some errands for Mrs. Hill, I found this letter upon the ground. I would have returned it inside the butchers except I saw the name of Bennet written upon it and since I can read that name thought I would bring it to you as it must concern your family."

"Thank you, Martha, you have done well, I shall see that it is returned to its rightful owner."

Martha curtsied and left Mr. Bennet to open the curious letter, not ten second later he was on her heel demanding where Jane and Mr. Bingley were.

"I know not sir, for I have just returned. Give me a moment and I will have them found."

"Never mind, Martha, I shall do it myself. Thank you that will be all."

This was the first time that Martha ever saw Mr. Bennet run in search of anything.

Almost two hours had passed since they had left Longbourn. Elizabeth had been informed of the long Darcy-Wickham past and she and Mr. Darcy had a wonderful discussion about their book "The Lady of the Lake". The conversation had ended though and they were presently sitting in silence. Darcy knew that Elizabeth's mind was disturbed from the way she was biting her lower lip.

"Elizabeth...?"

She looked up at him but did not say anything for a moment. Almost as if catching herself she said "yes, Fitzwilliam, did you say something?"

"Not yet, but I plan on it. Please come and sit here next to me." He grabbed her hand and before she could protest pulled her to sit next to him on the carriage seat. He untied and removed her bonnet, throwing it back on the seat across from them next to Georgiana. He then wrapped his arm around her and pulled her close, resting her back against his side and wrapping his arm around her. Leaning into her hair he whispered. "Fear not, dearest loveliest Elizabeth, love of my heart and keeper of my soul. No one shall harm you for they would have to go through me first and that will never happen."

Elizabeth loved having his arms around her but she needed to look at him so she unwrapped herself and turned to look at him.

"Fitzwilliam, I am glad that you love me as much as I do you and that we feel the same way, but I do not fear for myself, I fear for Georgiana. To be so young and have such a trial placed before her. No wonder she is so timid and fearful of making decisions. What she went through would break the most spirited girl and to have it occur to someone already afraid of so much. I begin to understand her more. It is my responsibility as her sister to make sure she is guarded from anything like this ever occurring again, and to also see that she makes honest and good friends who will not abuse her kindness and generosity, but help her develop into a wonderful woman."

Mr. Darcy was looking at her intently, praising the heavens for the woman sitting before him. He was surprised as she leaned in and kissed him. Then just about as quickly as it happened she turned and re-wrapped his arms around her as she snuggled in. Neither said anything for awhile both just savoring the delight of sitting together and touching.

It was not long before they too were asleep, Elizabeth wrapped in Mr. Darcy's arms and him resting his cheek on the top of her dark curls. This was the sight that Georgiana awoke to an hour later, which made her heart soar to see her brother so happy.

Georgiana could tell that the carriage was nearing London by the increased travelers seen on the road and the slowing pace. Not wanting prying eyes to look in upon her brother, she closed the curtains and let them continue to rest for another half hour smiling at the happiness that they had found in one another.

The November sky was darkening even more and the carriage was slowing, they had finally reached London. Georgiana determined that they were probably nearing Elizabeth's aunt and uncle's home so she decided to wake them.

"Brother," Georgiana said as she lightly touched his. Darcy opened his eyes and let them adjust to the darkness. "We are in London and I am sure we must be near to Gracechurch Street."

"Thank you Georgiana, I am surprised I slept as soundly as I did. I generally have trouble sleeping in a carriage."

"Well brother, I think it is understandable. This is the first time you have ever been comforted into sleep while in a carriage. It is only natural that you slept peacefully and soundly." Georgiana flashed him a smile so innocent he could not censure her for her impertinence.

"Elizabeth, we are almost to the Gardiners', you had better awaken and ready yourself."

"Ummm, I daresay I rarely sleep in a carriage, yours must be uncommonly smooth to allow me to do so."

Georgiana did nothing but smile as Darcy shot her a glance warning her not to speak.

"I daresay it is; I always instruct the driver to miss the ruts and potholes, thus making for a comfortable ride." Just as Mr. Darcy finished the sentence and handed Elizabeth back to the other seat next to Georgiana the carriage jerked as it hit a very large rut and pothole. All three burst into laughter, unable to hold it in after such an emphatic reply and contradictory occurrence.

Mr. Darcy leaned over to open the blinds in order to view the streets and determine their location. Just as the blinds opened the carriage came to a halt and Elizabeth exclaimed "Oh, we are here, I recognize the park just across the way. I take the children there each time that I visit. They love to feed the ducks at the pond."

The occupants quickly gathered their things and were ready just as the footman opened the carriage door and Mr. Darcy stepped down. He handed out the ladies and the three of them walked towards the entrance of the Gardiner's home.

"Miss Bennet!" The maid exclaimed as the door opened, "What do you do here?"

"I am come to see my Aunt and Uncle Gardiner. May we come in?"

"You may, but Miss, your Aunt and Uncle are away. They are not expected back for another two weeks."

"Two weeks, where are they?"

"Why, they traveled to Lambton to see Mrs. Gardiner's extended family. Do you not remember they do so every year at this time?"

"Oh yes, in my haste and excitement it absolutely escaped my mind, my father's as well."

Elizabeth looked at Mr. Darcy who could easily read her mind and nodded in agreement.

"Alice, when they return can you inform them that I am in town staying with the Darcy's at London House." Mr. Darcy handed her his card which she promptly passed onto the maid. "Upon their return you must tell my aunt straightaway and have her and my uncle come to the Darcy's that evening no matter the time. Will you remember to tell them, Alice?"

"Yes, Miss Bennet, I will tell them the moment that they arrive though right now I know not what day that will be."

"Thank you, Alice."

The three returned to the carriage and Mr. Darcy ordered it to London House, his residence. Secretly he was very happy that she would be staying with them.

"Mr. Darcy, I do hope that this does not inconvenience you or your staff by me staying at your home."

"Not at all, how could you even think such a thing? I could not be happier. Did the maid say that the Gardiner's were to Lambton?"

Elizabeth smiled and said "Yes, she did, my aunt was raised there as a girl."

"Ah, I see, did you know that Lambton is but five miles from Pemberley?"

"It is! Mr. Darcy, what a fine thing since my family visits the area every year."

"So it is. Shall we announce to the house tonight that we are to be married or wait until the morning, what is your desire Elizabeth?"

Elizabeth laughed lightly at his enthusiasm "I have no preference, Mr. Darcy, it is your house and your staff, what would you prefer?"

"It is not too late, and most of the staff will still be there since they have been planning for our arrival, let us do it tonight. I wish to share my joy with everyone and ensure they all treat you as their mistress and not as a guest."

It did not take long for Mr. Bennet to find Jane and Mr. Bingley in the garden on a walk at the pace he set out looking for them.

"Jane dear, will you excuse Mr. Bingley and me, but I have business we must discuss immediately."

"Surely, father, but what is the matter? You really look almost ill. Here, have a seat and let me fetch a glass of water."

"No, Jane, I am fine. You return to the house and Mr. Bingley and I shall follow shortly."

Jane did as she was told and once she was clear of the corner of the house Mr. Bennet immediately began.

"Mr. Bingley, sir, although I do not know you as well as I do your friend Mr. Darcy I do believe you are a man of integrity."

Mr. Bingley nodded his head, wary of the tone that was in Mr. Bennet's voice. "I am, sir."

"Good and you value Jane and her feelings?"

"Yes, I do sir, above anything else."

"Since you value her so much you would not like to see her upset or hurt in anyway?"

"I would not, sir. Mr. Bennet, what do you mean by all of these questions? Have I done something to lose favor with you, sir?"

"Well Mr. Bingley, I daresay I do not believe it is you; however, I greatly feel that it affects you."

Mr. Bennet withdrew the note from his pocket and thrust it into the hands of Mr. Bingley who read it immediately. Before he even quit the note he had headed for the stable, Mr. Bennet close on his heels.

"I believe I must take my leave sir, I have business that calls me away immediately. Please provide my best regards to Miss Bennet and her mother and let her know that I shall call on her as soon as I can. I trust you will keep this a secret, Mr. Bennet, in order not to injure the feelings of Miss Jane and her mother and sisters? I shall know how to act."

"I will keep it a secret as long as I can, but won't you come and say goodbye so that Jane does not worry."

"No Mr. Bennet, I am afraid time is of the essence. As much as I wish to I must be off." Mr. Bingley mounted his horse and galloped towards Netherfield with a look of sheer hatred towards his sister on his face.

Ten minutes after leaving Gracechurch Street the Darcy carriage was stopping outside a very elegant townhouse. Darcy first handed Georgiana out who ran directly up the stairs and into the house as the door was opened with impeccable timing by the butler and housekeeper, obviously they had welcomed home this duo many times. Darcy then handed out Elizabeth who stood eyes wide in amazement as she drank in the beautiful sight before her.

London House, as it was called, was a stately historic home built from dark red brick in one of the finest areas of London. The house stood five stories from basement to the top floor with large windows that overlooked a crafted and manicured garden. There was a walkway that at the end had a set of stairs that was topped with a set of elegant double doors. The doors opened into a sophisticated marble entry which had a grand staircase in the center that was wide enough for five people to walk up side by side. If you walked to the left and to the back of the staircase you were led to Mr. Darcy's public study, where he met for business dealings. To the right and under the staircase was a door that led below stairs to the kitchen and other places where the servants performed their duties and resided. To the immediate right was a glorious sitting room that Elizabeth ached to explore, from this vantage point in the foyer she could but see a few of the furniture pieces. To the left was a large dining room with a table that looked large enough to seat twenty.

Elizabeth began to wonder at the wealth of Mr. Darcy. *If this is his townhouse which I have heard tell is nothing to his estate, what must Pemberley be like?* Right about the time that she began to feel overwhelmed she was introduced to the housekeeper and butler.

"Mr. and Mrs. Robbins this is Miss Elizabeth Bennet." Elizabeth curtsied at the introduction and Mr. Darcy took a step closer to her, which put him very close. "She is come to stay with us for... well for this stay I am not sure exactly how long she shall stay, but upon her next visit she will be here indefinitely." This was said with such a smile that Mr. and Mrs. Robbins could not mistake his meaning but being the good servants that they are presumed nothing and must wait for his official declaration... but also being the good housekeeper that she was Mrs. Robbins felt confident that she could pry a little.

"Very good sir, I did not know we were to expect another so I only readied yours and Miss Georgiana's rooms. It should not take me more than a few minutes to have a guest room readied on the fourth floor; do you have a preference which room Miss Bennet shall reside in for her stay?"

"Yes, Mrs. Robbins I should like it very much if Miss Bennet could reside in the Lavender Room. I presume it is in impeccable condition and needs no special readying. I would prefer you to stay here and when we are ready we can escort Miss Bennet to the room together."

Mr. and Mrs. Robbins quickly glanced at each other in confirmation of their thoughts. The years together had taught them to understand each other perfectly and in this instance they both knew what the other was thinking.

"You are correct sir, it is in a perfect state and as I always do each week, it was dusted just yesterday." Mrs. Robbins was smiling to herself and to her husband, *the master has finally met his match and he has brought her here for a visit.* Few of the current servants were around when the late Mrs. Darcy had been alive, but Mr. and Mrs. Robbins had been. There were rumors surrounding the Lavender Room. It was commonly known around the house that the Lavender Room was the best, but no one for sure knew why as no one was ever allowed to go in the room, that is no one except Mrs. Robbins.

No one has ever stayed in the 'Lavender Room' since it was redecorated; the mistress had asked that the room be remade upon her last stay at London House. She died before ever returning to see it and to this day not a single person had ever been allowed to use it. The late Mr. Darcy would not allow it for it grieved him to see it and be reminded that his wife could not enjoy it, but when the current Mr. Darcy assumed responsibility he had told Mrs. Robbins that the first person to use it would be the next mistress of Pemberley and London House. He rationalized it saying that he would present it as a gift from his mother to his future wife since they would be unable to know each other. Until the day he was to bring her to London, the room was to remain uninhabited with the door securely locked. The only persons having access to the key that was hidden in Mr. Darcy's study being that of Mrs. Robbins and him.

"Mr. Robbins, could you call all of the servants to be ready in the foyer in an hour. I have an announcement to make. Mrs. Robbins, please retrieve the key and meet Miss Bennet and I at the Lavender Room."

Mr. and Mrs. Robbins, butler and housekeeper, smiled to each other knowingly as each ran off to perform their tasks, both knew the importance of their current tasks and both knew that this evening must be perfect.

Mr. Darcy took Elizabeth's hand and wrapped it over his arm. Together they began to climb the stairs up to the third floor where the family apartments were located. As they paused at the third floor Elizabeth commented.

"Should we continue Mr. Darcy, we would not want to keep Mrs. Robbins waiting. Did she not say that the guest quarters are on the fourth floor?"

"She did indeed, but why would you stay in the guest quarters, you are to be mistress of London House, you are to stay in the family rooms."

Mrs. Robbins reached the landing below the Master and Miss Bennet just as he began his tale. She stopped there to allow him privacy in his telling yet close enough to open the door quickly as he required.

"My mother had been in London at the beginning of her confinement with Georgiana. She ordered this room to be redecorated and then returned to Pemberley for the duration of her confinement. The room was readied for her just as she wanted, draped in the finest French silks and satins that money could buy. She had the bed, dresser, wardrobe, chairs and fireplace mantle designed and custom made by a renowned craftsman. Unfortunately she died before she could ever see the room. My father never once entered this room. He knew her hand was in every detail and it pained him to think of it. He had the key tied to a lavender piece of silk and hidden away in his desk. Georgiana and I never knew what the room looked like. Right before he died he told me of the room and the happiness that mother had in designing it. He told me that I could have no pain in using it and to have it reopened, perhaps moving Georgiana into it for her quarters until I married. I came here to view it and as I opened the door memories of my mother flooded me. She is in everything in this room. I can see her dresses as lavender was her favorite color, I can smell her in the dresser sachets as she always had the same. I can remember her favorite flowers as they are carved into all of the wood in this room. When it came right down to it I could not give the room to Georgiana, I again had the door locked and the key returned telling Mrs. Robbins that the first person to use this room would be the next Mrs. Darcy. Elizabeth, this room is my mother's gift to you, by exploring and getting to know it you will likewise get to know my mother."

This was Mrs. Robbins cue to move forward with the key. She held it out by the ribbon as Mr. Darcy took it and opened the door.

Mr. Darcy gently opened the door and escorted Elizabeth just beyond the threshold into the room. Mrs. Robbins waited in the hallway out of their way but close in case she was needed.

Elizabeth gasped as she entered the room. If she had thought that the entry and sitting room were elegant they were nothing compared to this room. The walls were painted pale lavender with a glaze that made them shine in the candlelight. She could only imagine what they would look like in the dawning sun. The bed was a large four-poster bed with a brocade silk canopy. Delicate Calla Lilly's were carved into the rich dark mahogany wood that made a perfect offset to the lightness of the walls and various materials. The mantle and other furniture were also all carved with the same delicate flowers. There was a large mirror above the fireplace mantle and a large painting hanging above the bed.

"This is exquisite Mr. Darcy, are you sure you want me to stay here?"

"Yes Miss Benet, I have never been surer. This room belongs to the Mistress of Pemberley and London House, although you are not mistress yet, you shall be very soon and I would like nothing more than for you to stay in this room." Darcy walked to her and kissed her forehead and then began to leave.

"I shall allow you time to get ready to meet everyone. We barley have half an hour now. Mrs. Robbins, please come here."

"Yes sir."

"Miss Bennet did not have her maid accompany her on this trip; I would appreciate it if you personally would assist Miss Bennet for tonight and tomorrow morning. We will decide tomorrow who will assist her for the remainder of her stay."

"Yes sir."

Mr. Darcy bowed to the ladies and left the room. Mrs. Robbins could swear she saw him wiping his eyes.

Chapter 22
Changes to More Than One Household

The three miles between Longbourn and Netherfield had never been covered as quickly as they were today. When Mr. Bingley arrived at the front of Netherfield he leapt from his horse and entered the house before a stableman was even there to take his horse. Charles hurriedly walked straight to the drawing room passing Caroline's main along the way.

"Pack my sisters trunks immediately with all of her belongings she shall be departing within the hour and will not be returning."

The maid curtsied with her eyes to the ground and then ran towards her mistresses rooms to do as she was told. Never in her life had she seen the serene Mr. Bingley in such a mood as he was today.

"CAROLINE," Mr. Bingley angrily yelled as he walked into the room, "you had best ready yourself because you are to go to Scarborough and not to return until Aunt Mary agrees that you are enough a lady to be fit for society."

"Charles, what are you droning about? I know not what you…"

Caroline's face paled as he thrust a very familiar letter into her hands.

"Charles please, let me …"

"No Caroline, you had best depart this room and this home and my life now. If you do you shall retain a portion of your allowance. If you do not I shall cut you off entirely for hurting my sister."

"Your sister? Why Charles, you are not making any sense for I am your sister and you are hurting me."

"No Caroline, from this day you are my burden but you are not my sister. I shall never tell another that I have a sister named Caroline. For I now have sisters aplenty to replace you."

Caroline was shocked and confused but said nothing as he continued.

"You had best be glad that this charade of yours did not cost me Miss Jane Bennet for if she or her father rescinds the acceptance of her hand in marriage you will be blessed to never see me again for if you do I will…, I will…, I will…, well I do not know what I will do, but I shall have awhile to consider it as you depart for Aunt Mary's and I stay here to beg Jane to forgive you and to continue loving me."

The full extent of his meaning set in and Caroline turned and ran to her room furious that she had been discovered.

One hour later saw Caroline and her maid in the coach escorted by Mr. Bingley's personal man, to ensure she arrived at their aunt's, letter of explanation in hand. Mr. Bingley had escorted her to the coach himself ensuring she left his house. As he did he explained to her. "Caroline, you will be receiving one correspondence from me containing papers regarding the full settlement of your inheritance upon you. You will no longer be given a regular stipend from me. You must learn to economize and budget for you are now dependent upon yourself. Expect the papers within the week."

It did not take long for Elizabeth to ready herself to meet the London House staff and twenty-five minutes later she was standing next to Mr. Darcy at the base of the stairs as all of the staff were assembling in order of their duties. Mr. and Mrs. Robbins were in the lead being butler and housekeeper.

"Good evening to each of you. I have called you all together to introduce you to a special guest." Mr. Darcy began.

"This is Miss Elizabeth Bennet." All of the London House staff bowed and curtsied appropriately, showing their respect for Mr. Darcy and his guest. They were amazed that he would gather them together for a mere houseguest; it was never done before, what made her so special? No one had to wonder long however for as soon as the completed their bows and curtsies Mr. Darcy continued.

"I want to be the first to inform all of you that Miss Elizabeth Bennet has done me the greatest honor in consenting to be my wife. We are to be married just before Christmas."

Applause and shouts of congratulations broke out throughout the foyer full of London House staff. Large smiles graced the faces of each person showing their happiness with the arrangement. All knew that there were going to be some changes to the household after having a reserved lonely bachelor and his shy sister as sole inhabitants, however instinctively they knew that this chestnut haired beauty standing before them blushing from head to toe peeking small admiring glances at the master would be just as good as the master to work for.

The applause finally calmed down and Mr. Darcy proceeded to give them the longest speech any had ever heard from a Darcy. The staff was more shocked by his speech than anything else as the master never told of his personal life and here in the next few minutes he opened it to ever person in the house. They all stood there listening and mesmerized at his story and clearly able to see his love for his future bride.

"You may all wonder as to the suddenness of my engagement and small amount of time before the wedding. Miss Bennet's family estate is in Hertfordshire where, as many of you know, I have been staying with my good friend and future brother Charles Bingley at his estate named Netherfield. Yes, yes, I see wide eyes, Charles and I are to be brothers for he has proposed to Miss Bennet's elder sister. Netherfield is but three miles from Longbourn, Miss Bennet's father's estate. We were frequently in company and in short matter of time both of us were lost. I convinced Miss Bennet that I could not do without her and she consented to be my wife. Georgiana and I had to return here to London for some pressing business matters and Miss Bennet came to stay with her family to purchase her wedding trousseau. Yes, I see wide eyes again. Miss Bennet came unexpectedly to her family; not knowing that they are away on holiday therefore will be staying with us until their return. I want each and every one of you to treat Miss Bennet with the respect owed to the Mistress of London House and Pemberley. Any changes that she requests to rooms make them. Any adjustment to schedules and duties fulfill them. Anything she wants or requests it is your personal mission to achieve it. Does everyone understand?"

There were nods all around.

"Miss Bennet, do you wish to say or request anything of the staff now?"

"Yes Mr. Darcy that would be nice. Thank you all for your warm welcome and acceptance. I am very happy to be here on a visit and getting to know each of you before I return home here as a new bride. Thus far I want to commend you on everything that I have seen. You all appear to take pride and joy in London House as it is the finest I have ever seen. I have no wish at this time to disrupt such a smooth operating routine and so all that I ask is for you to help me when I get lost and keep up the good job that you are already doing."

This was said with spirit and joy that only Elizabeth could produce and instantly the entire staff was put under her spell. Everyone was sure that the best mistress that could ever be found had just walked into the lives of everyone at London House.

With the announcement made Darcy and Elizabeth retired to the drawing room where Georgiana joined them for an hour or so before all retired early after a long day of travel.

As the evening came to a close Georgiana and Elizabeth were ready to retire to their rooms, each attempting to stifle yawns and not show their true fatigue. Mrs. Robbins came to assist Elizabeth.

"I hope you have enjoyed your first few hours at London House Miss Bennet?"

"Yes Mrs. Robbins I have, I could never have dreamed of being as happy as I am here with Mr. Darcy and Miss Georgiana. I have truly been blessed to have met Mr. Darcy."

"He is a wonderful master, mum; all here appreciate his generosity and steadfastness."

"I am so pleased to hear that."

Mrs. Robbins helped Elizabeth off with her gown and replaced it with her nightgown and a robe. There now, shall we take down your hair?

"Yes, that would be nice."

Mrs. Robbins began to hum a nice soothing tune as she pulled hairpins from Elizabeth's hair, until Elizabeth interrupted her.

"Mrs. Robbins, if you don't mind may I interrupt and ask a question?"

"Of course mum, anything you like, I will answer if I can."

"This is a magnificent painting here above the bed. I could never even imagine setting my eyes upon such a magnificent structure such as this one holds. It is exquisite how one painting can portray all of the seasons of a single location. The art master must truly be talented. If it is in this room it must have some significance. Can you tell me about it?"

Mrs. Robbins was gently laughing as she said "With pleasure mum. This painting is indeed special. This is the location where the late Mrs. Darcy felt most at peace shown in the glory of all four seasons. This is where she loved to wile away her time on long walks in the springtime collecting flowers, in the summer soaking in the heat of the days, in the fall admiring the colors around and in the winter praising God for the fresh cover of purity and goodness that graced the ground. This mum is Pemberley."

"Pemberley!" Elizabeth gasped the word as if in denial of the fact that it truly was, stepping closer to the painting to admire it more closely. "Surely you must be joking, that is Pemberley, I am to live with Mr. Darcy and Georgiana here?" Elizabeth pointed her finger at the painting as she looked at Mrs. Robbins.

Mrs. Robbins only nodded slightly.

Elizabeth returned her stunned gaze to the painting and just looked at it for many minutes before she whispered more for herself than anyone else. "I had no idea Pemberley was such a great estate."

This impressed Mrs. Robbins for it let her know that this lady was accepting her master on the basis of him and not the estate that he would be bringing to the match. Mrs. Robbins was caught in her own musings when she realized that Miss Bennet was looking a little pale.

"Miss Bennet, are you alright? Come, sit in this chair by the fire and calm yourself. Do you require anything?"

"No, I am just a little overwhelmed at all that I have just learned. It has been rumored that Mr. Darcy is wealthy and I had heard that his estate was grand, but I was not prepared for anything of this magnitude. Mrs. Robbins, my father's estate is but a small estate, my mother has taught my sisters and me all to run a household to the best of her abilities with the resources that she has had available, but I know nothing of running an estate of this size. What if I make too many mistakes and shame Mr. Darcy. I cannot do that to him, he has such faith in me. I cannot ruin all that he has accomplished. I know not even where to start."

Elizabeth had worked herself up to the point that she was just about in tears. "There now, no need to get all worked up. It will be well, both London House and Pemberley are such well oiled machines that they practically run themselves. In addition you have me and Mrs. Reynolds to help you."

"Mrs. Reynolds?"

"Yes, she is the housekeeper at Pemberley. We will not let you fail, because if you did we would not be doing our jobs. Plus, the master expects us as the housekeeper to ensure that you are informed of everything. Nothing will go wrong when we all work at it together."

"Thank you Mrs. Robbins, you have eased my mind greatly."

"Now off to bed with you, you have had a long day and I daresay tomorrow will be filled with house tours and shopping. You need to get your rest."

Elizabeth snuggled down between the bed sheets asking one last thing before Mrs. Robbins departed. "Mrs. Robbins?"

"Yes, Miss Bennet what is it?"

"I was wondering if in the morning I may have some paper and ink to write to my father. He is expecting me to be at my aunts but due to their departure from London I was brought here instead. I need to alert him of my location."

"Yes, I shall bring it up first thing in the morning."

"Thank you, I will see you in the morning." Elizabeth rolled over and was asleep by the time the door latched.

Mrs. Robbins stood outside Elizabeth's door with her head bowed in silent praise of the gift the master had brought to the household. She was sure that Elizabeth Bennet would make a fine addition to the Darcy family.

Mr. Wickham had left Meryton shortly after the Darcy carriage, only at the edge of town instead of veering towards London he hied his way towards Kent. He made quick time and not too late was ensconcing himself at the Inn at Kent, taking time to become presentable.

He garnered himself a table in the corner and sat down to a quick meal and some ale as he formulated his plan for an hour hence. Plan in mind and completing his dinner he retired to his room, gathered his calling cards and departed for Rosings Park for an evening audience.

As prompt as could be he alighted from his horse at the front steps and rang the bell. The butler answered and after being presented a card and inquiring to see her ladyship Mr. Wickham was seen into the drawing room where Lady Catherine sat on her throne reigning over the household.

"Mr. Wickham, to see you ma'am."

"My lady." Mr. Wickham purred as he bowed before Lady Catherine.

"What could you possibly want?"

"I have come to inquire as to the health and happiness of your family ma'am?"

"Do not play coy with me; I know you are not here merely to inquire about my family. Get to your point or leave, I don't have all day."

"Indeed, ma'am, that is why I have come. I was passing through Kent and heard of your nephew Darcy's engagement. Being as intimate with the family as I have been in the past, I know that he and your daughter have been engaged since infancy I thought I would stop and offer my congratulations to the happy couple. I had hoped to find him here since it was rumored that he is visiting with her and her family right now. Is he not here?" The last was said as Wickham looked around as if expecting to see Mr. Darcy and his fiancée.

"You say he is engaged?"

"Yes ma'am, you of all people should be aware of that."

"Indeed I am not. You say he is with her visiting family?"

"Yes, that was my understanding."

"You will come with me." Lady Catherine rose and crossed the room yelling for her butler. As he entered she barked her orders. "Ready my carriage, I am to London in half an hour. You Mr. Wickham will accompany me."

"Me, my Lady?"

"Yes you."

"I cannot, for I must return to my regiment. I am a soldier in her majesty's militia and I have only been spared a small amount of leave. I must return or else my wages will be cut. I cannot afford for that to happen."

"You WILL accompany me and if I must, you will be compensated for your troubles."

Very well my lady, however should we not wait until morning? It is late in the evening and dangerous to travel by night. I also must return to my lodgings for my belongings, yes tomorrow would be better don't you think?"

"I suppose you are correct; however you are to be here by six, for that is when we shall depart."

Hearing more orders being shouted by Lady Catherine, Mr. Wickham departed for his lodgings thinking that the audience could not have gone smoother.

Early the following morning the soldier's camp and Meryton were all abuzz with the news of a soldier's desertion. Colonel Forster was livid that a man under his command could condescend to leave without receiving leave to do so. It did not take long for Lieutenant Denny to crow all that he knew once someone mentioned that the two had been seen together in town yesterday afternoon. In no way did Denny try to make Wickham's excuses and get in trouble himself, he merely stated the facts that Wickham had left town towards Kent yesterday afternoon with the intent to return by this afternoon, he stated personal business as his reason to leave and that was all he knew.

With the knowledge that he was to return this very day Colonel Forster decided to await his return before taking action further then penning a note to Colonel Fitzwilliam and sending it express.

Thursday November 28th, 1811
Meryton Militia Camp
COLONEL FITZWILLIAM:
 Upon your last departure from town I told you that I would keep you apprised of Lieutenant Wickham's proceedings if they gave me cause to worry. Early this morning it was discovered that Lieutenant Wickham has left Meryton for Kent on a pretense of

personal business. He left with no word to his superiors or approval of leave. He is expected to return this afternoon.
CAPTAIN FORSTER

Moonlight still streamed through the partial opened curtain of the second floor window at the Inn in Kent. Mr. Wickham was just beginning to stir. He quickly realized where he was and what his errand was and leapt from bed with more energy than seen since he last tried to ensconce with Georgiana Darcy last summer. He grinned to himself as he readied for the day, packed his bags for his return trip and went down to the public dining room for a bit of breakfast.

By half past five he was dressed, packed, fed and on his horse towards Rosing's Park anticipating his arrival at exactly six o'clock, just when Lady Catherine de Bourgh was ready to depart.

He arrived in good time to join the carriage and by five minutes after six his horse had been tethered behind and they were on their way to London.

"If you excuse me Colonel, but you have received an express."

"Thank you Jones."

"Will there be anything else?"

"No, that will be all."

Colonel Fitzwilliam began to open the missive as Jones was leaving the room, instantly recognizing the sender as Colonel Forster. The missive did not take long to read and in even shorter time the Colonel had his horse called and was awaiting it being brought around at the front door.

No sooner had the stable boy handed him the reins and he was in the saddle did he spur the horse into a gallop, heading straight for the Matlock townhouse and some advice.

Colonel Richard Fitzwilliam wasted no time in arriving at the Matlock's London townhouse. He entered the house and sought his parents out in very quick order. They were still at breakfast although just about done.

"Father, Mother, it is good to see you this morning in such excellent health."

"Richard," his mother said her smile evident in her voice as she spoke, "sit down son, why you look tired. Will you have some breakfast? We are about done, but we will sit with you as you eat."

"No mother, I thank you I am fine. Once you are finished I have urgent business I need to discuss with you and father in the drawing room."

Lord Matlock looked at his son earnestly and announced, "I am done, let us go there now."

Offering his arm to his lady the three walked to the drawing room and gave orders not to be disturbed.

"Father, Mother, I have reason to believe that you may expect a visit from my aunt Lady Catherine as early as tomorrow."

"What, son you must be joking, Catherine has not left Rosings Park in well over ten years." Lady Matlock said laughing as she took her seat.

Lord Matlock instantly caught the seriousness of the allegation. "What makes you think so Richard, for something monumental would need to occur to make her venture forth?"

"You are correct father something monumental has occurred. Something I have not been given liberty to share though I will do so anyways."

Lord Matlock raised his brows curiously and looked at his wife who was all attention.

"Before I tell you please know that this is some of the most wonderful news and I am behind Darcy all the way,"

"Darcy, how does that boy do?"

Richard laughed "Extremely well I dare say, probably the best he has been in his entire life. Here read for yourself." Then handing Darcy's letter to his father and mother who moved close together to read he began to watch.

> *Tuesday November 26th, 1811*
> *COUSIN,*
> *I write this in great haste late in the evening. I must first demand your congratulations for I am the happiest of men. Miss Elizabeth Bennet has agreed to be my wife. We are to marry in one month's time. I know I have become an impulsive man under her expert tutelage, but the story shall be saved for another time.*
> *I also write this to inform you of our whereabouts. First thing in the morning I return to London with Georgiana and Miss Elizabeth. Yes Georgiana is here, yet another story that I shall not currently entertain you with. We come because it has been brought to my attention that Wickham may be trying to cause his usual mischief and this time may have an accomplice at Netherfield.*
> *We must return to London for everyone's safety.*
> *COUSIN F. DARCY*

"Engaged... Why who is she? Where is she from? Married in a month, preposterous, a wedding needs longer to be planned. Impulsive Darcy has never been before, what sort of influence could this girl have on him? Safety... what is going on?" All of this was coming from Lady Matlock as she read however Richard answered none of it. He saved his reply for his father.

"Richard, my boy, I presume you will explain how this relates to Lady Catherine and why Wickham's name is mentioned here."

"I shall, father, have you nothing to say for Darcy's news?"

"I have not, for I shall tell him my mind when I next see him."

Richard knew that it did not bode well, for had he been going to give approval he would have said so at once. He always gave approval quickly and disapproval waited until he had you in a position that he would be sure to win his point.

Richard, not having time to support Darcy further, told his father what he knew of Wickham in Meryton, his lies about Darcy and what he now appeared to be up to.

Lord Matlock agreed that this was one thing that would make Lady Catherine leave Rosings Park. They would handle it as best they could.

"Now Richard, tell me of this lady so I may be prepared to see Fitzwilliam."

"No father, you must meet her on your own. I assure you she is all you could expect from Darcy to marry in a wife. "

Lady Matlock interrupted. "But Richard, he has known her scarcely a month or two and now they are engaged and will marry in another month's time. Tell me, has he compromised her in some way and is her father forcing him to marry her?"

"Mother, how could you say such a thing? This is Darcy we are talking about. That thought is absurd, and you cannot truly believe it yourself so I shall dismiss it with no reply."

"It is not absurd; he is a man and has weaknesses such as any man may. He could have been bewitched by a pretty face and a well-placed comment."

"Again, mother, if it were me I would agree, but I say it again this is Darcy we are talking of, be serious."

Lord Matlock interjected here. "We are serious; Darcy must not know what he is about scampering off into the wilderness and getting himself engaged to some country girl. Why, we know nothing of her. I shall not approve of this; why, we all had such high hopes for him and one of our own fine London ladies. I shall not have some unknown fortune hunter joining this family because Darcy has a weakness for her eyes."

Richard started a little at his father's comment. "How do you know about her eyes?"

"What, what are you rambling about? I know nothing of her eyes. It is common knowledge that Darcy has a weakness for fine eyes. Why do you think that all of the ladies he sees walk up and bat their eyes at him?"

"Really I did not know it was common knowledge, but yes, as you say, she does have uncommonly expressive eyes."

Just then the door burst open and a haggard butler came rushing in ahead of Lady Catherine de Bourgh.

Chapter 23
Lady Catherine

Ten minutes into the carriage ride Wickham had decided he had made one of the worst mistakes of his life. No amount of money was worth enduring her ladyship in a confined carriage for this length of time. Her daughter slept and her daughter's companion silently knitted in the corner. That left Wickham to entertain her ladyship. To be honest, Wickham would have preferred it had he been the one to do the entertaining, but as it was he was forced to endure Lady Catherine's diatribe.

"This is not to be endured, it shall not be, my sister's son, offering marriage to a woman other than my daughter. He knows, as does everyone else, that they have been destined for each other since infancy. This shall not be borne, I will not allow it."

Wickham gritted his teeth and smiled as she continued.

"You must know that I take the trouble of knowing all of the ladies at court for my dear family's sake. I do that just so that I may prevent unfortunate happenings such as this from occurring. My nephews know not how to protect themselves from being ensnared by these fortune hunting man catchers, case in point being Fitzwilliam getting involved with some woman."

Wickham smiled in spite of himself. This only infuriated Lady Catherine further who completely misinterpreted his mirth.

"I suppose you are pleased with yourself."

"I am, for I know something that you do not."

"Oh, you think you do, well I highly doubt that, for there are very few things in this world that I do not know about."

"Well, I happen to discover last night who the lady in question is and know that you ARE aware of her existence, however knowing who she is will not make you any happier."

Lady Catherine glared at Wickham then spit out "Are you going to enlighten me?"

"Why you said that you most likely already know so I see no need to. It will come to you sooner or later."

"Mr. Wickham, let me be rightly understood. You will tell me said information at this moment or I shall have you thrown from this carriage."

Wickham smiled at the thought of getting out of Lady Catherine's presence; however his wallet had not been loaded yet, so he acquiesced to her demands.

"I have discovered that your nephew Mr. Darcy is to marry Miss Elizabeth Bennet. Miss Elizabeth, as I am sure you are already aware, is the second daughter of Mr. Thomas Bennet, cousin to one Mr. William Bennet Collins, the heir presumptive of Longbourn."

"This cannot be. It is even worse then I supposed, my nephew engaged to my clergyman's cousin. He wants to kill me, he does. This news shall be the death of me." Lady Catherine continued moaning about her death that her ungrateful nephew was causing for close to twenty minutes.

Wickham continued to half listen as he counted down the time before they would be in London and removed from the carriage. Through the depths of this near comatose state he heard Lady Catherine's emphatic exclamation.

"I suppose you are well pleased with yourself? If I remember right, you and my nephew have had some falling out and have not had contact for many years, though the particulars I am unaware of."

"I suppose you could call it a falling out; however the circumstances are so very trifling that I would not bore you with them. The particulars are merely that once we left school your nephew had an estate to run and I had a profession to obtain. We have seen each other often enough though. I have twice visited him at Pemberley to discuss my employment pursuits and we even crossed paths this past summer in Ramsgate. So you see, Lady Catherine, though we have not kept in constant contact as much as we should have we are far from being estranged from each other as you are led to believe."

"Oh, I see, I did not know."

"No my lady, how could you have known. Your nephew, if I am not mistaken, visits but once a year. Hardly enough time to hear all of one's comings and goings. One could not expect you to be so acquainted with all of his dealings. There are such better things to discuss, things such as family loyalty and all events that have taken place in the past year since your last meeting. Yes, I suppose with such neglect from your nephew one could not expect the two of you to know much of each other."

"Neglect, nonsense, I am nearly his closest relative and entitled to know all of his concerns. I keep in constant contact with him and am very diligent in knowing all of his comings and goings."

"Really, your ladyship, you were not informed of his engagement."

"Insolent boy, what gives you the right to address me in such a way? Who do you think you are?"

"Lady Catherine, I am a man who has come a long way to aid you and do yet continue to aid you. I speak as I find and no amount of intimidation from you will make me change my position. You had best get comfortable with it."

"I shall not get comfortable with it and you cannot make me. I shall know how to deal with you."

Wickham smiled with the knowledge that Lady Catherine would pout in the corner of the carriage the remainder of the journey to London. He was not scared of her, and soon he would be on his way back to Meryton. Fitzwilliam Darcy's life would be over as he knew it, and Elizabeth Bennet would be heartbroken back at Longbourn ready to be consoled. What pleasure, first to ruin all chances of Darcy's happiness and then to stomp all over his feelings by compromising the lady he will no doubt continue to love until he breathes his dying breath and quite possibly through his death and into the eternities. Yes, this was going to be grand indeed.

Lady Catherine looked at Wickham's face knowing that he had no idea what was soon to befall him in London.

A few hours later the de Bourgh carriage stopped outside of Rosings Place, a miniature rendition of Rosings Park, only set in London instead of Kent and without the park.

Lady Catherine invited all inside the house, assigning rooms for their stay and barking orders that they were to remain there until she returned from speaking with her brother.

The household was shocked at her arrival. She had not been there in over ten years and had not sent word ahead, and then as quickly as she had arrived she had departed leaving them to get her guests to their rooms.

Lady Catherine made good time in arriving at Lord and Lady Matlock's townhouse. It was but a few seconds later that she rapidly entered behind a haggard butler into the drawing room where Lord and Lady Matlock sat with their son Richard.

Without waiting to be announced Lady Catherine let known her demands.

"Richard, you will leave us now! I demand to speak with your parents alone." When no one moved she emphasized her point "This minute! Leave!"

Lord and Lady Matlock were shocked at her arrival. Although they had expected her to come no one anticipated it being so quickly. Although as it does, shock wears off and off it went.

Richard was standing to depart when his father stated. "No Richard, this is my home and your aunt has no right to dismiss my guests. I ask that you stay."

Richard nodded his head towards his father and resumed his seat. He was very interested at hearing the conversation and relieved that he could do so invited and not have to resort to eaves dropping which he certainly would have done.

"Very well brother, if you wish your son to know of the foolishness of his cousin I care not."

"If Anne has done something foolish I assure you that Richard will be able to..."

"ANNE! How dare you ever presume that my Anne would do anything foolish? I speak nothing of Anne; I speak of none other than your nephew Fitzwilliam Darcy."

"Yes, I presume you mean Fitzwilliam, as I have no other nephew that I know of."

Richard tensed at the mention of Darcy. He knew that was why Lady Catherine was here, but until that moment he had hoped that it was all for naught. He had not been able to get the point to his parents fast enough that he approved of the lady and so should they before Lady Catherine arrived and he feared that they would all agree and plot against Darcy. He had been unable to let them know that regardless of anyone's notions on the topic Darcy was marrying for love and therefore in true Darcy fashion, after his father, would not back down and if they did not embrace Miss Elizabeth Bennet as part of their family they had better realize that they will never see Darcy again, for he will stand by his lady.

"Well, brother, what say you to his foolishness?"

"Foolishness, why Darcy is such a strong and stalwart lad, I know of no foolishness on his part. You will have to inform me of your notions of foolishness."

"Brother, you are so tiresome. Surely you must know I am speaking of his presumed engagement to this young fortune hunter from Hertfordshire."

"Sister, I know not of what you speak. I know of no PRESUMED engagement to a FORTUNE HUNTER." Lady Catherine began to speak but he silenced her with a look and his hand held up in her direction. "I do however hear that he is engaged to a country gentleman's daughter who is known to be intelligent and have expressive eyes." Lord Matlock looked towards his son for confirmation. Richard just nodded in approval of the statement. "If they are in fact the same lady that we speak of then I suppose I have heard of our nephew's joyous news, how good of you to travel all this way to offer your congratulations in person."

"I do nothing of the sort. I came here to break them up and hear the truth, that it is all a huge misunderstanding. He must deny her and conclude with his family duty by engaging himself to Anne. You know as well as I do that this was our sister's dying wish. Would you deny her that?"

"I beg to have a different understanding, Catherine. If I remember correctly you expressed your wish of Darcy and Anne marrying to our sister as she lay dying. Anne's wish was that her son marries for love and that if your daughter Anne was the love he found then they should marry. However, if she was not then he should search her out. That is what I remember on the subject. If you recall that is also more in line with Anne's philosophy on life, for if you remember our own dear sister defied her family when she rejected her arranged marriage and sought her life next to her love, George Darcy. Correct me if I am wrong, dear sister, but that is how I remember her wishes. In fact, you should remember them as well, for her decision to marry for love left Sir Lewis de Bourgh in need of a wife, a title you proudly took."

"Brother, this shall not be borne. I shall not allow this to take place. I will send my informant Mr. Wickham on a little errand for me."

Lady Catherine turned in a huff and began to storm from the room in the same manner she had entered.

The mention of Mr. Wickham's name put everyone on edge. So it was true, he did head to Kent and address Lady Catherine. Their fears were becoming real right before them.

"Lady Catherine, did you say Mr. Wickham? Mr. George Wickham?"

"Yes, the very same, he was on his way through Kent when he heard of Darcy's engagement and news that he was visiting his fiancée's family. His long time acquaintance with the Darcys' made him assume Anne was the fiancée, so he stopped to offer congratulations. I have him staying with me at my townhouse. Once I return he shall be sent on an errand... I will not be upset in my determination to make Darcy see reason, acquit this scandalous presumed engagement, and marry my daughter. He is obviously blinded by a pretty face. It is a frequent fault with the Fitzwilliam men."

With her piece said, Lady Catherine turned and departed the room leaving behind a now furious Lady Matlock.

"Why the nerve of that woman, I have a mind to approve of Darcy's little lass unmet simply to put a burr in her boots. Oh the nerve of her to presume that the Fitzwilliam men are tempted by merely a pretty face. My dear, your Fitzwilliam TRUE ladies know that we must have a lot more than just good looks to entice our men. I daresay that I am come to the realization that our Miss Bennet must have more than just good looks if Fitzwilliam Darcy gave her more than one look, fine eyes or not."

Richard could not be happier but time was also wasting. "Father, Mother, as much as I enjoy this I must depart. Something has come up of an alarming nature that must be addressed immediately."

"Son, you cannot fool us, we know exactly what has come up, go, and take care. You shall update me upon your return. Be prepared for a large party at dinner for we shall send invitation to Darcy and his lady directly."

"Yes Father." Richard nodded at both and set out towards the door. Just as he reached for it he turned to his parents and said "Father, Mother, I know that twenty minutes ago you were less than pleased with Darcy's choice and that you are only supporting her because Lady Catherine was so wrong in her methods of refusal, but please know that you will not be dissatisfied or disappointed. As you say she must be more than just a pretty face, in fact at first Darcy scarcely thought her pretty, however she is much more than that. Her character, oh father, mother, she is truly one woman in a million and had I not seen Darcy's interest in her even before he himself did we may truly hate each other for loving the same woman. I am not ashamed to tell you, but Darcy truly is marrying his equal and should Lady Catherine succeed, which I assure you she will not, but should she, you will still need to welcome Miss Elizabeth Bennet into this family because kill Darcy or not, I would marry her in his stead."

Flashing his mother and father a quick glance he left them standing with their mouths open, shocked at what their son had just said. He ordered his horse readied and set off.

Lord and Lady Matlock looked at each other the shock still evident to both. Lady Matlock spoke first.

"Well my dear, I am astonished. Who could this little wonder be who grasps not only the heart of Fitzwilliam Darcy but also his cousin, two of London's most eligible bachelors in the palm of her hand and in such a short amount of time?"

"Yes, who is she indeed?" replied her husband.

After Richard left Lord and Lady Matlock he made short time in readying themselves for a morning call at the Darcy's London house.

Lady Catherine departed the Matlock residence in a rage and returned to Rosings Place no less fit. Never had she been so upset at her brother, if he would not assist her, she would just have to take matters into her own hands. As she entered Rosings Place she instantly demanded that Wickham be brought to her in the drawing room.

"You sent for me, Lady Catherine?" Wickham said as he entered the room.

"Indeed I did, come here at once. I am most seriously displeased: my visit to my brother was most distressing, he does not see reason to condemn the lady on my word alone, we must have substance. You will do an errand for me."

"No, I think I have done enough for you already. There has been nothing for me in all of this. I must return to my regiment."

Lady Catherine's eyes narrowed and her voiced dripped with animosity. "You misunderstand me Mr. Wickham, I am not asking you, I am telling you what you will do for me, or else there will be consequences. Am I rightly understood?"

Wickham was a little concerned with her tone as he knew her to be a formidable woman; however he maintained an air of indifference as he coolly said "Lady Catherine, until there is something in this for me I will do nothing that you ask. Am I rightly understood?"

Lady Catherine maintained her earlier look as she leaned back in her chair steepling her fingers to her lips. "Very well, Mr. Wickham, what is your price?"

"Twenty thousand pounds."

"Preposterous" Lady Catherine yelled in even more of a rage, "I will never pay that sum for some petty news I would have learned in but a few days. No, you will get no such sum from me."

"Alright, Lady Catherine, Let us first come to a price for the news already provided and then we can discuss this next errand, as you call it."

"Very well, Mr. Wickham, what is your price for the previous news?"

"Five thousand pounds."

"I must say, sir, that you have pretty high expectations for compensation. I will not pay that amount; I will however pay you fifty pounds for your efforts to relay the information to me in a most expeditious manner."

Mr. Wickham laughed "Fifty pounds, do you think me a fool? I will take not less than four thousand. The thousand I lowered is because I am humored at your presumption that you could get away with offering a mere fifty pounds."

Lady Catherine pressed her lips into a thin tight line, thought for a moment and then offered "Two thousand pounds."

"Well, I must say that we are getting a bit closer and reasonable in our offerings. Make it two thousand five hundred and we have a deal."

"Agreed, now let us discuss my next task for you. Shall we come to an agreement on the price first, since that seems to be all you really care about Mr. Wickham?"

"Certainly not, Madame, I must first know the task to know the importance when I negotiate the price."

Drat, Lady Catherine thought. She had wished he would agree. "Very well, as I said before, I need substance."

"Substance, my lady?"

"Yes substance, you are to return to Hertfordshire to search out any and all information that you can discover about the lady and her family. When I say information I mean scandalous information. I will give you two days."

"Lady Catherine, if I return to Hertfordshire I will not be returning here to report. I will be required to resume my duties in my regiment."

"That is your concern, sir, figure it out. You will report back to me here in two days' time and you will not see one farthing from me until you do."

"My Lady, you will be compensating me upon my departure for the information already relayed and while we are at it let us begin discussing my compensation for this new errand. Whether or not I perform the errand will depend on the compensation I am to receive for my efforts."

"Very well, what do you propose?"

Wickham eyed her ladyship greedily. He knew aiming high would settle him on a handsome sum and well above the amount he already had for the previous information, yet knowing instinctively that it would be below the twenty thousand pounds that he wished. With a quick smile he shot for the skies. "Twenty-five thousand pounds."

"No!" Lady Catherine stated quite unceremoniously. "In fact, this is highway robbery; I no longer require your assistance, get your things and remove yourself from my house."

"Very well." Wickham turned and began to leave. He knew she needed him and would not let him go far. He might as well play along - he was sure it would get him more money than arguing with her. At the door he paused and counted 1…, 2…, 3… before reaching for and turning the doorknob.

"Wait, let us discuss this a bit further."

"Alright, what do you propose?" Wickham said smiling, pleased that she had called him back.

"Well, I am a reasonable woman, after all, and realize that the future information is of more import than that already relayed so let us start there, that is, if you are reasonable as well."

"Very well, what is your amount, Lady Catherine?"

"Three thousand pounds, in addition to the two thousand five hundred you are already getting."

Now we are getting somewhere, Wickham thought to himself.

"My lady, do you not think that the information that will condemn the lady that your nephew loves and make him turn to his cousin for solace and to become his future wife is not worth at the very least ten thousand pounds? By marrying Mr. Darcy your daughter shall be gaining that amount on an annual basis. I daresay it is but a trifle."

"Perhaps if Mr. Darcy were paying you that would be the case, however he is not. For me it is more than a trifling sum. I refuse to pay it. You will receive four thousand pounds."

"Four thousand my lady, you insult me. That is not acceptable. At the very least you must offer double the amount that you are already paying me because the information is of double the importance. To be honest, even that amount is not enough. I will however perform this errand for the ten thousand I previously stated."

Lady Catherine was getting impatient and this gardener's son was wearing on her patience. She stood up and playing her last card walked to the door. Wickham got a worried look on his face wondering if he had pushed her too far. "I will pay you ten thousand, for both the previous information and the future errand, however the stakes just got higher. Now you will not only retrieve information for me, if there is not any you will create it by whatever means possible. But no matter what, Miss Elizabeth Bennet is not to marry Fitzwilliam Darcy. In addition, I am feeling kind, so I shall also not tell them where I got the information once provided to me. This should satisfy you, am I correct?"

Lady Catherine narrowed her eyes and pursed her lips in a manner that Wickham had never seen before. He went pale, that was one aspect he had forgotten, just assuming she would never tell, now he realized she would tell, and it would all be placed on his shoulders. Fitzwilliam Darcy would kill him for sure and if he did not then Richard Fitzwilliam certainly would. He knew that the ten thousand pounds were all he would get and he was mightily pleased with himself. "It is my lady. I shall pack my things and begin your errand at once. I will meet you in your library to receive my check and then be on my way to return in two days."

Wickham got up and brushed past her to retrieve his things. Lady Catherine retired to the library where she went to her desk, withdrew her bank book and prepared a bank note in the amount of ten thousand pounds. She then sat waiting for Wickham to return. Her mind raced and maybe, just maybe she even felt a little guilt at what she was doing. No, I have to do it, for Anne... both Anne's. For I know the truth. My sister wanted her son to marry my daughter. Ten thousand pounds is a small price to pay to have Anne as the mistress of Pemberley, something I never was, but was always jealous of. Anne Fitzwilliam Darcy married for love, and what did I get, her left over arranged marriage to a man twice my age that never loved me and always compared me to others? I doubt I shall even lose this ten thousand, after all Richard knows of Wickham. Regardless of losing it or not she thought *Anne shall be Mistress of Pemberley and I shall never feel guilty at achieving her happiness, no matter the cost.*

When Wickham returned Lady Catherine addressed him. "Now sir, I have written one bank note and you shall have the entirety in full now." Wickham smiled at this. "However, my man James, who is a retired assassin, shall accompany you until you return. He shall present himself as your man while he is with you, however if you try to renege with my money then he shall take appropriate actions to ensure my interests."

"Very well my lady you will not be disappointed." Wickham pocketed his ten thousand pounds and turned to leave, hearing her final parting words.

"While you are at your task I shall return to my brother's home to work on him and my nephew who were both so adamant but an hour ago."

"Both? I thought that you said you only visited your brother earlier?"

"No, I said I was upset at him for I saw him and his wife along with their son Richard. Are you familiar with the colonel?"

"Indeed I am, I am also in his Majesty's army as you know."

"In fact, I dismissed Richard before I spoke with my brother," Wickham visibly relaxed in the first second, but then instantly tensed again as Lady Catherine continued, "but he very unceremoniously contradicted my order and made Richard stay so I told them both my reasons."

"You did, and what did they have to say on the matter?"

"Oh nothing of consequence, that is until I told them how I would act on the matter."

"And what, might I inquire, did you say you would do?"

"Why exactly what I am doing, seeking information about Miss Bennet."

"Lady Catherine, it is imperative that I know this so that I may work around any obstacles put in my path. Did you tell them how you would obtain your information?"

"Of course not, I merely told them I would have my informant do a little more research for me."

"Do they know who I am your ladyship?"

"Of course they do, as you said you have been a long time family friend. It was only natural for me to tell them of your visit to offer your kind congratulations upon hearing of Darcy's engagement. I daresay the colonel was interested; however, my brother cared nothing for knowing who you are. Now off with you, you are wasting precious time." Lady Catherine smiled her evil smile and pushed him out the door, shutting it behind her. She instinctively knew that the bank note would never be cashed since Wickham would most likely not make it back in London's borders with the Colonel in his tracks; however, James would ensure that any information he learned would be returned to her. She laughed to herself as she remembered the look upon his face when he learned that the Colonel knew he was her informant. "This will teach him to take advantage of a de Bourgh" Lady Catherine said as she walked to the window to watch Wickham depart.

The Colonel's horse was quickly readied in a short amount of time and he was off towards the general's office. Support was what he needed; taking Colonel Foster's letter and his personal information that Wickham did not in fact directly return to Meryton, but was here in London, he presented Wickham's case as a deserter for papers to be drawn up. The letter along with Colonel Fitzwilliam's personal knowledge that he was not in fact directly returning to his regiment and that he had lodgings here in London saw the papers in his hand in fifteen minutes. His Majesty's government did not approve of deserters and quickly took action against any of them.

With papers in hand and soldiers to back him up, the Colonel led the way to Rosings Place.

Less than an hour after leaving the Matlocks' London residence, Colonel Fitzwilliam and his men were scattered about the park across from Rosings Place; a few were then sent to the back to guard the alley and even more sent along the street both to the north and the south.

Now all they had to do was wait, and wait they did, but wait long they did not, for a scant ten minutes after their arrival Wickham emerged from Rosings Place.

Lady Catherine was watching from an upper window. Two steps past the Rosings Place front gate she saw in excess of twenty militia men converge on Wickham, who already had his hands in the air, admitting defeat as he looked up at the window to nod with cruel disdain at Lady Catherine.

It took but a moment to have him in custody and all of his belongings confiscated and searched.

Colonel Richard Fitzwilliam returned to his aunt's door with a look of hatred and disgust on his face. He addressed his aunt. "Lady Catherine, we have just taken into custody a deserter of His Majesty's army and found upon his person this bank note that he shall no longer need. I shall retain it for the purpose of evidence against him in his trial for theft, for I am sure he is a thief, for no such sum could have been freely given him. It must have been stolen or removed from you by some duress, either way it is evidence."

Lady Catherine attempted to take the bank note, no remorse upon her face, but Richard was quicker and turned and walked away, note in hand, not looking back.

Chapter 24
Elizabeth's First Day at London House

Thursday dawned a beautiful day and Elizabeth was excited as it was her first full day at London House. She quickly got up and began to ready herself for the day, ringing the bell for Mrs. Robbins. Mrs. Robbins promptly arrived with a large smile.

"Good morning, Mrs. Robbins."

"Good morning, Miss Bennet, I trust that you slept well."

"Oh yes, what a divine bed. It provided such a restful sleep after such a long and tiring day yesterday."

"Wonderful, I am happy that it did. I was afraid when you rang so early that you had not slept well."

"Early? Is it not already a little past seven o'clock?"

Mrs. Robbins laughed, "Yes indeed, it is a quarter after. Are you generally an early riser then?"

"Why yes, in fact I have slept in today."

Mrs. Robbins smiled at Elizabeth's response.

"Mrs. Robbins, this room, it is utterly amazing, I knew when I saw it last night that it would be exquisite in the daylight and I was not wrong. Seeing the sunrise against the glazed walls truly is a beautiful and fantastic vision."

"I shall take your word, Miss Bennet, for no one has ever seen it but yourself."

Elizabeth smiled and blushed, amazed that there was anything that she could experience here in London House first. "I did take the opportunity to tour the room a bit more this morning and discovered that behind that lovely pale curtain there is an exquisite door. It was locked so I could not tour it, but may I ask where it leads?"

"Yes, Miss Bennet, it leads to the private sitting room."

"The sitting room, why there is another? Why should a guest chamber require two?"

"Well, this sitting room is the sitting room for this chamber, each chamber in the house has its own, however there is one set of chambers in the house that also has a private suite, including a sitting room connecting the two chambers."

Elizabeth blushed now understanding. "Ahhh, I see, so I am not ensconced in the best guest room in the house I am in half of the master suite."

"You are correct for the most part. You are residing in one room of the master suite; however you are not in half of it. The master suite at London House consists of nine rooms in total. There are only two entrances to the rooms, this one and the one at the end of the hall, which is the room the current Mr. Darcy has occupied for the past five years. Both of your doors are locked and no one has entered any of the central rooms except to clean them since Mr. George Darcy died. Between the two rooms is a large sitting room with four doors. Two doors lead to the individual master's and mistress's chambers including their private sitting and dressing rooms. The other two doors lead to another larger chamber and a nursery."

Elizabeth was intent on listening to Mrs. Robbins and keenly interested in the rooms beyond the door. "Do you think I shall tour the rooms, Mrs. Robbins, or shall they be reserved for our return after our marriage?"

"I do not know, Miss Bennet, that shall be a question for Mr. Darcy."

"Has Mr. Darcy arisen yet, or does he still slumber?"

"He is awake and in his study. Would you like me to show you the way?"

"Yes, that would be nice, thank you, Mrs. Robbins."

"You will also have stationery and ink there. I informed the master of your wishes and he has it all readied for you whenever you are ready to write your father."

Mrs. Robbins showed Elizabeth the way to the study and after asking the master if anything was needed departed to go about her duties.

"Thank You, Mrs. Robbins; we shall breakfast at half past eight."

"Yes, sir." Mrs. Robbins curtsied and went about her duties after informing cook.

"Elizabeth…"

"Yes, Mr. Darcy."

"Fitzwilliam, please call me anything but Mr. Darcy. I can handle it from anyone but you. To me you are Elizabeth and to you I would wish to be Fitzwilliam."

"Yes, Fitzwilliam." Elizabeth had walked closer to him and leaned against his desk as he sat at it.

Darcy cleared his throat "I hope that the room was to your satisfaction, that you slept well."

"Oh yes, most assuredly, I have never slept upon such a soft bed. I felt as if I were sleeping on a cloud, wrapped in the most exquisite silk. It truly is the best bed ever; perhaps you should sleep there and try it yourself."

The last was said innocently with no innuendos, but it affected Darcy none the less. He could not speak and as he began to stutter over his words Elizabeth realized her blunder and instantly became crimson with embarrassment. "I am sorry Fitzwilliam, I did not mean to imply, what I meant was, oh never mind, just forget it."

"Fear not, Elizabeth, I am not offended, I merely had to reclaim my senses as I considered what it would be like to sleep in such a place, upon a cloud wrapped in silk." Adding under his breath. "With your soft body wrapped in my strong arms as I hold you tightly pressed against me all night long."

Although said quietly and to himself Elizabeth heard every word and could see his chest rise and fall as his breath quickened, his knuckles tense and whiten as he gripped the chair he was sitting in and his dark eyes penetrating her, sharing every thought and desire in him with herself. She could not say anything; all she could do was return his intense look, her desires mounting as each second passed. It was a stand-off for each, neither wanting the moment to end, but also knowing that they were walking on dangerous ground. Elizabeth was becoming flushed and embarrassment was beginning to take over. She broke eye contact first and began to move towards the window. Before she could make it there Darcy was on his feet with Elizabeth in his arms embarrassment now being the furthest from her mind as she felt his warm lips upon hers.

"Elizabeth, I am very happy that you agreed to be my wife."

"As am I, Fitzwilliam."

"Now, let us ready for breakfast to further occupy ourselves."

"First I must write a quick note to my father. Do you have something that will suit for a few minutes?"

"Surely, your stationery is just there."

Elizabeth sat to write her letter and once done they stood and Darcy escorted her to the breakfast room, where each sat and began to fill a plate. Darcy was informed that Georgiana had called for a tray to be sent up, as she was still tired from yesterday's journey and so he and Elizabeth would eat alone.

"Elizabeth, what would you like to do today?"

"Well I am not sure, but I suppose I would like to see the house and have a nice walk through the park."

"I assure you that can be arranged. What say you of visiting Lord and Lady Matlock this evening so that I may introduce you?"

Elizabeth smiled, "Fitzwilliam, I would enjoy meeting your beloved uncle and aunt. I think tonight is perfect."

"I suppose while you are here you must shop for wedding clothes since that is your true purpose. When would you like to start?"

"I think I must wait for my aunt and uncle to return. I need my aunt to go with me. I know it will mean we will have only a small amount of time to accomplish it, but I have no other option."

"Yes I see what you mean, very well, until then we shall have to occupy your time with tours of the house and have you begin redecorating to match your desires."

"Fitzwilliam, I could not imagine changing a thing. Everything I have seen so far is exactly to my liking."

"Elizabeth, my dear, for one, you have not even seen the house yet and secondly nothing has been redecorated, except the lavender room and a few small places Georgiana frequents, since before my own birth. I had hoped that you would redecorate a great many things for no other reason than to let me see some changes around here."

Elizabeth laughed and said "As you wish sir, but it would help me if during the tour you let me know which ones you are most tired with, so that I may have an idea of where to start."

"Very well, I can do that."

The two finished their breakfasts and the tour of London House began at a leisurely pace. Elizabeth was in awe of all that she saw. The house was exquisite, she could barely comprehend that she was to be mistress of it. Frequently she caught herself wondering if this was real or whether she would soon awake to discover that it had all just been a dream. That in fact there was no London House, no Pemberley, and worst of all, no Mr. Fitzwilliam Darcy.

With tour completed Darcy addressed Elizabeth. "Well, Elizabeth, what do you think? Do you know where you shall start with the household changes?"

A sly smile crept across her face as she replied, "I do and I shall be sure to tell you just as soon as we begin our walk. For now I shall go ready myself and meet you in the foyer in twenty minutes."

Twenty minutes passed quickly as they both readied themselves for a November walk. Dress changed, coat, hat, scarf and gloves donned, Elizabeth headed to the foyer to meet Fitzwilliam.

"Elizabeth, you look like a winter angel. Are you ready?"

"I am."

The two headed for the front door. Just as the butler opened the door Elizabeth laughed and exclaimed "Fitzwilliam, you asked earlier what I wanted to change first at London House. I have my answer for you."

Darcy stopped and looked at her. "What is that?"

"I want to change only one thing…" Darcy raised his eyebrows at her. "I want to change the eligibility of London House's master."

Darcy let out a hearty laugh as he took her hand drawing her nearer to him. "That you shall, dearest Elizabeth, that you shall."

Darcy laid a very passionate kiss on Elizabeth and then turned to depart the house only to walk straight into a very astonished Lord and Lady Matlock who had heard and seen the entirety of it all.

Not missing a beat or embarrassed in the slightest, which also astonished his aunt and uncle, Darcy addressed them.

"Lord Matlock, Aunt, how fortunate it is that you have arrived as you have, for we were just about to depart on a lovely walk." The two were still speechless so Darcy continued. "I hope it is alright if I take a moment to make some introductions. Elizabeth, this is Lord and Lady Matlock." His familiar address of the lady did not pass them unnoticed, but further astonished them. Was this truly their uptight nephew? "They are the parents of Colonel Fitzwilliam. Aunt, Uncle, this is Miss Elizabeth Bennet, my fiancée."

With their senses slowly coming back to them Lord Matlock reached out his hand to take Elizabeth's. She flashed him a dazzling smile as she offered her hand to him.

"Miss Bennet."

Elizabeth took a chance and addressed him. "Lord Matlock, it is my pleasure to make your acquaintance. Mr. Darcy has told me much of your family and his love for you all. I am indeed pleased to finally meet you. Lady Matlock, it is indeed a pleasure to meet you as well. Mr. Darcy speaks highly of you, why almost as if you were his own mother." Elizabeth curtsied and smiled at her, hoping that she would not let Mr. Darcy down. She knew this meeting was monumentally important and that it meant a lot to Fitzwilliam.

"Thank you, Miss Bennet, I think of him as one of my own sons so it pleases me that he shares the sentiment."

"I know we were on our way out, however Mr. Darcy if you do not mind we should postpone our outing and retire to the drawing room for refreshment. Would you care to join us, Lord and Lady Matlock?"

"Yes, that would be lovely." Lady Matlock responded.

Just as they were beginning to take off their winter coats Georgiana joined them.

"Aunt, Uncle, you are here, how good of you to call on us. I see you have met Elizabeth."

"Yes Georgiana, we have just met. Will you join us for tea? Just let us all remove our outer clothing."

Georgiana rang for tea and Lady Matlock took a good look at Elizabeth as she discarded her outer clothes.

Elizabeth was dressed in a simple yet fashionable pale pink gown. Her hair was adorned with pink satin ribbons that left bouncing chestnut curls peeking out under her charcoal bonnet with a bit of pink lace. She had charcoal-colored kid leather gloves and a charcoal wool-lined long-coat that hung past her knees. The colors offset her complexion to make a very cheery sight. Her cheeks were flushed with a little embarrassment, yet her eyes spoke of her confidence and self-assuredness.

It took but a second for the assessment to take place before Lady Matlock smiled in spite of herself and began removing her own outer clothing.

Once in the drawing room everyone sat and Elizabeth and Georgiana poured tea.

Darcy began the conversation, aware that his uncle and aunt had not been as open to Elizabeth as he had wished. He had envisioned more congratulations and possibly even a strong hand shake or if he was very lucky an embrace. None of this had happened. Only looks in each other's direction. "Uncle, Aunt, what brings you here this crisp day?"

"We had a visit from Richard who mentioned you were in town. Since we were about this morning doing a few errands and a bit of shopping we decided to stop by and invite you and Georgiana to dinner. Of course, Miss Bennet is invited as well."

"Thank you, uncle, we are happy to attend."

"Very good, we dine at seven."

"Now tell me about your trip to Hertfordshire. I see that it was eventful."

For the second time since their arrival Darcy laughed. Not just the slight twitch of the lip and small noise that they generally heard from him, but a full laugh, a laugh that had not been heard in many years, not since he was a young boy. Each smiled in spite of themselves.

"Indeed it was, indeed it was."

Darcy narrated his time visiting Bingley in Hertfordshire, telling of the sport and riding paths, conveniently forgetting all that they wished to know. As the conversation progressed, Lady Matlock became irritated and when he paused for breath she began on her own.

"So, Miss Bennet, you are from Hertfordshire, Meryton is it?"

"Yes ma'am, my father's estate is Longbourn and it is but one mile from Meryton and three miles from Netherfield, the estate your son and Mr. Darcy inhabited on their visit to Mr. Bingley."

"Longbourn, Bennet, I have heard neither name before, does your family not frequent London?"

"No ma'am, we do not. Although my mother would have enjoyed it, I am afraid that my father would not. He prefers the quiet of his family party and library."

"Do you have a large family, Miss Bennet?"

"Some may think so, but I believe it is perfect. I am the second of five sisters."

"Five sisters! Have you no brothers?"

"No, not one."

"Is your entire family still at home?"

"Yes, I have four sisters along with both of my parents still at home. My eldest sister is also newly engaged and shall be joining us in London tomorrow."

"Who has she become engaged to?"

"Mr. Charles Bingley, I believe you are acquainted with him?"

"Yes, indeed I am. He is a close friend of Fitzwilliam and Richard, a very amiable young man."

"Yes, he is perfect for my sister Jane."

"So it seems like the society in Hertfordshire was quite agreeable to all this fall was it not?' This was said with a look at Darcy.

"Indeed, I think you must be right." Darcy replied.

Georgiana could not help but laugh a little here.

The visit ended shortly after with adieus until dinner.

Upon departure Lord Matlock addressed his wife. "Well, my dear?"

"Well what? Twenty minutes of trivial conversation is hardly enough to base an opinion on but if I must give one I shall say that she has worked wonders on Fitzwilliam, so she must have something to her. Did you hear his laugh? He has not done thus for many years. For that aspect alone I adore her. As for the rest we shall see, we shall see. Husband, can you believe that these two previously unknown Bennet ladies from Hertfordshire could capture of hearts of not one, not two, but actually three of London's most eligible bachelors?"

"No, wife, if I had not heard it firsthand myself I would not believe it."

"Poor Richard!"

"Yes, poor boy indeed, he will just have to find another though, he is young and will rally quickly enough."

Upon their departure Elizabeth and Darcy re-prepared themselves for their outing and upon opening the door were met with another visitor.

Elizabeth laughed and turning to each gentleman said "Well, Mr. Darcy, it appears as if everyone has conspired against our taking a walk. Colonel Fitzwilliam how are you today."

With such a greeting Colonel Fitzwilliam could not help but smile at the lady.

Darcy quickly explained about his parents' visit and invited the colonel in.

"I apologize, Miss Bennet, generally I would never dream of intruding and making you forgo the enjoyment of a walk, however I have some pressing news about... well, suffice it to say that it is important news that I must share with Darcy this instant. Could I beg your forgiveness and steal him for some... business." By the way he was stuttering over the sentence Elizabeth knew very well what the business was and wasted no time in acquiescing to his request.

The two men headed for the library, once inside with the door closed the colonel said nothing, he just looked at Darcy and handed him a bank note.

Darcy's face clouded over, anger and hurt rising to the surface. "Richard, perhaps you should have a seat and tell me about your morning." The colonel sat and began.

"Darcy, this has been a day let me tell you. This morning I received a letter from Colonel Foster." Richard handed the note over and nodded his head towards it in indication that Darcy should read it. He continued as Darcy read. Upon reading it I instantly set out to my parents to warn them of Lady Catherine's imminent arrival as I was sure it would occur. I wanted to prepare them, to ensure that they allowed Miss Bennet the opportunity to prove herself before they received a tainted opinion. Let me say, it was fortunate indeed that I showed up when I did, for not five minutes after my arrival and telling them of your engagement Lady Catherine burst in. I was still answering many of my parent's questions."

Darcy interrupted here "So that is why your parents called here this morning. They already knew of my engagement. I wondered how they could have already learned that I was in town."

"They called here? What did they say? How did they act?"

"Lord and Lady Matlock were fine; they met Elizabeth, talked for a few minutes and then invited all of us to dinner. We shall attend them at dinner tonight. Will you be there?"

"I would not miss it for the world. I will be there."

"Very good, now finish telling me all."

"Yes, where was I, oh yes, as I was saying Lady Catherine burst in and let all of us know her..., passionate..., views of your engagement that she had been informed of by our dear friend Mr. Wickham. Well, it turns out Mr. Wickham accompanied her back here to London."

"He did? But why?"

The colonel proceeded to tell Darcy all, right down to the recent arrest and confiscation of a bank note for ten thousand pounds from none other than their own Aunt Lady Catherine de Bourgh. Darcy was rightly furious.

A knock came upon the door "Enter," boomed Darcy, his mood portrayed in his voice.

"Sir, an express for Colonel Fitzwilliam was just forwarded from his quarters." exclaimed the servant.

"Very well, bring it to him." The servant did as he was bid.

Colonel Fitzwilliam tore the message open and chuckled at the contents. "I daresay it reached me a little late. The event is already taken care of. It is from Colonel Forster, a follow-up after yesterday's letter, informing me of Wickham's desertion."

The two continued discussion for a bit longer and then returned to Elizabeth and Georgiana, who had settled in the drawing room for conversation.

The afternoon walk was forgone and the afternoon was spent leisurely until it was time to prepare for dinner with Lord and Lady Matlock.

Chapter 25
Angry Jane

As Bingley awoke Thursday morning many of the events of the previous day flooded his mind, all except the one that he most wished for, the one that you would expect a newly engaged man to be dwelling on. This fact only made him more furious. His first instinct was to rush to Longbourn and be with Jane, thus soothing his troubled mind, but instinctively he knew that she would directly read his mood and then inquire about it. He did not want to disclose events yet, but knew if he saw his beloved Jane he would reveal all to her gentle inquiries and natural inquisitiveness. His thoughts were of the pressing business in London that he needed to attend to immediately.

Jane was indeed inquisitive and after breakfast she accosted her father in his library "Father, I demand an explanation. Yesterday afternoon you come out into the garden in quite a state, dismissed me and then not five minutes later, from the house, I see my Mr. Bingley, whom I might add has only just asked me to marry him, gallop away from Longbourn as if he was greatly upset. You then come and tell me that he has left on urgent business and did not leave any indication when he is to return. You will answer me directly Father; did you retract your consent for me to marry him?"

Mr. Bennet could not help but slightly laugh despite his most angelic daughter's anguish. "No my child, I did not retract my consent."

Jane stared at him, willing him to continue, but he did not. Letting out a near angry breath and strengthening her tone as Mr. Bennet had never before heard from his sweet Jane she said "Father, you must, I demand that you tell me at once what occurred yesterday between the two of you. You know that I would normally never dream of confronting you over your personal business; however this affects me as it affects Mr. Bingley. We are engaged and I will not see him injured by one of my thoughtless family. Tell me at once what you said to him."

"Well Jane I daresay that you are angry, good for you." Jane gave him an icy glare as she turned to leave the room.

"Very well father, if you will not tell me I will know how to act."

Ten minutes later, Mr. Bennet heard the family mare Nelly whinny in the front of the house and a moment later, the front door slammed. Mr. Bennet looked out his library window to see Jane atop a saddled Nelly and gallop from Longbourn in the same manner as Mr. Bingley had yesterday and in the same direction. Mr. Bennet wondered to himself "I knew not that Nelly could travel so fast." Then he groaned and called for his horse to be readied. He knew Jane was upset and he had never seen her thus, so he knew not what to expect, however now he knew he must follow her or else; depending on what occurred at Netherfield the night before there could be more emotions flying and despite the neighborhoods general opinion, Mr. Bennet did care for his girl's emotions.

Jane arrived at Netherfield at record speed and was quickly at the door slightly requesting, slightly demanding an audience with Mr. Bingley. Many of the house staff had resided in the neighborhood their entire lives and knew the Bennet family very well; the butler was just such a man. Never had he seen the quiet and serene Jane Bennet in such a state. This made him hurry all the more. "Mr. Bingley sir, there is a Miss Jane Bennet here to see you."

"What, she is here?"

"Yes sir, may I show her in?"

"Yes, please."

Jane was shown into the library. She took a nervous stance just inside the door, suddenly conscious of her actions as she realized where she was and wondered how she would explain herself. She nervously addressed Mr. Bingley. "Mr. Bingley, sir, I have come to... well that is to say, sir, I need to speak... what I am trying to..." Jane looked at her hands timidly and Mr. Bingley was upon her in an instant.

"Charles, my name is Charles to you, dearest. What is it that makes you so shy with me today? We have always been able to speak to each other. Ah, let me guess, I left in haste and did not bid thee farewell and you have come to terminate our engagement as a penance for my thoughtless actions." Despite how he was feeling Charles was trying to make light of the situation since Jane was clearly affected and he was afraid that before it was over she would be even more so.

Jane looked up scared that her actions had been interpreted thus. "Charles, no, please do not think I have come to break our engagement, nothing could be further from the truth. I have been so worried, and my father..."

Another interruption occurred as the door was opened and Mr. Bennet entered, "Yes, yes Jane, your father is such an inconsiderate man, for he would not settle your nerves and impart the gentleman's business, so you rush over unannounced in a manner befitting none other than your mother."

Jane looked down ashamed of how she had acted and her father's callousness towards her mother.

Mr. Bingley smoothed all of it over as he declared "Miss Bennet, Jane, could never offend me in any way. She is well aware of the fact that this is her future home and therefore she may visit it at any time night or day." Mr. Bennet winced at Mr. Bingley's words, but Mr. Bingley did not see it for he was grinning heart Jane like a lost schoolboy before continuing. "In fact, I am very glad that you both have come here for I need to speak with both of you. Jane, as your father I am sure imparted to you yesterday, business called me back here to Netherfield unexpectedly." Looking at Mr. Bennet he then continued "The same business I am afraid calls me to London immediately."

Jane looked as if she would cry, afraid that everything was falling apart around her. That was until Mr. Bingley finished his statement.

"I know we are scheduled to depart tomorrow, however I am afraid we must leave today; as soon as possible in fact. I do hope, sir, that this does not inconvenience you any and that Miss Bennet may still attend London for her trousseau with me today instead of tomorrow. In addition, my sister will not be joining me as she was unexpectedly called away yesterday to attend our Aunt Mary in Scarborough, therefore Miss Bennet will require an escort. If you have not a maid to send with her I will arrange for one of the maids from Netherfield to attend her."

Mr. Bennet knew that the business in London must have to do with the fact that his sister was now in Scarborough and knew that he needed to consent so that Mr. Bingley could accomplish his business and his Jane could get her serenity back. "Very well, Mr. Bingley, when do you propose departing?"

"Within the hour sir, that is if Miss Jane can be ready by then."

"An hour, why I can barely return home and call for my trunks in such a time, I suppose I can try, if I leave this instant." Jane was already standing to depart with a look of happiness and concern on her face.

Mr. Bennet laughed, "Jane dear, why don't you sit at the table over there and compose a list of the items that you want packed for your London stay. I see you are already attired sufficiently for travel, if Mr. Bingley can locate a maid to accompany you then you may depart for London with Mr. Bingley without returning home. I will deliver your note and have your trunks packed. They will be delivered to London this very day. I know that will inconvenience you as you will not have a dress to change into after your travels but I daresay with this late of a departure you will arrive in little time for evening appointments, your trunks will be there by morning. I am sure Lizzy will have something suitable for you to wear."

Jane jumped up excitedly and kissed her father. "Thank you, Father."

Less than an hour later, with a list made, a maid located and Mr. Bingley's belongings packed a carriage was on the road to London and a lone rider was pony-ing an old mare to Longbourn in the other direction.

Four hours later saw the Bingley carriage pulling up in front of Gracechurch Street.

"Miss Bennet!" A very confused maid exclaimed as she opened the Gardiner's front door. "What do you do here?"

"I am come after my sister Elizabeth to stay with my Aunt and Uncle Gardiner. I know I am not expected until tomorrow but I am come a day early. May we come in?"

"You may, but Miss, your Aunt and Uncle are away and Miss Elizabeth went to stay with the family that delivered her. Mr. and Mrs. Gardiner are not expected back for another two weeks."

"Two weeks, where are they?"

"Why, they traveled to Lambton to see Mrs. Gardiner's extended family. Do you not remember, they do so every year at this time?"

"Oh yes, I'm afraid it has escaped everyone's mind."

The maid smiled, "Yes Miss Bennet, your sister said the same thing,"

Jane looked at Mr. Bingley who smiled, "Well it appears as if I will be escorting you to Darcy's London House as well."

"Alice, when they return can you inform them that I am in town staying with Elizabeth at London House. Mr. Bingley, do you have a card to leave for my uncle?"

Mr. Bingley handed his card to Alice as she responded. "Yes, Miss Bennet, I will tell them the moment that they arrive though right now I know not what day exactly that will be."

"Thank you, Alice."

They returned to the Bingley carriage and directed it towards London House.

Mr. Bennet returned home to a household that was in a very agitated state. He had not seen fit to inform Mrs. Bennet of either his or Jane's departures earlier and therefore Mrs. Bennet was in full thralls of a fit of nerves that defied any fit she had ever had to date.

"Oh Mr. Bennet, you are come, I have been searching for you all day." Mr. Bennet rolled his eyes at his wife since it had not yet been two hours ago he had been sitting in his library.

"We are all in an uproar, Jane is missing."

"Missing of what do you mean, why I just sent her off in the coach to London with Mr. Bingley less than half an hour ago. Has something befallen the coach, has she been kidnapped?"

Mrs. Bennet sat with her mouth open trying to process the information that was related to her. Mr. Bennet just stood there smiling.

"Mr. Bennet, of what do you speak, Jane is not to leave until tomorrow. Why is she gone already and without taking leave of me? That is not like her."

"Well my dear, Jane and I had unexpected business with Mr. Bingley this morning and while there, Mr. Bingley received a note that called him immediately to London. I had to make a choice my dear, either refuse to allow Jane to go purchase her trousseau in London or allow her to leave within the hour with one of Mr. Bingley's maids as escort. Why I have a note from her here detailing the items she wants sent after her. I need them gathered immediately so that I may send her trunks with Mr. Hill to London this very afternoon."

"Why Mr. Bennet, what a good father you are, always watching out for your girls' best interest. Here, hand me that letter." With that Mrs. Bennet stood, snatched the letter from Mr. Bennet's hand and began yelling for Mrs. Hill.

"Hill, Hill, oh where are you. Yes, yes there you are. Fetch Miss Jane's trunks for me immediately, we must get them packed so that they may be delivered to London."

Mr. Bennet retired to his library to await the announcement that Jane's trunks were ready. He sat at his desk and noticed a letter addressed to him from Lizzy.

Oh, what a good girl to send word of her safe arrival to me, he thought as he opened the letter. The contents however caused him to call Mr. Hill to ready his trunks as he would be delivering Miss Jane's trunks to London himself.

Mr. Bennet located Mrs. Bennet to impart his plans. "My dear, I fear I must also hie to London for I have just received word from Lizzy that Mr. and Mrs. Gardiner are on their annual trip so Lizzy and Jane cannot stay there. Instead they are being lodged at Mr. Darcy's London House. I will be delivering Jane's trunks to London myself so as to also be able to ensure that they have the proper chaperones for their residence there. If there are not sufficient chaperones I fear that I will either be forced to return with the girls with me or stay there with them myself."

"Oh Mr. Bennet, why don't we all go?"

"Because the wedding is too close and I fear the girls will not have a proper ceremony if someone does not stay here to oversee it. No my dear, you must stay here to ensure a wedding fitting men of Mr. Darcy's and Mr. Bingley's stations is planned. I will however deliver a note to them by you if you prepare one."

A few hours later Mr. Bennet was riding in his carriage two trunks strapped to the back, a letter not for his daughters, but instead for Mr. Darcy secure in his vest pocket and a large smile upon his face. If all went his way then he would be residing in London for a few weeks, at least enjoying his days in the London House Library.

The party at London House was just breaking up to prepare for dinner when Mr. Bingley and Jane were announced.

Elizabeth rushed to her sister. "Jane, what do you do here? We did not expect you until tomorrow, and in fact in all honesty I was not sure father would let you come after he receives my letter stating that the Gardiners are away from town."

"Well something unexpected arrived and Charles was required to return to London today. We departed before any post was received. We are only just arrived but we did stop at Gracechurch Street."

Jane looked at Mr. Bingley. "Darcy, I have urgent business and I must discuss it with you soon, however first I would ask if Miss Jane can stay here with her sister. I unfortunately do not have a chaperone for her beyond the maid we brought from Netherfield as Caroline is in Scarborough with Aunt Mary for an undetermined amount of time."

Darcy looked at Bingley slyly. Darcy knew that Caroline hated Aunt Mary and had in fact been avoiding her visits to Scarborough for nearly ten years. She certainly was not there willingly and Darcy knew it must have something to do with Bingley's urgent business.

"Yes of course, Miss Bennet is welcome here, you need not even ask."

Mrs. Robbins was called. "Mrs. Robbins, would you prepare another room for Miss Jane Bennet, she is come to stay here with her sister, Miss Elizabeth. Please see that her room is near Miss Elizabeth's and have her things delivered directly."

Jane blushed and responded to Mr. Darcy's request to the housekeeper, "Um… Mr. Darcy… there is no need as my trunks will not arrive until this evening or even tomorrow. Mr. Bingley I am sure will tell all." Then turning to Elizabeth she said "I am afraid, dear sister, that I must beg a dress from you."

"Oh Jane, you know you need but ask. In fact if you recall I borrowed one of your dresses so you may wear your own. Come let us get you refreshed. Mr. Darcy, Georgiana and I are attending dinner with Lord and Lady Matlock but I daresay you will be comfortable waiting our return."

"Elizabeth-" Darcy interrupted. "if your sister is not too tired I will send a note to my Aunt and Uncle announcing an enlargement to our party. What say you, Bingley, Miss Bennet?"

Jane and Bingley nodded at one another "Very well, Darcy, if they approve then we accept."

Darcy wrote a quick note to his aunt and uncle requesting an enlarged party and it was not acceptable that they reschedule. They quickly responded that Mr. Bingley and his soon to be bride and sister to Miss Elizabeth Bennet were welcome at their table any day. The fact of the matter was they were dying to see the eldest Miss Bennet, second to steal the heart of one of London's eligible bachelors, Mr. Bingley, and what better way to get an early introduction.

Elizabeth and Jane departed to prepare and Bingley took some time to inform Darcy of everything that had occurred the last two days. Darcy was shocked and angered, yet he kept himself in check, for he could see the pain and anguish on his friend's countenance.

"Bingley, man, I will attend your solicitors with you if you wish. I see that by allowing your sister to go on paying court to me as she has for years without letting her know my true feelings, might I add that I did that for fear of hurting her, that I have caused part of this disharmony. I will aid you in making it right. I commend you for your actions and agree with your methods; this is best for you and your lady."

"Thank you, Darcy, I would like that. Now, I must get ready as well. I have my belongings, would you mind if I used a room to ready myself as well, as I have not time to return to Grosvenor Square presently?"

"Certainly, follow me."

An hour later saw the entire party refreshed, dressed, and ready to depart for the Matlocks' London residence.

Upon arrival in front of the Matlocks' all removed themselves from the carriage and Darcy led the way, escorting Elizabeth and Georgiana on each arm. Bingley followed close behind, escorting Jane.

The entire party was shown in and outerwear was removed. Lord and Lady Matlock, along with their son Colonel Fitzwilliam, were just entering the foyer as the task was completed.

"Aunt, Uncle, you of course remember Mr. Charles Bingley, well, this is his fiancée and sister to Miss Elizabeth, Miss Jane Bennet."

Jane curtsied in the acknowledgment of all.

"Welcome," boomed Lord Matlock. "You are of course all welcome."

"Come, join us in the drawing room" said Lady Matlock, dinner should be ready shortly.

Everyone entered the drawing room and took their seats on the comfortable sofas and beautiful armchairs.

Lady Matlock had been able to inspect Elizabeth earlier that day, so her attention was on Jane. She was easily able to view her as they all walked in and sat down. On the surface Jane was everything and more than the lady expected to come from a small country town in Hertfordshire, as was her sister Elizabeth. Lady Matlock was pleased with all that she was seeing of this remote family so far. Appearances can be deceiving, though, so it took a good ten minutes of light questioning before Lady Matlock had confirmed her initial opinion that the ladies were women of good breeding and that they each held true affection for the men that had asked for their hands. Lady Matlock could not ask for anything more for the two young men who despite not being her own sons in flesh, were by heart.

The dinner bell rang and all adjourned to the dining room for a pleasant dinner and conversation. Near the middle of dinner the butler entered with a note for Mr. Darcy.

Mr. Darcy read the note, slightly chuckling to himself.

"Aunt, Uncle, it seems I must beg you allow an addition to the party, or else depart immediately."

Lord Matlock looked at his nephew inquisitively and inquired "If you feel it is necessary you know you may invite anyone to join us, but may I ask who and why?"

"It is a Mr. Thomas Bennet, father to Miss Elizabeth and Miss Jane. It seems he received Miss Bennet's letter this morning announcing that their Aunt and Uncle Gardiner who reside here in London were unable to receive them due to their being away from home and so it seems as he states here, "I have taken it upon myself, difficult task as it may be, to either return directly with my daughters to Longbourn sans trousseau or take up residence in the Darcy London House Library, ensuring proper chaperones are available at all times." He leaves it up to me to decide which fate he will have."

Although the Matlock's did not know Mr. Bennet they could tell by the light air that their nephew was portraying while reading the note that he was a teasing and fun-loving sort of man. In addition, with two such amiable daughters how could he be anything but a proper gentleman?

Lord Matlock turned to his butler and stated "Show him in."

Mr. Bennet was shown into the Matlock dining room, making the appropriate bow to all in the room. Mr. Darcy instantly greeted him like a long-lost friend despite the fact that they had seen each other only the day before and Elizabeth looked on the pair, pleased at how well her beloved father and intended were getting along.

Mr. Darcy made the introduction of Mr. Bennet to Lord and Lady Matlock and Colonel Fitzwilliam and a plate was added next to Colonel Fitzwilliam so that Mr. Bennet could eat with them.

Lord Matlock began the conversation. "So, you have come to keep an eye on your daughters, have you, Mr. Bennet?"

"Indeed, I received Elizabeth's missive late this morning telling me of her change of residence and since I had also just sent Jane off as well a few hours earlier, I thought it best to come and ensure their proper accommodations or escort them back home." Mr. Bennet looked at Mr. Darcy as he stated "proper accommodations" and was pleased to see the gentleman blush a little.

Lord Matlock picked up his glass of wine in order to hide his smile at the subtle insinuation that Mr. Bennet did not fully trust his two daughters into the hands of their intendeds so easily.

Mr. Darcy interrupted Lord Matlock's musings as he addressed Mr. Bennet and the ladies. "I assure you, sir, that your daughters have proper accommodations and chaperones; however we are pleased with your coming. I would hope that you and the ladies decide on staying at London House instead of rushing back to Longbourn. It would be a pity to come all this way and not allow the ladies time to shop for their trousseau."

"Yes, yes, thank you for your benevolence, Mr. Darcy, I am sure you have nothing more in mind except that the ladies here have adequate trousseau upon entering the marriage state."

Lord Matlock laughed aloud at such a statement, he could not help himself. Glancing around the table he could see flushed faces on many of those in attendance.

Mr. Darcy, who had colored as well, was composed enough to answer, although coloring even more at the statement. "As much as the Miss Bennet's trousseau interests me, it is their pleasure with this trip and even more a practical issue that is my primary interest."

"A practical issue, well, be sure to enlighten us."

Everyone was interested in what he would say here.

"Well, sir, Miss Elizabeth has only been able to have a small preliminary tour of London House, her future home. As of yet she has not told me which alterations she would like made."

Lord and Lady Matlock each almost choked on a bite of dinner as this was said and Elizabeth colored. None of this was lost upon Mr. Bennet.

He began to speak but was interrupted by Mr. Darcy. "I might add that it would please Mrs. Bennet to no end to know that I ensured her daughter Elizabeth had every chance to redecorate London House in any way that she sees fit."

"Ahhhh, I see your point Mr. Darcy, in fact I have a letter here for you from Mrs. Bennet. I shall give it to you this evening when we discuss this further. For I gather another discussion is needed if the response of many here at the table is any indication. It appears if there may be more to this redecorating business than meets the eye."

Elizabeth was studious of her hands and Mr. Darcy simply looked at her, smiled, and stated "It would be my pleasure, Mr. Bennet.

Dinner came to an end and the men all adjourned to the library. Once the door closed Lord Matlock positioned himself next to Mr. Bennet. He knew that this position would be where he would obtain the most enjoyment from the evening. "Mr. Bennet," he began "it is indeed a pleasure to meet you; I met your lovely daughter Miss Elizabeth this morning as she was informing Mr. Darcy of her first change to London House. So I am assured of the fact that she has at least begun to tell Mr. Darcy what changes she would like to make."

This was said as he watched Mr. Darcy out of the corner of his eye. Mr. Darcy had his glass of port halfway to his lips when he stopped and stared at the two gentlemen astonished that his uncle would broach such a topic, especially in company, even company as intimate as theirs.

"Indeed, Lord Matlock, which room was it that Lizzy wanted altered. Knowing my Lizzy she has shocked you with wanting to alter Mr. Darcy's study or library or some other room that she should not be worrying about."

"No, quite the contrary, Mr. Bennet, no such rooms were on her agenda, she only voiced her opinion to changing the state of one thing in the entire house… that of Mr. Darcy's marriage eligibility status."

Mr. Darcy was thoroughly embarrassed, the Colonel was raging with laughter, Bingley slapped him on the back and said "Good for you, old man." Mr. Bennet laughed as he said "Yes, that sounds like my bold Lizzy."

"Oh, but there is more." Lord Matlock stated.

All eyes looked to him inquisitively. "The two were getting ready to depart on a walk when we arrived and the door was ajar when she said this. Upon completion of her acknowledgment, Mr. Darcy praised her decision in the best manner possible with the front door ajar for all and sundry to see. I must say it was quite a sight to walk up the front steps hearing this acknowledgment and then to see Fitzwilliam here worshiping her face as he was."

The Colonel and Bingley were whooping at Darcy, slapping his back and congratulating him on stealing a kiss.

Mr. Bennet could not resist adding to the story "Is that all, Lord Matlock, well I suppose we can let this pass for the time being as it is nothing compared to the scene I caught them in at Netherfield the night of the ball. It is a good thing he had already asked her to marry him or else we may not all be meeting on as friendly of terms, for he would be marrying her at the point of my shotgun."

Mr. Darcy felt it necessary to defend Elizabeth here as this was getting a little out of hand. "Uncle, Mr. Bennet, I assure you both that Miss Elizabeth is a lady and that she would never allow anyone, even me, as her intended to soil her reputation in any way. She has been raised by you as a gentleman's daughter and I pity the fool who tries to impose himself on her and I would pity myself, if I were to push her past the bounds of propriety that she is well aware of. I am sure I would be sporting the shape of a lady's hand across my cheek if I attempted more than I ought."

Mr. Bennet felt it necessary to ease his troubles "Yes, son, you are correct; my Lizzy would not stand for it, would she? You are a good man, I trust you and am sure that your uncle, cousin and friend here know you well enough to know that you would never do such a thing. We are just having sport with you. In fact, knowing you better then even I do they are probably astonished that you even came close to kissing a lady, let alone an entire session of it that had to be interrupted by her father and another in front of an audience."

All men laughed for a few minutes and then settled into amiable conversation; it was but a few short minutes until the conversation made it to the reason all were in London. Colonel Fitzwilliam began the ill conversation.

"Father, Mr. Bennet," and then nodding at Mr. Bingley he continued "earlier this day I made an unfortunate discovery. I have already informed Darcy about this however I feel both of you should also be aware. I apprehended Mr. Wickham here in London."

The men interrupted him with exclamations of joy until they noticed Darcy and Fitzwilliam were not joining them in their joy.

"May I continue?"

"Indeed, son, go on." Lord Matlock said apprehensively.

"As I was saying, I have apprehended Mr. Wickham; however upon apprehension of him I discovered a ten thousand pound note on his person from our aunt and your sister Lady Catherine de Bourgh. It appears as if she had paid Wickham to ensure Darcy and Miss Bennet's wedding does not occur." The colonel pulled the noted from his pocket for all to inspect.

Heavy breathing was heard around the room but silence otherwise. Finally Lord Matlock spoke. "I shall know how to handle this. Thank you, boys, think no more of it. You shall not be bothered anymore. Let us have more pleasant conversation by joining the ladies."

"Gentlemen, before we depart may I speak?" inquired Mr. Bingley. The gentlemen all nodded their approval. "Unfortunately my business here in London overlaps with some of yours." Bingley informed those in the room who did not already have knowledge of Caroline Bingley's doings of what had been done. It was decided that Mr. Bennet and Mr. Darcy would accompany Mr. Bingley to his solicitor for a joint purpose; that of his sister and his marriage, to aid him in his settlement of her inheritance onto his sister and also to complete the marriage documents for his marriage to Miss Jane Bennet.

Discussions coming to a close the gentlemen joined the ladies in the drawing room.

The conversation in the drawing room was of an infinitely more amiable topic. The ladies had entered and had five minutes of trivial conversation on the weather, their travels and general topics normally discussed in a parlor of women who were just becoming acquainted with one another and who were respecting the differences of rank and station.

Elizabeth was the first one brave enough to address her ladyship instead of just responding to her. "Lady Matlock, I would like to thank you on two accounts this evening. First of allowing us to invite my sister Jane and Mr. Bingley with such little advance notice and second for allowing our father to join us uninvited and in the middle of your dinner party."

"Fear not, Miss Elizabeth, you are to be a part of our family now and by extension your family is also a part of us. They are welcome in our home at any time. Not to mention Mr. Bingley is practically another son."

"Thank you, Lady Matlock."

"Aunt, you may call me Aunt, just as Fitzwilliam and Georgiana do."

"Thank you, Aunt."

"So you have an aunt and uncle that live here in London, do you?"

"Yes, Edward and Madeline Gardiner, my uncle has a very successful warehouse and resides near it, in Gracechurch Street."

"Madeline Gardiner? Is she the same Madeline Gardiner from Lambton in Derbyshire?"

"Yes, the very same."

Everyone's interest was growing.

"Why, she is your aunt? Wonderful, she and I went to the same ladies' school growing up! I was years ahead, however she and I have met many times over the years at charity aides and fundraising events. I am proud to say that she is one of my friends. She is very active in the London community and your uncle is known for his generosity of donations to our auctions and fundraisers. What a coincidence, I am more and more pleased that you have such an amiable family."

Relief was evident on Elizabeth's face. She had heard of many noble families that spurned their sons and nephews marriage choices on the grounds of family connections. As Lady Matlock had asked her questions Elizabeth's concerns had risen, however at Lady Matlock's response her fears eased and she began to feel truly comfortable with her future aunt.

"So your aunt and uncle are on holiday are they?"

"Yes, they were to visit family in the North. They make the journey every year, however in our haste to come to London we forgot."

"Do you expect them to return soon?"

"Soon enough, I suppose, they are to be away another fortnight, however we will either just be returned to Longbourn or very soon to be returning upon their arrival in town. I suppose we will miss them this trip."

"I seem to recall the purpose of your attendance here in town is to purchase your wedding trousseau. Shall you still be able to make the necessary purchases?"

"Yes, I daresay we will. My father is here now, he will see to it that someone attends us shopping or else call our mother to town for the purpose."

Jane interjected here. "I am sure mother would be more than pleased to make the journey."

Elizabeth rolled her eyes at her sister, which was not unnoticed by Lady Matlock. "Yes, Jane, I am sure she would be more than eager to attend to us." In lesser company Elizabeth would have followed the comment with another retort that she preferred that her mother not come but instead stay home and plan the weddings; however, she did not want to provide her ladyship the wrong impression either of her mother or of her respect for her parents.

Elizabeth's rolling of her eyes had been noticed though, and Lady Matlock's interest was piqued. "So your mother enjoys coming to London?"

"Yes, she enjoys it very much; it is usually our father who prefers the quiet solitude of his library and our mother the hustle and bustle of town."

"I daresay that her accomplished shopping skills would help you at this time."

"Yes, I am sure they would, however Jane and I generally prefer to shop with our Aunt Gardiner and let our younger sisters keep up and attend our mother."

"So your mother is a lively shopper, is she?"

Elizabeth laughed at such a comment. "Indeed, she is a very lively shopper. She can make it through three or four warehouses before luncheon seeing and noting each and every thing in each warehouse. She can then return home to remember which bolt of fabric or skein of lace she wants and which warehouse it was in, frequently down to the location of the item within the warehouse."

Lady Matlock smiled, "What a talent."

Jane and Elizabeth simultaneously said "Yes, it is."

"If it would be acceptable to you and your father I have some shopping to do this week before the winter sets in too much, I would be happy to accompany you and assist in any way possible."

Jane and Elizabeth sat gaping at Lady Matlock. They never dreamed of a lady in her situation wanting to assist them with their purchases.

Georgiana had been listening to the conversation desperately wanting to say something this was her opportunity. "Aunt, may I attend also? I would love to go shopping with all of you."

"Yes, Georgie dear, if Fitzwilliam approves you may attend us as well. We shall make a week of it, meeting each day for shopping and then lunch."

A little more discussion was had by the ladies until the gentlemen appeared. It was decided what time that they would meet to begin their shopping and agreed upon by all that they would be a very merry party.

Once the gentlemen returned, the remainder of the evening passed first in informing all of the ladies' plans and then in pleasant conversation until the Darcys', Bennets', and Mr. Bingley all retired to the Darcys' London House.

Soon after arriving, the ladies excused themselves for the night and the gentlemen settled into the library for an evening of amiable discussion and port.

Chapter 26
Friday Morning

Friday met a whirlwind of activity at London house, even before breakfast. Mr. Bennet knew his girls, especially Lizzy, were early risers, so in order not to draw attention to them he requested early audiences with the ladies in Mr. Darcy's library.

Jane and Elizabeth met each other as they left their rooms and walked to Mr. Darcy's library together.

"Oh Jane, I hope we can stay in London for a few days at least. I would prefer not to return to Longbourn yet."

"Yes Lizzy, I am of the same opinion. Let us see what father has to say on the matter. He may very well just want to discuss his plans for his sojourn in London."

Lizzy smiled in spite of herself, "I daresay he plans on occupying the large leather lounger that sits in front of the fireplace in Fitzwilliam's library with a book in one hand and a drink of some sort in the other."

The two arrived at the library and their discussion ended. Lizzy knocked lightly on the large, solid door. They were bid to enter by their father.

Jane and Elizabeth entered, but could not help smiling and raising eyebrows at each other. There sat Mr. Bennet in the large leather lounger in front of the fireplace with a book in one hand and his morning coffee in the other.

"Jane, Lizzy, come here, my dears."

The girls walked to their father and each gave him a morning kiss upon the cheek as they had done since girlhood.

"You wanted to speak with us, father." Jane said as she sat on the settee closest to her father.

"Yes girls, you mentioned last night that Lady Matlock had offered to attend you shopping today. Is that correct?"

Lizzy spoke here "Yes, father, she has."

"Very good, now I come to the main point. Her ladyship I am sure frequents an entirely different set of shops that what your mother and Aunt Gardiner frequent, shops that are most likely of an infinitely better quality than those you two are used to. I want you to not be distressed by this. Although I have in no way set aside enough money to bribe wealthy young men to marry you I have set aside enough to send you to the ones you caught clothed well enough." The ladies smiled at their father as he finished. "I want you to have fun shopping with your future family." Mr. Bennet choked a little on his words and Lizzy laid a hand over his. He quickly pulled away, reaching for his vest pocket. "And make sure you purchase everything here on these lists from your mother as I do not want to have to return to London because we missed something."

The girls smiled and took the lists from their father. "Now off with you and leave an old man in peace."

Jane and Lizzy stood to leave. "Actually, Lizzy my dear, if you have a few minutes I would like you to stay. I have something else I would speak to you about."

Jane departed to breakfast, but Lizzy sat to speak further with her father.

Mr. Darcy awoke refreshed and happy. The Mr. Wickham problem that had plagued him yesterday had been solved, his Elizabeth was even right now under his roof and her father, whom he had grown to love as much as any dear friend, had arrived and agreed to stay for awhile to let the ladies' shopping continue as planned.

After readying himself, Mr. Darcy sought his study to accomplish some morning business, primarily responding to Mrs. Bennet's letter, before the ladies were expected to breakfast. As he settled into the library he could hear light speaking from behind him. To those not acquainted with the mysteries of London House, they would wonder at what they were hearing; but to Mr. Darcy he knew exactly what was occurring. Mr. Darcy's personal study was off of the front of London House so as not to allow business persons to walk clear through the house, however to reach the library one has to follow a number of hallways weaving to the back of the house and then to the front again. The result being that the study and library shared a wall, a false wall to be exact. A false wall, in the form of a bookcase, that sat behind Mr. Darcy's desk in the study, the furthest back wall of the library.

Mr. Darcy stood, walked to his study door, and promptly locked it. He then went to the bookcase and paused. Never before had he used this London House secret for eavesdropping purposes, he generally used it for quick access to the library when he was alone and had no desire to walk all the way around. He hesitated to consider whether he should eavesdrop or not. Part of him knew he should not, but the other part of him was desperate to hear every word that his Elizabeth ever uttered and it was clear she was one of the persons in attendance. So Mr. Darcy removed two large books that housed the handle to open the bookcase and the view hole. He now had a full view of the library and although muffled, he could hear all that was going on inside.

Jane was just leaving the library, but Elizabeth was staying to talk further with her beloved father.

"So, Lizzy, now that you are beginning your second day here at the Darcy's London House what think you of the place?'

Darcy could not be more pleased with the question he was dying to hear her honest answer to her father.

Elizabeth blushed a little, which Darcy could not see, but her father could. "I like it very well, father."

Mr. Bennet smiled in spite of himself. "Just very well, Lizzy, come my dear, I know you better than that I am sure you have a dozen different opinions on this one room alone. You cannot tell me that your only response is that you like it very well."

"Oh, father, do not tease me. You know what I mean."

"No Lizzy, I am afraid I do not, you will have to enlighten me."

"Father...," Lizzy let out a distressed breath, "must you press me?" Mr. Bennet just smiled and waited. "Yes I suppose you must. Well, as I said, I like it very well. Did Mr. Darcy tell you that I am in a special room?"

"No, he did not. What is this special room?"

"Father, it is just so exciting and flattering. I am in the 'Lavender Room'. The room was redecorated at Mr. Darcy's mother's request prior to her illness and death. She never saw the room, as she died before returning here. Both Mr. Darcy and his father had the room locked up and my Fitzwilliam presented the room to me as a gift from his mother to the new Mrs. Darcy. The future Mrs. Fitzwilliam Darcy was to be the first person to ever step foot into the room besides the housekeeper to clean it and Mr. Darcy himself to view it."

"Well, my dear, I can see you are pleased by this."

"Oh, father, it is all so very romantic."

Mr. Bennet laughed at his daughter's dramatics.

"The rest of the house is well I suppose. You know I care not for the house or furnishings father, I am marrying Fitzwilliam because I love him, he has earned my respect and esteem and I want to be with him and please him for the rest of my life. I would marry him and live with him in a broken-down cottage if that was all he could offer me. I will say though that his painting in the gallery is rather fine to look at and there is another in my room of a most beautiful and magnificent estate manifesting itself in each of the four seasons. I have learned that it is Pemberley and if it is even one-tenth as wonderful as that painting portrays it to be then we shall not spend much time away, as I will be content to stay in Derbyshire the rest of my life."

Mr. Bennet's eyes glistened at his daughter's honest reply.

"Oh, father, I hope I did not distress you."

"No my dear, that was the answer I envisioned from you, I just did not realize that hearing you praise another man and his estate so much would have such a profound feeling of loss to myself. I shall miss you dearly, Lizzy."

Mr. Darcy was more than well pleased at hearing Elizabeth praise him and his estate but most of all at her saying that he had earned her respect and esteem and that she loved him. Darcy knew Elizabeth was always frank with her father and knowing this made all she said that much more important to him.

"Father, I shall miss you too. I am sure Fitzwilliam will let you come and stay with us anytime you wish and with no notice at all."

"Yes, my dear, I am sure he will. Now let me discuss with you the real reason I wanted you to stay behind. As I said before you and Jane will be shopping at exquisite establishments that cater only to certain individuals when you shop with Mr. Darcy's aunt today. You were both told that I have allocated additional funds to each of you for purchasing your trousseau; however I want you to know that I have set aside even more for you my dear. I also want you to add this list of purchases to the one from your mother."

Lizzy started to reject what her father was saying but he interrupter her.

"No, Lizzy, you cannot argue with this. I know a bit more than you do what is required of a lady of your future station. You shall need additional items, more than what Jane will need being at Netherfield. Plus you are heading to the North, it is much colder there in the winter months and you are going to need to add items that are not necessary for Jane. Plus, Mr. Darcy, I am sure maintains many social engagements with persons in very high stations, you are going to need to have your gowns made of finer quality materials and with much higher quality adornments and embellishments." Lizzy looked puzzled towards her father. "Yes, yes, do not look at me like that I have learned something of women's finery these past twenty plus years listening to your mother's and sisters' blabbing about lace and what not. You only assumed I was not listening."

"Oh father, you truly are the best man."

"Well, well, off with you now. I am sure your young buck is out searching the halls for you already this morning."

Lizzy rose to leave. "Thank you, father, I truly do appreciate it."

Lizzy shut the library door behind her and went towards the dining room.

Mr. Darcy had just started to return all of the books to their proper places when he saw his good friend wipe a tear from his eye and respond to the closed door. "I shall miss you dearly, my dearest Lizzy. What shall I do without you at Longbourn?"

Each minute around Mr. Bennet made Mr. Darcy have a renewed appreciation for the jewel he was to steal away from Hertfordshire in less than a month.

Elizabeth and Mr. Darcy reached the entrance to the dining room at precisely the same moment on account of Mr. Darcy's exceptional timing.

They bowed-curtsied to each other, Elizabeth smiled brightly and Mr. Darcy could not resist reaching for her hand and bringing it to his lips for a soft kiss.

"Good morning, Fitzwilliam."

"Good morning to you, my Elizabeth. Are you just coming to breakfast?"

"As you see; you have impeccable timing, sir."

"Yes, yes, I am sure it has nothing to do with my TRYING to synchronize our eating schedules."

Elizabeth laughed "What a happy thought, I am so glad that you have. It will make breakfast all the more better."

Fitzwilliam offered his arm and the two entered to join Jane and Georgiana, who were already eating.

Breakfast had been concluded but all in attendance were still sitting at the table talking amiably when her ladyship entered.

Elizabeth, Jane and Georgiana were concerned that they had not been watching the time and eagerly jumped up to go ready themselves for their outing.

"Aunt, oh we did not expect you so soon. If you will excuse us we will all just take a few minutes to prepare ourselves." Elizabeth stated in a somewhat hurried fashion as all three were eager to exit.

"Do not distress yourself; I am here early to speak with Fitzwilliam. Take your time readying yourselves."

The three ladies went to get ready and Lady Matlock began to address Mr. Darcy. "Fitzwilliam, I received your note early this morning. Why is it that you wish to speak to me about?"

"Aunt, would you mind accompanying me to my study?"

"Surely nephew." Lady Matlock responded. As the two walked to the study they passed Mr. Bennet walking towards the dining room, paper and cup of coffee in hand.

"Good morning Mr. Bennet" Lady Matlock addressed him.

"Ah, good morning, my lady, how do you do this fine day?"

"Very well thank you. Just this morning as I was leaving my home I ran into Lady Russell. I mentioned to her that my nephew and his best friend are marrying the nieces of Madeline Gardiner and she was quite excited. I hope you will not mind if I take your daughters to tea with a few friends today."

Both Mr. Bennet and Mr. Darcy starred large eyed and open mouthed at her ladyship. "Madeline, Mrs. Edward Gardiner, you know my sister-in-law."

"Of course, did not your daughters tell you last evening?" Both men shook their heads in the negative as she continued. "Madeline and I both attended a ladies' school in Derbyshire and are both avid volunteers for the London community. Mr. Gardiner is known for his generosity in items for our auctions and fundraisers. Why, his warehouses are the only warehouses many of us use as our modesties will only purchase their fabrics from him. He is known for his high quality of merchandise and honesty."

"Yes, he is." Mr. Bennet replied dully as he was still trying to comprehend.

Mr. Darcy was still in shock.

"Why, sirs, do not look so surprised."

Mr. Bennet recovered first. "Indeed we are surprised Lady Matlock. The ladies mentioned nothing of this last evening and it is one of the last things I anticipated hearing this fine day. I would not have thought that you would know any of our relatives as their situation in life is decidedly different than yours."

"Mr. Bennet, I will excuse the statement on the fact that you are shocked and do not know me well, but I would hope that no one, especially someone in my family would discount anyone on account of their position in life. Some of my dearest friends are those who are in trade or law or some other profession. I base my friendships on the merit of the person alone."

"Yes, your ladyship, I see that you do and I am very happy for it. I had no intention of offending, I was surprised, that is all."

"As am I, Aunt." Mr. Darcy had finally recovered and looked a little sheepish at Mr. Bennet as some of his aunt's accusations fairly fit him not too long ago.

"Fitzwilliam you astonish me, you have known me your entire life. You know I base all relationships and connections on the merit of the person." She breathed in a heavy breath, "You men are exhausting. Now, Fitzwilliam, we had best get to our talk or else the ladies will be ready and I will not be."

Mr. Bennet knew his cue so he bowed and departed. Fitzwilliam led his aunt the rest of the way to the library.

Upon entering both sat down and Mr. Darcy began.

"Aunt, I daresay I am a fool. Not too long ago I thought the majority of our family would scorn connections solely based on position and wealth. I nearly walked away from Elizabeth because of it and now here it is known that her family connections are some of those that are dearest to my family. What a fool I almost was."

Lady Matlock was beginning to see all now. "Think no more of it, Fitzwilliam, the fact is that you did not walk away and now Elizabeth is to be your wife, and a fine wife she will make. I am sure when you meet her aunt and uncle you will love them as I do. They are well-educated amiable people. Yes they are in trade, however they are successful and live a very comfortable and modest lifestyle. Although I have only been to Madeline's once she has been to our townhouse many times. You shall love them when you meet them."

"I am sure I will, aunt. I am glad to know all of this; however this is not why I asked you here today."

Lady Matlock just looked at Darcy imploring him to go on.

"Aunt, since you know the family a little and you have now met Mr. Bennet you are aware as I am that Elizabeth does not come from a family as wealthy as ours. I am marrying her for love, not for the dowry she will be bringing to Pemberley. With that said I also know her father has set aside what he considers a considerable amount for Elizabeth's trousseau. I do not know what he considers a considerable amount, however I know the bills that I receive from Georgiana's shops after you take her shopping and regardless of the amount Mr. Bennet has set aside, I do not want him to receive invoices of those amounts. I would ask you to request in private to the proprietors while the ladies are being fitted that they split the invoices, sending only half of the amount to Mr. Bennet and the other half directly to myself. Tell them to set an account as they have for Georgiana under Elizabeth's name for any future purchases that she makes as Mrs. Darcy. I am sure you shall have no problem accomplishing this."

"It shall be no problem, nephew. I do see your point; in fact I had intended already to do this only having the tab sent to your uncle instead. Your uncle and I discussed it this morning. I shall do as you wish, however there may be a few items that we pick up as a wedding gift to your bride, so be not surprised if the accounts are smaller then you anticipate."

"You need not do that aunt, unless you wish to. I am more than happy to pay all of Elizabeth's purchases, because it just reinforces that she is soon to be my wife, a day that I can hardly wait for."

"Yes, I can see the happiness that has been brought to you since she has entered your life. She is good for you nephew, a rare jewel among mere stones. Your uncle and I like her very much and are a fair way onto loving her as a member of our family already. We can see the joy she brings to you and Georgiana and we are so very thankful for her. We have tried for years to bring you happiness and all we can do is temporarily fill a small part of your void. She has filled it now and we can see your happiness overflowing. Marry her, love her, and never let her get away."

"Thank you, Aunt" was all Darcy could say. His aunt stood, kissed his cheek, and walked towards the door.

"Well, I think the ladies will be waiting for me. We shall not be back before lunch..." With a smile over her shoulder she then said "In fact, you may want to hold dinner." She chuckled and then turned to face the ladies who were in the foyer bidding adieus to Mr. Bennet and Mr. Bingley.

"Are we all ready for a day of shopping?"

Smiles lit upon each face and Georgiana responded "Yes, we are," in a voice of confidence rarely heard from her.

Lady Matlock smiled and winked at her nephew as she led the ladies to the coach.

Charles Bingley was up to an early start Friday morning. He wished to reach London House before the ladies left to go shopping. He wanted to see Jane and he had a task for Georgiana. He made good time in getting there, however upon arrival he was informed that the ladies were just finishing readying themselves for departure and that Darcy was speaking with his aunt privately in the study.

Charles asked if Miss Georgiana could be informed that he wished to speak to her for five minutes before the ladies left.

Georgiana came down directly. "Mr. Bingley, what do you do here? Have you come to see Jane before we depart for the day?"

"Yes, that is one of the reasons, but the other is to make a secret request of you."

Georgiana got excited, "Yes, anything for you Mr. Bingley, shall we discuss this in the drawing room?"

Mr. Bingley followed Georgiana into the drawing room and once seated began. "I would like to you take note of a few things the next few days that Jane particularly likes, but decides not to purchase for whatever reason it may be. I then want you to provide the proprietors my card and have them send me a bill for the items and have them delivered to me at Grosvenor Square. Can you do all of this?"

"Yes Mr. Bingley, I would love to, what fun!"

Mr. Bingley handed Georgiana a few of his cards and thanked her for her help.

The two exited the drawing room just as Elizabeth and Jane were coming down the stairs.

"Charles, you are here." Jane exclaimed happily.

"Yes, Jane dear, I am glad I am able to see you before you depart for the day. I have business with Darcy and your father and thought that coming a few minutes early would behoove me more than not."

They reached each other and Charles took Jane's hand and kissed it and then wrapped it around his arm. "May I escort you to the front of the house?"

Jane smiled sweetly "Of course."

Once all of the ladies were situated in the coach Mr. Darcy securely closed the door and stepped back as it departed for a day of shopping. The gentlemen returned inside and Darcy spoke first. "Charles I did not know you were here."

"Yes, I just, I wanted to see the ladies off this morning and of course see Jane's sweet smile to buoy me for the more arduous tasks of today."

Darcy shook his head in acknowledgement and Mr. Bennet just laughed. "My boy, you two are a sorry lot, come let us decide what we are to accomplish today."

All three men entered Mr. Darcy's study and took a seat. Mr. Bennet began the conversation. "Well I think we ought to start with the most important business first. We need to attend Mr. Bingley to his solicitor and sort out the business of his sister. While there we will; that is if you want to; draw up and finalize the marriage documents."

Bingley interjected here "Of course I want to. Let's get that done straightaway so as to have no impediments to Jane and me marrying."

Mr. Bennet smiled at the young man's enthusiasm.

"Then, I suppose, if there is time we shall attend Mr. Darcy's solicitor and do the same."

"Actually sir, I have already contacted him and he is unavailable until next Tuesday. I do hope this will not inconvenience you and you will be able to remain in town at the very least that long."

"Yes, yes I am sure we will be fine. The ladies plan on shopping at least today and tomorrow for the larger part of their purchases. The items will require fitting in the week to come, we shall stay at least a week, I am sure of that."

Both men smiled at their future father-in-law's admission.

"So, gentlemen, do we have an exact date yet?"

Both men looked at each other. How could they have been so foolish as to not have set a date yet? Mr. Darcy responded. "Miss Elizabeth and I have discussed no further than a few days prior to Christmas, however…" Mr. Darcy walked to the calendar on his desk. "… Christmas day is on a Wednesday. It takes two days to travel to Pemberley on good roads, three on poor. The roads are unpredictable this time of year, so we should plan on three. In addition we need at least two days at Pemberley prior to the holiday event to ensure that all is well at the estate for the season. Unfortunately I have been neglectful of late and have not returned there. I accomplish all by correspondence by mail and it shall remain that way until I return after my wedding. I would wish to marry on about the eighteenth of December to ensure I have enough time to accomplish all that is needed prior to Christmas and that our travels may be made in safety and not haste. I do believe we should consult the ladies as well"

"Well that is scarcely three weeks away."

"It is nineteen days Mr. Bennet."

"Very good, I see your preciseness Mr. Darcy; we had planned on staying in London for two weeks, which will leave just five days at Longbourn to finish all necessary arrangements. I think it is a bit close. If the ladies approve of the date then I shall write to the rector of Longbourn and request that Wednesday December eighteenth be reserved, however we shall have to depart London no later than the eleventh in order to not cause a stir with Mrs. Bennet. I suppose the ladies will be able to accomplish all in this time."

With plans in order the gentlemen set out for their appointment with Mr. Bingley's solicitor.

Friday did not dawn pleasant for all of London's occupants, Lord Matlock had plans to visit his sister on a task he would rather have foregone, but he had no choice, his family was being too affected.

He first ate a pleasant but unusually quiet breakfast with his wife, then seeing her off in the direction of London House; he turned and went in the opposite direction to Rosings Place.

Lord Matlock arrived to find a house that was being reined by chaos supreme. Apparently Lady Catherine's ire had not abated, but instead had risen with anger towards her nephew and his fiancée with each passing hour.

Lord Matlock did not spare any time; he sent a message to his son at his quarters to attend him directly at his Aunt's residence and then he entered to approach his sister.

Despite his desire for a civil conversation, Lady Catherine would not have it any other way than shouting, and the more Lord Matlock attempted to reason with her the more passionate and obstinate she became.

Thirty minutes into their meeting Richard arrived and the conversation turned worse. She had not forgiven him for walking away from her yesterday. Richard, of course, could not let such arguments go unanswered and confronted her with the accusation of paying Wickham. The two shared words of malice and hate for five minutes and it would have continued had not Lord Matlock interceded and gained control of his son. He never did gain control of his sister.

Lady Catherine blackened the name of Darcy, Bennet, and even Fitzwilliam. She accused Darcy of denying his dying mother's wish and declared that she would have her justice upon him. He would rue the day that he ever crossed her path. Lady Catherine was determined to ruin him and anyone who supported him. She also declared her intention of thrusting Anne at any man between the ages of thirty and ninety who had a title and a need of a well-dowered wife. Anne would be married by summer's end, regardless of her feelings and opinions on the subject.

Anne had seen her cousin Richard arrive and had come below stairs to speak to him. Hearing the arguments inside the drawing room and having no desire to be a part of them she sat upon the settee outside the door to await his departure. Hearing her mother's accusations against her cousins and her boisterous declarations as to her own felicity in marriage, Anne's ire was raised as it had never been before. Anne was proud of her uncle and cousin for defending her choice and happiness but becoming angrier at her mother with each declaration. Her twenty-five years of pent-up anger and opinion spilled over as she stepped into the room and addressed her mother.

Lord Matlock and Richard were surprised but pleased at Anne's ability to defend herself, Richard was openly admiring her when he was rudely taken aback at the sight of Lady Catherine reacting by striking her daughter across the face leaving a large, red, inflamed hand print. Richard instantly went to Anne's side and comforted her while his father grabbed his sister's arm and addressed her in a harsh tone. "Catherine Fitzwilliam de Bourgh, as head of this family I demand that you apologize to your daughter."

Lady Catherine was in a rage, but menacingly laughed out her reply "You demand it. Very funny, brother, I shall not now, nor shall I ever apologize. She had no right to speak to me in the manner in which she did. I have a right to treat her in any manner and with any method that I see fit. If you do not remove your hand from me at this moment you shall also learn firsthand how I see fit to deal with you, brother."

"Catherine I am warning you, this is your last chance to repent or I shall know how to act."

"No brother, I shall know how to act. Fitzwilliam shall rue the day he ever met that Bennet woman for he shall never see Georgiana again, I shall remove her from his charge and ensure she has a proper education and coming-out. By the time I am done there will be no one in London who condescends to associate with the likes of Mr. and Mrs. Fitzwilliam Darcy." The last was spit out as if venom was in Lady Catherine's mouth. She truly hated Darcy and it showed in every action and word she spoke.

With a hand still grasped on his sister's arm Lord Matlock addressed his son. "Richard, please see that Anne's belongings are packed and removed to our townhouse." Richard and Anne left the room to follow the directions of Lord Matlock: the look upon his face made it clear to both of them that their presence was no longer needed. Then turning towards his sister, Lord Matlock looked sadly upon her as he replied "Catherine, sister, you have made your position abundantly clear, now let me make mine." Lady Catherine tried to interrupt him but Lord Matlock would not allow it. "First of all neither your daughter nor Fitzwilliam have ever wanted a match between them. I should have put a stop to your marriage nonsense years ago. Second, you shall never lay another hand upon Anne as long as you live, and third I shall ensure that you never malign the name of Fitzwilliam, Darcy or Bennet ever again."

Lady Catherine finally could control her anger no more and challenged his authority. "And just how to you think you will ever accomplish that, brother, I would surely love to see you try."

"I shall accomplish it easily sister because this evening you shall be accompanied by me to the docks where you board a ship for the Americas in the company of one who you are well acquainted. Mr. George Wickham."

Lord Matlock turned from his sister and left the room, he ordered her trunks packed, her servants into his employ, declared she was not to leave the house under any circumstance until he returned, and departed to purchase her ticket and prepare to never see his sister again.

Chapter 27
London Shopping

The Matlock carriage was abuzz with maidenly shopping conversation. It was earlier discussed, primarily between Georgiana and Lady Matlock, that the best place to purchase trousseau items would be Bond Street.

Jane and Elizabeth were glad their father had talked to them or else they would be disturbed shopping at Bond Street, for it is known to have the most elite shops in all of London. No one from their family shopped on Bond Street.

"So Elizabeth, Jane, have you decided on your wedding gowns yet or is this shopping trip just for your trousseau?" Asked Lady Matlock.

Elizabeth answered "It is for both, Aunt. We are newly engaged as you know and came straight to London. In addition, there is no one in Meryton our Mother would have make our gowns. She prefers that we obtain them here."

"Very good, I know just the place. We shall order wedding gowns first, as they are the most important."

The excitement showed on the faces of both ladies.

Not long after, the carriage pulled to a stop on Bond Street. Lady Matlock and the ladies were let down by the footman and Lady Matlock turned to address him. "We shall walk the street to the various shops; however please have someone attend us between each shop to return our purchases to the carriage and have the carriage ready in case we need to attend the warehouses for fabric selections."

"Very well, My Lady."

Lady Matlock turned towards the ladies. "Shall we?"

"Yes Aunt, lead the way."

Lady Matlock led the way past ten or so shops and then stopped and turned to enter "Modiste Belle," the shop of the French modiste known from her intricate and much sought-after work. Elizabeth and Jane had heard of "Modiste Belle," however had never seen a piece of her work in person. Never would they have dreamed it possible that she would be commissioned to make their wedding gowns.

As they entered Lady Matlock and Georgiana were both greeted as dear old friends.

Lady Matlock introduced Elizabeth and Jane. "Miss Belle, this is Miss Elizabeth Bennet, she is to marry my nephew Mr. Darcy and this is her sister Miss Jane Bennet who is to marry Mr. Darcy's best friend Mr. Charles Bingley."

"Welcome to both of you."

"Miss Belle, the ladies have just come to London and we have need of two wedding dresses."

"Ah, my specialty, you have come to the right place. We shall make you both the most exquisite brides ever seen, though from the looks of you this shall not be hard as both of you are quite beautiful. Let's see, would you prefer to look at patterns and models first so that the materials may be narrowed down for you or select fabrics to have a wider assortment of textures, but a smaller assortment of designs once the fabric is chosen?"

The girls looked at each other and smiled. They knew what they wanted. Elizabeth looked to her aunt. "If it would please you Aunt, we would like to look at fabrics first. One of the most horrible things is to find the most exquisite fabric and then be told that it will not work for the design of your dress." The ladies laughed at Elizabeth's explanation nodding in agreement for everyone had experienced a similar situation in the past and knew how frustrating it could be.

"Very well, fabrics it is. Miss Belle do you have time to attend us to the warehouse or shall we go and make our selections and have them sent back."

"Lady Matlock I am at your service today you decide whether you would have me attend you or not."

Elizabeth nodded a yes to her aunt who had looked at her and it was done.

"I think we would like you along for your expertise and advice."

"Very well, ma'am, let me just tell Nelly and we shall be off."

The ladies departed the shop and quickly saw their carriage. They crossed the street and entered. Lady Matlock gave directions and they were off.

"Miss Belle, I assume we are to the regular warehouse that you attend."

"Yes ma'am, I use none other than…"

"Very well." Lady Matlock had cut her off before finishing, something rarely done to Miss Belle by her ladyship. Plenty others disrespected her like that, but not Lady Matlock. Something must be going on. It did not take long for Miss Belle to discover it.

"Lizzy, look where we are at." Jane whispered to her as they pulled to a stop outside of Gardiner Warehouses.

"Aunt, are we to look at the fabrics here?"

"Yes, Elizabeth, we are."

There was a huge smile on the girls' faces, which Belle was soon to discover why when she entered.

"Good morning, Miss Belle, I see you have brought some ladies to look at fabrics?"

"Yes, this is Lady Matlock and her nieces. Two of them here need fabric for wedding dresses."

Belle stepped to the side so that Jane and Elizabeth could be seen.

"Why Miss Bennet, Miss Elizabeth, what do you do here? Wedding dresses, why, do your Uncle and Aunt Gardiner know?"

"No Jonathan, as you know they are on holiday. We only became engaged this week and arrived in town but a few days ago. Aunt and Uncle Gardiner have not yet been informed."

"Aunt and Uncle Gardiner? Why, you are nieces to Madeline and Edward Gardiner, how wonderful."

The girls just smiled and nodded their heads. "Why wonders never cease. This day just gets better and better."

"Well, ladies help yourselves, do you need to be shown around or would you just like to look as normal."

"We shall be fine, Jonathan, if we need anything we will call for you."

The ladies began their fabric excursion and an hour later after browsing Jane had selected her fabrics and Elizabeth had narrowed hers to a few choices.

Jonathan gathered the bolts and took them to the sitting area for the women to look them over and discuss.

Belle eyed each bolt that Jonathan placed in front of Jane. "Miss Bennet, I see that you have an eye for shiny fabrics. I would love to hear what you have to say about why you have chosen these fabrics and the design you would like, and then I will tell you my ideas, for upon seeing this top fabric they are running wild. I have such an idea in mind for a dress for you." Belle's excitement could be seen by everyone.

"Miss Belle, you are by far a better judge of fashion than me and I am sure can come up with better designs. I would love to just hear your idea straight away and then tell you my opinion of it." Jane stated.

Everyone could see how pleased Miss Belle was with Jane's response.

"From listening to you describe fabrics, textures and styles with your sister and friends here today I have been able to gather that you have generally worn simple yet pretty dresses. Well we are going to make this dress everything that those were not; this dress shall be exquisite and elegant. You will be divine while wearing it."

Jane's face shone with excitement as she dreamed of such a dress; by the time Belle was done she was amazed that such a dress could exist.

"Yes, an apt description, Miss Belle, Mr. Bingley will be unable to tear his eyes from you." Georgiana chimed in.

"Belle, do you think you could make the veil to match the dress as well with this chiffon?"

"Yes Lady Matlock, I shall do just that and it will attach to Miss Jane's hair with some rose clips."

Jane turned towards Elizabeth, "Lizzy, I am so excited, oh to own such a gown."

Few knew Lady Matlock was also prudent in addition to her intelligence, despite her wealth. "Belle, the ladies will be frequently in London after their marriages, I wonder if this gown could be used as an evening gown as well as a wedding gown? That would be the most prudent thing to do so that such a design does not go unseen after the nuptials and I am sure Miss Jane will wish to wear it often."

"Of course ma'am, it will be perfect for balls, parties and trips to the theatre and opera. She will be the best dressed.'

"Oh Belle, I shall wear this dress with pride. It sounds better than I could have ever dreamed. I shall be the most beautiful bride ever seen. We shall truly surprise Mr. Bingley."

Belle nodded her head in agreement.

"Now Miss Elizabeth what have you chosen?"

"Well Belle, I could not decide so I had Jonathan bring several fabrics here for you to see, but after listening to the divine dress you have come up with for Jane I am all in anticipation of what you shall come up with for me."

"Ah, the pressure is on, for the future wife of Mr. Darcy of Derbyshire must be seen in nothing less than a masterpiece."

Belle quickly stood to inspect all of the different fabrics that Elizabeth had gathered. Shaking her head and turning a little to look at Elizabeth she began but was surprised as Jonathan hesitantly interrupted. "I am sorry to interrupt Miss Belle, but Mrs. Gardiner will be very distressed if Miss Elizabeth's dress is commissioned without using some fabrics that she has had set aside these past few years."

Elizabeth looked surprised and declared "Jonathan, what do you speak of? I know of no such fabric."

"Oh yes, it does exist, please wait, I will go get it and tell you all." Everyone sat in silence with their eyes upon Jonathan as he walked away.

Jonathan entered Mr. Gardiner's office where a very beautiful armoire was situated. He opened it and gently gathered the delicate fabrics into his arms and then returned to the ladies. Jonathan lovingly carried the fabrics to the sitting area, as he walked through the door a gasp was heard and silence fell upon the room as he began a short tale. "Years ago, when Mr. and Mrs. Gardiner were visiting Paris they stopped at a fabric supplier for the purpose of arriving at an agreement to sell the fabrics here in London. While there Mrs. Gardiner browsed the bolts of fabrics and came upon some that she claims spoke your name to her. She at first did not purchase them, but for an additional two days the fabrics would not leave her mind, she says they begged her to return for them. After talking it over with your uncle it was agreed upon that they would return for the fabrics and purchase them for your future wedding dress." Jonathan placed the fabrics into Elizabeth's hands as she wiped a tear from her eyes.

They were the most exquisite fabrics that had ever been seen and only a few select people knew they existed. Jonathan just happened to be one of them. The room was silent yet everyone leaned towards Elizabeth to get a better look at the magnificent fabrics.

Feeling every emotion that was in the room Belle hesitantly broke the silence by approaching Elizabeth and picked up the first piece of fabric, gently unfolding it for everyone to get a better view. "Long have I imagined a dress that I would someday find the perfect fabric for, I believe today is the day my design comes to life. Shall you like to hear about your wedding gown, Miss Elizabeth?"

Elizabeth nodded her head in agreement, unable to say a single word.

"This" she said as she continued to unfold the fabric "shall be the main dress, which will just lightly grace the floor. In addition to being the dress it shall also be your cape train." The fabric was shimmery silver lamé with the most delicate metallic threads weaved through in various swirl patterns that sparkled in the sunlight from the nearby window. It was neither soft and flowing nor stiff, it would just move with the person who wore it in such a way that one could not describe. "If you are to show this dress off beyond your special day then the train must be able to be removed so that it will not inhibit your movement and cause worry when wearing. I shall not describe all of the details of the dress to you because it is to be a surprise. I shall only let you know the essentials."

Picking up a second piece of fabric Belle began to describe it as well. "This tissue shall be under your dress, but protrude from the bottom of the dress, the sleeves and neckline, embroidered with an exquisite stitch that I shall amaze you with. The dress and cape shall be trimmed with this." Bell said this as she picked up yet a third fabric, an exquisite Brussels lace. "We shall also use this to create your veil, which will also train behind you longer than even the cape shall. Lastly the cape shall clasp around your neck using this." Belle unfolded the final diamond encrusted ornament pin from some white satin and held it up for all to admire.

Lizzy was finally able to gather her voice. "Oh Belle, the dresses sounds absolutely divine. Jonathan, I can barely believe Mrs. Gardiner saved this fabric for me. Jane and I shall be dressed beyond out mother's wildest dreams. Are you sure you have the time to make such a dress as you have begun to describe."

"Yes, I shall work day and night if I must, but you shall have a dress as no one has ever seen before."

"Shall we make our purchases and return to Belle's to finalize everything?" Inquired Lady Matlock.

"Yes Aunt, we shall. Jonathan, can you send the bill to our father?"

"Surely Miss Elizabeth, but I shall not do it until your uncle returns. I feel it safe to say, knowing your uncle and aunt as I do that your father shall not see a bill. Your uncle will undoubtedly want the fabric for his favorite nieces' wedding gowns to be a gift, especially yours Miss Elizabeth."

"Thank you Jonathan, however if he does not then just send the bill on to father."

"Yes, Miss."

"Jonathan."

"Yes, Miss Elizabeth."

"Thank you so much for your help and assistance today, not to mention your kindness. We shall return again in a few days to select fabrics for the rest of our trousseau."

"I shall be ready to assist you again on whichever day best suits your schedule."

Jane and Elizabeth both smiled to Jonathan and all the ladies left the warehouse to enter the carriage and return to Belle's.

Lady Matlock stayed just a moment longer than the rest to speak to Jonathan.

"Jonathan, you can expect us again after lunch to shop for the girl's ready-made items. At that time I would speak with you about a private matter, a matter relating to gifts for the ladies."

"Yes, Lady Matlock, I shall be at your disposal."

Lady Matlock entered the carriage and it departed to return to the modiste shop. Just as the carriage was stopping Belle addressed Lady Matlock. "Lady Matlock, it shall take us one week to complete Miss Jane's gown with a fitting mid-week, say on Wednesday. Miss Elizabeth's main gown shall be done for her to fit, although I shall need a second week to complete it and the cape. Will there be a problem with that?"

"No Belle, there is not problem, we shall be here for Jane's fitting and if it is alright with Miss Elizabeth Lord Matlock and I shall transport her gown to Meryton is she leaves before it is completed." Lizzy shook her head in agreement. "Do you need anything else from us today?"

"No ma'am, I shall leave you now."

"Thank you Belle, we look forward to seeing your masterpieces."

Belle smiled, thanked Lady Matlock and entered her shop delighted at the commission she had been entrusted with by the ladies. These truly would be dresses to be remembered.

"Aunt," a very happy Georgiana inquired "where shall we go next."

"Georgiana, I believe we have agreed to meet Lady Russell for tea and lunch at Wagner's. Shall we?"

"Oh yes, I adore Wagner's. Lizzy, Jane, have you ever been to Wagner's?" All of this was said as the party began walking to the corner where they could already see the tea and sweet shop.

"No Georgiana, I do not believe we have, but I am sure we shall enjoy it."

"Oh yes, they have the finest chocolates and sweets one has ever tasted."

They had just arrived at Wagner's and were being seated near a window at one of the tables when Lady Russell arrived.

"My dear Lady Matlock, what a pleasure it is to meet you today."

"The pleasure is all mine, Lady Russell. May I present my niece, Miss Georgiana Darcy, and my future niece and her sister, Miss Elizabeth and Miss Jane Bennet."

"Miss Elizabeth, you are to marry Mr. Darcy. Well my dear, what a fine accomplishment for you." Lady Russell stated.

"Thank you Lady Russell, however I do not see it as an accomplishment. I see it as a privilege. He truly is a wonderful man and I am blessed to have been chosen by him on the basis of mutual affection and a likeness of minds."

Lady Russell and Lady Matlock exchanged amused expressions. "Yes, yes, my dear. All newly engaged women feel as such, but I assure you he is a prize and every woman in London, perhaps in most of England, will be angry at you for winning despite the fact that Mr. Darcy never even considered them in the race." All of the ladies at the table were smiling at this and Lady Russell continued.

"Miss Jane, I hear congratulations are in order for you as well. You shall also be marrying another of London's finest gentlemen. He gets a lot of attention for the sole fact that he is Mr. Darcy's closest friend. The two are always seen together and near inseparable."

"You are correct, Lady Russell, I am to marry Mr. Bingley at the same ceremony as my sister and Mr. Darcy."

"Goodness, best friend marrying sisters and in the same ceremony, mind you. This shall cause a stir about town now won't it? What a fine thing for the two of you, marrying best friends. At least now you shall know that your husbands will always welcome one another. It is so common for sisters to marry men that hate the sight of one another and then end up estranged. I am glad for your sakes that this is not the case."

Lady Matlock laughed "So true Lady Russell, for think of dear Mrs. Grange. She and her sister were so close their entire lives and when her sister married their husbands are each so stubborn and can agree on nothing, not even the weather and thus they have been estranged these twenty years at least."

"Pity, it is." Lady Russell responded. "I also hear that the Miss Bennets here are the nieces of Madeline and Edward Gardiner."

"Why yes, we are... news does travel fast in London doesn't it?" Lizzy stated.

"Indeed it does." Lady Matlock responded.

The ladies continued talking of various topics for close to an hour until the party broke up.

Lady Russell smiled, waved a gloved hand, entered her carriage and was off.

All of the ladies stood, gathered their belongings, and exited the tea and sweet shop.

The remaining ladies all smiled and looked to Lady Matlock. Georgiana began, "Thank you for tea and lunch aunt. That was splendid. What are our plans for this afternoon?"

"Well Georgie dear, we have the wedding dresses taken care of, now we can more leisurely shop for trousseau. I suspect each of the Miss Bennets have a list their Mother has helped them prepare."

Elizabeth responded, "Yes Aunt, we do. My Father brought the list here to us. Do you know best where to begin?"

Lady Matlock smiled and said "Perhaps we should pay Jonathan another visit."

All of the ladies giggled and Elizabeth replied "Yes, perhaps we shall."

The carriage arrived again at the Gardiners warehouse; the ladies exited and quickly entered the warehouse. Jonathan was ready, awaiting them.

"Ah, you have returned. I hope lunch was good."

"Thank you, Jonathan, it was." Lizzy replied, some of her vivacity shining through.

Lady Matlock began by addressing Jonathan. "Jonathan, as I mentioned before we departed earlier we have returned for wearables. I thought today could be spent gathering the items that do not require fittings so that they can be out of the way. Then next week we shall be able to expeditiously shop for the remaining requiring fabrics."

"Yes my lady, while you were to lunch I gathered a few items I suspected the ladies would prefer and put them in the sitting area. Some of these I know Mrs. Gardiner herself would recommend to any of you, and the other items I know the ladies would love, since I am familiar with their shopping habits."

"Very good, Jonathan, I appreciate your attentiveness. Let us accompany the ladies to the sitting area and then I wish to speak to you in private about some of my own purchases I shall need."

Jonathan bowed and led the ladies to the sitting area. He pointed out the tables he had arrayed for each Jane and Elizabeth and which items he was confident Mrs. Gardiner would recommend and those he himself had chosen based on his knowledge of each lady. He then encouraged them to browse anything else they wanted.

"Lady Matlock, if you are ready I shall accompany you to Mr. Gardiners office where we may talk."

Lady Matlock followed Jonathan to the office and took a seat. Jonathan took one across from her and nodded for her to begin.

"Jonathan, thank you so much for the thought and preparation you put in before our arrival."

"You're welcome, my lady. I would do anything for those two ladies. They are indeed favorites of their aunt and uncle. I think I know what Mrs. Gardiner would want for them and know for sure at this happy time that she would want them having attention."

Lady Matlock smiled warmly at Jonathan. "I appreciate that, but now I must speak seriously on two matters. First of all Lord Matlock and I want to provide some items to Miss Elizabeth as a wedding gift. So before we leave I shall indicate which items you are to send the bill to me."

"Very well, my Lady, as I prepare the invoice just indicate them to me, in some manner, and those items I shall send to you instead of Mr. Bennet."

"Thank you, the second item is this, my nephew, Miss Elizabeth's intended, wishes that some of the invoices be sent to him instead of Mr. Bennet, particularly fabric purchases. He wants Elizabeth to choose among fabrics of the finest quality and does not want Mr. Bennet to pay for all of them."

"Lady Matlock, I shall try to aid you, how I shall do this is to send the entire fabric bills to each gentleman, however Mr. Darcy show get half of the fabrics and Mr. Bennet the others."

"Yes, that shall work. Please create an account in the name of Elizabeth Darcy for anything Elizabeth purchases now or in the future."

"Yes, ma'am, I shall do that."

"Wonderful, shall we return to the ladies?"

"After you, my Lady."

Jonathan and Lady Matlock returned just as the ladies had finished looking at the items in the sitting room.

Jane began "Oh Jonathan, you truly know us, don't you? The items set aside for me are perfect. These here I shall purchase, and these over here I shall return to you. They are lovely; however I shall not need them all. I would however like to browse further."

"Yes Miss Jane, just leave it all there and I shall have everything ready for you when you complete your shopping."

Elizabeth was next "Jane is right; you really do know what we prefer. It is amazing that over the years you've been able to discern our taste despite our mother's shopping antics."

Everyone laughed.

"Yes Miss Elizabeth, I hope I have. Do you like the items I set out for you?"

"Yes, I do. In fact I think I've completed the majority of my trousseau shopping. I only have the few remaining items. Like Jane does, I have two piles, though my take pile is a bit larger. I shall purchase these and returned these." Elizabeth said as she pointed out each pile.

"Alright, I shall ready them as I do Miss Jane's, feel free to shop some more."

Lady Matlock and Georgiana remained sitting until the ladies departed into the shop area. Then Georgiana spoke.

"Jonathan, my brother's friend, and Jane's intended, Mr. Bingley, placed a charge on me. I am to give you his card and select some items for Miss Jane. The items that I select are to be billed to him and sent directly to Grosvenor Square addressed to Jane. He wishes to present them as a gift for their wedding."

Jonathan smiled and nodded as he accepted Mr. Bingley's card.

"Three of these items," Georgiana pointed to the pile "Miss Bennet liked exceedingly well but did not choose them for one reason or another. I would like them sent to Mr. Bingley."

Georgiana selected the items to show Jonathan and then placed them back in the pile.

"I shall see to it, Miss Darcy. Is there anything else?"

"No, I shall go shop with them and see if anything else catches her eye." Georgiana entered the shop.

Lady Matlock had begun to look through Elizabeth items and had selected four of them as gifts from her and Lord Matlock and two of them to have the bills sent Darcy. She informed Jonathan and went to join the ladies.

"Well ladies, how are your purchases going?"

"Very well Lady Matlock, I suspect that we should have everything except the dresses from our lists today."

"Excellent, I knew the Gardiner's warehouse would be able to supply us. This is the only place to shop."

The girl's beamed brightly and nodded their heads in agreement at the praise for the aunt and uncle.

"Collect your additional items and proceed to Jonathan, he will record our purchases for the invoices."

The girls collected their last items and began to congregate in the front of the warehouse.

"Elizabeth, my dear, may I have a word with you?"

"Certainly, Aunt."

The two stopped at the sitting area near the front of the warehouse and sat down.

"My dear, your future uncle and I would like to purchase some of your trousseau items as a wedding gift to you."

Elizabeth began to protest that her family could well provide for her.

"Nonsense, stop protesting, I shall not listen to it. It is already done. I spoke with Jonathan already. From the items you selected earlier I chose those that I particularly liked and had him place them on my tab already. We planned on providing you with a wedding gift regardless, why not have it be something that I already know that you like."

"Thank you, Aunt, that is very kind of you. You need not have done that, but since you already have I shall just thank you again. Thank you."

Lady Matlock leaned over to hug Elizabeth as she said "You are welcome, think of it this way. You can either just allow them as a gift or if you are bound and determined to spend all of your father's money you have more funds available for additional shopping."

Both ladies laughed and stood to join Jane and Georgiana. As they entered Lady Matlock leaned over and whispered one more thing into Elizabeth's ear. "Welcome to the family, my dear. We are so glad that Fitzwilliam chose you."

All Elizabeth could do was smile and blush from ear to ear becoming happier and happier with her new family.

After finishing up and wishing Jonathan a good day, the ladies entered the carriage, Georgiana lagging a little behind.

"Jonathan, I was hoping that you could add two more items to Mr. Bingley's gifts for Miss Jane."

"Surely Miss Darcy, just tell me which."

"I would love it if you added the dainty cream fingerless gloves and matching wrap hanging on the far wall."

"Oh yes, what a beautiful set. Those have just arrived from Paris. Even Mrs. Gardiner has not seen them yet."

"Yes, Miss Jane just adored them, but concluded that they were not on her list of purchases. I am absolutely positive that Mr. Bingley would want her to have them. In addition, I would like something added to my own account. As you know Elizabeth is soon to be my sister. I want to get her a gift."

Jonathan just smiled and nodded at Miss Darcy.

"I would like to get her the charcoal fur lined hand muff with a matching hat. It is lovely and I know it will match her overcoat and gloves and I adore the hat much better than her bonnet that she has. It shall make a striking presence on her, plus I saw her admiring them today."

"Very well, Miss Darcy, I shall have it sent to London House."

"Thank you Jonathan, please send it to me so that I can present it to her myself."

Jonathan bowed as Miss Darcy left the warehouse. He was pleased that the favorite nieces of his esteemed employer were marrying into such pleasant families."

The carriage departed the warehouse for the Darcy's London House, arriving just in time for the ladies to change for dinner.

Chapter 28
Bingley's Solicitor

Twenty minutes after leaving London House the Darcy carriage arrived at Bingley's solicitors.

"Mr. Bingley, Sir." Watson said as the three men entered the office.

"Mr. Watson, I presume you remember Mr. Darcy?"

"Yes, good day to you, Mr. Darcy."

"Good day Mr. Watson."

"And this, sir, is Mr. Bennet, my future father-in-law."

"Good day to you as well, sir."

"Good day" said Mr. Bennet.

"Mr. Watson, as I stated in my note, I come to you for two purposes. The first is my sister Caroline and the second is a matter entirely more pleasant, my upcoming nuptials to Miss Bennet."

"Yes, Mr. Bingley, which shall we discuss first, and would you prefer to do it in the larger meeting room or would you prefer the two of us retire to my private office?"

"We can talk in the conference room with Mr. Bennet and Mr. Darcy. They already know all of the matters that we are to discuss."

"Very well than, follow me." Mr. Watson led the way into the room where all were seated and he shut the door.

Mr. Watson began. "With which item of business would you prefer to begin, Mr. Bingley?"

"Let us begin with the least pleasant, my sister Caroline, and end with the happy discussion of my wedding."

Mr. Watson smiled at his declaration and began. "I received your note earlier and began looking into Miss Bingley's inheritance as you requested."

"Good Watson, what did you determine?"

"You have the ability to transfer the entirety of Miss Caroline Bingley's inheritance to her at any point after her twenty-fifth birthday. I believe she has already passed this age and therefore there is nothing to question here. But there is another provision that your father left should the transfer of her inheritance occur prior to her marrying."

All eyes turned to Mr. Watson wide and curious about this unusual development that Mr. Bingley previously knew nothing about.

"It appears as if the late Mr. Bingley was concerned with his daughters' - yes both daughters' - extravagance prior to her death. This provision was for both ladies, but as Mrs. Louisa Bingley Hurst married prior to the transfer of her inheritance it became void on her part. It seems as though you may transfer her inheritance in full, however she will still not have access to it in its entirety. If she lives with family she is to live off of its interest along with one hundred pounds per annum until she is thirty years of age. Upon her thirtieth birthday she shall receive interest and five hundred pounds per annum until her thirty-fifth birthday where she shall regain full rights to her inheritance. If her inheritance is transferred to her and she does not live with either you, Mr. Bingley, or another family member than her allowance shall increase by two hundred fifty pounds per annum, coming from her own funds. The interest on her funds amounts to approximately six hundred pounds per year at this time. You Mr. Bingley have formerly allowed her an allowance of fifty pounds per month or six hundred pounds per year, however the past four years she has exceeded that by more than double, without you curbing her spending habits. Should you transfer everything to her and you discontinue your allowances to her, she shall live on about half of what she is used to until her thirtieth birthday whereas she shall return to her current level. At the age of thirty-five, she shall do as she pleases."

"Well, Mr. Watson, you have certainly surprised me. Is there anything else?"

"One final item, sir, Miss Caroline Bingley is required to retain the services of either myself or one of two other solicitors' firms, whom your father chose. Upon her marriage the funds will transfer to her husband with similar stipulations as those upon Mrs. Hurst."

"If there are provisions such as Louisa's, then should there not be another major provision on her current inheritance for children?"

"Yes, there is, but by my calculations mentioning the other provisions is worthless because if she does not marry and have children before the age of thirty five then it becomes void when she gains full control, regardless of your father's desires. It is just the way that the law works."

"I see, thank you, Watson."

Darcy was curious what the last provision was and inquired.

"Mr. Bingley replied. Ten thousand pounds must be retained until my sister reaches the age of forty. If she has children then the money is to be their dowry, however if there is no children then she shall have the money. Each of my sisters have twenty thousand pounds, this means that half of their funds must stay in reserve. Should Caroline receive all of her funds today and continue to spend as she has in the past by the time she reaches the age of forty she shall have less than five thousand pounds to her name."

"Actually Mr. Bingley, if she were to spend as she has she would have less than one thousand pounds."

"Very well, Mr. Watson, let us do this. Caroline has walked her own path; I shall not feel sorry for her. Let us see how she manages on her own. I presume I can still receive updates as to how she is doing even though I have signed her inheritance over to her?"

"Should she retain my services, shall I keep you abreast of her situation?"

"Very well, can I also add to her provisions?"

"Yes, to the extent that they do not interfere or substantially change your father's."

"Good, without Caroline knowing I would like another one hundred pounds per year added to her inheritance if she adheres to her allowances voluntarily. This should provide her another one thousand pounds upon her thirty-fifth birthday, if she learns from all of this. I of course hope she marries, but at this point I cannot imagine a man who would want such a wife."

"Very well Mr. Bingley, I shall add that. Now let us speak of more pleasant things, what of your bride?"

"Mr. Watson, I am to marry an angel. Miss Jane Bennet is the eldest daughter of Mr. Bennet here." Mr. Bingley indicated towards Mr. Bennet as he said this.

Mr. Watson smiled and turned towards Mr. Bennet. "Is this true sir, is she truly an angel, or is this young man blinded by love?"

"He indeed speaks the truth, she is truly angelic. The only daughter I have that I can say this about, and I do have many of them."

Mr. Watson laughed "Good, good, now to business. I have already drawn up the settlement papers from Mr. Bingley's perspective; all we need to do is insert dowry amounts and provisions that you require sir and final allowances from Mr. Bingley."

Mr. Bennet pulled some documents from his vest pocket and handed them over to Mr. Watson who read them aloud. "Miss Jane Bennet is to receive one thousand pounds upon the death of her mother and a lump sum of ten thousand pounds upon her marriage. Eight thousand pounds is to be retained for future children with the interest from it being added to the remaining two thousand pounds that may be used in any manner as deemed appropriate by Mr. Bingley in supporting his wife the future Mrs. Jane Bennet. Upon the death of Mrs. Bennet the one thousand pounds is left entirely to the discretion of Mr. Bingley to use with as he deems necessary for the goodwill of the Bingley household."

Mr. Bingley and Mr. Darcy sat shocked. It had circulated through Meryton that the Miss Bennets' would be lucky to receive their share of five thousand pounds upon their mother's death and maybe fifty pounds per annum if extremely lucky. It seems this was not the case. Mr. Darcy recovered first.

"Clearly Meryton gossip is not to be trusted, Mr. Bennet."

"Clearly Mr. Darcy." Mr. Bennet said in a dry voice that all had learned was full of mirth. "Tuesday you shall receive the same for Miss Elizabeth and someday when some unwitting sap comes to claim the others they shall likewise be duly compensated for removing the ladies from my endless burden." He laughed at his own joke. "I trust you gentlemen can keep this a secret. I have done this to keep away the unworthy. If everyone knew that my beautiful daughters were to receive eleven thousand pounds each I would have more bucks knocking on my door than I would prefer. This way I know that they at least marry for some esteem."

Mr. Bingley finally regained his voice, if not entirely all of his senses. "Certainly Mr. Bennet, may I ask how? I mean, never mind, oh forget I said anything." Mr. Bingley was still reeling at the news and not in full control of his person.

Mr. Bennet laughed, "How my boy, well economy, that and a bit of deceit I suppose. Mrs. Bennet of course prefers shopping, however if she thought I had a small estate then she would not overspend. Sure, there are some elders around who knew what the estate made under my father's management, but they just assumed that I squandered all of the money and eventually stopped even considering it. Truth be told, I was a second son who often quarreled with my brother. From the coming of age I saved my money just in case my elder brother cut me off with the death of our father. As a professor I boarded at the university and still made a handsome wage. Upon my marriage I had already invested about twenty thousand pounds and then just added Mrs. Bennet's five thousand to it. It took some funds to restore Longbourn from disrepair when I inherited it, but not too much so as to set me back, like the neighborhood generally believes. My estate brings in about five thousand pounds per year, about the same as Netherfield. I remove two thousand from the profits and set it aside, for at least the past twenty years, for another forty thousand pounds. In all total I have fifty five thousand pounds for my five daughters and another ten thousand for Mrs. Bennet should she outlive me. If I should outlive her then the ten thousand shall be divided evenly between all of my grandchildren or I shall pass on Longbourn and live on it myself."

Mr. Darcy and Mr. Bingley sat starring at Mr. Bennet, amazed by all that they had just heard.

Mr. Watson was the first to interrupt. "I see this comes as a shock to both of you, Mr. Bingley and Mr. Darcy, but we really must proceed, how much would you wish to settle on Miss Jane Bennet for her monthly allotment and household accounts?"

"I would like Miss Jane to take responsibility for all of the household accounts as they stand. Mr. Bennet, I assume Miss Jane is familiar with accounting for funds and also economizing?"

"Yes, Mr. Bingley, I can assure you and Mr. Darcy both that my girls were instructed in all of the proper household functions required of a lady. Both Jane and Elizabeth are good with their funds and do not spend frivolously."

"Wonderful, then I would like Miss Jane to have full access to the household accounts and also her two thousand pounds plus another five hundred pounds per year. I daresay, with Caroline gone I shall be saving money. If she requires more, we shall adjust. Do you think this fair, Mr. Bennet?"

"Yes son, currently my Jane barely spends one hundred pounds per year; I am sure she shall do very well and have much remaining at the year's end. It is most generous of you."

With settlement papers completed and signed the men returned to their carriage a scarce two hours after leaving it.

"Where to now men, shall we lunch at my club since I am sure the ladies are still out shopping?"

"Certainly man, let's go." Bingley replied.

The three men arrived at White's, exited the carriage and entered the commons area. Mr. Darcy was greeted by the man and led to his usual room, where the three occupied a private screened sitting area in the back. The three men sat down in the dark leather chairs, ordered lunch, and began amiable conversation.

Half way through their lunch Lord Matlock and Colonel Fitzwilliam arrived at White's. They saw Darcy and his group and proceeded to join them.

"Well men, I assume from the merriness here that your day has proven pleasantly productive."

"Truly Uncle, have a seat and join us. We have just been learning the antics of our ladies."

"Ah, so you take advantage of their esteemed father to gain insider information that the ladies would otherwise wish to remain private, do you?"

"Certainly, what good is it to be on common footing with their father if we do not exploit it?"

All five men laughed, but then Darcy saw it, that look upon his uncle's face. Becoming serious, he inquired. "Uncle, what is it that distresses you? I know that look despite your efforts to hide it."

"Darcy, why do you have to be so observant? For once could you just worry about your lady and forget an old man."

"Nay uncle, I must know, let us be of assistance to you. We are practically all family here; let us share your burdens."

Lord Matlock laughed. "Darcy, you already share this burden whether you wish to or not."

Colonel Fitzwilliam took over the conversation at this point. "Darcy, my father and I have recently removed Anne from Rosings Place, that is, the London home of Lady Catherine." He said to ensure Mr. Bingley and Mr. Bennet were not left to wonder of Rosings Place. "We can now assure of Anne's safety and also ensure that Lady Catherine will never interfere in yours and Miss Bennet's life."

Darcy began to be concerned with the assurance that his cousin was portraying. "Cousin, you know I would never doubt you and I am pleased with such a happy turn of events, but how can you be so sure that Lady Catherine will not disturb us? She is hardly likely to keep her word and why would you be concerned for Anne's safety? What has happened?"

Lord Matlock stated in a matter of fact manner "She will not interfere because she is bound for the Americas with one Mr. George Wickham on tonight's departing vessel."

"You cannot be serious!" exclaimed Mr. Darcy.

"Oh, indeed I am nephew."

"Why? How? I mean I do not desire her interference; however I do not wish her exiled from England. I can protect my family from her."

"No, I will protect my family from her. Darcy you must understand, she threatened Georgiana and Miss Elizabeth. Still worse yet, she truck Anne. Generally we take her threats for naught, but she crossed the line this time and I fear for all of my nieces. Yes, I see you are surprised, Anne is not safe."

"What is to happen to Anne?"

"She is of an age to inherit without her mother and thus she shall. Today she took full control of her inheritance, Rosings Park and Rosings Place. She is officially free from her mother and I must say I have never seen her in better health. I believe you described her as 'bright as any ornament I have ever laid eyes upon is that correct, Richard?"

Richard cleared his throat and even blushed a little, "Ummm, yes father I believe I did. Is a cousin not able to comment on his fair cousin's state of health without drawing an eyebrow?"

"Surely, Richard," Lord Matlock tenderly began, but he could not help adding a bit more. "However I doubt that ever before has said female cousin drawn as much inspection from said male cousin as was done today when she exhibited youth, vibrancy, energy, and passion, yes passion. It appears as if Anne's sickly demeanor has been a pretense and Richard saw it and I dare say admired it instantly. I dare say my sister may have set her cap on the wrong cousin." Richard glared at his father who innocently responded with a weary smile upon his lips "Have I misspoken?"

Richard stuttered to answer in a non-eloquent manner "Yes, father, you have misspoken. I believe you are allowing your mind to run wild."

"Uncle, Richard, I am indeed sorry that Lady Catherine caused such an event to occur, however for Anne's sake" and stealing a sly look at Richard "and Richard's, I hope it is for the best."

All of the men roared with laughter at Darcy's comment and then continued to talk and tease for another two hours before the party retired.

As they were all departing for their carriages, Mr. Darcy inquired of his uncle. "Uncle, I have been thinking that we should attend the theatre while everyone is here in town. What think you of this idea?"

"Sounds good my boy, which play shall we see?"

"I believe Romeo and Juliet by Shakespeare is currently playing."

"Oh yes, a romantic play for lovers it is. What day is it playing?"

"I believe each Saturday."

"Well it is a little too short of notice for tomorrow. You know how ladies make such a fuss on such short notice, but I suppose next Saturday shall be ideal."

"Very well uncle, Saturday the seventh it is then. We shall inform the ladies this evening at dinner. Also, shall you, Aunt Matlock and Anne join us at London House for Sunday dinner? You too, Richard, if you are available."

"Yes we shall, I will inform your aunt."

"I shall if I am able." The colonel replied.

The men parted and each returned to their respective homes. London House was filled with enjoyable conversation, reading, and business correspondence as they awaited the arrival of the ladies.

Chapter 29
Back at London House

Friday November 29, 1811
MR. GARDINER,

Sir, I hope that your visit in Lambton with the family of Mrs. Gardiner has been a pleasant affair. I apologize for this interruption, but want to assure you that all is well here in London at your place of business. The purpose of this letter is to inform you that your nieces, Miss Jane and Miss Elizabeth Bennet are in town for the purpose of purchasing their wedding trousseau.

This may come as a shock to you and I apologize that it is me informing you instead of your esteemed family; however I thought it best that you be made aware of the developments sooner rather than later.

Although I do not know the exact date, I am led to believe that they are to be married sometime in the first part of December.

In case you have not been previously informed Miss Jane Bennet is to be married to Mr. Charles Bingley of Netherfield near the Bennet's own home and Miss Elizabeth is to marry Mr. Fitzwilliam Darcy of Pemberley in Derbyshire, very near to your own current location.

As I said before I hope this letter finds you well and pleased with the contents that it relays.

Respectfully,

JONATHAN STEARNS

Please advise Mrs. Gardiner that I took the liberty of presenting Miss Elizabeth with the French fabrics and Brussels lace from the armoire in your office. Modiste Belle has been commissioned to fashion the wedding gown and if I may be so bold, the design she has envisioned shall do the fabrics every justice that they deserve. I hope that Mrs. Gardiner will be well pleased and not offended by the presumption I had in presenting the fabrics, but under the short timeline in which the dress is to be commissioned I felt I had no other choice.

Jonathan looked over his letter one final time before sealing it and posting it express to Lambton. He truly hoped the news would bring joy to the Gardiners.

The ladies returned to London House packages abounding all of their arms and those of the footman, with promises of more to follow.

"Daughters, I see you had a productive day shopping and from the looks of the stamps on the wrapping we shall make your uncle a very rich man." He kissed each of his daughters on the cheek as he reached them.

"Yes father, it appears as if it is commonly known that the best warehouse is uncle Gardiner's. Jonathan helped us very well today."

"Yes, well I know Jonathan and his aptitude for selecting pretty things for my girls. He always has had a soft spot for you two adorned in finery."

"Oh, father, stop teasing."

"Well off with you, put your purchases away and prepare for dinner, it is in less than an hour."

Jane and Elizabeth headed towards their rooms packages in hand with maids and footmen following. Georgiana lagged behind and bid Lady Matlock farewell. She had just left when Darcy and Bingley entered the foyer.

"Brother, Mr. Bingley, oh what a wonderful day we have had." Both looked upon Georgiana smiling and invited her into the drawing room. Mr. Bennet took this opportunity to prepare for dinner.

"I am so glad, Georgiana."

"Brother it was more fun than any shopping I have ever done. I hope to repeat the event many times in the future."

Darcy laughed as he responded. "So you shall, dearest, though I doubt that my pocket book can handle it. How many items did you purchase for your closet today?"

"None for me brother, this day was all about Jane and Elizabeth."

A very shocked Darcy responded "None, how in the world did you accomplish that? I have never heard of you returning with nothing. Are you ill?"

"No of course not Fitzwilliam, I am perfectly well. I said that I did not purchase anything for me, not that I returned empty handed."

A large smile crossed Darcy's face. "I see what you mean. I must learn to take your words literally. So what did you purchase?"

"It is a surprise for Lizzy, I shall not even tell you."

"Oh, what a fierce creature you are."

Mr. Bingley happily chimed in here. "Did you only purchase gifts for Miss Elizabeth or were you able to fulfill my task as well?"

Darcy looked at his friend, realizing, that Bingley had set Georgiana on the same task that he had given his aunt.

"Yes, Mr. Bingley, I selected three items for Miss Bennet's trousseau that she had liked very well but had decided to forgo due to the cost that she labeled extravagant. I then accompanied her around the warehouse and watched her eye and touch the most beautiful French gloves and shawl set that she never considered purchasing, but that I could tell she absolutely adored. I recommend that you give it to her as a particular gift upon your wedding. They shall all be delivered to Grosvenor Square."

"Thank you Georgiana, thank you so much. I cannot tell you how much I appreciate this."

"Anytime Mr. Bingley, will that be all or should I continue in this manner as we complete shopping throughout the week?"

"By all means look for more. I would like you to identify about ten items to be sent to Grosvenor Square."

"If I may Mr. Bingley, and you too brother, remember the name of Jonathan at the Gardiner warehouses. He has a particular knack of selecting items that your ladies love. Particularly Miss Elizabeth, he truly knows her taste. He will be most helpful in the future for recommending all of the best and most fashionable items for gifts."

Georgiana winked at her brother and departed the library before either could say another word.

"I dare say Darcy; she gets more animated each day. You had best train your hounds to chase off suitors."

"I believe you are correct Bingley, let us ready ourselves for dinner."

Dinner was a pleasant affair as everyone enjoyed the company of each and every other person at the table.

The ladies were notified of Sunday's intended dinner guests and their intent to visit the theatre the following Saturday with not a little pleasure.

As the dinner party broke up and everyone went their separate ways Elizabeth approached Darcy.

"Fitzwilliam, have you any commitments this evening or are you free to talk?"

"Elizabeth my love, I am free and at your disposal."

The two entered the library and sat in chairs facing one another near the fire.

"Fitzwilliam, with all that has occurred the past two days I feel I have barely even set eyes upon you."

"I feel the same Elizabeth, but let us talk now. Are you enjoying your time spent here in London?"

"Oh yes, I am enjoying it very well. Your Aunt is the most wonderful woman; I am truly blessed to have made her acquaintance. Are you aware that she intends to purchase some of my trousseau items as a wedding gift to me?"

"Yes, she made me aware of her intent this morning. I hope that it does not offend you in any way?"

"No of course not, it was just surprising. I know my father may not have the means that you and your family has, but he has informed me that he has enough for my trousseau and I need not worry about the expense. He said I may need additional items for the cold in Derbyshire and for various events that we may attend that I may not be used to from my limited exposure to town events."

Darcy hated knowing information and being unable to share it with those that he loved and whom it affected. He spoke directly to Elizabeth but did not look her directly in the eyes as he usually did.

"Elizabeth my love, your father is correct; you need not worry about the expense of the trousseau. Even if your father could not afford it, which I assure you he can, I would bear the expense of anything that you desire. In fact I also had my aunt set up an account for you in the name of Mrs. Darcy with your uncle's warehouse for any future purchases that you desire."

"Fitzwilliam, are you not telling me something?"

"No dearest, what do you mean?"

"Fitzwilliam please look me directly in the eyes and tell me that you are not hiding any information from me."

"Elizabeth, I assure you there is nothing."

"Fitzwilliam I told you to look in my eyes and say it, not at your hands, not at my feet, not at the wall, but in my eyes."

Just then there was a knock at the door and Mr. Bennet entered.

"Oh Mr. Bennet, you are here, I was just assuring your daughter that she should allow any present my aunt wishes to give her and not worry about the trousseau expense for you are able to afford it and even if not that I would happily pay it. She thinks that I am for some reason hiding something from her do you think that I am?"

Mr. Bennet clearly caught the meaning of Mr. Darcy's words and responded. "Mr. Darcy, I tend to agree with you, and I will join you in assuring Elizabeth that all you spoke is true. As to the secrets, I suppose Mr. Darcy does have a secret, but I suppose if you were to promise secrecy as well he could share it with you as could Mr. Bingley with Jane. Perhaps we should gather the other two here and just tell our secrets one time."

Mr. Darcy physically looked relieved at this idea and instantly called the footman to fetch Bingley and Jane. Elizabeth sat and looked at the two curiously.

Bingley entered quickly with a look of concern upon his face. He instantly addressed Mr. Bennet. "Mr. Bennet sir, Jane and I were just discussing how happy I am to have all of the marriage settlement papers signed. She has gotten it into her pretty head that I am not fully disclosing the particulars of today's events to her and would be most appreciative if you could assure her of today's success."

"Certainly Mr. Bingley, I think Mr. Darcy is also having a similar problem here with Elizabeth. Well I believe I should have known my two smartest girls could read you two bucks like a book. I suppose I shall have to break the news to them."

Distress instantly spread on each girl's face which their father laughed at. "Do not look so gloomy girls, I am not rescinding my blessing of your marriages, I am only here to tell you that each of you shall have a dowry of eleven thousand pounds apiece."

Elizabeth and Jane's eyes opened wide in surprise and neither could say a word. Mr. Darcy and Mr. Bingley just laughed as the shock began to wear off. Mr. Bennet continued to relay the particulars to both of the girls. By the time his story ended the girls had recovered their senses and of course Lizzy had questions.

"Father, why did you never tell us? Does mother know?" Then realizing what she had just said Elizabeth shook her head in the negative and answered her own question. "Of course not, she would never be able to keep such information secret from the neighborhood in general. She would declare it from the rooftops hoping it would attract some suitor. Yes father, I see your motive and I must say I agree."

Mr. Bennet answered her first question and then a few others that she thought to ask. When all of the questions were answered he excused himself and left the four lovers to themselves in the library.

All four sat down and Darcy began. "I am very well pleased that your father told you I would hate having to try to keep that a secret. I would surely make myself sick."

Bingley laughed and said "No such thing, man, I was just going to break my promise of secrecy and tell Jane, I was about to break it when we were called in here, I am just glad I did not have to break the promise with knowing it less than twenty-four hours. What a poor excuse of a gentleman I am." He laughed at his own statement and Jane of course came to his rescue stating that he was a gentleman and all other manner of comforting words.

The ladies were further informed of the wedding date which they agreed with and the two parties broke to opposite corners of the room, Jane and Bingley to sit by the window and Darcy and Elizabeth to stay by the fire.

"Fitzwilliam, I am shocked beyond words, I had no idea my father had set aside such funds, but I agree no one should know of this so that my younger sisters have a chance of matches of esteem, not those tainted by the thoughts of wealth."

"Very well, we shall tell no one."

"Thank you, Fitzwilliam."

"So Elizabeth, you began to tell me of your shopping with Aunt Ellen before we met with your father. So you have had a good time?"

"Oh yes indeed, she is very good to escort Jane and me in our purchases. I am very happy to have her support at this time."

"But...?" Darcy knew something was on her mind and he wanted her to confide in him.

"But, Fitzwilliam, she is not my Aunt Gardiner. I have told you before how dear my aunt is to me, in fact she is more my mother than my mother is my mother. I dearly wish that she were here with me and with Jane too of course. I miss her Fitzwilliam, I want to share my joy with her, have her meet you and love you as I do."

"Elizabeth, I share that desire with you. Your Aunt Gardiner must be a remarkable woman to be able to hold such a high regard with you. I desire to meet her and welcome her to our family."

"Thank you, Fitzwilliam, I was afraid you would not know what I meant when I tell you that I am beyond happiness and sorrow right now. I am so happy to be engaged to you and here with you, but so sorrowful that I cannot share it with one of the people I love most in this world. My heart is almost breaking over it." A tear had begun to fall from Elizabeth's eye as she spoke of her beloved aunt. Darcy reached towards her and wiped it away with his thumb, keeping his hands lovingly on her shoulders.

"Elizabeth, if this distresses you too much let me have you consider another option. I know I have requested that we marry as soon as possible, but I would not have your dearest aunt miss anything. Do you want to postpone the wedding so that your shopping can be finished with your aunt and you can have her be a greater part of our wedding preparations?"

"Oh Fitzwilliam, you are the best of men to offer this." Elizabeth reached for his hand and placed a kiss on it as she continued. "But no, I would wish to marry on the eighteenth. My aunt and uncle shall return by then and be at our wedding. Nothing will stop them from attending I am sure. I want to marry soon as well."

Darcy had been holding his breath while waiting for her to answer. He wanted to offer, for her peace of mind, though in no way did he agree with the idea of postponing the wedding. He was pleased that she wanted to marry him as soon as he wanted to marry her.

Their discussion continued pleasantly and teasingly when Elizabeth remembered her room.

"May I ask you another question, Fitzwilliam?"

"Yes, anything."

"Am I ensconced in London House's mistress's chambers?"

Darcy looked at her a moment and replied in confidence as he moved a little closer to her. "Yes you are. I want you where you belong, you are not some guest, even if you are not yet my wife in name you are my wife in my mind and therefore you deserve the best that London House has to offer. The Mistress's chambers are the best and rightfully yours. I want you there."

Elizabeth saw the love and determination in his face and heard it in his voice. "Thank you; I do love the room so much. May I tour the rest of the master suite chambers?"

Darcy reached for Elizabeth's hand and held it in his caressing her palm. "If you truly want to tour them now I will arrange it, however I wish to show them to you myself on the day that we marry. If you were to tour them now I could not see your reaction at your first sight of them as I would not be able to accompany you. Please choose to wait."

"With such a declaration how could I do anything except wait? I would never choose to see them without you. I shall wait the day that we marry and return here together to view them.

Darcy was so pleased with her response that he tightened his grip upon her hand, pulling her close to him. He leaned in and kissed her ever so gently that she could not doubt how happy he was in her decision.

The two talked for another two hours about everything they could possibly think of and finally retired upstairs to their respective rooms. Darcy had escorted Elizabeth, stopping outside of her bedroom door. He leaned towards her and whispered into her ear. "Elizabeth, dearest, loveliest Elizabeth, I have the greatest desire that our wedding day will soon arrive so that I may accompany you beyond this door. When I do rest assured we shall not only tour the master suite together." With statement said Darcy leaned in and placed the most passionate of kisses upon Elizabeth's lips. "Until tomorrow my love, dream of me as I shall dream of you." Darcy turned and went quickly down the hall to the next door, the Master's chambers, and entered with one last passionate glance at Elizabeth still standing in the hallway looking back at him as he entered his room.

Friday evening was one of the darkest ever in the life of Frederick Richard Fitzwilliam, currently known to all as Lord Matlock. He stood at the edge of Pier Street looking over the railing to the ships below as his only living sibling boarded the *Rhemalda*, a ship that would set sail carrying her and not stop until it landed on the shores of the distant and unknown lands of America.

He was distressed, grieved, but it had to occur, it was for the best. How could he allow her to stay when she had threatened the lives of three of the most precious women in his life, his nieces, Miss Georgiana Darcy, Miss Anne de Bourgh, and Miss Elizabeth Bennet, soon to be Mrs. Fitzwilliam Darcy.

The harbor master blew the harbor horn indicating that all had boarded and that departure was imminent. Frederick Fitzwilliam eagerly searched the ship's deck for a final sight of his sister but he could see no sign of her. The ship's ropes were untied and it departed the shores of England. Frederick Fitzwilliam stayed and watched until the ship was beyond human sight; he then fell to his knees and wept.

Chapter 30
Lord's Day

An expressed arrived in Lambton Saturday evening, causing a stir and a discontinuation of a most pleasant trip.

"Madeline my dear, a most unexpected and happy affair has just been brought to my attention by Jonathan. Would you care to read this letter?" said Mr. Gardiner to his lady.

"Yes, my dear, I would." said Mrs. Gardiner as she reached for the letter in his hand.

As she read a smile crossed her face. "Oh I am so glad I showed that fabric and lace to Jonathan, what a tragedy it would have been had it not been able to be used. I am so glad that Miss Belle is commissioned to fashion the dress. What an unexpected event. I had no idea that Fanny was familiar with Miss Belle. Come, we must return to London at once."

Mr. Gardiner lay a hand on her arm "My dear, is that the only news you gathered from this letter or did you also note who it is that your favorite nieces are marrying?"

"I see, Bingley and Darcy it says here, hmmm where have I heard that name recently?" Then it dawned on her. "Darcy! Elizabeth is to marry the Master of Pemberley! Edward, do you think this is correct?"

"It must be my dear; however we shall not announce it in case no one is to know yet."

The couple left the room and called for their trunks to be readied for departure first thing in the morning.

Although it was not a custom for the Gardiners to travel on the Lord's Day this was an emergency and they were desirous of reaching London no later than Monday.

Saturday passed much as the day before, with shopping, dining, and entertaining, pleasant for all in attendance.

Sunday morning dawned cold but beautiful for the first day of December. All of the carriages were readied and occupants bundled in their Sunday best.

News had spread rapidly around London that the hearts of Mr. Fitzwilliam Darcy of Pemberley and his best friend Mr. Charles Bingley had been captured by two country beauties from Hertfordshire with not a little interest. That interest had brought out all of the town's residents for a chance to see the ladies at church.

St. John's chapel was near full when the Darcy and Bingley carriages arrived. The occupants departed the carriage and gathered on the walkway to enter the church together. All could tell that the church was bursting with people despite the cold day and Darcy commented on it. "Well, it appears as if the service shall be a full one today. Let us go in and see if our family pew was left unoccupied or if there was someone bold enough to take it." Darcy smiled and led the way with Elizabeth on his arm, Mr. Bennet followed escorting Georgiana and Bingley finished the line with Jane on his arm as the last of the party to enter the chapel.

As soon as the party entered all eyes settled upon them and the room became quiet except for a few whispers made to their neighbors about the pretty appearances of the ladies who entered on the gentlemen's arms.

The entire party sat in the Darcy family pew and enjoyed the services. When the rector had completed his message and the final hymn had been sung the Darcy party arose to return to the carriages. Darcy escorted Elizabeth with the rest of the party following just as they had entered the church.

They were not far beyond the chapel doors when introductions were required to be made. Everyone, who could contrive any association whatsoever with the Darcy's or Bingley's, approached to offer congratulations and tried to get updated information with regards to London's latest gossip firsthand.

It took the group a quarter of an hour to walk from the chapel doors to their waiting carriages and had it not been for Mr. Darcy and his adeptness at little or no conversation it would have taken significantly longer.

The Darcys' and Elizabeth entered the Darcy carriage and Bingley, Jane, and Mr. Bennet the other. No sooner had the carriage door closed than Mr. Darcy tapped his walking stick on the roof and the carriage departed for London House.

The Gardiners had gotten an early start for their return trip to London, leaving the "Lambton Inn" by six in the morning. They were blessed with good weather and relatively dry roads considering the time of year.

Mrs. Gardiner was very eager to return home and be with her favorite nieces at this happy moment in their lives. They were every bit as dear to her as her own children and she was almost distressed that she was missing some of the events already. If Jonathan was correct the wedding dresses were already planned and she was not there to offer support and advice.

Mr. Gardiner could see his wife's gentle agitation and tried to soothe her as best he could. Happily for him, she was an even-tempered woman and instantly saw the folly of her worrying, settling down to enjoy the journey, realizing that nothing could be done until their return.

As evening was approaching they stopped at a country inn for the night, bedding early so that they could again set off early enough to make it to London in time to still call on their family.

Lord and Lady Matlock arrived at London House as punctual as ever for dinner. "Uncle, Aunt, we are so glad that you could join us this evening." Said Darcy as he walked into the room with Elizabeth on his arm.

Lady Matlock could not but smile at the sight of domestic felicity upon the countenance of her nephew. Never had he looked so at ease in the presence of anyone, even his own family... my, was that a smile upon his face? Seeing the smile was all she could handle. She could no longer refrain from embracing her nephew, so letting go of her husband's arm she advanced upon Darcy and his love.

"Nephew, niece, how it pleases me to see the two of you so happy together here in Darcy's home, I knew one day Darcy would find a woman to bring him such happiness." By now Lady Matlock had reached them and wrapped her arms around both of them at once.

Elizabeth let out a little laugh and Darcy looked at his uncle inquisitively who merely shrugged his shoulders as if to say that he still did not understand the fairer sex.

While all were still offering good wishes and removing their outer attire the bell rung again to admit a handsome sight, Colonel Richard Fitzwilliam accompanying a very elegantly adorned Anne de Bourgh.

"Cousins, how happy I am that you could join us." Darcy went to Anne to address her, first offering his apologies regarding her mother which she quickly brushed off.

Anne was glad that her mother was gone. No one, simply no one could ever imagine what she had been through the past twenty-five years and if they did they would not condemn her for her loss of feeling towards he mother's present circumstances. Luckily good did triumph over evil, her mother was now gone from hurting her and she was allowed to return to Rosings Place and eventually Rosings Park alone and able to restore order and love to places that had for too long been devoid of it. This day being alone at Rosings Place, only being visited by Richard had been near heaven itself.

"Nonsense, Darcy, I wish it not mentioned this evening. I simply must meet your Miss Bennet. I am eternally grateful to her for stealing your heart since I must admit, as you most certainly know that I did not want it, despite my mother's insistence." Darcy noticed Anne's eyes drift a little to Richard and then quickly snap back to him making him almost wonder if he had imagined it.

"Certainly, Anne, come. Elizabeth, may I introduce you to my cousin Miss Anne de Bourgh, Anne, this is Miss Elizabeth Bennet, my fiancée."

"Miss de Bourgh, I am so pleased to meet you. Colonel Fitzwilliam and Mr. Darcy have told me much about you." Anne blushed slightly but confidently responded.

"Thank you, Miss Bennet, I am indeed happy to make your acquaintance as well. I have heard much about your beauty and talents. I dearly hope that I may hear you play and sing sometime soon."

"I daresay they have exaggerated my talents for some mischievous reason, however I should be delighted if the opportunity arises. Come; let us retire to the drawing room while we wait dinner. Georgiana and Mr. Bingley are already there with my sister and father. Are you acquainted with Mr. Bingley?"

"Yes, I am, for he is a great friend of both my cousins. He has come with them to visit at Rosings on their annual visits. He is an amiable man."

"You are correct, he is truly amiable. Come you must meet some of my family then. Fitzwilliam, we are to the drawing room to meet my family."

"We shall follow. Aunt, Uncle, Richard shall we?"

The remaining four turned and followed Elizabeth and Anne into the drawing room, where introductions were made and pleasant conversations was had among all.

Dinner was announced and Darcy led the way to the dining room with Elizabeth on his arm, followed by Lord and Lady Matlock, Mr. Bennet and Georgiana, Richard and Anne and lastly Mr. Bingley and Jane. Everyone took their seats at the table and dining and conversation commenced.

Such a perfect dinner group one could not wish for. With dinner completed the men retired to Darcy's library for drinks and Elizabeth led the way to the music room for the ladies to talk and await the return of the men.

"Uncle, Richard, I am so glad that you could join us this evening. It has been a most enjoyable dinner."

"True, Darcy, I have never known a better dinner group." announced Bingley.

Lord Matlock simply nodded his head in agreement. The past few days had been trying for him, first sending off his sister and then all of the thoughts of guilt that had plagued him since. Darcy noticed all of this and approaching his uncle he extended his sympathy.

"Uncle, please tell me you are well and that you are not unduly distressed. You have done what you had to and must not think on it too much."

"Yes, yes, Darcy, it is done and for the best. I do not regret my decision only the fact that it had to occur. I worry for her despite it all. She is my sister after all. What is to become of her? How shall she live? I know not. I have provided her some money to make her way and live when she reaches the Americas, but I am distressed. I wish I could have prevented it all, but I simply could not. I cringe to think of what she may have done if I had not taken the actions that I did."

"What uncle, tell us so that we may share your grief and lighten your burdens." All nodded in agreement to Darcy that they would share anything that they could to aide their uncle, father, and friend.

"No, it is bad enough that Richard and Anne had to bear witness to such hatred and cruelty. I wish for nothing more than for it to never be spoken of again. Am I understood? No one is to ever ask me again."

His eyes penetrated everyone in the room as each nodded their solemn promise to never speak of it again.

"Come, let us be happy, this is a time of rejoicing and celebration. I shall not allow my mood to affect everyone. I shall be fine; I just need time to adjust. Come Mr. Bennet let us tease these young men and tell them what they are soon to be in store for as the delightful Miss Bennets' change from being accommodating young fiancées to the ever powerful wives that have dominion over our homes and can bring us to our knees with nothing but a nod of their pretty heads." Lord Matlock stated. Everyone in the room laughed and took a seat. The atmosphere was already beginning to lighten.

Mr. Bennet smiled his agreement and settled into his already favorite chair ready to be entertained. His short acquaintance with the Fitzwilliam and Darcy families had taught him of their easy teasing dispositions, and if his senses were correct then the three men before him were to be targeted. Yes, three, for indeed Colonel Fitzwilliam was not to be left out.

"Richard, son, I noticed you had an early departure after this morning's services and I have not seen hide nor hair of you until you showed up here in pleasant female company."

The Colonel simply nodded his head knowing that any reply would only stoke his father further.

Darcy having a bit of pity on him began "Richard, is Anne as well as she seems under the present circumstances of her mother?" Then looking at his uncle for fear he had just approached the subject all had promised to never speak of, he was relieved that his uncle nodded his continuance. "I spoke with her momentarily and it seems she is more pleased then distressed."

"You are right, Darcy, it seems she is. I have spent much of today in her company and have learned but little. From what I gather Lady Catherine has hurt her in many ways over the years and she is indeed more happy than sad at her mother's departure."

Lord Matlock frowned deeply at this and became serious in his reply "Richard has she indicated in what manner she has been hurt? Is it beyond what we all see in having her life stifled and ruled over?"

"Father I cannot say for sure, but I believe that Anne has been hurt in many ways, I dare say that yes beyond being stifled and ruled over, though I cannot say in what manner. She is happy that she is her own mistress now and that her mother has no control over her. Throughout just today I saw her confidence rise and her personality begin to shine. Truly she is an amazing woman."

Lord Matlock smiled and his mischievous nature took over "Woman, then, not girl, lady, or cousin."

The Colonel instantly saw the mistake that he had made in praising his cousin so. "Yes father, I know you are trying to trap me in some sort of word play, but I will not have it. Anne has been through a lot the last few days and the last thing she needs is you speculating about her."

"Calm yourself my boy, now you even jump to conclusion and come to her defense. I was not speculating or making reference to her, I was making reference and speculating about YOU. I think you are more lost then you want to admit, defending the lady even when it is not needed."

"I agree, Richard; I think you have taken to her defense. Why just days ago I remember Darcy doing the same for Miss Elizabeth," Bingley interjected.

Mr. Bennet could not help himself "If memory serves me correct, Mr. Bingley, you yourself were quick to jump to your lady's aid when confronted in my library. Puppy Dog Bingley was nowhere to be seen, but Big Dog Bingley was readily there. Look at the man you have grown into the past week all because of the love of a Bennet lady."

Bingley was red from head to toe when he responded "I suppose I am a lost hopeless man, but as long as I am lost to her I would not want to be found."

"Well said, Charles, but I want to get back to the topic of my son. Already we know that we are to wish you and Darcy joy in your impending nuptials, but Richard, when are we to offer you felicity and happiness in your choice?"

"Father, you have overstepped your bounds. You know nothing of the sort has occurred. Anne is in a distressing situation just losing her mother and all. I or any man would indeed be callous to take advantage of her in such an unpleasant situation."

"Well I dare say that Anne is not grieving from what I have seen and I think it is very thoughtful of you to give her a few days to grieve, but what about tomorrow? I think she will be well enough recovered if you wanted to approach the subject, and very willing I dare say from the looks of it."

Mr. Bennet happily added to the conversation. "You know, Colonel, we already have the church booked, dresses are being ordered, and all of the family will be in attendance at this double wedding, why not just make it a triple?"

Lord Matlock jumped at the plan "Splendid idea, Thomas, I could not have thought of a better plan myself. What say you, Richard; shall we make it a triple?"

Darcy and Bingley kept their mouths shut, this had indeed been taken a little further than any teasing had ever gone it the past.

A tight lipped and stone faced Colonel Fitzwilliam stood and went to the door "No, Father, we are not to make it a triple." He opened the library door stepped out and quickly closed it. They had hit too close to his feelings and he could not have it. None followed him, wanting to give him a wide berth; however laughter could be heard in the library following his departure.

Colonel Fitzwilliam approached one of Darcy's footmen and asked him to have Miss Anne step out for a brief conversation.

Anne was summoned and joined Richard in the foyer outside the drawing room. "Cousin, you asked to speak with me."

"Yes, I did. I must depart this evening and wanted to inquire whether you would have my parents escort you home or if you desire to return now by way of my escort. I understand that it is still early in the evening if you wish to stay."

Richard wondered if Anne felt for him what he had begun to feel for her and was using this as a sort of test. Normally a lady in love would not decline an offered escort from her interest, but a mere cousin would.

"Are you well, Richard, I hope it is nothing serious?"

"Yes, yes, I am well, it is just that tomorrow I must meet with my regiment and I must prepare a few items this evening."

"Tomorrow, you are not leaving are you? It is just a meeting is it not?" Anne was slightly distressed at this thought and Richard could see it and hear it in her voice. He did not respond just nodded to her as she came to her senses of what she was saying and responded. "Would you mind if I asked you to escort me home, I mean would it take you too long away from your duties?"

"No, I mean, you may ask and I shall be happy to take you home Anne. My duties will not require so much time as to not allow me to escort you to Rosings Place."

"Very well, I wish for you to take me home. I shall inform my Aunt and return directly."

Anne turned, entered the room to inform all and was very quickly back to an awaiting Richard.

Richard had called for the carriage and already put on his outer wear. He then picked up Anne's in his hands, holding it ready to place over her small and delicate frame when she returned. He could smell her perfume on the garments, yet again reminding him of the woman she had become.

She returned and he helped her into her coat and handed her, her bonnet and gloves, his hand slightly touching hers as she took them. Once she was bundled and well guarded from the cold he offered her his arm and the two stepped out to the awaiting carriage. The drive to Rosings Place was short and was done in almost complete silence. What a contrast to the rest of the day the two had spent together in amiable and free conversation. Richard departed the carriage and helped Anne down walking with her up the walkway and into the foyer of the home.

"Cousin, Richard, do you have time for an evening drink or must you leave directly?"

Richard stood in the entry, twirling his hat in his hand. Already she had pleased him by wanting him to escort her home and now she was inviting him for a drink should he accept or not. His reply did not come quickly and Anne began to worry that she had been too upfront.

"I will understand if you must go sir, I just..."

"I am sorry Anne, I did not mean to not answer I was just calculating the time in my head. Yes, I believe I can stay for a drink." Richard shed his outer jacket and lay it on the bench in the foyer as she handed hers to the butler. Richard followed Anne into the library where they settled into the chairs in front of the fire and enjoyed a glass of wine.

They sat mostly in silence for near ten minutes enjoying each other's company, but not needing to speak. Richard had almost finished his glass when he turned his body in his chair and leaned towards Anne. "Anne, what are your plans now that you are on your own? Where shall you live, how shall you spend your time?"

"Oh, I do not know. I suppose I shall stay near family here in London at least until after Darcy's wedding and then I shall probably return to Rosings. The household has had no reprieve in many years and I would not want them to continue on as they have without my mother. I wish to simplify things a bit and live in peace."

"Yes, I am sure you will love having a peaceful life. But will you be lonely? You could live in London and get out into society and meet ladies and gentlemen that you could be friends with, begin to go to balls and parties and things of that sort."

"Yes, I suppose I could, but Richard I have no desire to flaunt myself about town and see and be seen. I truly want a quiet and peaceful life. I shall return to Rosings Park and live there in quiet and solitude."

"You would not always want to be alone though, would you Anne?"

"No I suppose I would not, but I also have no intent to throw myself upon the London ton."

"Would you allow visitors at Rosings Park?"

Anne smiled at him. She had been hoping his conversation was for his own interest and not simply for her to get out and meet people. For she already had chosen who she wanted to enjoy her days with.

"Yes, I suppose visitors would be welcome, at least for short stays, and some of them would be more welcome than others."

"Are family visitors welcome visitors?"

"Yes, some more than others." Anne could not believe how bold she was being.

"Would I be a welcome visitor?"

Anne's smile became so large that even the Colonel could not miss the joy showing upon her face. "Yes, Richard you would be a most welcome visitor at any time and for any length of stay."

"Any length of stay?"

"Yes."

Richard swallowed the rest of his drink in one gulp and then leaned forward. "Anne I know that in the past we have not spent any great amount of time together, even when I had wished it your mother..."

"I know Richard, she always wanted me to spend time with Darcy, but she is not here now, do not mention her at such a happy time." Anne put her drink down and leaned forward in her chair reaching across and touching Richard's hand. "Please go on, I want you to go on."

Richard did not miss her meaning. "You do, you want me to?"

"Yes, I want you to."

"Anne, if you desire, I would be a permanent guest at Rosings Park. Then I could offer you protection and company."

Anne misunderstanding his meaning quickly took her hands from his and with a bit of hurt and anger replied "Guest, Richard, I do not want you as my guest to offer protection and company to me I want you as my husband to offer me love and affection. I had begun to think that you felt the same way about me that I feel for you. Are you merely offering support to a cousin or do you wish to love and comfort a wife?"

Anne was embarrassed and hurt, but it must be said, Richard Fitzwilliam may be able to fight battles in war, but in matters of the heart he was completely inept.

Colonel Fitzwilliam did not respond, he simply stood and pulled Anne to him and kissed her with a passion he did not know even existed in the race of man.

"Anne, dearest, I was proposing, I was just making a mess of it. Thank you so much for doing it so much better than me. I accept, I accept with all of my heart."

Both began laughing as they realized Anne had proposed to him but then quickly sat back down moving their chairs closer so to be able to still touch hands as they sat.

"Richard, I know you must leave to prepare for tomorrow, but I also wish for us to discuss what is to happen in our future. I want to talk before we make any announcements to the family. Can you return tomorrow evening?"

"Anne, I can stay and talk now. I do not have commitments this evening; I simply had to get away from my father. He had guessed the intentions of my heart and I could not be around him any further without being embarrassed and mortified. I wanted to be with you and was so glad that you wanted me to escort you home and not my parents."

"Oh, what would you have done had I decided to stay?"

"I would have been jealous that you enjoyed their company more than mine and returned to my quarters a jilted and hurt man."

Anne playfully slapped his arm. "You would have done nothing of the sort."

"Surely I would have, but since that is not what occurred we must not dwell on it. How shall we begin to decide our future? When do you wish to marry?"

"Richard, I do not want a large wedding I want it a small family affair and if you do not think me too bold I would wish for it to take place soon."

An enormous smiled crossed Richard's face. "What about December the eighteenth?"

"The eighteenth, that is scarcely days away, how would we ever prepare in time?"

"Could a dress be made in such an amount of time?"

"Yes, I suppose a dress alone could be made, but what about the church and the flowers and the breakfast?"

"It is already done, for have you forgotten that it is Darcy and Bingley's wedding. They have already offered a third wedding that day even if it was done in jest. We could be married all of us together. That is if you would not object?"

"Object, no, why I would never dream of it. I cannot imagine how it could be made any easier or more expeditiously performed. It is perfect"

"It is settled then, we shall be married on December the eighteenth." Richard leaned in and sealed the date with another kiss from Anne.

"Richard, there is one very important thing I wish to discuss with you?"

"What is that?"

"I wish to discuss your position as a Colonel. Do you want to retain it or would you be happy becoming a country gentleman over Rosings Park?"

"Which do you prefer Anne, a husband in uniform or one at home under foot."

"I think there is more to this than what I prefer. As any wife, I would prefer my husband with me, but Richard I know how you love what you do and you are very good at it. The question is what you would prefer. I will follow you."

"Oh Anne my sweet, you are so wonderful to be thinking of my needs. An army life is not for you. You were born into fortune and convenience. I would not take that from you. I too was born into convenience and had to learn the army life. But if you remember right my father groomed not only my brother but also me in the art of property and estate management. I should be much happier and comfortable at Rosings Park with you than I ever would be in an army encampment. I shall give up my commission tomorrow and stand with you by my side as we manage Rosings Park as Mr. and Mrs. Fitzwilliam."

Anne was so happy all she could do was smile at Richard.

"How long have we been here, Anne?"

"I think about half an hour."

"So it has not even been an hour since we left London House?"

"I believe you are correct."

"Shall we return there and announce our good fortune to everyone? If we are to marry with Darcy and Bingley the earlier we all begin preparing for it the better."

"Yes, let us return."

The two hurriedly prepared and returned to London House. Upon entering the room, they saw that Elizabeth was performing for everyone.

The two applauded her performance and all occupants in the room turned, just noticing their arrival. Shocked at their return Lady Matlock invited them to come and sit.

"Father, Mother, Anne and I have come to announce to you and everyone that we are to be married and we have chosen to share Darcy and Bingley's wedding day as Mr. Bennet so kindly offered to me earlier this evening." Richard was grinning at everyone's faces and Anne beamed up at him.

It took but a moment for the shock to wear off Lady Matlock and for her to rush to the couple. Kissing and hugging out her congratulations to her son and future daughter.

"Oh I am so happy, I can hardly contain myself. Come and tell us all how it is to be."

The couple sat down and the rest of the evening was spent in planning an additional couple into the wedding.

Additional shopping was required for the following day.

Chapter 31
The Gardiners' Return

Lady Matlock could not be happier with the developments in her youngest son's life. She had often thought over the years that Catherine had set her cap on the wrong nephew for her daughter, Anne. Lady Matlock and Anne have had many conversations over the years that led her to believe long ago that Anne had a high regard and feeling for Richard. About the time that Lady Matlock came to that realization she also came to another. Anne de Bourgh was not as sickly as she was generally thought to be; she used it as a ruse to avoid prolonged interaction with her mother. No matter what anyone would think she did not condemn her for it either.

Lady Matlock had often seen in Anne qualities that she knew Richard admired in women and had been aware for the past five years at least that Anne was in love with him and not her cousin Darcy. She was so happy that all was working out as it properly should. Even better for herself now that her son would be away from the harm that an army life inflicts on a person. She had never approved of Richard becoming a Colonel, but he was a second son and that was what he had wanted and Lady Matlock never interfered with her children's choices. Too often she had seen the harm that came when one did.

Thinking of someone who interfered in her children's lives, her thoughts naturally turned to Catherine and likewise in response to her own precious husband. Lord Matlock had been solemn since his return on Friday. Last night she had seen a little of himself in his actions but too much the past days he had been out of spirits and distressed. It pained her to see the love of her life in such a state. When he returned Friday night he looked haggard and aged. He said nothing but walked up to her embracing her in such as way that had she not known better she would fear that she would never see him again. Then in the next moment his embrace turned to one of a man in need, as if he was just returning from a long sojourn and needed the assurance that his wife and love was there and indeed real.

Lady Matlock had led him to his room and dismissed the servants. She stayed with him assuring him in every way possible that she supported him and would always be there for him. After a distressing few hours in which additional tears of pain and regret were shed Lord Matlock fell asleep with his head on his wife's lap, his arms wrapped around her as best he could, her reclining against some pillows as she stroked his hair and lightly hummed. Lady Matlock eventually also fell asleep against the pillows as she watched her husband. She could tell that he was not sleeping restfully but hoped that he would soon recover from this trying and harsh event.

This had been almost three days ago. Last night he had indeed looked better than he had all weekend. The announcement of Richard and Anne's engagement had raised his spirits while in company but then when they returned home he had again been distressed.

"Ellen, oh what have I done? Catherine is to miss the wedding of her only daughter. What if I had waited but two days to send her away? Perhaps the news would have softened her and she would never carry out her purpose."

"Husband, hush, you know as well as I do that her purpose would never change. She would not accept Richard and even worse she would have hurt all of the girls. You did what was required and I will not have you regretting that decision."

Lord Matlock had remained distressed but agreed with his wife. "I know you are correct, Ellen, I just wish that I could get her from my mind, it is just not so easy. I fear you will despise me if I tell you but it was easier to get over the loss of my sweet sister Anne at her death than it is now to get over Catherine. Anne was loved, she had a beautiful family, and her death ended her sickness, her pain, and her suffering. I know that she went to a better place and is able to watch over her precious son and daughter that she loved so much as they undertake life. Ellen, I know she is happy with how they have turned out and I know she would approve and love Miss Bennet as we do, but Catherine; she has wounded my heart and my soul. Ellen, shall I ever recover?"

"Oh Frederick, I shall never despise you and you shall recover. You are the best brother and she does not deserve you. Although I have never loved Catherine as I did your sister Anne she is still my sister as well, and I, like you am also distressed by the need to dismiss her as we did, but it had to be done. I care for Anne and Georgiana and now Elizabeth too much to let a spiteful woman hurt them because she cannot get her hands on Pemberley. You know as well as I, that Pemberley is all she wants. She wants to control Darcy's beautiful estate. Her hurting those girls would indeed distress me more than anything. Those girls depend on us; they cannot protect themselves from such a woman. Do you understand Frederick, they need YOU. It is you who have saved three women from the harm of an old and bitter woman. Have you also thought that it is you who have also saved the hearts of so many more who would have been affected had they been harmed. Do you understand, husband? Your act was selfless; a lesser man would have shunned the decision and not made it because it was hard, but you took it upon yourself to make the impossible decision and have saved so many others' feelings in the process. You have saved the hearts of Fitzwilliam, Richard, Mr. and Mrs. Bennet, their other daughters, Bingley, and oh so many others that we cannot begin to name. You are the better man and I love you."

Lady Matlock hoped that her words penetrated his mind and soothed his soul. She reflected back on her words and remembered that she had seen him relax a little, but the stress of recent events still showed around his eyes. This would take time for him to recover but she would be there to help him through every moment of it.

She would also be there to help the girls in whatever they needed, and right now it was shopping for the remainder of the wedding clothes.

Lady Matlock had picked up Anne on her way to London House, arriving in good time. All of the ladies were prompt and ready for another day filled with shopping and entered Lady Matlock's carriage with high spirits.

Soon after the ladies left for another day of shopping, first in order being Anne's wedding dress.

The Gardiners reached London in good time, it was barely Monday mid-day and they were anxious to see their nieces. Alice greeted them at their arrival, at first shocked at their early return but then understanding as she imparted the news that their nieces were in town and them responding that they already knew.

They refreshed themselves and put the children down for a rest in the nurse's care and then dismissed themselves to call on the Darcy's and their family. It was early enough that a visit should not interfere with the household schedule. Mr. Darcy and Mr. Bingley had both left their cards with directions and invitations to call upon their return so they did not concern themselves with calling on an unknown family as they normally would have. The couple called their carriage and made short time of the pleasant journey across London to Darcy's London House.

The ladies were still shopping when the Gardiners arrived; however, the gentlemen were in the library enjoying the company of one another when the butler announced them.

"Mr. and Mrs. Gardiner, to see you, sir."

Mr. Darcy looked up and began to rise, but Mr. Bennet was already up and ahead of him.

"Edward, Madeline, what do you do here? We had not thought you would return for another fortnight?"

"Thomas, how good to see you brother. Jonathan sent us an express with your family's good news and of course Madeline here was distressed at missing the events so we left immediately and just returned this very day."

"Oh, we are indeed glad to see you." Then walking to his sister-in-law to give her a welcoming embrace he told her. "Madeline, you must know that the girls would never allow you to miss the event. They would rather stall the weddings then not have their most beloved aunt in attendance. Fear not, you have only missed a little shopping and I daresay there will be plenty more for you to partake in"

"Yes, Thomas, thank you for the comforts, but Jonathan has already told me of their shopping and had it not been by fortune that they went their first for the fabric for their wedding dresses and by fate that Jonathan was there instead of one of our other workers then we would already have a tragedy with Elizabeth's dress. Oh Thomas you must know that these two girls are almost as my daughters and I would not miss a moment of this. I can help them, aide them and most of all it will ease my mind for I want to do this with them."

"Sister, fear not, you shall be here for them. I am sure they will be so pleased that you have returned. Lizzy has told me already that she misses you being with her."

The two smiled an affectionate sibling smile and Mr. Bennet continued. "Oh, where are my manners, what is to be done with me. Here we are standing in the middle of the doorway and I have not even introduced you to their fiancés."

Turning towards Mr. Darcy and Mr. Bingley who were standing behind them he made the introductions.

"Brother, sister, this is Mr. Fitzwilliam Darcy and Mr. Charles Bingley, boys this is Mrs. Bennet's brother, Mr. Edward Gardiner, and his wife Mrs. Madeline Gardiner."

Mr. Darcy stepped forward to welcome them to his home. This was the woman Elizabeth loved as dearly as her own mother It would be important to her for them to feel welcome in his, soon to be their, home and he did everything in his power to welcome them. "Mr. and Mrs. Gardiner, it is indeed a pleasure to have you in my home. Miss Elizabeth has told me so much about you that I feel I know you and love you as family already. Come in and have a seat."

The Gardiner's looked at him slightly shocked at such a pronouncement. What man would ever welcome them almost as family with no prior interaction, especially one of such a station as Mr. Darcy? Mr. Darcy must truly cherish Elizabeth and be a remarkable man.

As they were sitting Charles spoke up as well, not wanting to neglect this Aunt as his dearest Jane had also spoken often and fondly of her. "I also feel honored to meet you. Miss Jane has spoken highly of you since the time we have met. I daresay your arrival will please her greatly. You will be welcome at any time in my home either here in London or in Hertfordshire."

The entire party sat and had pleasant conversation until the ladies returned from shopping. With each passing minute Mrs. Gardiner was more and more pleased with the men that her girls, as that was how she had for many years thought of them, had chosen as future companions.

When the ladies arrived back at London House it could not be missed. The doors to the house burst open and the stillness was interrupted with feminine laughter and the music of their voices. The halls sang out with the joy of five ladies who spent a day happily in each other's company. The men and Mrs. Gardiner heard them and stood to leave the library and join them in the foyer.

Elizabeth was walking towards Mr. Darcy when she caught sight of her Aunt and went to her almost running. "Aunt Maddy, you are here, you are come. Jane, look who is here." Jane instantly dropped all that she held and went to embrace her Aunt as well, tears of happiness overflowing her delicate feelings. "Aunt, I am so glad you are here, I fear we made you cut your visit short, but can I admit for myself that I am so happy that you did and that you are here. I have dearly wanted you here with us at this time."

"Jane dearest, you could not imagine that after I discovered yours and Lizzy's engagements that anything would keep me from returning and sharing your joy." Looking up shocked she noticed her dear friend standing next to Mr. Darcy smiling.

"Lady Matlock, Ellen, my friend, what a pleasure it is to see you. What do you do here?"

"Madeline, you will not believe this but I am the Aunt to Fitzwilliam Darcy. It seems as if we are to become more than friends, we are to be family."

"Ellen, you tease me do you not? Oh, the joy I felt hearing of my nieces' betrothals is nothing to know that they shall be part of such an excellent family."

The two had walked to each other and embraced as only the closest friends do.

Everyone watched with smiles upon their faces as the two addressed each other.

As everyone settled down Darcy invited everyone into the drawing room for refreshments. The rest of the afternoon was spent updating Mrs. Gardiner of what purchases had already been accomplished and which ones remained to be made.

Mrs. Gardiner also requested and was told the stories of how the couples met and fell in love and how each was proposed to. She was smiling with pleasure as Jane repeated her proposal in the most romantic and angelic way and a little shocked when Lizzy spared no details and mentioned her father catching her and Darcy in a passionate kiss. All in all though she could not be more pleased with the happiness that both of the girls had achieved, and was even slightly pleased at the breach in propriety that Mr. Darcy and Elizabeth were caught it because it showed that Mr. Darcy had passion, an element that Mrs. Gardiner has always known Elizabeth would need in a marriage partner to have true happiness.

Tuesday and Wednesday were spent primarily purchasing the remaining items needed for the ladies trousseau. The entire party shopped together, however Lady Matlock primarily assisted Anne while Mrs. Gardiner aided Jane and Elizabeth.

Each evening the ladies returned and showed off a few of their packages and stored the rest to be viewed at a later time, it was evident that happiness was overflowing in mirth.

Finally the ladies had a few days to relax before returning to Longbourn and the excitement that was sure to take place there. Likewise the gentlemen had concluded all business except for Colonel Fitzwilliam. He was learning that there was a lot to do when giving up a commission and even more as he was taking over Rosings Park with his new wife in scarcely a fortnight.

Two couples could often be seen walking in the park across from London House or just relaxing and talking in some remote corner of an obscure room, but most of all they were avoiding company. Very few introductions were made as they tried to walk in secluded areas of the park. Callers at London House were turned away with excuses by the butler and no calls were returned in the days that preceded the weddings. But they could not avoid society forever, for Saturday must arrive and the theatre must be attended.

Chapter 32
Theatre

Saturday evening arrived after a week of activity and anticipation. The women retired to their rooms to eat and dress in a leisurely fashion, thus ensuring that they would be well rested for the evening events.

Elizabeth sat in a hot tub of water taking a refreshing bath. She was musing at her good luck at finding the exquisite gown she was to wear this evening at Belle's earlier this week.

Elizabeth and her party had entered Belle's with no purpose other than to be fitted for their wedding gowns, have some final measurements taken for the other gowns they had ordered and give their opinion of what they saw, but before Elizabeth had entered the shop two steps her eyes had caught sight of the gown draped over a model near the window.

Slowly Elizabeth walked admiringly over to the gown and gently touched the fabric. Belle joined her with a smile on her face. "Miss Bennet, how do you do today?"

"I am wonderful Belle, and you?"

"Thank you, I am well. Would you like to see your wedding dress?"

"Yes Belle, however may I ask you a question first?"

"Yes Miss, anything."

"Is this dress on display here as a model for sale, or was it commissioned by another patron?"

"A little of both." Belle responded. "The dress was commissioned for a lady; however she was not pleased with the gown and would not honor our arrangement. Rather than take a loss on the gown I refused her it and now am hoping another will enjoy it in her place someday."

"Oh I would love to try it on, it is simply breathtaking."

"Yes Miss Bennet, I shall ready it for you."

Belle smiled as she removed the dress from the model, she hoped the dress fit Miss Bennet and that she would want it because there could be no other lady that would look half so well in it or deserve it as she does.

Elizabeth first tried on her wedding gown and blushed and smiled as everyone commented on its beauty. The dress had turned out better than Mrs. Gardiner could ever have imagined and tears filled her eyes as she looked at it draped upon Elizabeth.

Next, Elizabeth tried on the window gown, it fit as if Belle had made it special for her and as she stepped around the corner to look in the mirror she knew she must have it.

As Elizabeth repositioned in her bath she laughed at her reaction to the dress.

"Belle, would you establish an account for me in the name of Mrs. Darcy and place this dress on it as my first purchase? I daresay Mr. Darcy will not object when he sees it, he is after all constantly telling me these past days to establish accounts everywhere I go."

"Yes Miss Bennet, I would be happy to do that."

The dress was now her's and she was excited to surprise Mr. Darcy with it.

Wednesday as the ladies had returned from shopping Elizabeth had approached Fitzwilliam to tell him of her new account. She was a little unsure of how to approach the subject despite him repeatedly telling her to create them. She should not have feared though, for he actually appeared happier at her spending his money.

"Fitzwilliam."

"Yes, beautiful?"

"We have returned from shopping." Elizabeth said as she entered with a few parcels in her arms.

"Yes I see that. Did you enjoy yourself?"

"Oh yes, immensely, my wedding dress is almost complete, I am sure you will love it."

"Elizabeth, I will love it because you will be wearing it."

"Thank you for the compliment but I think it is lovely even just being on the model. I am truly blessed to have a caring aunt that saved this fabric for me. It is far more beautiful than anything I have ever set eyes upon."

"I am sure it is. I see you have some parcels, were you able to finish your trousseau shopping or do you have more to purchase?"

"I finished today, now I shall have a few days to myself or to spend more time with you."

Darcy smiled and sweetly kissed her.

"May I see what you have in your packages?"

Elizabeth opened one or two of them and showed him the contents. "What about that big one there, may I see it as well?"

"Oh yes, I was meaning to mention that one to you. No, you may not see it yet, however it most concerns you."

Darcy smiled a little curious and inquired?

"So you have bought me a gift have you?"

Elizabeth became a little distressed that she had not thought to get him a gift after all of the gifts he had given to her and worried that he was expecting one. The thoughts showed instantly on her face and Fitzwilliam acted quickly to put her at ease laughing as he replied.

"I can see you have not gotten me a gift. Perhaps I should stop guessing and just let you tell me."

"Fitzwilliam, I hope you will not be upset, but no I did not get you a gift, I wanted to let you know that the item in that package is the first thing I have purchased in the name of Mrs. Fitzwilliam Darcy. I have created an account and that purchase was added to it." Darcy was smiling from ear to ear but Elizabeth did not see, she continued to ramble at a fast pace. "I know that I am not yet Mrs. Darcy, yet you have mentioned that you would not be displeased if I set up an account. I also know that the item was not needed; and that my trousseau purchases were already complete, but it is so beautiful that I could not pass it up. If it distresses you I will speak to my father and he will pay for the item."

Darcy hushed Elizabeth with a kiss. "Elizabeth, I am not upset, you have made me so happy that you are comfortable enough to establish accounts in the Darcy name. I wish you would open even more."

Elizabeth laughed slightly. "When you get this bill you may not have that same wish."

"I shall always have that wish and I doubt a few items no matter how frivolous you think they are will break my accounts. Now, may I see this frivolous item that Mrs. Darcy purchased?"

"No, you shall see it in due time, but not now. I shall tell you though, that it is nothing more than a pretty gown. I shall wear it when you least expect it and surprise you."

This surprise was just what Elizabeth had waited three days for.

Finally clean and relaxed Elizabeth exited the tub and Sarah entered to aide her in getting ready. As Sarah put the finishing touches on her hair, Elizabeth took a long look in the mirror.

"Miss Bennet, you truly are a vision. Mr. Darcy would have to be blind not to notice your beauty tonight."

Elizabeth laughed lightly "Sarah, I have no doubt that he will notice. In fact it was my purpose in buying this dress, to have Mr. Darcy notice…, well everything."

The entire party, except for Elizabeth was gathered in the foyer below stairs. Sarah descended first carrying Elizabeth's outer clothing and stepped to the side to await her mistress.

Mr. Darcy had watched Sarah arrive and knew that Elizabeth would be there shortly. He already had his eyes at the top of the stairs when she entered his view. No one else noticed her until they heard Fitzwilliam's labored breathing and then saw nothing more than his black long coat swish past them as he raced to her side.

"Elizabeth, if only…"

Mr. Darcy stopped himself and replied quietly to her "You look magnificent, by the end of the night I shall probably be established in ten duels to fight off all of the men that I catch admiring you."

"No Mr. Darcy, you need not fight any of them, just smile, for you have triumphed over them already. It is you and none other that I allow in my heart."

Darcy kissed her at that response for all to see.

The Darcy, Bingley, and Gardiner carriages pulled up outside of the theatre. Anticipation was thick as it was the first time that the bachelors had been in public with their intendeds since the banns were posted in the 'The Times'.

Fitzwilliam first handed Georgiana down from the carriage and then did the same for Elizabeth. The same could be seen occurring at the Bingley and Gardiner carriages. Mr. Bennet approached to escort Georgiana. This was becoming quite a habit of his and he was very pleased with the young girl he already loved as another daughter.

The ladies all straightened their gowns and cloaks and once ready took the arms offered by the gentlemen and walked towards the theatre entrance. Half way there they were met by the Matlock's, Colonel Fitzwilliam, and Anne coming from another direction. Greetings were exchanged, a few hugs made and the large party finally complete entered the theatre.

Lady Matlock had sought out Elizabeth trying to whisper in her ear as she nodded towards her dress. "Well my dear, what did Fitzwilliam think?"

Elizabeth blushed as the man himself spoke.

"The truth, aunt, or what I am allowed to say in polite company?"

Lady Matlock raised her eyebrows at his emphatic reply and firmly responded. "Why, nothing but the truth my dear boy, I demand the truth."

"If you must know then, aunt, I had inappropriate thoughts that the only way Elizabeth and this evening could be more perfect was if she no longer bore the name of Bennet and we were instead heading to the Master Suite at Pemberley instead of the theatre with a bunch of relatives."

Elizabeth turned a few shades of red but smiled agreeably at Darcy.

Lady Matlock had expected such a reply and nodding her head at the two replied "That will do, Fitzwilliam, that will do." She rejoiced inside herself that her son, for that is how she had thought of him these past years, had made a mutual love match. Lady Matlock hurried to Lord Matlock's side at the front of the party as they entered the theatre.

The gentlemen quickly removed their long coats and turned to assist the ladies. Not one of the party, except Lord and Lady Matlock, realized every eye in the theatre was turned to them to catch the first glimpse of the ladies.

Elizabeth and Jane stood next to each other and both reached up to remove the hoods of their cloaks as they turned their backs to the room and allowed the gentlemen to help remove them.

The first sight the room beheld was of their backs. All admired the forms in front of them with politeness until they turned around.

Mr. Darcy stepped forward head held high and a slight smile upon his face as he escorted Elizabeth through the throngs of gaping-mouthed, wide-eyed theatre patrons towards his box, stopping only a few times to accept the congratulations of a few who were bold enough to stop his progress and offer it in hopes of being introduced to the beauty on his arm. Generally, their courage was rewarded and Mr. Darcy introduced Elizabeth to them, however none were provided the details that they had hoped and were therefore left to conjecture them on their own.

The party finally reached the Darcy's box and took their seats, aware that the entire theatre below had their faces turned towards them, many being as bold as to point. If the reaction of the crowd, especially the gentlemen, was anything to go on, the Bennet ladies had easily gained the approval of the ton, with nothing more than their pretty looks. Mrs. Bennet would indeed be proud for more than one fellow had looked with jealousy upon Mr. Darcy and Mr. Bingley.

The theatre lights dimmed and Romeo and Juliet began. Elizabeth could see the tension release from Darcy's face, neck and shoulders as no one could see him any longer. Pleased that he was finally comfortable she reassuringly touched her hand to his. He caught her hand before she could pull it away and kept it in his for the entire first act; he only moved her hand once to remove the glove that kept him from touching her warm skin.

Darcy had never experienced anything as perfect as holding hands with Elizabeth in a darkened theatre and was only distressed when the first act ended and everyone stood to get refreshments. He kept hold of her hand, raising it to his lips for a kiss before putting her glove back on and placing her perfect hand on his arm. The entire action had been witnessed by the Matlocks', Gardiners', and Mr. Bennet as they all exited the box with slight looks to each other, but not one said a word.

The lobby was full of theatre patrons lingering around the refreshment tables as they discussed the play, politics, weather and news.

That was until Mr. Darcy entered, from that point on he and the beautiful woman on his arm were the topic of all conversation. Who is she? Where is she from? Is that other woman her sister? Do you think there are more of them? These were questions that could be heard being asked and discussed all around the room. It was evident that the men admired the Bennet ladies and the women instantly despised them yet promised that they would be their best friends by the end of the season.

The intermission ended with pleasure for the Darcy party and they returned to their seats. For the other patrons though it ended in wretchedness, for they had learned barely anything of the ladies and what they had heard was unreliable at best.

The second through fifth acts began much the same as the first. The lights dimmed, Darcy removed Elizabeth's glove, and they held hands through the entire act. Likewise the intermissions were the same as well. Darcy kissed Elizabeth's hand, replaced her glove, and escorted her to get refreshment. The Darcy party kept primarily to themselves and by the end of the night a significant number of the ton were disappointed at their lack of knowledge. Although with Fitzwilliam Darcy as the man in question, it was not unusual that he kept his private affairs to himself.

The following days until the party left for Hertfordshire on Wednesday would keep them all on their toes to avoid having to entertain curious visitors.

The entire party was well pleased with the play, never had such a congenial party attended together. The evening was late and soon after entering the house Georgiana and Mr. Bennet excused themselves for the night, but Darcy, Elizabeth, Bingley, and Jane all headed to the drawing room for some late private conversation.

Bingley and Jane took up the sofa near the window and Darcy and Elizabeth occupied another in front of the fire. Neither of the couples wanted to leave one another and talking was the only way they could stay together.

"Elizabeth, beautiful."

"Yes, Fitzwilliam."

"Thank you for allowing me to hold your hand the entirety of this evening. It gave me great pleasure." He reached for and held her hand again as he said this.

"You are welcome Fitzwilliam, I enjoyed it immensely."

"Of that I am grateful, I hope that we can make this a tradition and always hold hands at the theatre."

"If you wish, I should like that."

"I do, I wish a great many things."

"A great many things. Why, Fitzwilliam, what could you possibly wish for that you do not already have or cannot just snap your fingers and have brought to you? You are a man with everything."

"Elizabeth, you of all people should know what I wish for."

"No, I suppose I do not know for my knowledge is that you have everything that you wish for."

"No certainly not. I wish to be loved."

Elizabeth interrupted. "You are loved, for I love you immensely and I know your sister, aunt and uncle, cousin and many others love you as well."

Darcy looked intently at Elizabeth begging her to understand "Elizabeth I wish to be loved as only a husband can be loved, and love you as only your husband should."

"Oh…" Elizabeth blushed as she finished "and you shall, in eleven days Fitzwilliam."

"I also wish for you to love Pemberley as I love it. To rejoice in the peacefulness there, to be comforted in its sturdy walls and allow it to protect you from all of the cares of the world as it does for me." Elizabeth listened intently. "I wish that I could introduce you to every place I have ever been, replacing my memory of being there alone with a memory of being there with you. I wish you could have known my father and mother and that I could see how much they love you as already the Uncle Frederick and Aunt Ellen do. I wish to know how many young Darcys' we will have running around Pemberley. I wish I could see you right now with your hair cascading down your back and to run my fingers through it as I breathe in the scent of lavender that I have been tempted with all evening. I wish so much, some of it may soon come to pass and others may never happen, but most of all I wish for you, right now."

"Fitzwilliam, I share your wishes." Elizabeth said as one hand stroked the side of his face and the other reached for her hair. "Though we cannot fulfill all of them tonight, I believe one of them can not hurt us too much." With that said she removed one pin from her hair and then lightly shook her head. Her long hair fell in tendrils down her back almost to her waist. "I have recently discovered the merits of a ladies maid that has been educated in the art of one pin French hairstyles."

"As have I." Darcy huskily breathed as his left hand reached for a particularly tempting curl that had fallen just in front of Elizabeth's eye. He leaned forward further as he played with the curl and breathed into her ear. "Your lady's maid shall have any amount of money at her disposal for any form of education that expedites undoing your hair or anything else she can arrange to be undone fast."

Then quickly straitening himself he stood and offered his hand. "I fear it is late, you need to rest."

"Fitzwilliam, I am fine I assure you, we can talk a little longer."

"No, Elizabeth, you must retire now." Fitzwilliam quickly but passionately kissed her and then finished "If you beg my pardon I shall not escort you to your chamber."

Elizabeth was on the verge of asking what she had done to offend him and he knew it so he softly whispered to her.

"Elizabeth, I see your distress, fear not you have not offended me, far from it in fact, but if you do not go to your room alone and this very minute I am afraid I shall not be gentleman enough to control myself and not offend you. I have every intention of you and I making it to our wedding day with all honor intact and no regrets. With scarcely eleven days as you pointed out it would be a shame if I allowed passions to rule." With one final stroke of her chestnut hair and a whispered kiss she left his ears burning with a promise for eleven days hence.

Jane had seen Elizabeth depart and it was but a moment until she walked past Darcy towards her room, cheeks aglow in shades of pink and red.

Bingley approached Darcy and grasped his shoulders with a firm hand. "This is going to be the longest week and a half of our lives, is it not?"

"Indeed it shall, indeed it shall. Can I offer you a drink, Bingley."

"Yes, the strongest one you have."

"Amen to that, brother, amen to that."

The two sat in the chairs just opposite the couch Darcy and Elizabeth had shared and tried to drink away the thoughts occupying their minds. Unfortunately for both of them it did not work. The inebriation and lost control of their minds only made their dreams more vivid and torturous. By morning both were hoping the days would go faster and the more they anticipated and dreamed the slower the days progressed.

Chapter 33
The Ensuing Days

Despite the gentlemen's longing for the days to ensue at a more rapid pace they passed as all days do and soon enough Wednesday was upon them and everyone entered three carriages bound for Hertfordshire.

The past weeks had allowed Georgiana and Elizabeth the time to get to know one another on sisterly terms. They were comfortable in each other's presence and happy that they were soon to be sisters. They did not stand on ceremony with one another, therefore Georgiana was not shocked when Elizabeth gave up the seat next to her in favor of the one beside her brother, neither was she shocked when scarcely a mile from London the two had securely closed the carriage curtains and nestled into one another's arms, sound asleep just as they had been on their arrival two weeks earlier.

Georgiana was constantly studying Elizabeth, observing the teasing manner that she displayed towards Fitzwilliam and how he reacted to her. She was learning that a fiancée and wife could treat a man much differently than a sister could. His reactions were such that Georgiana had never seen in him before. Some emotions that she saw from him the past days she would not have ever dreamed he possessed in the weeks, months, and years prior to meeting Elizabeth. Seeing the two together made her learn things of her brother that she had never known and brought the two of them closer together in the process.

Georgiana was indeed grateful for the presence of Elizabeth in their life.

The carriages stopped at the usual resting place between London and Meryton where the party could refresh and have a bite to eat. They took their time making sure everyone was well rested before setting out again, this time the Bennet carriage in the lead.

All three carriages pulled onto the grounds at Longbourn scarcely behind midday and were quickly greeted by an ecstatic Mrs. Bennet who barely acknowledged the return of her husband and daughters but instead showered her two future sons-in-law with questions about the pleasantness of the trip, the comforts of their carriages and insistence at knowing if her daughters' presence had pleased them.

They both assured her that the trip was pleasant, the carriages were well sprung and very comfortable and that nothing could please them more than travelling with the Bennet ladies. He face brightened at their proclamations and she began to usher everyone into the house.

Bingley sent his carriage on to Netherfield with the Hurst's so that they could attend themselves and stayed with the Darcy's at Longbourn. Georgiana had opted to refresh with the Bennet ladies and remain at Longbourn rather than further her trip to Netherfield immediately.

Mrs. Bennet did credit to her housekeeping skills and had an elegant but not too ostentatious dinner arrangement prepared for the party once they had been refreshed. She occupied the entirety of the dinner conversation making sure everyone was in complete knowledge of every detail she had prepared with regards to the wedding each day of their absence. By the end of it everyone knew what was to be on the menu, how the church was to be decorated, what colors of dresses the bridesmaids would wear, how their hair was to be done, who had been invited and where they would sit in the church and most of all how jealous the entire neighborhood was that she had two daughters engaged to such agreeable men. Everyone was seeking her advice on how to catch a rich handsome husband for their daughters, but of course none of them would succeed for none were half as handsome as her Jane or near as witty as Elizabeth.

Everyone at the table looked upon each other with raised eyebrows and shrugged shoulders as Mrs. Bennet continued for close to three hours, the only break being the departure from the dinner table into the drawing room, Darcy and Bingley began to wonder that anyone could speak so much and so fast; their heads were beginning to spin.

Georgiana loved every second of it and had quickly become a favorite of Mrs. Bennet. She was even invited and accepted the invitation to stay at Longbourn instead of returning directly to Netherfield. She was to be their particular guest, of which she was proud.

Mr. Bennet finally interrupted his lady to announce the addition to the wedding, one that shocked his wife into silence for a moment, allowing the occupants of the room to disperse to the corners.

"My dear Mrs. Bennet, I fear I have been a negligent correspondent and completely forgot to tell you. There is to be a third couple sharing in this blessed day."

"No there cannot Mr. Bennet, for Mary, Kitty, and Lydia has been here with me. I know not of any suitors for any of them unless you have brought one home for my dear Mary. Oh what a good father you are. You knew she would not find one here in Meryton and so while you were in London had Mr. Bingley and Mr. Darcy help you find a husband for our dear girl. What a good father you are. Mary dear, come here, Mary."

"I did NOT find a suitor for Mary and have no intention of ever doing such a thing. The marriage I speak of is another. Colonel Fitzwilliam, the friend of these two men," he indicated towards Darcy and Bingley "has also gone and gotten himself engaged, to Miss Anne de Bourgh. The couple has decided that they also wish to share in the most joyous of days and will be marrying alongside our girls."

Mrs. Bennet stood, unable to speak for a full minute, giving all of the room a chance to depart to separate areas of the house, thus giving at least some of them peace and quiet when she came to and decided who it was that required her attention.

Happily for the couples it appeared that Mr. Bennet was the one with the information so she followed him to his library questioning him for the remainder of the evening. Mr. Bennet groaned inwardly but allowed her questions to assail him. His daughters would pay dearly for the time he was giving them free of their mother.

The evening passed as all evenings do, and the men had to depart for Netherfield. The Darcy carriage was called and the ladies escorted the gentlemen to the door, each providing sweet goodbyes that would carry the men until tomorrow.

The following days passed much the same as this one. Visits from the gentlemen, updates from Mrs. Bennet about the wedding details, and sweet goodbye's at the door each evening. If the ladies were unable to attend the men, then they either stayed home to catch up on business before the wedding or sat with Mr. Bennet in the library acting lovesick.

It was almost more than Mr. Bennet could bear, and if he were not as fond of the boys as he was he would not have allowed it. Great was his relief Monday when the Matlock and Gardiner parties arrived, from them he would at least hear sense and with Lord Matlock and Mr. Gardiner's assistance he would also have a little bit of sport with the gentlemen's sensibilities. And sport with them they did, they even went so far as to occasionally tease the ladies. Elizabeth took it in stride, but Anne and Jane were mortified. Not half so mortified as when their mother joined them Monday evening to provide a little motherly advice prior to their wedding that was to take place in a little less than thirty-six hours. Jane was distressed and Elizabeth was close to laughter as their mother blushed and stumbled through some incoherent statements thrashing her hands around like a wild woman. When she finally stood, straightened her dress and calmly asked if they had any questions, Jane could scarcely lift her eyes from her lap and Elizabeth wanted nothing more than for her mother to leave.

Jane and Elizabeth looked at each other and both knew what they should do, they quietly went to their aunt and uncle's room and asked their Aunt Maddy to join them for a little while.

Madeline had informed Edward that Mrs. Bennet planned to talk to the girls this evening and both knew that in the morning that Mrs. Gardiner would need to have another discussion with them, setting both of the girls at ease, letting them know that the acts of marriage were nothing to distress themselves over that instead they should look forward to the pleasure, joy and love that they would instead share with such marriages. They were both pleased that the girls had come directly to their aunt, and Uncle Edward relinquished his wife readily to go and put the girls at ease earlier rather than later.

Emma Hox

The final day before the wedding had arrived and Longbourn was in a tizzy. Mrs. Bennet commanded and demanded better than any army general, for everything must be perfect for her girls. Unconscious that her actions were causing more strife then good, but to the relief of all, Mrs. Gardiner was going behind her to clean the tears of everyone, from the housekeeper and maids to her nieces. Finally she called her husband and insisted that Jane's trunks should be delivered to Netherfield this moment by him and that her nieces should accompany him for "There is some reason that I cannot remember at this moment but I assure you she is needed there and it would be best for Lizzy to attend also."

Mr. Gardiner instantly understood and went to collect the teary-eyed girls.

"Jane, dearest, it is time to load your belongings and take them to Netherfield. Mr. Hill is busy so I thought I would do it for him. I also have heard that you are needed there to inspect something or another that Mr. Bingley has purchased and so thought you should attend me." Jane's face lit up with happiness but Lizzy's fell and Mr. Gardiner saw it.

"Lizzy, I think Mr. Darcy would use me as his prey in our next hunting trip if I arrived with Jane and no Lizzy, so you had best grab your cloak as well. I think a little time away from Longbourn could do you both some good."

Both of the girls fell on their uncle hugging him and then quickly gathered their outerwear and met him in the driveway. They were off to Netherfield in less than five minutes.

The short ride to Netherfield revived the ladies and they were ready again to meet their fiancé's and converse sociably by the time they arrived.

The butler opened the door and in but a moment Mr. Bingley was in the foyer, happiness all over his face at the arrival of the party. He called over his shoulder to Darcy who came almost running to join them and greet his lady.

"Mr. Gardiner, Elizabeth, Miss Jane, what a pleasure to see you, what do we owe this honor to, for we did not expect to see you until later when…"

Confusion was on the ladies faces for they were sure their Uncle said Jane was needed at Netherfield, but Mr. Gardiner interrupted while throwing some winks and sly looks that only the men could interpret.

"Mr. Darcy, did Mr. Bingley not tell you he sent a message forward early this morning that Jane was needed to inspect something or another or speak with the housekeeper or something such. I know not for sure since I could scarcely read the missive through the blots, but here they are. I brought them just as you requested." Mr. Gardiner was pleased at himself for his quick thinking and remembering that Mr. Bingley had recently been teased about his poorly written letters.

Mr. Bingley looked a little confused and started to contradict Mr. Gardiner but Mr. Darcy understood instantly. "Oh Bingley, what are we to do with you? Miss Jane, you are truly going to have your hands full with this forgetful old goat. I assure you Mr. Gardiner is correct, Mr. Bingley was just telling me this morning of a new table that arrived and he needs your assistance in the best placement of it. I believe it is in the drawing room. Why don't you and Elizabeth head in there and we will join you just as soon as we direct the footman with your belongings."

Darcy had seen the footmen enter with trunks and easily put it together.

272

The girls stepped away and Mr. Gardiner addressed them "Thank you, Mr. Darcy, it seems as if Longbourn is in quite a stir early this morning. Mrs. Gardiner found both of the girls in tears and thought it best not to have them around this morning. If you would entertain them here say until it is time to ready for dinner tonight we would be most appreciative. I trust it will not be an imposition." Mr. Gardiner looked at them with a crooked smile, knowing full well that the men were very pleased to have the ladies in the house, even if they had not been expected.

Mr. Gardiner entered the drawing room and informed the ladies of his return to Longbourn and that the gentlemen would deliver them before supper. The ladies began to object that they must help their mother but he easily told them that it was their time to relax and enjoy their betrothals one last day before their lives changed forever. He and Mrs. Gardiner could well handle anything Mrs. Bennet threw at them.

The girls smiled their thanks and their uncle was off, returning to the mayhem of Longbourn.

It look no more than a few minutes for the couples to properly greet one another and even less time for them to settle into their respective areas of the home. Jane and Bingley began in the drawing room with quiet discussion but were soon walking Netherfield from room to room making sure everything was ready for Jane to arrive on the morrow.

Darcy and Elizabeth however headed straight for the library where they could be found reading, discussing or just being comfortable in the presence of the other for the majority of the day. Periodically another member of the household would enter and have a few minutes discussion with the couple, but ultimately they would leave the two to themselves.

The day passed altogether very amiably, more so than if the couples had been separated by the short distance of Longbourn and Netherfield and the ladies had been left in the clutches of Mrs. Bennet. All good things must come to a close however and it was time to return to Longbourn for supper. Darcy could tell that as the time neared their departure that Elizabeth stiffened and became less relaxed. She fidgeted more and became restless. As he led her to the foyer he whispered to her, "Elizabeth, calm yourself beautiful, this is the last time you shall return to Longbourn bearing the name Bennet, for tomorrow you are a Darcy and by my side forever. I shall be with you the rest of the evening until it is time for you to sleep, your mother will have no time to upset you and most of all I shall not allow it."

Elizabeth looked up at him all of the love she had for him shining on her face. "Fitzwilliam, dearest, how do you always know just what I am feeling and able to say the perfect thing?"

"I only have such abilities with you dearest, because I have you here." As he said the words he put his hand over his heart and then pulled her tightly to his chest in an embrace as he kissed the top of her head.

The rest of the party was joining them to load into the carriages so they parted their embrace, but Elizabeth took his arm, holding a bit tighter then she normally would.

The carriages made quick time reaching Longbourn and the entire party had a very amiable supper. It was evident that someone had spoken to Mrs. Bennet about her manner of addressing the ladies, the servants and the other members of the household for she was constantly catching herself mid-sentence and changing her mind about the statement. Mr. and Mrs. Gardiner would secretly look at one another and smile at her display but pleased that she was not offending anyone.

The Gardiners feared that no matter how close it was to the wedding that if Elizabeth was made too upset that Mr. Darcy would sweep her up and elope, without a second thought. It was evident to the Gardiners', Matlocks' and Mr. Bennet that Darcy was protecting his lady from her mother, always ensuring that he was placed between the two and constantly redirecting her attention if ever it landed on Elizabeth. Elizabeth, instead of being impertinent and sticking up for herself as she normally would, was fully content to allow him to protect her for the evening, never leaving his side until it was time to depart.

The Matlock carriage left with Lord and Lady Matlock and Mr. Fitzwilliam and his fiancée Anne, returning to Netherfield and retiring for the night before the Darcy carriage even left the Longbourn drive.

The two men who would share the Darcy carriage could be seen on opposite sides of Longbourn's foyer each with a lady standing in front of them, but neither even noticing the other couple. It was too cold to walk the grounds yet they still wanted to linger together. Darcy and Elizabeth were making promises for the morrow, Darcy showing a bit of his teasing manner.

"Elizabeth, beautiful, you will meet me at the church tomorrow will you not?"

"Of course I will, Fitzwilliam."

"Promise, no changing your mind tonight."

"I promise. I shall be there on the arm of my uncle dressed in the finest dress you ever laid eyes upon."

"I care not what you wear, you could arrive in a potato sack and I would still think you are the most beautiful creature I ever laid eyes upon."

"Thank you, but I am happy nonetheless that I shall have a dress more exquisite than anything you ever laid eyes upon."

"That could not be for the dress you wore to the theatre could take any man's breath away, most of all mine."

Elizabeth smiled up at him as she walked him closer to the door, kissing him as she whispered "That was nothing compared to what you will see tomorrow."

Darcy quit breathing for a moment, knowing full well she meant the dress but his mind running wild to everything he would see tomorrow that would be more exquisite than the dress she wore to the theatre.

All he whispered hoarsely in return as he turned towards the carriage was "Promise?"

Jane and Elizabeth stood in the doorway waving until the carriage was out of sight and then turned to go to their rooms to rest for tomorrow.

Darcy and Bingley just sat back in their seats with looks of anguish. Bingley spoke first.

"Tomorrow cannot come soon enough."

"Amen to that, brother, amen to that."

Silence reined the rest of the night except for a few words of goodnight as they arrived at Netherfield and each separated to his respective room.

Chapter 34
Wedding

Happy for all of the neighborhood's feelings was the day on which such an important wedding took place in Meryton. Three extremely anxious bachelors stood at the front of the church in anticipation for the first glimpse of their soon to be brides. The anxiousness showed on the emotions of each in extremely different fashions.

Mr. Bingley of course was overflowing with happiness, grinning from ear to ear and happy enough to tell each and every person of his good fortune at winning the hand of the most angelic and beautiful Bennet lady.

Mr. Fitzwilliam fidgeted with his jacket, his trousers, his timepiece, and anything else that was within his reach including his cousin's jacket. He was constantly looking around at everything and everyone in a nervous and hasty fashion. Darcy feared he would cause himself harm and have the wedding postponed.

Mr. Darcy stood tall and still, not moving except to swat at the hand of his cousin as it assaulted his person. One would have thought he held no emotion surrounding the day if they were not watching him as the doors to the church opened and his lady entered.

For those who had been watching Mr. Darcy, such as Mrs. Gardiner it was evident that Fitzwilliam Darcy's dream was coming true. His face instantly grew soft and held such a look of pleasure that Mrs. Gardiner instantly got choked up and had to catch her breath. She was very happy for her niece to have made a love match every bit as strong as her and Mr. Gardiner's. In the few days that the Gardiners had been blessed to be around Mr. Darcy and Mr. Bingley they had become extremely pleased with the gentlemen who were gentle and solicitous to their nieces. They could not have chosen better matches had they chosen the gentlemen themselves. The families were pillars of London and afar and some of the dearest friends of their lives.

It was time, the entire congregation stood as Mr. Bennet walked down the Longbourn Chapel isle with Jane on his arm. He was followed by Mr. Gardiner escorting Lizzy and Lord Matlock with Anne.

Mr. Darcy had just finished swatting at Richard's hand when from the corner of his eye he saw the door at the back of the chapel begin to open. He instantly stood with his eyes transfixed searching to be the first to see his bride. Then in an instant she was there, radiant on the arm of her most beloved uncle.

All coherent thought left Mr. Darcy's mind as he watched Elizabeth float into the chapel and up the aisle. Never had he seen her look as magnificent as she did today and his mind stowed the image of her perfectness alongside the others of her singing in the tree at Oakham Mount, of her after any number of walks, of her dancing with him at Netherfield, of her coming down the stairs to attend the theatre and of her with her hair down in the drawing room. This was another instance where his breath was taken away by her beauty and a soft smile spread across his face. The dress was indeed exquisite.

Lady Matlock had delivered Elizabeth's wedding gown as she promised. It was more beautiful then she had remembered and her mother fawned over it half the evening. The dress bodice was stitched in such a way that it created diamonds that erupted off of the fabric. Each diamond point was adorned with a diamond shard that sparkled in the sunlight. Satin was inlaid into the dress just over Elizabeth's bosom and attached to the remainder of the bodice made of an exquisite layered silver tissue. The neckline was neither a traingular, rounded, or squared neckline, it was nothing anyone had ever seen. It was high in both the front and the back, nothing more than an opening in the fabric for Elizabeth to slip her head through. The width of Elizabeth's neck kept it open to expose just a little of her neck and a small bit of shoulder. The tissue was also ruffled under the dress, protruding slightly from the bottom, the mid-arm sleeves and neckline, giving it an elegant yet exquisite touch. The layered tissue also made up the skirt of the dress with a little flow and movement, but not too much, it perfectly showed Elizabeth's fine figure. It lightly skimmed the ground and was perfectly complimented by the shimmery silver lamé overlay.

The silver lamé was made with the most delicate metallic threads weaved through in various swirling patterns that sparkled in the sunlight from the nearby window. It began where the bodice left off and lay over the silver tissue in one long flowing manner. It was cut up the front and edged with sparkling silver lace, which allowed it to float behind as Elizabeth walked.

Elizabeth's veil was made of delicate Brussels lace. It attached to her head with gorgeous diamond clips at the base of her hair, and trailed behind in a train ten feet long.

Unseen, as she had already removed it, but later to be seen by all, there was also a silver lamé cape lined with white fur that clasped around Elizabeth's neck with a diamond encrusted ornament pin.

She was a vision of beauty and everyone in the room was caught by it, but Mr. Darcy scarcely saw it, all he could see was the dark pools of Elizabeth's eyes that looked upon him with love and the soft red lips that were more intoxicating than any liquor. It required all of his strength to offer only his hand as she met him at the end of the aisle, for he wanted to offer her his entire being right then and there, regardless of all the people in attendance.

Each lady was left with a kiss on the forehead from her escort as her hand was placed into the hand of the man that had earned her love. Mr. Darcy gripped Elizabeth's hand as if it was his lifeline and she in return squeezed his with equal force and vigor, from this point forward they would never be parted.

The ceremony progressed with each couple taking their turn to recite their vows and pledge their enduring love to their future spouse. Mrs. Gardiner often wondered how Lizzy and Mr. Darcy ever made it through the ceremony as absent they were with anything around them except each other but somehow they did.

The reverend pronounced the three men and wives, and offered for the gentlemen to kiss the brides. Each man did so in relation to their emotions and sensibilities. Jane and Bingley had a kiss of happiness and joy, putting on a little show for the audience as their smiles were so wide that kissing was a bit awkward but those in attendance loved it. Richard and Anne felt shyness in front of the audience, so their kiss was a quick one of tenderness and less of passion, very few in the audience thought of it, especially when their eyes caught sight of Mr. Darcy and Elizabeth. The two displayed neither happiness nor shyness, all you saw was energy and passion, caring nothing for the relations and friends looking upon them. The kiss was long and full of every promise of a long, happy, and passionate life together. The two would not have ended their kiss if it were not for Richard clasping Darcy's shoulder and whispering in his ear, "Hold on, cousin, she is yours but why not wait for everyone to leave before you prove it any further." Darcy looked at him out of the corner of his eye and relinquished his demands on Elizabeth's lips. Elizabeth unwrapped her arms from around his waist and removed her hands from the tight grasp of his back and settled for his arm instead. The grip in which she held him though let him know she approved of the kiss and that she would soon welcome another.

The three newly married couples walked up the aisle towards the doors that a scarce hour before had brought them here single. They entered their carriages and set off towards Netherfield where the wedding breakfast was to take place.

Jane and Bingley's carriage transported a couple that smiled and laughed as much as anything else. They occasionally stole a quick kiss and Bingley promised Jane that he was positive that she would love THEIR home as much as he.

Richard and Anne's carriage carried a couple who had a little polite conversation about their future together and one lingering kiss as the carriage pulled up on front of Netherfield, but the Darcy carriage was silent of all conversation. Darcy had directed his footman to have all of the carriage curtains drawn closed and that warming stones and blankets were to be in abundance. No sooner had the doors of the carriage closed then the two found a comfortable and convenient position to resume their previous chapel activity. The rapidness of the journey from the church to Netherfield had never annoyed anyone as much as it did the Darcys, but as they pulled up the Netherfield drive the two composed themselves and Elizabeth quickly rearranged her hair as best she could. They departed the carriage with dignity and no one but Lady Matlock and Mrs. Gardiner suspected a thing. Those ladies exchanged happy knowing smiles with one another and followed the three couples into Netherfield on the arms of their most beloved husbands.

To Mr. Darcy it seemed the wedding breakfast would never end. He would have heralded to the world Mrs. Bennet's event planning skills had she canceled the wedding breakfast and sent the couples off with a farewell from the Longbourn Chapel steps. He was desperate to be off and on his way to London House with no one except the new Mrs. Darcy. The words she had spoken November twenty-eighth still rung in his head daily and he was ever grateful that his torture would end and he could act on them. He never would forget her embarrassment and naivety as she explained her good night's rest upon the bed in the Lavender Room. *Oh yes, most assuredly, I have never slept upon such a soft bed. I felt as if I was sleeping on a cloud, wrapped in the most exquisite silk. It truly is the best bed ever; perhaps you should sleep there and try it yourself.* He also could not forget his wish to personally show Mrs. Darcy the master suite on the day that they marry…, today.

Lost in his introspections Elizabeth approached him, touched his arm gently and then stood on her tiptoes to whisper in his ear. "Fitzwilliam, husband, what is it that is bothering you? The last ten minutes your face has been a mixture of pain and pleasure. I do not know whether I should laugh or be concerned. Please share your thoughts with me."

"Oh my dearest, beautiful Elizabeth, wife, I am not bothered by anything other than my own thoughts and desires to escape this place with no one but you." Elizabeth blushed pink at his pretty words and Fitzwilliam pulled her into his arms, leaning his mouth close to her ear as he whispered. "For weeks now I have thought of nothing but this day and I promise you those thoughts were not of us sitting and socializing with what seems like hundreds of neighbors at an insufferable breakfast. The thoughts were more to the effect of having you in my arms and your lips upon mine and escorting you into the master suite at London House to make you part of my world. To experience the pleasures that only a man and wife who love each other as we do can experience."

By the time Fitzwilliam had stopped whispering in her ear and looked upon Elizabeth's face he had to catch his breath for he easily saw the passion in her eyes that was felt throughout her entire person. It was all he could do to refrain himself from whisking her away that moment. Then his every wish for that moment was fulfilled by her.

"Fitzwilliam, if you would please call for our coach, I will tell my mother of our departure. I feel that the events of today have been tiring and with such a journey before me I fear we must leave post haste or else I shall be too tired to fulfill my duties of the wife of a man worth ten thousand a year. I am sure she cannot object to such a sensible suggestion." Elizabeth looked upon him with such a look that he quickly kissed her as he anxiously started towards the door.

It did not take much for Elizabeth to find her mother in the crowded room. She was standing next to Lady Lucas and Mrs. Phillips loudly speaking of the good fortune of her two perfect daughters. Part of Elizabeth cringed at the baseness of her mother while the rest of her melted with affection at the lady who despite everything would do anything for her daughters who she loved so much.

Elizabeth put her hand softly upon her mothers are as she approached her. "Mama, Mr. Darcy and I really must be getting on our way to London.'

"Oh Lizzy my dear, must you leave already? Why I have barely got to see you today in your exquisite gown. My dear, I am so happy for you. I was just telling Lady Lucas and my dear sister Phillips, was I not?" Both ladies eagerly nodded their heads in agreement.

"Yes mama, I am sure that you were, but as it is I feel that today has been a long and eventful day though it is only late morning, and Mr. Darcy and I have such a distance to travel and you know how tiring travel can be. Well I thought that based on your motherly advice last evening that we should depart sooner rather than later so that we may arrive at London House in time for me to rest before I am required to perform all of the duties that I must as Mrs. Darcy."

"Yes my dear, I am glad to know that you have heeded my advice. What a good girl you are. Come; let us find your father so that he may gather everyone's attention for your farewell."

"No mama, I mean I would love to find papa, however do not draw everyone's attention. You know how much Mr. Darcy hates to be the center of attention. Let us quickly say our goodbyes to those we love and then we shall sneak away without another thought of us."

"Very well, my..., oh come, there is your father now..." Then shouting above all the crowd Mrs. Bennet exclaimed. "Mr. Bennet, oh Mr. Bennet, you must come and see Lizzy off, she and Mr. Darcy are ready to depart for London."

Mr. Bennet walked towards Lizzy with his arms outstretched as he reached her she melted into his arms. "Papa, I shall miss you so much." She whispered to him.

"And I shall miss you too, my dearest girl. I have already spoken to Mr. Darcy and have an open invitation to visit London House or Pemberley without so much as an invitation. I daresay you should beware, you may see more of me than you ever desire."

"Nonsense papa, I could never tire of seeing you. You shall be as welcome to me as you are to Fitzwilliam. Papa, thank you so much for all that you have done for me over the years as I have grown. Most of all thank you for your support as I chose Fitzwilliam to be my husband. It pleases me that you two get on so well together. Thank you, Papa."

Mr. Bennet was not generally an emotional man, but giving up his Lizzy and hearing such words of tenderness from her he was very much affected. Her little speech had him tearing up so much that he had to wipe his eyes with his handkerchief.

"Off with you, go and say your sentimental goodbyes to Jane, for she shall appreciate them more than me." Although his words seemed harsh, Mr. Bennet had kept Lizzy in his embrace and his voice was tender and loving. She was not deceived by his words and kissed him again as she left his loving arms to find her sister.

Mr. and Mrs. Bingley were standing on the far side of the room together with a crowd of well wishers. The angelic nature of Jane and the amiability of Charles made everyone want to be around them. Jane saw Elizabeth approaching her and knew that her sister was coming to say goodbye. She had been anticipating the Darcy's early departure as Charles had told her it would most likely occur. She walked towards her sister and the two fell upon one another in a quiet tearful embrace.

"Jane, sister, what shall I do being apart from you for so long?"

"Lizzy, we shall be together in thought and spirit each and every day."

"Yes, Jane, but it is not the same."

Tears were rolling down Jane's face at this point and she had attracted the attention of Charles. He came to stand next to her as her support, just being there in case she needed him. The ladies stood together embracing, tears rolling down their faces and not saying a word for quite some time. Finally Mr. Darcy walked up and he and Charles exchanged a farewell embrace of best friends and now brothers and then gently pulled their weeping wives apart. Mr. Darcy was the first to speak.

"Luckily for us the roads between Netherfield and Pemberley are good and the stretch from Grosvenor Square to London House is nothing but a short jaunt. You shall see each other often, for Charles and I have constantly been in each other's presence these past years and marrying sisters will hardly discontinue that practice. You will barely have time to miss one another before you are together again."

Charles piped in as well, "Darcy speaks the truth; in fact we are so much in each other's company we plan our times to be apart just so that we may have some peace and solitude."

The girls smiled up at their husbands who were trying so hard to console them. Elizabeth tried to explain their tears to their husbands. "We know, it is just that every time we have been apart in the past we knew exactly when it was that we would see each other again, leaving today we know not when it is to be and so we cry at the thought of it being a long time."

Darcy being the solution driven man that he is quickly responded "If that is all, then I have a simple remedy, when do you next want to meet, pick a day and we shall make it come to pass."

"Good idea, man." Charles responded. "Jane, when would you like to visit your sister?"

"Oh Charles, do you mean it, we can choose a time now?"

"Yes, any time that you want. Darcy and Elizabeth plan to be back at Pemberley for the Christmas and New Year holidays. Perhaps we should attend them just after New Year. That way each of us can have our first holidays as man and wife but then rejoice in the New Year together."

Elizabeth was excited at the idea of hosting her sister and brother-in-law at Pemberley, "Brother, that sounds perfect, please say yes, Jane."

"How could I not, I have heard such wonderful things about Pemberley from Charles and now Elizabeth shall be there, I can hardly wait for the day. Yes, we shall come."

All four passed farewell hugs around and then Darcy and Elizabeth said goodbye to everyone else including Mr. and Mrs. Richard Fitzwilliam. They were also invited to Pemberley for the days following New Year, but were unable to attend for matters known only to them. Darcy and Elizabeth walked out to the carriage, with many followers. Everyone stood on the stoop to wish them farewell, but no one stayed to wave as long as Charles and Jane.

Once the house and Jane was out of sight Elizabeth sat back onto the bench of the coach and wiped at her moist eyes. When she finally looked up she saw Mr. Darcy looking at her with a soft and kind smile.

"Fitzwilliam, I promise that I am not normally this silly."

"I know Elizabeth, I know. Today has indeed been a day of change. All in one day you changed your name, leave your family that you have always known and take up a new family, you are also required to quit your childhood home, and unlike your sister who is staying in the neighborhood you are off to live in a place that is barely known to you. You are very strong to handle it as well as you have."

"You give me too much credit, Fitzwilliam; I am not at all handling it well."

"You do not give yourself enough credit, Elizabeth; you are indeed handling it very well."

Mr. Darcy swiftly moved from his side of the carriage to hers and wrapped her in a warm embrace. He first removed her slippers and placed her feet upon the heating stones, he then covered the two of them in blankets that had been previously warmed by the footmen and they both reclined to sit in amiable silence for a few minutes until Elizabeth spoke, asking questions about Pemberley.

Still holding her in his arms Fitzwilliam began to tell her all about Pemberley in the various seasons, often exhibiting his excitement to explain to her some particular aspect on a walk or from a tree. No other person and definitely no woman could respect the view from the grand oak tree at the northernmost part of Pemberley property they way that he anticipated Elizabeth would. His appearance under so much excitement brought out features Elizabeth had never seen before. As he spoke he also touched and caressed her as he had never been allowed before. Elizabeth first was stiff and fearful of the emotions being discovered, she did not know that she could feel more than she had already felt as the two kissed and held each other the various times that they had teetered on the verge of propriety prior to their marriage. It did not take long for Elizabeth to become accustomed to the touches and again melted into Fitzwilliam's embrace. Somewhere along the way Elizabeth became comfortable enough to return the touches that he was offering, becoming bolder with each mile closer to London house, only furthering the intimacy that they had begun to feel.

Mr. Darcy was exercising every effort in his being at doing nothing more than touching Elizabeth during their travels; her actions however were straining his resolve. Already the two had experienced the fire and passion of their mouths intertwined. Now they were experiencing the intensity of touch. In no way did Mr. Darcy want them to experience the intensity of the two combined until they were in the confines of their private rooms at London House. He knew that with the level of desire he felt for Elizabeth that once begun he would be unable to restrain himself until he had discovered every part of her. He wanted it beyond anything but not here, not now, he had a plan and if all was orchestrated as he directed this was to be the best day of both of their lives.

The couple in the carriage bound for London talked for close to an hour until their weariness of the day caught up with them and still wrapped in each other's arms and the intimacy of sharing a blanket they fell asleep.

Mr. Darcy awoke first to the sounds of London emanating from outside the carriage. It took him a moment to adjust to his good luck of having his wife in his arms. He smiled lovingly at her sleeping form and gently placed soft gentle kisses on the top of her head.

Elizabeth awoke from her pleasant dreams of being held in Fitzwilliam's arms. She was a little disappointed as she thought it was just a dream, then her mind cleared and reality began to invade as she remembered her wedding of today. Her eyes opened and she felt two sturdy arms wrapped around, holding her close in a warm embrace. She tightened her grip on his arms and he returned the pressure and addressed her.

"Elizabeth, dearest wife, we have just entered London. We have about ten minutes before we arrive at London House."

Very well husband, I will just remain here until we are much closer. It is too cold and I am much too comfortable to give up my personal warming stone."

"Warming stone, why Elizabeth is that all I am too you, a warming stone."

"Indeed not, for you are also useful for reaching books off of the upper shelf in the library, providing me with lovely gifts and making me swoon with your intoxicating kisses."

The first two replies made Mr. Darcy screw up his face with fake indignation; however the final response had no reply other than to kiss her quickly so as not to break his previous resolution.

The Darcy carriage shortly pulled up in front of London House where every servant in the place had gathered in straight lines on each side of the houses entry in order of rank to view the arrival of their master and new mistress. The majority of the servants had already met Miss Bennet while she stayed at London House during her trousseau shopping visit, but this was not Miss Bennet, this was the new Mrs. Darcy and everyone was ready to see her as such.

Elizabeth straightened her pelisse and Mr. Darcy placed her bonnet on her head, tying it under her chin and then pulling her to him he whispered as he kissed her forehead. "Welcome to OUR home Mrs. Darcy."

The carriage door was opened by the footman and Mr. Darcy stepped down. He turned to hand out Elizabeth, but instead of handing her down he scooped her into his arms and began to carry her up the walk to the front steps. She laughed and scolded him, but never asked to be put down. If he was comfortable enough to display in front of his servants then she certainly was to.

Pausing at the front door Mr. Darcy addressed Mr. and Mrs. Robbins. "If you please, Robbins, invite everyone into the foyer to reassemble in the warmth of the home and I shall address everyone."

"At once, sir."

Mr. Darcy entered the house with Elizabeth still in his arms, he told her a quick story as he walked. "Every bride that has ever entered London House or Pemberley for the first time has done so in the arms of their husband. By doing this we invite love and happiness into our home. My father once told me that if you are not ashamed to show your love to each and every servant, then that love will be enough to sustain you through any trial that may come your way."

"I know that our love is that strong, Fitzwilliam, thank you for loving me and marrying me."

Darcy gave Elizabeth a kiss, not a quick chaste kiss, but one full of promise and hope for a long and happy life together. He then turned around and began to address the London House staff.

"Thank you all for gathering here on this momentous and happy day. I cannot tell you the joy that I feel in presenting to you Mrs. Elizabeth Darcy, Mistress of Pemberley and London House."

All of the servants began to clap and shout congratulations to the couple.

"As you know we are to be staying only a short time before departing to Pemberley on Friday. I do not expect that we shall be requiring much assistance during our stay, and as of now I do not have an anticipated date of our return from Pemberley, but I trust that London House will remain in your capable hands until we return." Then addressing Mrs. Robbins he continued. "We shall take all meals while we are in residence in the Master Suite's sitting room and I trust that my directions sent ahead were attended to and that the rooms are ready for our arrival."

Mrs. Robbins smiled with warmth at Mr. Darcy. "Of course sir, exactly as you wished and I have already readied a light repast in your rooms and dinner shall be served by me later this evening."

"Thank you, Mrs. Robbins, I appreciate your diligence."

Mr. Darcy took Elizabeth's hand and saying his final goodbyes to his staff for the evening led Elizabeth to the master's chambers. Although it was barely four in the afternoon they were not to be seen for the rest of the night or the entire following day.

Pausing in front of the master suite Mr. Darcy again picked up Elizabeth to carry her over the threshold to their rooms. Elizabeth began to laugh. "Is this a continuation of another Darcy tradition?"

"No, this is a beginning of a Darcy tradition. No London House or Pemberley husband that I know of has carried his wife across their bedroom threshold," Then lowering his voice a bit and looking directly into Elizabeth's eyes he continued. "however I surmise that if it brings love and happiness to carry a new bride into the home then it must bring passion and exhilaration to carry her into the master suite, and even if it is not the truth it is what I shall tell all our sons when we have them. Welcome to the Master Suite, Mrs. Darcy".

The two entered together to embark upon a long and joyful life together. With Jane and Charles and Richard and Anne they were always the best of friends, meeting often and exchanging letters in between. It was evident to anyone who met them that all three marriages had been for nothing but the deepest love.

The End

Breinigsville, PA USA
10 December 2009
228982BV00002B/2/P